ást
EMBERONIUM

EMBERONIUM

SRINIDHI THANGA THIRUPATHI

PARTRIDGE

Copyright © 2016 by Srinidhi Thanga Thirupathi.

ISBN: Hardcover   978-1-4828-8435-7
         Softcover   978-1-4828-8434-0
         eBook   978-1-4828-8433-3

All rights reserved. No part of this book may be used or reproduced by any means, graphic, electronic, or mechanical, including photocopying, recording, taping or by any information storage retrieval system without the written permission of the author except in the case of brief quotations embodied in critical articles and reviews.

Because of the dynamic nature of the Internet, any web addresses or links contained in this book may have changed since publication and may no longer be valid. The views expressed in this work are solely those of the author and do not necessarily reflect the views of the publisher, and the publisher hereby disclaims any responsibility for them.

Print information available on the last page.

To order additional copies of this book, contact
Partridge India
000 800 10062 62
orders.india@partridgepublishing.com

www.partridgepublishing.com/india

Note From The Author

I wrote this book *Emberonium* which is my debut novel when I was doing my twelfth standard. That is the most crucial year in anybody's life. Only our twelfth board exam marks decide the roads in which we are allowed to travel. If one gets good marks in these board exams (which I call as an exam to test your 'Memorizing and Vomiting' skills) he is allowed to enter the best colleges and universities in the nation. Nowadays the students (not to forget the parents too) are in an insane abstraction that only taking up Engineering and Medicine will give them a comfortable life. And the key to a well settled future life is the marks in these Board exams.

Though I knew the seriousness of that academic year I couldn't prevent myself from writing this book as I am really addicted to writing. The parents of the students doing their twelfth standard consider their children as 'Mark Yielding Machines'. I really thank my parents that they were not one among them. They were really loving and caring. My dad Thanga Thirupathi was a busy bank manager and my mom Ratnapathi was a teacher. They didn't force me to get full marks, or 90 percentage or state rank or school rank. They just wanted me to lead a happy life. Though my father did not expect any results he would ask me to just study my lessons without wasting my time.

He is my Idol. No matter how poor I perform in my exams he would give me all sort of entertainments like picnics, abroad tours, a movie a week, eating out at a fancy restaurant during week ends and so on. He is really a gem of a person. He is like my BFF and we share a lot during our regular morning walks.

Though that academic year was crucial, our atmosphere at school didn't seem so. Daily it was just the same pointless talks, giggles, mocks and fun with my school friends. In fact we were enjoying our days like never before in our school life and we did a lot of crazy stuffs. Moreover our school books were our worst enemies and the equations, formulae, derivations in those text books were like the knives with two sharp sides. So I didn't dare to learn them. Even if I had the interest to learn them I was squashed by several factors.

I can't believe my own eyes. I was quite good in my studies when I was young. I even got 95% in my tenth public exams. But to my dismay, I failed for the first time in my entire lifetime! It was a Chemistry test. I thought that my parents would be mad at me. But their reaction was not like I had expected. They celebrated it. Infact my mom made me Gulab Jamun!

My studies went drab. But my parents never scolded me. They just wanted me to put up my efforts without wasting my time.

I tried to do what they wanted me to do. But, suddenly my mom fell ill. She got Jaundice and my Ammamma came over to our house to take care of her. I was disturbed by her illness. I just needed some distraction. My text books were not helping me.

It was the month of August. As usual I was having a gala time with my friends. Suddenly something struck me. Why can't I write something! How about a novel! I had the outline of Emberonium for quite a long time. I think I am always over imaginative. Emberonium was deposited for a long time in my bank of imaginations. I used to entertain my classmates with a few of such imaginative stories during free time and some girls really enjoyed it. Once, I had shared this imagination with one of my friends. She said to me, "It will be really nice if this particular story is taken as a movie or written as a book."

So, I just took a new note book from my bag (Luckily I had brought a new note that day for Maths!) and just scribbled down the second chapter of the book. I decided that I could learn my lessons at home and write at school during the free time.

My Mom was delighted when she saw it and she motivated me to continue my works. She herself is a writer and her works had come out in some of the famous Tamil magazines too. But my Dad felt that it would be a distraction for my studies. But my Mom supported me and defended me. She promised Dad that I would get extraordinary marks in my upcoming quarterly exam.

Yes! My Quaterly Exam marks were Extraordinary! But they were extraordinary in the wrong way. My Dad was not cross. But he asked me to suspend my writings. It had been just a month since I had started it and I was about to reach the climax of the book. I could have completed it if I had just one more weak. But I didn't have the heart to disobey my Dad.

So, I just suspended my task. But I couldn't focus on my studies. After a few weeks I decided to write my book during the lunch hour and keep my work secret. So, it was a top secret mission! I used to eat my lunch in exactly 3 minutes and I would start writing the book. My family knew nothing about this. I decided to elaborate the story.

My friends really motivated me to write my book. Some would proudly say, "We have got a budding writer in our class!" Some would say, "Srini! You have to dedicate this book for us! We are allowing you to write no!" Some close friends would say, "You should call me for your book launch, no matter what." Some would praise my mom and they would say that my Mom will be very proud of me.

I had a very good friend who would ask me to stop writing my book and start learning the lessons. She is really a true friend and really hard to find. She is a well wisher. Some girls would tease me. But they did not have the guts to tease me face to face. Even if they do I will never bother about them. I like to be what I want to be and I would never ever change my thoughts or acts for someone's comments or wishes. Of course my parents are exceptions! They are my best friends and guides.

Once I lost my note book and I couldn't find it. I thought that it was a punishment for my crime and I decided to drop my task. I had actually misplaced it somewhere and my friends had taken it and kept it safely for me. If they had not done it then I would have lost my note and thus my interest to write the book. I am really thankful to them.

Within a month I completed my book. When I read it to my mom that evening she was on cloud nine. I promised that I would sit for preparing for my public exams.

Then I was pestering my mother to type my manuscripts. This work was affected by various factors like perpetual power cuts, my mom's sleep, our good old computer's malfunction (the computer was bought before seven years) and several other factors. I can never repay my Mom for the typing and editing works she had done for me. We decided to publish the book after my public exams were over as it would be a huge distraction for me.

Though the works associated with the book was over I enjoyed my life like a happy butterfly. I was hopping here and there, least bothered about my studies. Our whole class was like a garden with happy butterflies. Singing crazy songs and talking crazy talks and laughing merrily like idiots.

But when I woke up to face reality I had to face my pubic exam! The worst nightmare! I had two volumes in Physics, Chemistry, Maths and Computer Science. Most of all I had 21 lessons in Chemisty. And knew not a single word from any of these eight books. And all I had was just 50 days in my hands!!!

I had to face my exam (doomsday) in 50 days! However by God's grace and from the guidance of some great people I did my exams well and I got **90%** marks. Let the dead past bury itself.

So, I was really happy that I had written Emberonium. And my grandparents and parents were much happier. So let us go nowhere but up.

Readers, it's time to meet Bindu and save the Earth. Welcome to the world of EMBERONIUM.

Never bend your thoughts and burn your dreams!!

Acknowledgements

Thank you God! Thanks for being there with me and showering me with your blessings.

A verbally inexpressible Thanks to my Mom Ratnapathy for not only typing my hand written manuscript but also being my backbone and bestie. I could never express my love for you Amma! You are the best.

A million Thanks to my Dad Thanga Tirupathi, who always made me his priority. I am so fortunate to have you in my life. I can never tell you how thankful I'm for everything. No Dad can be like him!

A sweet Thanks to my Sis Sri Indhumathi, who was always my secret partner in crime. An excellent critic of my story too. My crazy, annoying bestie.

To my cousin Rashmi, for unlocking the doors of the world of novels and holding my hand and guiding me to become a novel reader from a short story reader. Only reading inspired me to write.

To my Grandparents for their blessings. To my Maternal Grandma Jagadambal for appreciating me over my first writings and both my Grandpas for celebrating my first book.

To my Best friend Harshitha, for being there for me during ups and downs; the only person who can tolerate all my mokkais.

To my lovable Josephites (St.Joseph's Matriculation Girls' Hr. Sec School, Madurai), for being listeners to my story. For motivating me and allowing me to carry out my secret mission.

To my teacher Mrs. Vasanthi (St.Joseph's, Madurai) for trusting me and giving me full freedom and hope, even when I hit rock bottom in my academics. Thank You Mam! You never complained even once and kept on motivating me that I would balance both studies and my writing well.

To Chinmaya Vidyalaya Rajapalayam and Palayamkottai for giving me the platform to exhibit my writing and oratory skills during my childhood days.

To Dr.ML.Stephen Raj, The Head of Department of Biotechnology and Mr.G.S.Suresh of English Department at Mepco Schlenk Engineering College for motivating me to continue my reading and writing.

Above all, I dedicate my whole hearted Thanks to Partridge Publications for their never ending support.

1
Conference In The Clouds

It was chill and warm at the same instant. I was floating in the air. My feet were not touching the ground. I was free of gravity. A very divine and enchanting music filled the air around me. The music was mesmerizing and it made my heart float with happiness. There was white mist everywhere, and it seemed that I was among the clouds. The air around me was enriched by a very pleasant odour. I was moving randomly amidst the clouds. Suddenly I heard a loud sound of laughter. I moved towards the direction of the laughter. It seemed that many were having a gala time. Suddenly I could see golden chairs among the clouds at a distance and I moved towards it. As I went near that area I could see that the chairs were not vacant. Each chair was occupied by a man or woman wearing a lot of golden ornaments. It was really strange.

When I went closer a man dressed in tiger hide became clear to my vision. He was having a snake around his neck. He had a trident in his hand. He had smeared three horizontal white marks on his forehead. He had an eye on his forehead! Could this be lord Shiva? The god of destruction! He resembled him.

Suddenly a man with four heads and long white beard in each of the heads said to him in a loud voice, "Oh! Lord! Can you please tell us the reason behind this sudden meeting?" Now it is very clear without any doubt that he is Lord Shiva, the god of destruction as per the Hindu Mythology. I guess the four headed man must be Lord Brahma, the god of Creation.

Hindus believe in the trinity of Brahma, Vishnu and Shiva. It is believed that Lord Brahma performs the duty of creating life and Lord Vishnu performs the duty of protecting the lives on the earth and Lord Shiva performs the duty of destroying the lives. I think that the one sitting to Shiva's right must be Lord Vishnu, because he has the Sudarshana chakra in his right hand and a white conch named Panchajanya in his left hand. There were a number of gods in the meeting. It was really strange and peculiar. I was completely puzzled.

Lord Shiva began to explain, "I feel that the human beings are really becoming smart!" Goddess Parvathi, Lord Shiva's wife and Lord Vishnu's sister spoke, "You mean the domineering living creatures in the planet Earth of the Solar system in the Milky way galaxy?" Lord Shiva nodded his head.

Goddess Parvathi was wearing a red colour silk saree and she was adorned with innumerable jewels. Lord Muruga, their son said, "Yes, what is wrong with them. They are more pious and devoted than any other living species in any other galaxy. They really believe us and pray to us."

Lord Shiva explained, "I am afraid only about their growth, unlike the creatures in all other galaxy the human beings are really smart. They do unbelievable stuff with the help of their knowledge of science. They are trying to solve all the puzzles of nature by their intelligence. Now-a- days they casually send rockets, satellites and even set up space stations. They have started to explore the other planets in their solar system and now, they are trying to explore their Milky Way galaxy. They know the existence of other galaxies too, and soon they will explore them too."

The goddess of wisdom, Saraswathi who is Lord Brahma's wife said, "Yes, their growth is really marvelous and incredible. I am really proud of them. I am really happy when a child prays to me for the growth of his wisdom and knowledge. In fact, in the nearest future these children are the ones who are going to bring about some amazing s developments!"

Lord Shiva interrupted, "Can't you people see it? Don't you understand the impending threat to us? Their inventions and discoveries are going beyond the limit and I fear that they will soon discover us!"

Lord Vishnu butted in, "Why do you fear about that now? In fact, a young chap from the earth had already discovered us many years back! Have you forgotten that? What danger had he brought up on us? Nothing! So don't worry unnecessarily."

Lord Shiva said, "Yes! What you say is absolutely right! But he was a good man and he promised that he would keep the truths about us a secret. It was a long time back. Then, moral values were considered more important than life. But today the scenario has changed! If any other human being of this period finds us he will not be like that young man who visited us before. What was the name of that young chap? Hmm… Yaah! I got it! It was 'Rama' I think. I interacted more with him. He was of very good nature. You cannot expect every human being to be like him today. If they discover us then, that will lead to many problems. Listen to my warning."

Lord Brahma questioned, "So what have you planned?" Lord Shiva said very clearly in a serious tone, "I am going to wipe out the earth!"

At once Lord Muruga shouted in shock, "Father! Are you insane?"

Lord Shiva turned to him angrily and said, "You are always the rebellious child Muruga. See your brother Ganesha. He never opposes me under any circumstances. But anyway, what I am going to do is the only way to safe guard ourselves. We have no other choice!"

Goddess Saraswathi said in a pleading manner, "Is intelligence such a sin? Is death the punishment for wisdom? Then I am the one who is to be punished! Human beings pray me before starting to learn. I grant them knowledge and brain power. So spare them and punish me! Will you be happy if all the humans become idiots? Will you be satisfied if they have no knowledge of their potential? Already you clear out human population periodically in the name of natural calamities and sweep off the knowledge gathered by many generations in a single second. But the next generation arises and rediscovers its glorious past. We all have been silent spectators of this drama again and again." All were listening to her intently and nodding their heads in agreement.

Lord Shiva said in a fed up tone, "Don't be so weak at heart Saraswathi! Our protection alone is not the reason behind my plan. Human beings have changed a lot today. They have no fear for us. They do all sorts of crimes and have no morality. They are committing sins after sins. Their sins have become intolerable and mother earth is crying in pain! They hurt their fellow beings physically and mentally and even kill them. So they ought to be punished. They have to face the 'doomsday'. This is their end."

Lord Vishnu said, "Oh! Come on Shiva! You cannot punish everyone for this. Even Mother Earth will not be happy about your decision. Don't decide in haste. What about the young babies and innocent kids? What sort of sins did they do? Why should they be punished? Show some mercy on human beings! They are like our children. Just for our safety, security and secrecy we cannot destroy them completely. They have toiled for generations and developed the present world with all comforts. Are we going to kill them just like that? They pray to us with faith and belief. Is 'dooms day' a reward and an answer to their prayer? There should be some other way. Calm yourself down and consider our views."

Soon most of the gods in the meeting accepted what Lord Vishnu had said and they tried to convince Lord Shiva. After a while Lord Shiva said, "OK, since you all don't want to punish the whole of the human population, I have decided to turn all the grownups into ashes. There is a way……"

2
A Narrow Escape

"Bindu! Bindu!" Someone whispered. Suddenly all those figures of the deities were blurring. The clouds around me disappeared. Someone was pinching my arms. I didn't want to wake up. The pinching became harder and it was more painful. I shuddered off from my sleep and opened my eyes to face reality.

Oh! Gosh! Have I been sleeping again? Mrs. Mathi was standing there and staring at me. Oh! That trouble shooting toad! We have been calling her 'toad' since our seventh grade. We don't know who the creator of this incredible name was, but it spread as fast as wild fire as it sounded funny and was apt for her voice.

Did she see me sleeping? Yeah! I'm sure she did. I could see that from the way my classmates are staring at me. I was sure I didn't droop and fall off while sleeping. I am an expert in sleeping with my eyes wide open. Who knows? May be I was a fish in my last birth. She should have seen me. But I bet that she couldn't have found out that I was sleeping. Why are they staring at me like this?

Priya was giving me 'You silly sleepy idiot get up!' look. Priya, Shalini, Raj, Diya, Krishna and Meena were all staring at me. Or, did I blabber something in my sleep? I sometimes sleep talk. "Can you hear me?" shouted Mrs.Toad. Oh! Then toad must have asked me some question. I just nodded. Mrs. Toad yelled, "Then, open your mouth and tell the symbol for Tungsten", as she approached my seat. I am sure that the Latin name of Tungsten is Wolfram, but am not sure if its symbol is 'W' or 'Wo'. She has been waiting since eighth grade to find some fault in me and punish me. I can't let that happen and now she is approaching me with a stick in her hand. How am I going to escape?

Mrs.Toad bellowed like a bull. "Fool! Open up your mouth and answer!" God! I need to escape one way or another. I read everyone's face. Everyone was staring at me. Raj was giving me some kind of signal. He was moving his lips and showing up some letters with his finger. I think he is signaling me the answer. I read his lips. He mimed, "W". Then my first guess should be correct.

Mrs. Toad again bellowed, "What girl? Do you know the answer or not?" Is he really trying to help me or setting up a booby trap? I hope he is not taking his vengeance now. We both are friends, but not when it comes to studies and impressing our teachers. Can I trust his answer? Now it's all in God's hands.

I muttered, "W". Toad bellowed," Sit down", in a disappointed and arrogant accent because she couldn't punish me. That was a narrow escape. It's awesome that I am a good lip reader. This talent has helped me under many circumstances. It is so good that Raj has saved me today. Though we are friends, we always fight over our marks. We always have this competition 'Who gets the teachers attention!' and 'Who is in the teachers' good books!' We both compete in trying to impress the teachers by answering all the questions quickly and correctly.

If he had not helped me now, I would have been a prey to Mrs. Toad's vile intentions. Anyway I need not be thankful to Raj as I had already guessed the answer. But for the sake of courtesy I should thank him during the lunch break. And what is that bizarre dream I dreamt? All those 'Dooms day','Sins', 'New world' 'Young generations','Gods' and 'Ashes'. Whatever it is, never mind. I tried to ignore the peculiar dream and concentrate in my works.

3
World's End

Next we had English class. Mrs. Crow is our English teacher. Obviously, Mrs. Crow is not her original name. Her hair style, voice and the way she looks at students reminds definitely a crow! She is known for her stylish pronunciation and accent of the language. But what the students hate about her is that she appreciates and patronises only her niece 'Hana' from our class. She always loves to sing in praise of Hana. But Hana doesn't deserve that.

Hana is a pure 'over acting' type girl. She is a fraud. She always steals my answers. Mrs. Crow is so partial. Hana borrows my project for 'reference' and her project turns out to be a mirror image of mine. She is a copy cat. I know that God is up there and he will have his own measures for her plagiarism. I believe in Gods, but not in religions.

Though Raj and Diya are my best friends since childhood, I considered all other students of my class also as my friends. But I didn't encourage anyone else to get too close to me. Maybe it was because of the way I grew up. I don't believe anyone easily and get too close to them quickly. Anyone who meets me for the first time would often think that I am a rude and unfriendly girl. But I am not so, though I have my own rules to let someone into my circle.

I, Bindu Thirupathi am a sixteen year old girl who spend much time on scientific researches; love to enjoy with my family; do not bother about the gossips and back bites done by the other girls in my class; do not get involved in groupism; and I have no time to waste on silly matters. All I have is pleasant memories of 'general friendshipism'.

Apart from studies I am interested in dancing, painting, swimming and cycling. But above all I forget myself when I am involved in scientific researches. I was awarded the 'Young Scientist of India' title when I was in my 7th grade. There was a tough competition for that title between the aspiring young scientists from all over India. Raj was also in the race. But I won the title at last.

Why am I boasting about this? Because, that success has changed my life in a wonderful direction! The topic I chose for my research impressed the world famous scientist Professor Ramanujam and he volunteered to accept me as his apprentice! So I am a busy student with a tight schedule of school, extra-curricular activities, plus my researches with Professor Ramanujam.

Oh! My God I have drifted away from the class for quite a long time! Have I missed anything important? Not at all! Mrs. Crow is still praising Hana and her wonderful project which is without any doubt a replica of mine. The bell went. Most of the students went out of the class room to have their lunch in groups. Everyone was with at least 4 or 5 of their friends. Some were in a big group of even 10.

I don't prefer to sit with others because I don't like groupism. So, I sat all alone in my place and opened my lunch box. A gang of boys and two gangs of girls were also sitting on the floor of the class room and eating. Diya was also sitting with one of the groups. She came to me and said," Bindu! Come with us and eat."

Though she was my only close friend and she always cared about me, I did not like the company of the other girls who were sitting with her. They used to chat about certain things which I felt unnecessary. So I used to avoid their company. But Diya came in the same van with them and she had to maintain cordial relationship with them.

So I said, "It's okay Diya. I've got some works to do. You carry on with others. Maybe I'll join you some other day". Diya had to run as Hana shouted, "Hey! Diya! Hema has finished half of your lunch! If you don't come now your box will be empty soon!" There was a roar of laughter from that gang.

I love my school and its location. Our school is located at the foothills of the Western Ghats. I am happy that I don't learn in a concrete building but in a pleasant and natural atmosphere. We have uncountable number of trees and plants. Squirrels, jungle fowls, monkeys, rabbits, parrots, woodpeckers, peacocks and don't panic please, snakes are also the common inhabitants of our school premises. It's simply like an eco-park.

Students prefer to sit under the trees and have their lunch. They go to the dining hall or stay in the class room only when it rains. I usually sit in the class and read a story book while eating or just look around and observe whatever is in my vicinity. Today I am watching the girls who are eating in the class. Mostly all girls in my class were flirts, and the boys hated it. It is so funny to see these girls flirting and the boys' repulsive reaction to their flirts.

I had almost finished eating when a group of students suddenly entered the class room noisily. Some of them were shouting, "The world is going to come to an end!" and some shouted randomly, "Its dooms day!" I was completely puzzled. They were all jumping randomly like monkeys, yelling slogans about the world's end. Could it be true? Is the world really coming to an end? Then, is my dream true? Are the Gods behind the world's end? Is the end of the world approaching?

My thoughts were interrupted when a boy's voice informed, "Attention everybody! Mrs.Mathi is coming to the class." It was Yogith. He is a silly boy. He is famous for backstabbing others. He makes silly and false complaints about students to teachers. He is a nerd, but he always complaints about everyone. He is a pessimist and is believed to be the teachers' spy. He listens to all the gossips around the class and reports them to the teachers. So no one in the class likes him.

If Yogith is announcing a teacher's arrival, then he should have made some fake complaint to her and the teacher was coming to enquire about the problem. So everyone seemed tensed. Suddenly

Ann shouted, "What does that 'stupid toad' want now?" Yen stared at Ann. There was anger and cunningness in his look. I think he has plotted something against Ann.

Ann is one of the smart girls in our class. She used to be a good girl. But nowadays, the company she keeps has spoilt her. She is a 'cup cake' in front of the teachers by talking like cream and honey. Once she comes behind them, she uses all sorts of repulsive words. She also bullies the other students of the class. She is a 'plastic' and makes the other normal girls feel weak and vulnerable. So the girls act as her slaves, praise her and treat her like a princess. She could achieve anything by her acting. She is good in studies too.

She thinks that she has very good friends. She considers Usha as her BFF. But Usha is always jealous of Ann. Usha does all sorts of backbiting and backstabbing to pull down Ann. All Usha worries about is her beauty, looks and style. She secretly waits for a chance to overtake Ann. Ann completely trusts Usha and is ignorant of the backbiting.

Meena is Ann's side kick. Meena is a selfish girl. She is always ready to backstab Ann and Usha. But Ann thinks that Meena is an innocent girl. All girls act too good to Ann as she is beautiful, popular and intelligent. They think that her company would gain them popularity.

Ann believes that everyone admires her. But everyone secretly hates her. In the beginning, Ann wanted me to join her gang. She liked me for my intelligence, smartness and other talents. As I was against groupism, I politely rejected the offer and withdrew from her. Any other girl in my class would have sold all her possessions to be in Ann's gang.

As soon as Ann finished her remark about the teacher, all the girls around her made a fake roar of laughter. I could see that Ann was pleased, happy and proud with her slaves around. But in Yogith's eyes I could see the joy of victory that he had actually found a real complaint to present to Mrs. Mathi.

Mrs.Mathi came into the class bellowing, "Has everyone paid money for your group photo copies?" Oh! Then actually Yogith hadn't made any complaint. Phew! Everyone shouted in relief, "Yes Mam."

Toad replied, "OK! Maintain silence in the absence of the teachers!" and she was about to leave the class.

But Yogith rushed to her and whispered something into her ears. I could see the anger in Toad's face. Yogith pulled back and retreated to his place. As he neared his place, he saw Ann and made a scornful expression.

I heard Toad bellow again, "Ann, come out and meet me". Oh! God! Yen must have complained about Ann. Ann is dead!

Ann silently muttered something to her slaves and they made a fake chuckle. Guess she must have cracked some silly jokes. She heroically got up from her place and marched out of the class. Bell rang and the students rushed to their places.

4
The Decision For Destruction

As we settled down, our Maths teacher entered the class. She was famous for the colorful outfits and make up she wore. She was too fast in speaking, that most of the class couldn't understand her coherently. She was too fast for a Maths teacher. Though the students disliked her way of teaching they used to appreciate her dressing sense. As usual she was trying to complete a full chapter, very fast in a period. All students were passing secret written messages about Ann and the paper slips were passed on from one desk to the other. I couldn't concentrate in the class. My mind drifted somewhere else. I was thinking about the strange dream. Ann hadn't come back. I think Yen must have given some extra fittings to the complaint. Ann shouldn't have affronted Mrs. Mathi in front of Yen.

Thank God! The bell has rung. Everyone jumped up from their places and ran out of the class. It is games period. All evacuated the class and Usha accompanied me to the playground. All girls were talking about Ann. Yogith was coming a long way behind us. Actually he was trying to overhear the conversation among a group of boys.

When we reached the play ground we could see Ann running round and round the track. She was enjoying her punishment. As she saw the class approach she began to wave her hands and run in a heroic manner. She came running towards us in slow motion with a victorious smile on her face.

The difference between normal people and 'plastics' is that while normal people are ashamed of committing mistakes and getting punishments, plastics put up a scene as though it is no big deal for them. They even take pride in it. As she came near us, a group of girls mostly her slaves ran towards her and gathered around her. She started narrating something so dramatically and they began to roll with laughter. Usha pouted.

To distract her I asked, "Usha shall we play throw ball?" She smiled at me and said, "Sure." We both started walking towards the games room to grab a ball. We heard some strange sound like thunder. The distant sky was rumbling.

Usha jumped in joy, "Wow! It will be so nice if it rains now!" I lifted up my head to see the sky. Suddenly everything became blurred. I heard some other unclear voices now.

Soon the voices became clearly audible. "No! No! We cannot do something like that!" boomed a strong male voice. A very sweet female voice sang, "Yes! But we are Gods! We have the freedom and authority to do anything!"

Another strong female voice shrieked, "What do you mean by that? There is no such thing as Gods! We are just 'Mutants' with special powers! We exist between dimensions and so we are invisible to human eyes. We can see them; hear their mind voices and thoughts and even reveal ourselves to them only if we wish. We have the ability to help them with our extra powers. We control the natural elements. It doesn't mean that we have the right to destroy them completely. We cannot erase this form of life on the earth altogether. They have their freedom to live here happily."

Another male voice talked soothingly, "Sweety! You don't get it. We are not going to completely destroy the earth. We are just going to turn all the people above 25 years into ashes by using Emberonium."

The strong female voice retorted, "But why?"

The male continued, "You know, the population of the senior citizens is very high today. Modern science has increased the life span and the earth is overcrowded today. It's time to clean up! We should also test the ability, will power and potential of the younger generation. We are going to let them live free and bring out the best of them. I'm sure that the younger generation will survive and come out in flying colours. Let us eliminate the negative elements altogether. Moreover the humans will never know that the damage is done by us."

The female voice surrendered in a low tone, "Ok! But don't damage the spirits of the young ones."

The male voice commanded, "Well! Now everybody get ready to send giant Emberonium rocks to the earth! Be careful! The huge rocks should not collide with the earth. They should just land gently on the earth. The meteorite should reach closer to the earth's atmosphere at the highest speed but once it enters the earth's atmosphere the speed should be made nil. Search for the right spots so that the human population throughout the earth's surface is evenly under the impact of the radiation from Emberonium."

A new polite and feeble voice said, "Adhivega is the quickest in travelling and Anjanaiputra can lift up any huge mass. Can we seek their help?" The male voice said, "Very well! Adhivega shall move the Emberonium meteorites near the Milky Way Galaxy and the rest shall be continued by Anjanaiputra. You all shall ensure that everything goes on as per our plan". Mixed voices of a group shouted, "Yes Lord!" A female voice tried to interrupt, "But..."

After this some sharp peculiar sound pierced my ear drums and no more voice was audible. My head spun very painfully and everything went black. When I tried to open my eyes I heard many voices shouting, "Bindu! Bindu!" "What's wrong with her?" "Hey don't push yaar!" "Ouch! Don't stamp my foot! I may fall over her!" Raj's voice commanded clearly, "Don't crowd around and suffocate her. Let her get some fresh air". Someone splashed cold water on my face.

I opened my eyelids with difficulty to see the curious and panic-stricken faces of my class mates. My head was rested on Usha's lap and Raj was having a water bottle in his hands. Everyone was staring at me. I felt quite embarrassed and sat up erect.

Raj handed me over the water bottle and said, "You fainted and fell down. You were blabbering a lot incoherently when you were unconscious."

I felt quite ashamed that this had happened in front of my class mates. I tried to stand up. But I couldn't as I felt very tired and dizzy.

Diya insisted, "It's OK! Don't trouble yourself! First drink some water!" I drank some water quietly. All were looking at me with concern and Diya questioned, "What is wrong with you Bindu? What were you trying to say?"

I tried to look normal and said slowly, "I don't remember anything Diya!" Ann, Diya and Usha slowly walked me to the class and they shooed away Raj who tried to accompany us. The crowd around me dispersed to continue their games. When bell rang all students rushed out of the school.

5
My Sister Indu

As I packed my bag, I was wondering. 'Why am I getting such bizarre dreams again and again recently? I think I must go to a doctor. Though I have never ever heard or read anything like Emberonium, the same word is heard by me often. Is this some sign or premonition or a warning?' After collecting my things I walked slowly towards the school gate.

I could see my sister Indu waiting for me impatiently near the gate. We usually walk home together. No student was allowed to use bikes or cars. We could use the school bus or cycles or walk. We both usually enjoy our walk home. Indu is also a lover of nature and we both used to just enjoy the sight of the mountains far away and the paddy fields on the way.

As I neared, I saw that my sister's face was red with anger. Oh! God! I'm late. As I approached her, she yelled, "Why are you so late?" I replied, "I fainted during games period Indu. I thought my friends would have informed you."

She stared at me and asked, "Really? Is that true?" I shared the gist of the conversation I heard when I had fainted. I couldn't judge whether it was a dream or my own imagination.

Indu listened to me with suspicious eyes and finally asked, "Are you making up some stories?" I snapped back, "I don't have to." She thought very seriously for a minute and then said with the confidence of a doctor predicting an ailment, "Then you must have got EIP!"

I laughed and said, "Hey! It's not EIP! It's ESP! Do you mean Extra Sensory Power that gives someone the power and ability to foresee the future? I don't know if I have ESP or not."

Will it be some extra sense as she says? She said with a mischievous smile, "I did not mean ESP! I said EIP as I am sure that you have some Extra Imaginative Power!" and she chuckled. She added, "It has taken you this much time to understand that I am making fun of you! Great! How come you are a scientist?"

I stared at her angrily. Stamped my foot and began to walk fast ahead of her. I am never going to share my problems with her. She is teasing me when I share my intense problem with her. She came running fast, laughing aloud and joined me. When she tried to hold my hand, I pulled back and walked fast. Before she could try to convince me, we had reached home and Indu rang the bell.

Mom opened the door and welcomed us warmly. She asked eagerly, "Did you enjoy your lunch?" I replied, "It was delicious Mom! I enjoyed it!" Indu continued, "Yes! It was very delicious Mom! The peacocks and monkeys in the campus enjoyed it!"

It took a second for Mom to understand the scenario and she shouted, "What! You spilled everything to your pets there?" Indu laughed and said, "Yes! But don't worry! They all are alive and quite well! They are surprisingly strong enough to survive even after eating the dishes cooked by you!"

Mom began to breathe heavy; her nostrils flared; she stared at Indu angrily and she held Indu's ear in her fingers. Indu ran off from her hold and Mom began to chase Indu around the house. It seemed like two kids playing around in a silly way.

I used to envy my mother for her childishness. She is a happy home maker. She is happy and contented with her life always. Very simple things give her extreme happiness. Though she is well educated and has the ability to choose a profession, she prefers to stay home and enjoy. She is short and a bit chubby. She has long hair and beautiful eyes. She is known for her gorgeous laughter. She always makes her surroundings also happy by cracking jokes and being funny. She goes mad sometimes at my Dad when he fails to come home in time to fulfill his promises of outings like temple, cinema or any family functions. Otherwise she is a perfect match to my Dad and a loving mother to us. She enjoys like a child with us and sometimes I used to wonder if she was our mother or a friend to us.

The laughter of Indu and Mom rang around for a while and finally Mom gave up as she could not catch up with Indu in speed. Indu came and sat near me panting and giggling. Mom brought two big glasses of freshly prepared apple juice for us. She placed it on the teapoy and sat on the couch. As usual Indu began to hug and kiss our Mom and Mom tried to squeeze out of her grip.

Indu has grown taller than Mom and me. May be I am short and chubby like my Mom and Indu is tall and lean like my father. Finally Mom shouted, "Enough Indu! Go and refresh yourself! You stink of sweat and dirt. Have a wash and both of you eat the curd rice that I have kept on the dining table. Dad will come soon and as soon as he comes we shall go to the movie!"

Wow! It's Saturday. Our 'Movie Day'. We usually go to theatres on Saturday and watch a movie. Indu ran in after finishing her juice.

I asked, "Mom to which movie are we going today?" She replied, "Dad said something like 'Dooms Day' and don't ask me anything more than that. I don't know the name of the hero or heroine."

Oh! God! What is this? Is this mere coincidence or is it another sign that indicates something to me? Is the world really coming to an end?

"Mom..." suddenly Indu's howling interrupted my thoughts and we both rushed to her room. The whole room was a total mess. She had scattered out all her clothes from her cupboard and was sitting in the midst of them with tears in her eyes. Oh! Oh! The drama queen has started her play.

She said between sobs, "I'm not coming to the movie. I don't have any nice dress to wear out. Always she gets many costly clothes. I don't have anything that fits me!" and pointed towards me. This has become her habit nowadays. She thinks that I get the best always and she is given the inferior quality in everything. But our parents treat us both equally.

Seeing me she yelled at the top of her voice, "I don't like you. Get out of my room. Mom, I am not coming to the movie." I opened my mouth and started, "Indu…" But before I could say something she shouted,' Shut up your bloody mouth! You are the reason for everything. The first child gets the best! You are selfish! I don't like you!"

I could not tolerate it any more. I walked out of her room and drank my juice. Mummy began to console her. I went to my room and had a bath. I dressed up in a purple colour cotton tops and black jeans. When I came out of my room, Indu was completely ready and sitting on the dining table. My mother was feeding her curd rice as though she was a baby. Seeing me Indu pouted her lips. Before I could make some funny comments my phone rang. I ran to my room to fetch it. It was Diya. She enquired about my health and was happy that I was alright. There was also a message from Professor Ramanujam.

Well! Professor Ramanujam is a world famous scientist. He is very intelligent and interesting. He is very old. I am proud to be his apprentice. Every Sunday I go to his research lab and do some projects under his guidance. I learn a lot from him and it is my pride and pleasure to work under him. I opened up the message. It read:

'Meet me at 8 am tomorrow in my lab. Bring your last week's report.'

Oh! God! I have forgotten to complete the report on mutation. Every day I had spent some time on it. But still there is some final touch up work. If I don't submit the report Professor will be mad at me. OK. Let me finish it after coming from the movie.

As the calling bell rang, I went to open the door. It was Dad. He was in his formal office wear; a striped white shirt, tie, black pants and shiny black shoes. Dad is very tall and lean. He is fairer in complexion than my Mom. He loves spending time with us whether it is a shopping or any form of outing. He is always fit, smart, active and energetic. He has an attractive smile and he easily makes friendship with everyone.

He is the manager of a private sector bank and he is known for his friendly and warm approach to his customers. He is a very responsible, matured and thoughtful person. He always says that life is to live happily. I learnt from him that whenever a problem arises we must not moan over the problem, but search for the solution which will be right in front of our eyes. He loves me very much and gives me freedom to pursue my dreams. But he keeps on advising me and insists me that I should know my limitations and I should be always alert to be on the safer side.

On seeing me Dad smiled broad and exclaimed, "Wow! Darling! You are ready! I will get ready in no time and we shall go out" I replied, "OK Dad. But Indu is out of mood. She will be alright if she sees you!".Dad went inside. I sent a reply message to Professor.

'OK Sir!'

I came to the dining hall and had some curd rice. Dad was ready in a blue jeans and a colourful checked cotton shirt. He drank the apple juice that Mom gave him, and he asked, "Shall we go?" I replied, "Sure Dad". Mom locked the house and we got into Dad's car. And unbelievably Indu was cool now. My thoughts began to waver here and there and finally came back to my bizarre dream.

6
Dooms Day

Dad went to get the tickets. We waited for him. After he returned back we all entered the movie hall. A huge group of college girls and boys were sitting behind our row. They were discussing loudly about the Mayan's calendar, the signs that predict the end of the world and the different means of its final destruction. That was quite annoying, but they stopped their clattering as soon as the movie started.

The movie was about a scientist who predicts the end of the earth five years earlier and takes all steps to save his family. Just like Nova's arc he builds a ship secretly and collects many species of plants and animals. When the earth is being engulfed by water he saves his family while all other people die. The film was a visual treat with the graphic works done very effectively.

Mom and Indu liked the story very much and they were continuously chatting about it on the way home. To my amusement Dad drove us to a boutique. I had planned to reach home early and complete my assignment. Why on earth are we going to the dress shop at this time?

Daddy said to Indu, "Look honey! You can select any dress of your choice now! Don't feel that we are partial. OK!" He looked very concerned. With a victorious look and smile Indu moved towards teen's section. Oh! Now I get the reason for our sudden shopping. Mom must have told Dad about Indu's tantrums.

Dad whispered to me in a low voice, "Bindu dear! You can also buy some dress if you really need them."

I just nodded my head and moved around without much interest. I randomly scanned the shop and my eyes rested on a blue tops with bead works. I liked it but decided not to buy it now, as it would irritate Indu and provoke her anger. May be next time I shall get it. Indu was beaming as she carried four new dresses when we came out of the shop. When she showed them off to me with delight and joy, my thoughts were hovering around my project.

We had dinner at the roof top garden of our favourite restaurant and returned home. Throughout this evening Indu was hanging around Mom as though they had been glued together. This is the usual scenario. Mom showers some extra love, care and attention as Indu is more demanding than me. When Mom and Indu were sleeping I was working in my lap-top to complete the thesis. Dad was watching TV in the living room. I didn't want Professor Ramanujam to be cross that I was incomplete in my works.

Last week he had explained me about mutants and the theory of mutation. Surprisingly we had many living evidences for the gradual evolution of mutants from human beings. But all these details are confidential matters that are to be kept secret. Until today I am the only person who has the freedom to enter and exit 'Ramanujam Valley' the private property strictly prohibited to other people. Professor is not just my mentor but he is more like my guardian and God father. He has become our family friend since the day I got the 'Young Scientist of India' award from him.

When I finished up all my work the time was 2a.m. I began to think about my peculiar dream and the movie I saw. The hero of the movie saves only his family when the whole of the earth faces its Dooms Day. How selfish he is! I didn't like this attitude of the hero of the story. Why doesn't he find a solution to save the whole earth?

Any natural disaster affects all the living organisms alike. But in my vision only the living beings above 20 are destined to die. How is it even possible? I was totally confused. I decided to share this to Professor. He might give me some clue about this dream.

My head was swirling. I felt very dizzy and sleepy. There was no sound from the living room. Dad must have gone to bed. I walked to the bed room like a sleep walker. Indu was babbling something in her dream and was occupying her lower bunk as usual. I climbed to my upper bunk and fell like a dead log. After resting my head, I was worried that I had not set the alarm in my cell phone. But my eyelids never allowed me to open my eyes.

7
RV

My alarm was buzzing. I tried hard to wake up and as soon as I saw the time my mind became alert. Oh! No! The time was already 7am! I have to be in Professor Ramanujam's research lab at 8am. I could hear Mom humming devotional songs in the kitchen. She has woken up early as usual and started her works.

I jumped out of the bed and rushed to the bath room. After refreshing, I dressed myself in a pink chudy. I applied very light make up and kept a pink colour sticker bindi with shining stones on my forehead.

Seeing me Mom said, "I thought of waking you up. But I did not want to disturb you from that deep sleep. You seemed really tired. How do you feel now?" I smiled but said, "You should have woken me up Mom! See now I have to rush up!"

She said convincingly, "OK! Hereafter I will wake you even if you are looking sick. Now what would you like to have, coffee or breakfast?"

Without answering her, I kissed her and said, "Don't worry my dear Mom. I will take care! Now I am in a hurry to leave." I just grabbed 3 idlis and put them into a box. I poured sufficient amount of chutney and sambar over them and stuffed the box into my backpack.

I went into the bed room and kissed goodbye to Indu still sleeping in the shape of letter 'S' and smiling in her morning dream. I waved bye to my Dad who was reading newspaper after his morning walk. I rushed out and jumped into my Audi. I kept on chanting 'I shouldn't be late' and drove fast but with my concentration on the road. I crossed the city limits and entered the forest area.

Soon I was able to see the 3 dome shaped structures roofing the magnificent buildings that stood tall and clear with the green background of nature. There were 2 white domes and a silver dome. The silver dome is Professor's observatory and it stands much taller than the other two. One of the white domes is his lab and the other in the middle is his residence. He lives all alone. He has a tennis court, a spa, a swimming pool, a helipad and an animal confinement with a varied range of reptiles, birds and animals. The whole area called 'Ramanujam Valley' also has a falls, a brook that overflows during rainy season, a dairy farm, a pond and a barn. Ramanujam Valley is shortly called 'RV'.

Professor owns the forest area and everyone would open their mouth in awe admiration when his name was said. He has a very good name and reputation in the society. Though he is always immersed in his researches, secret philanthropy is his hobby. As far as I know he doesn't have any relatives. Three years before, we celebrated his hundredth birthday. Though Professor Ramanujam is one hundred and three he looks very smart and energetic as though he is in his fifties. He is more steady and balanced than me when we work in the lab. He is well versed in not only all fields of science but also in Vedas and Puranas. I used to admire his memory power and ability to retain so much of information in his brain. I often wonder why he never has anyone with him except his close companion 'Aadhmi'.

I used to envy Aadhmi's abilities and talents. Wait! Wait! Aadhmi is not a human being. It is the most advanced Super Humanoid Robot created by Professor when he was 14. Aadhmi is a living proof; Err.... I mean 'a non-living proof' for Professor's extraordinary intelligence even at that young age. Aadhmi is not just a piece of nickel and aluminium. It is made of the strongest alloy and has sensory power more advanced than human beings. Actually Professor named his special software as 'Aadhmi' as it was destined to be of service to mankind. Aadhmi is not just a single robot. There are many hardwares of Aadhmi. They take care of Professor Ramanujam and his valley. Not even a fly could enter RV and exit it without Aadhmi's knowledge.

The whole RV is always under the scanning of Aadhmi's bio-thermo sensory scanners. Aadhmi can understand and react to all human emotions too. It can even make facial expressions. Professor Ramanujam never has the need to visit a doctor. Aadhmi's advanced technology bio sensors can identify even the slightest change in his body conditions and strictly prescribe him the suitable medications or plan a suitable diet to cure his physical and emotional discomforts. Aadhmi sticks on to Ayurvedic treatments to keep Professor fit as a horse. Though I knew less about Humanoid Robots, Professor enriched me with his knowledge, findings and ideas. I have freedom to access all areas of the lab except the closed room labeled 'Secret Research'. Initially I was curious to know what was in there. But Professor has strictly forbidden that from me and I gradually stopped pressing him. May be he has something very confidential or dangerous there.

I drove near the security gates and passed the scanning system. A voice greeted me, "Hello Bindu! Good morning!"

It is Aadhmi. I replied," Hai! Aadhmi!" It said in its robotic tone, "It seems that you haven't eaten anything in the morning."

I said, "Yes. Can you please open the gate?"

Aadhmi replied," Sure! But not until you finish eating the 3 idlis you have brought. You will get the carbohydrate, protein and minerals you need if you eat them. It will give you enough calories to work for 4 hours."

It can scan even people's thoughts. It might have read everything in my memory lane. With a sigh and without another word, I took out my box and started eating. Aadhmi has become more intriguing nowadays. It tries to dominate me in everything. This is not the first time it puts me some silly conditions to enter the gate. I think it is bullying me. I finished my idlis and showed the empty box like a KG kid. The gates opened.

I drove in and asked Aadhmi, "Where is Professor?"

It replied, "He is in the house." I drove towards the middle dome and parked my car in front of the building.

Aadhmi's metallic body was shining and reflecting the sunlight. In no time it was standing near me. Aadhmi is too gentle, but very fast for a Robot. Its facial features resembled humans and it observed me with its intelligent eyes. Ignoring it I walked past the portico where Professor's entire collection of cars was parked. They were lined up neatly on 4 levels. He has about 300 cars. He is a lover of cars. His collection includes BMWs, Limos, Ferraris, Lamboganis, Audis and many other varieties. All were very neat and sparkling as fresh deliveries. His favourite was the car which stood in the middle. It was made out of pure gold! He calls it Sorna. He has allowed me to drive some of his other cars. But he has never allowed me to go near Sorna. I too love cars and I love very much the Audi I own. But still, I crave to see the interior of Sorna and its efficiency.

Professor uses Sorna when he goes to meet our President. He and our President Dr. Abdul Rahman are good friends. This is the second time Dr.Abdul Rahman is elected as our President. I have heard that he was the President before some 10 or 15 years. Professor had once told me that our President owns a Sorna too and also that Sorna can travel not only on land but also in water and in air and even in space. But I have never seen or experienced the incredible travels. So I even had a doubt that it may not be true. How is it possible for a car to travel in space?

I walked past the fountain. The fountain was made of platinum. There was an idol of Lord Krishna in the middle. The fountain splashed coloured water on his face and body depicting the festival of colours 'Holi'. The statue kept on rotating on its platform. There was a flute in the idol's waist and periodically the statue moved its arms and pulled out the flute. Slowly the flute was lifted by the idol to the lips and a melodious music filled the air. After a few minutes the flute went back to the waist. I felt that Professor was a man of art.

Then I walked past Professor's indoor lotus pond. The pond had lotuses of different colours like purple, green, blue, orange, indigo, saffron, peach, metallic blue, yellow and various other colour combinations which I couldn't express. All these flowers had been created by Professors research on hybridization.

I walked straight into the living room. Professor was not there. I was puzzled. But I was relieved when I heard the friendly familiar voice saying, "Hi Bindu!" from the drawing room. I ran into the drawing room. He was sitting in front of the study table and he looked at me through is spectacles.

Professor is very tall, fair and lean. He is slightly bald headed, but not much. He always wears white pants and white cotton shirts with half sleeves. Though he is simple and his life style is simple, he is a billionaire. He spends a lot for his researches, charity and the various scholarships he awards to students of all age.

I greeted him, "Good morning Professor! How are you?" He replied warmly, "Good morning Bindu. I'm fine. Can I see your assignment on genetic mutation?" I said, "Yes Professor," and took out my laptop from my bag. Then I opened up my presentation and placed the laptop on the table.

He went through my presentation while I waited restlessly, admiring the beautiful and exquisite paintings on the walls of the drawing room. How does he remember everything so clearly even at this age? He could tell the names of all the famous paintings here and their painters. If I asked for any doubt, he would even share something special from their lives too.

After 25 minutes he took his eyes off my project and looked up at me. Is he satisfied or not? He made a grin. Oh! Thank God! He said, "Well done!" with a widening smile. All the wrinkles around his eyes and in his forehead became prominent. I controlled my pleasure and said humbly, "Thank you Professor!"

8
Liquefaction

Thank God! If he is not satisfied with my work, he will make me do it again and again. There is no worst punishment than that. So I was happy that the task was over. He said, "I have kept some gases in huge cylinders in the laboratory. Can you please liquefy them?"

OMG! He had taught me liquefaction of gases some 6 months back. I remember it only vaguely. But I have to try. So I replied, "Yes Professor."

Without waiting for any more instructions I began to walk to the lab. I walked past the beautiful flower garden and then the garden filled with carnivorous plants. To keep away from those peculiar parasitic plants, I walked in the middle of the pavement. After a long walk I came to the lab.

Professor had taught me 3 methods of liquefaction of gases. Claude's process, Linde's process and adiabatic demagnetization. I vaguely remember Claude's process.

As I entered the lab Aadhmi's laboratory hardware was standing near the cylinders. It said pointing to some cylinders," You should liquefy the gas in these cylinders."

I nodded and began to recollect the procedure. Claude's process is based on two principles. I was thinking deeply to organize the procedure.

Suddenly Aadhmi's laboratory hardware said, "Observing your brain functions it seems that you don't know how to liquefy the gas."

I was completely annoyed and gave it a frustrated look. It is always interfering in my business. Reading my thoughts it keeps on disturbing me. Aadhmi! You notorious robotic rascal! Stay out of my head! Or else I'll throw plates on you.

Catching up my mind voice Aadhmi replied in its robotic tone, "If you throw plates on me, the plates will be severely damaged. They will become unfit for eating. If you get this much anger, your blood pressure will increase. So don't be tensed. Moreover don't scold me in your mind. I can hear it."

I rolled my eyes and said with irritation, "Aadhmi can't you stay out of my head?"

It replied, "Not at all possible. I have to monitor all your actions. Your actions come out from your thoughts. So it is impossible to stay out of your thoughts."

I hate this robot. I will really respect it and like it if doesn't disturb me. I controlled myself and thought about Claude's process. The principle behind the process is Joule Thomson effect. Compressed air is allowed to do mechanical work by expansion.

Aadhmi's metallic voice again started, "You are an incapable student. It has taken you 3minutes, 11seconds, 5milliseconds and 23microseconds to recall the principle."

That's all. I had no more patience. I yelled, "Aadhmi stop it!" It yelled back, "Stop what?" I yelled again, "Stop monitoring me. I am a human being! Not a super computer! Our brain is not a processing unit with speed, accuracy and versatility. We forget things. Do you get it?"

Aadhmi said in its robotic tone, "Is it so? But a great man had said 'Human brain is the best computing device and no robots can replace him'. Whose words should I believe?" It voiced the quotation like a man. I stamped my foot and moved away.

I tried to concentrate on my work paying a deaf ear to its silly comments. I somehow recalled the experimental set up and managed to start the work while Aadhmi kept on trying its futile attempts to disturb me.

I arranged the experimental set up and when the process was going on I went to examine the different prototypes of the cryogenic engines which were made of an alloy that could withstand extreme heat and extreme cold temperatures. I was working on the cryogenic engines to improve their efficiency. These engines could give maximum thrust to rockets to reach greater heights and also to lift up satellites with transponders that may weigh more than hundred thousand tons. With the help of Aadhmi I liquefied oxygen to -223 degrees and hydrogen to -253 degrees and use them as a fuel for these engines. I went around the lab and then came back to the table where the process of liquefaction was going on.

9
Repeat Treatment For Aadhmi

Once all the gas was liquefied I measured the quantity to prepare the report. Aadhmi was continuously trying to make me converse with it. It wanted to build another word war with me. I said, "Aadhmi sir! I have completed my job Sir! What should I do now Sir? Shouldn't you report it to Professor, Sir?" I pretended to be modest and added the word 'Sir' with each sentence to please Aadhmi.

But aadhmi paid a deaf ear to my words. Usually I am supposed to report to Aadhmi and it will convey the message to Professor. But today Aadhmi is not doing so. I think it has decided to play pranks on me. With a bossy tone it said, "Sure! But you have to promise me one thing." I rolled my eyes and snapped, "What?" in an arrogant tone.

It happily wailed, "Tongue Twister!" Oh! Not the tongue twister again. Aadhmi always says some sentences in its robotic speed. Before I had understood even a word from it, it would have finished repeating it 3 times. Then it would pester me to repeat those sentences in the same way it had said. I go wrong always and I have never ever won in this game. Whenever I lose, it used to give me crazy punishments. This silly playful robot! Last time it made me twist my tongue with my fingers for 10 minutes as a punishment. It is a meddlesome and irritating robot!

I said, "Aadhmi! Please!" and put up the most piteous expression on my face. It said in a commanding voice, "No please!. Only tongue twisters." I sighed and gave up. Aadhmi said, "Try to repeat this. 'How much wood would a wood chuck chuck, if the wood chuck would chuck wood'" It said this tongue twister so fast 3 times and looked at me with a triumphant smile.

Wow! I know this myself. Thanks to my extra efforts to win Aadhmi and 'The Book of Tongue Twisters'. Aadhmi! You are dead today! I happily repeated the tongue twister three times. Even before I could open my mouth, Aadhmi read my mind and wore an expression of defeat on its face. It was shocked. Aadhmi! This is the expression that I have craved long to see on your metal face! As I am the winner my punishment to you is 'Repeat Treatment'.

Reading my mind, it asked slowly, "What is 'repeat treatment'? Why am I dead today?" It was really a fun to annoy Aadhmi. The puzzled expression on its face was such a wonderful scene. My plan was working well.

Aadhmi said, "Bindu! Please!" in a disturbed tone. I too tried to imitate the same tone and repeated, "Bindu! Please!" I was really irritating Aadhmi as my answers confused it. But I should control my thoughts and keep them blank; otherwise it will read my thoughts. Aadhmi said, "Don't". I repeated, "Don't". Aadhmi said, "Think about something. Think about that 'repeat treatment'. Don't keep your mind blank." With a roar of laughter I too repeated the same. Poor Aadhmi! It looked like a child lost in a crowded carnival.

Suddenly Professor Ramanujam called Aadhmi's laboratory hardware through the internal communication system. A live 3D hologram image of Professor appeared on a water-vapour layer and he asked, "Aadhmi is the liquefaction process over?" Aadhmi answered, "Yes Sir." I too repeated, "Yes Professor."

He said, "OK! I am coming to the lab." Once the call was over his image on the water-vapour screen vanished. Aadhmi again pleaded, "Please Bindu! Don't do this. This is making me crazy." I repeated, "Please Bindu! Don't do this. This is making me crazy." It said, "What should I do to make you stop?"

I repeated, "What should I do to make you stop?" It sighed and said, "Please, I'll do anything!" I too sighed and repeated the same. It said in a defeated tone, "Anything! Please cut it off!"

I think it really means what it says. I thought for a while and finally said, "OK. No more tongue twisters!" It asked in a shock, "What?" I said, "Yes. If you wished to play the tongue twister game ever again, then I'll give you this 'repeat treatment'". Aadhmi giggled and said, "So this is the 'repeat treatment' you were thinking! OK! I agree. No more tongue twisters". Well, one irritating problem is settled.

10
Nose-Poker Aadhmi

As we were talking Professor entered the lab swiftly. He was sturdy. His walk was firm and confident. He said in a brisk tone, "Can I see the liquefied gas?" I replied, "Sure Professor" and showed him the containers. He examined the quantity and remarked, "Fine".

Aadhmi interrupted and complained, "Bindu took 3minutes, 11seconds, 5milliseconds and 23microseconds to recall the principle."

Professor laughed and said, "Aadhmi human beings always take their own time to recall the information previously stored in their memory lanes. So this is not a mistake. It's quite natural. This speed is also not standard. It varies from individual to individual." Aadhmi went mum. Good! Nice nose cut to Aadhmi!

"Bindu did you enjoy the movie yesterday? What is the name of the movie?" Professor asked me casually. He knew very well that I go to movies on Saturdays with my family. I replied, "'Dooms Day' Sir. The story was OK. But I enjoyed only the graphics very much."

He smiled and said in a coming back to business tone, "Well. Today shall we discuss about surface chemistry?" But as soon as I said 'Dooms Day' my thoughts had drifted to my bizarre dream. Will it be correct if I discuss my strange dream with Professor? He has done research on dreams too. Probably he may even identify the reason why I have these dreams. He may even guide me to get rid of them. But will he believe that it is only a dream and not my imagination? Is my vision a premonition? What if my visions come true? Is the world coming to an end? I don't know and I have never seen my imaginary element in the periodic table. I have an uneasy feeling whenever the thought of the dream comes.

Professor had already started to discuss about surface chemistry and nothing had entered my mind. I have to put an end to this disturbance and distraction. I have to share this to Professor. But will he think that I am making up some stories? Even my sister doesn't believe me. We usually don't keep any secrets between us. But even she says my whole vision is a nice fiction. Shall I open up this matter now or later?

Suddenly Aadhmi interrupted in its robotic tone, "Professor Bindu is not listening to you. She is thinking about…" But before it could finish, Professor said, "Aadhmi how many times should I tell you not to sneak into Bindu's thoughts? It's not a good manners. Don't you understand that human beings can do multitasking?" Wow! Today Aadhmi gets a lot of nose-cuts and that too because of me! It's a lucky day I think!

I shut my thoughts and began to listen to Professor. He explained about the structure of colloidal solutions and the methods of preparation of colloids. I concentrated for 2hours and finally he gave a break. Not a break actually, but time for a little experiment. He wanted me to prepare the colloidal solution of Platinum. The method is easy. I have to do it by Bredig's Arc method.

Professor said to Aadhmi, "Now listen carefully Aadhmi. This is a strict order from me. You should never try to read Bindu's mind. Don't disturb her while she is doing the experiment. Once she completes the work she will report to you and you have to report that to me. Don't mess with her. Try to be polite to her." Then he left the lab.

Professor knew very well that I and Aadhmi were like Tom & Jerry. He did his best to keep us from quarrelling. Aadhmi is very quite now. I started the preparation. I took an electric arc and stuck it between Platinum electrodes. I placed the set up under water. I added a little amount of an alkali in the water to act as a stabilizing agent. I immersed the whole container in a cold bath. The arc became so hot and the intense heat vapourized some of the metal from the electrodes. The vapour condensed due to the cold water forming the colloidal solution of Platinum.

11
Puper

When everything was ready I informed Aadhmi, "Mission accomplished." All the while Aadhmi had kept mum. Professor is the only person in the world who can control Aadhmi. Aadhmi observed the colloidal solution and then informed it to Professor through its communication chip.

After a minute of listening, it replied, "Bindu Professor is in the observatory. You can go and meet him there after taking Puper with you." I said, "OK" and walked out of the lab to the animal confinement to take Puper.

On the way, I saw the temple of Lord Vinayaga and walked towards it. Lord Vinayaga is the deity of wisdom. He has the body of a man and the head of an elephant. He has big belly and long trunk. He has four arms. A serpent is tied around his waist. He sits on a small rat. He is the son of the God of destruction Lord Siva and the Goddess of power Parvathi.

I believe that there is some power superior to us and we name it as God. In my vision the Gods said that they were mutants. Could Lord Vinayaga be a mutant? May be! This change can happen to even human beings over a long period of time. Only necessity leads to genetic mutation and modification.

I stood in front of the temple and observed the statue. It was a marble statue decorated with golden jewels. The Lord was sitting on a golden platform. I prayed with joined palms and closed eyes.

'God! Please give me strength to accept everything that comes in my life. You know what is good for me in my life. Never allow me to take a wrong path. Always guide me in the path of righteousness. Give me the courage to face and win my difficult tasks.'

How good it is to surrender ourselves to some higher power! A baby has no worries as it surrenders itself to its parents who have more power. God is some sort of security like that. God has solutions to all our problems. Whenever I pray I never ask God for any materialistic things, but surrender myself at his feet. I felt very calm and relieved.

Then I walked towards the beautiful glass building. It was Professor's library. He had a wonderful collection of books from all over the world. Every month I have to read a book suggested by Professor and prepare a report on it. He himself was a voracious reader and he was happy that I was too. Through the glass walls I could see Aadhmi's library hardware. It was dusting and stacking the books. I walked past the library to the animal confinement.

In the animal confinement all animals are kept in a natural environment. It is a perfect zoo. All animals live and breed happily in this atmosphere. The vast forest extends up to many acres giving a lot of free space for all the animals here. Very rare species of plants and trees are abundant in this forest. Professor has a collection of many species of animals. The most important animal here is Puper.

Puper is a very cute extinct species. He is a saber tooth tiger cub. Animals like mammoth and saber tooth tiger existed only during the ice age. After the ice age they became extinct. Professor Ramanujam created Puper before 3 months and I had assisted him in that project. We studied all varieties of wild and domestic cats in detail. From fossil collections we decoded the saber tooth's DNA. We modified the DNA of related cat families and created Puper.

Though it sounds simple it was a 1 year project that took up most of Professor's lab time and all my vacations. The reward was miraculous. I became world famous because of my assistance. My pictures came out in all news papers and magazines. But not a single image of Puper came out as Professor Ramanujam was afraid to reveal Puper to the evil world. But somehow the curiosity of the media grew wild and the reporters were buzzing around me trying to get information about Puper.

It was really a good experience to work under Professor. Professor had modified the genes of the original tigers and created this saber tooth tiger. Puper's growth rate is restricted considerably so that Puper looks almost like a big kitten now. His eating habits have been altered too. I don't think of Puper just as some animal we use for our research. I love him so much. He loves me to. He is always happy to see me.

A hardware clone of Aadhmi takes care of all animals including Puper. But Puper dislikes Aadhmi. Though Aadhmi tries to be friendly with Puper and tries all tricks to impress him, Puper keeps away from Aadhmi. When we were under the project of creating Puper, I thought that the saber tooth tiger cub will be very wild as per its nature. But Puper is not a wild cat. He behaves like a domestic pet. Its behaviour and activities are under observation. Whenever I come to RV I spend some time with Puper. I carry him with me like a kitten.

I came to the area where young ones were kept. I went past many exhibits. I finally came to the glass cabin where I saw a yellow and white ball of fur with two micro small teeth protruding out. His eyes were sharp, bright and shiny as usual. I went to the entrance of the cabin and entered the password 'fluffy pants'. The door opened with a low buzzing sound. Even hearing that slightest sound, Puper stood up and ran towards the door. He jumped on seeing me. I am delighted to see his enthusiasm. I am so happy that he enjoys my visit. As soon as I knelt down he raced to me and jumped into my arms. My joy is boundless when I hold him in my arms. I lifted Puper and cuddled him. I gently rubbed his soft, silky and fluffy fur. He purred and gave a look of smile. I asked," Puper shall we go to the observatory to meet Professor?" He just smiled again.

12

Advancing Meteorites

I took Puper in my arms just like a baby. His claws scratched my skin. But I didn't mind. He was continuously trying to touch my face with his arms. Though Puper was 3months old, he was just the size of a domestic cat. His DNA has been altered by Professor to make such modifications. With Puper in my arms, the walk to the observatory didn't seem much long. I walked into the observatory and searched for Professor. He was sitting behind a huge pile of papers and drawing something. He is a good artist too!

Seeing me he smiled warmly and said, "Bindu I saw the colloidal solution. It is perfect!"

I said, "Thank you Professor."

Then he saw Puper who was trying to climb on to my neck from my arms. He remarked, "Puper has grown a lot. He likes you very much". I smiled.

Aadhmi alarmed Professor, "The time is 1 O'clock. It's time for lunch. Please come to the dining hall." Professor got up and said, "Bindu I am hungry. I'm sure that you are also hungry." I nodded in agreement. "So let us go to eat."

We started to walk. I was still carrying Puper in my arms. He had started to sleep and was slightly heavy now. Professor Ramanujam walked faster than me. Suddenly he turned back and exclaimed, "Bindu Puper is not a human baby. Don't spoil him. He can walk. Come on! Put him down. You should see him walk."

Puper had opened his eyes hearing Professor's sound and he stretched in my arms. I gently placed him on the ground. Professor chuckled on seeing me treating him as though he is a delicate doll. Puper began to walk with me very majestically. I admired him very much. It was so nice to watch. I've never seen him walk or may be I've never let him walk.

Professor started with a puzzled expression, "Bindu I saw something incredible through the powerful telescope in the observatory." I asked, "What is it Professor?"

He replied, "I observed four objects moving at very great speed. They seemed very large. I think they must be meteorites. They were nearing Neptune when I saw them. I've seen a lot of meteorites in my life, but nothing as big as these. These are very different. I'll have to keep on observing them in the following days." He began to think deeply as he walked.

This is so weird! No other scientist in the world could have seen these 4 meteorites as Professor has the most powerful telescope. If these meteorites come closer still, the whole world will know about it and start worrying about it. At present only Professor seems disturbed. Could these be the meteorites that come in my vision? If it is so, will they fall on the earth? Oh! God! Then what will happen to us? I think I must tell about my dream to Professor immediately. Now I am absolutely positive about certain facts. Firstly, I am having visions predicting the end of the earth; secondly, my imaginary element Emberonium not known to the world does exist; thirdly it is coming towards the earth in the form of huge meteorites; and fourthly, I may be becoming insane or going crazy as I imagine things!

We neared the house. Professor still had the confused expression on his face. As he was immersed in his own thoughts, we silently entered the magnificent house and walked to the dining room.

The dining room walls are completely covered by glass cupboards. All the cutlery collections are arranged neatly. Professor's favorite set is a crystal cup set embedded with jades, rubies, diamonds, emeralds and sapphires. It is exhibited on the top most shelf. Aadhmi has set the table for us already. We both sat down silently. Suddenly coming to his senses, Professor said, "Bindu, wash your hands before eating. You were playing with Puper and lifting him." I walked to the wash basin in the corner. Puper followed me and he tried to grab my legs. I smiled at him. We both walked back to the dining table. As soon as we sat, Professor called out, "Aadhmi". Within a fraction of a second, an old hardware of Aadhmi appeared from the kitchen. This is the oldest hardware of Aadhmi created by Professor Ramanujam when he was 14. Professor gets a surplus supply of all the basic requirements like fruits, vegetables, cereals, pulses, milk, meat, fish, egg etc. come from the farm lands in RV. In RV everything is cultivated and processed by the various hardwares of Aadhmi. Only organic method is followed. So the food here is always tasty and healthy.

Aadhmi served red rice and chicken gravy in Professor's plate. It came to me with a plate covered by a silver lid. It said, "Bindu I have brought something special for you." I wondered what that 'special' item may be! Very humbly it placed the plate in front of me and opened the lid. It has kept me some cabbage, a slice of carrot, a slice of beetroot, some unknown green color leaves and a ring of onion. I was completely shocked.

"Calculating your height and weight, your BMI (Body Mass Index) your weight is not appropriate for your height. You are slightly heavy. To say in simple words, you are moving towards obesity. You should not eat carbohydrate, fat and sugar. If you eat you will become fat and plumpy like a pumpkin. Eating these raw vegetables will reduce your fat, provided you must do regular exercise. Never even dream about eating chocolates and ice creams! I have fore warned you! If you do not follow my advice, you will become like an inflated pillow or a balloon." Saying so it moved back, pretending to be very humble and polite.

You metal head! How dare you comment on my height and weight? I know I'm slightly short and a bit chubby! But I am not a goat to eat these leaves and raw vegetables. May be I can have them as salad. But where is my main menu? Aadhmi is purposefully showing its vengeance. I couldn't open my mouth and say a single word in front of Professor. It is very cleverly touching me in my weak point. Professor Ramanujam came to my rescue.

He said, "Aadhmi serve rice and chicken in Bindu's plate. You very well know that she likes them." Aadhmi protested, "But Professor she is fat. She must eat only vegetables. I have…" Before it could finish Professor interrupted, "Aadhmi it is an order! Do what I say!" At once Aadhmi stood in attention and said, "Yes Sir!"

I chuckled and said, "Thank you Professor." Aadhmi served me delicious red unpolished rice and chicken curry. It placed a bowl of milk in front of Puper and tried to gently touch him. At once Puper sneered. Professor said, "Aadhmi leave him alone." Aadhmi pouted like a child and went into the kitchen. Puper never accepts Aadhmi though it takes care of him.

Professor leaned forward and said in a whispering tone, "I feel so sorry that I gave human feelings, emotions, thoughts and intelligence to Aadhmi. It is behaving more and more like a human and annoying us very much. It is always jealous of you and more intriguing in your matters. Don't worry about its nuisance."

We both chuckled secretly. I thought to myself, "How nice it would be if Aadhmi is physically more human. I could throw plates on it and even screw its ears!"

Aadhmi yelled from the kitchen, "Bindu! I can hear your thoughts from anywhere! Puper, your thoughts too!" We chuckled louder now. Puper must have thought something funny about Aadhmi to irritate it. It is so angry now!

13

Sharing The Dream

As soon as we finished eating, I started, "Professor, you have told me that you have done researches on dreams…." Even before I finished, he started enthusiastically, "Aah! Yes! That was some 50years back. That gives me some interesting memories." He smiled to himself thinking of something.

I didn't want to beat around the bush. So I said, "I have been having some strange dreams lately." Professor asked with concern, "What sort of dreams?" I replied with uncertainty and hesitation, "They are really strange. You wouldn't believe them."

He sat erect briskly and said, "Try me! You can say anything to me Bindu. I am ready to listen to you. OK. When did you have this dream first?" I replied, "During my physics class." He looked at me in a questioning way and said, "Were you sleeping in the class?" I replied, "Yes Professor." We both laughed.

Professor again came to the same point. "What was your dream about? Explain it to me in detail."

I just nodded and started, "I dreamt about Gods. In my dream they were having a chat." When I paused, Professor asked, "What were they talking about?"

I replied, "They were planning to destroy the earth." Aadhmi interrupted from the kitchen, "So without listening to the teacher you were imagining some stories?" I was totally pissed off.

I blurted out, "Shut up Aadhmi!" It wouldn't give up and started again, "But Bindu sleeping in the class is…" It was cut off by Professor's warning tone, "Aadhmi! Don't force me to dismantle you!" and he nodded to me, "You continue Bindu."

"When all Gods wanted to destroy the whole earth, the God who looked like Lord Vishnu convinced them that, only the people above 25years may be destroyed." Professor's eyes widened as he listened to the word '25years' and he eagerly asked, "Then!" "Then… I woke up!" "Did they say 25years? Are you sure about it?" I don't understand why he is giving more importance to that word '25years'. I said, "Yes Professor. I am sure" with a puzzled look on my face. "Is that all? Is your dream over? Have you missed any details?" I simply nodded as I have never seen him this much excited before. His eagerness faded. I continued, "But Professor again during the games period, I had a kind of vision. Actually I fainted…"

Aadhmi interrupted, "That's strange. When you fainted, you would have fallen down. Isn't it?" I replied a cold "Yes." Aadhmi exclaimed, "Wow! What a miracle! You fell down! But what a wonder! The earth is still safe and sound. It is impossible! Your fall must have created a tremor like earthquake or Tsunami. May be your friends must have experienced that." I butted in, "Shut up Aadhmi!" Aadhmi is always ready to tease me about my size. But I am not really that fat! Professor burst out, "Aadhmi stop it!" and gave out a sigh. He turned to me and said with concern, "Were you hurt badly? Are you alright now?" I said quickly, "Oh, nothing serious Professor. I am fine. Can I continue?" He nodded swiftly.

"I heard the voices of some Gods this time. I didn't see anything. I could only hear their voices. The Gods said that they were mutants with special powers and they existed between dimensions. They…" Professor butted in, "Really! That's incredible!" Somehow he controlled his emotions and asked me to continue. "They said that they were going to reduce the population of the earth in such a way that no human beings will get a clue that the Gods are behind this. They said about something called 'Emberonium' and that's all." I decided it would be better to skip the meteorite part.

14
Professor's Emotional Outburst

Suddenly I was shocked when I saw Professor's face. He was in tears. Why is he crying? Aadhmi shouted, "Professor she must have sneaked into your secret research room. She must have seen your research on Emberonium and on Gods." Why is Aadhmi saying like this? Is it crazy?

I shouted back, "No Aadhmi! I did not sneak into any room! I don't even know what you are talking about. I don't know anything about Professor's research but whatever I said is from my visions only."

Aadhmi argued, "No! How is it possible that you alone get such visions? How did you sneak into the secret research room without my knowledge? Tell me! How did you fool my security system?" during our word war, we both had totally forgotten Professor. Tears were flowing down his wrinkled cheeks. I turned to him and said, "Professor I swear! I didn't go in to the secret research room. I saw all these in my visions." He replied, "I trust you" in a very low voice.

Puper too became restless and tried to console Professor by rubbing his nose in Professor's legs. But Professor is still crying. Oh! God! Why is he crying like this? I've never seen him as a man of emotional weakness.

He said in a croaky voice, "Bindu please get me a glass of water." Even before I could understand what he said, Aadhmi handed him the glass of water. Professor's hands are trembling. He got the glass and drank a sip of water. Slowly he finished the glass and placed it on the table.

Aadhmi turned to me and said, "Sorry Bindu. You have never gone into Professor's secret research room. You are innocent. I read your mind. You should tell Professor about the meteorites too. Don't hide any information from him. All details are very important now. As you said very clearly some facts that Professor had proved by his researches I mistook you. I'm sorry." I replied, "It's OK Aadhmi." Why is it acting so polite?

Professor's hands are still shaking. But he has calmed down a bit now. He cleared his throat and spoke in a hoarse voice, "Bindu I trust you. Firstly, I am sure that you have never sneaked into my secret research room. Secondly, I believe that your dream is true. Thirdly, from my researches on dreams, I believe that your dreams are premonitions or signs that predict the nearest future. Fourthly, you have to trust me and confine in me. You should tell me everything." He stressed the word everything.

A started my narration again. I told everything that happened in my dream during physics period, without missing even single information. I told him everything about Gods; ashes; Dooms Day; Adhivega; Anjanaiputra; rocks; meteorites; new world; young generation and 25years. I told him each and every word. I told him about 'Emberonium' which is going to be sent to the earth in the form of meteorites.

I suddenly asked him, "Professor is there any element by name Emberonium? I have never seen any such name on the periodic table." Again his eyes were filled with tears. I don't know what made him cry now.

I felt very uncomfortable and said, "Professor, why are you crying? Please stop crying and tell me something." He controlled his tears.

15
The Tragedy

He simply had his eyes closed for a while and began to speak, "For generations our family had been doing scientific researches. All our family members lived together here as a big joint family. My grandpa, grandma, uncles, aunts, father and mother lived under one roof with love and affection binding us together. Each day was a day of celebration and joy with our new scientific inventions and discoveries. I was the youngest and as there was no young competitor in the family, I was an apple to every one in the family. We had a dog named Rex. He was my buddy and my lovable companion.

We had very little contact with the outer world. We didn't reveal all our inventions and discoveries to the outer world. We did not do researches for name, fame or money. Basically everyone in our family was genetically very much interested and well versed in Science, Maths, Vedas, Puranas, and Ayurveda. My uncle, father, mother and I concentrated more on space research. We all invented a new space ship and named it 'Prapancha'. Prapancha could travel even across the galaxies. We used Tritium as the fuel for Prapancha. You couldn't imagine the speed of Prapancha. It is faster than the speed of light. So we had to take so much of precautions before we began our adventure. Prapancha could also glide at a snail's pace. It could sail between dimensions too.

My uncle Prem was just 5years elder to me and we were good pals. He and I were the passengers of Prapancha's maiden voyage. We went at a moderate speed as it was the maiden voyage. We travelled for nearly 3months and fled past the Milky Way Galaxy. After touring Andromeda for more than 2months, we finally came to Kaala Galaxy. There were only two planets in Kaala Galaxy where we could land. Mostly all other planets were burnt and were looking like ember.

We landed on one of the two planets and named it 'Embera'. We wanted to collect samples of soil and rock for research purpose. We wanted to study the planet and know more about it. The rocks looked peculiar. We could collect only a pea size sample of a rock as it was too hard to break down. Then we returned back to the earth. We were happy to be home. We shared about our amusing space voyage to our family members.

My mother, father and two of my uncles were very much interested to study the pea size rock we had brought. We named it Emberonium. To our wonder it was so soft and spongy, very different from its hard state when we collected it. We were sincerely working on it to study its age, composition, atomic structure, atomic mass etc. 6days had passed after our return. Though we got some idea about its physical structure, we couldn't predict its true nature. The 7th day was the worst day of my life. It turned everything upside down."

He seemed as though he was reliving a painful moment. Uncontrollably tears began to roll down his eyes. He sobbed like a small child and burst out, "Why the hell did I bring that Emberonium to earth? Why the hell did I bring it home? I am a murderer! I did a massacre! I killed my family!" I was shocked and taken aback. What is he saying? Has he gone mad? Or is he really opening up the truth hidden deep inside him? How am I going to console this broken down man?

"Do you want to know what happened on the 7th day of Emberonium's presence in our lab? I still remember that cursed day. As usual we were in the lab. My uncle and I were playing arm wrestling on a table. Mom and Dad were preparing a report on its atomic structure. The room was filled with laughter and joy without knowing that a clock was counting down our seconds of happiness.

Suddenly, I felt a sweep of heat wave and to my horror, everyone around me turned into ashes. Yes! My father, mother and uncle just like that turned into ashes. I was still holding my uncle's arm and he crumpled to bits right in front of my eyes. What is happening here? Am I dreaming? I cried out loud and ran to see all other family members. To my horror they were also dead!

How is it possible? Why is it happening like this? I ran here and there crying like a child. I thought that I had gone mad. I was just 19 then. I knew no body other than my family. Why am I alive and how am I alive? Why are all elders dead? How will I live alone? Why the hell should I live alone? I heard the barking of Rex somewhere. Thank god! At least one living soul is with me. Of course, Aadhmi had always been with me and he was with me then too. He tried his best to console me and convince me.

I was very angry that I had lost everybody on a single day, all of a sudden. It was so painful to lose all beloved ones on a single day. I had no more tears to drain down my sorrow. Aadhmi was with me throughout my turmoil. Though it could not understand the real impact of my loss, it pretty well understood the seriousness of the situation. I am alive today, only because of Aadhmi's love, care and concern for me. It saved me from all my suicide attempts. It saved me from dying of fasting.

It took me some time to accept that I was an orphan now. I was all alone. When I wandered around my house, I found some animals dead and some animals alive in RV. Some trees were also burnt down to ashes, while some plants and trees stood normal. What is the mystery behind this? To my amusement the pea size Emberonium had vanished completely giving no clue about its disappearance. I soon learnt that the whole world around our area was normal. This abnormal destruction was observed only up to a radius of about 20km from our lab. After that radius, all plants and animals were normal. There was not even a single abnormal death reported beyond that limit.

I understood that Emberonium was the cause of this destruction. But how and why?

I thought about it over and over, until I became crazy. I forgot food, water or sleep. Emberonium had not affected non living things. So I sent Aadhmi again to Embera to collect another sample of Emberonium. When I analyzed the range of age of the survivors and the age of the organisms that were destroyed, it was clear that only the living organisms of age above 25 years had been destroyed. Now I was sure that Emberonium had not affected me as I was below 25.

The Emberonium sample brought by Aadhmi posed no threat for 6days. But as usual it vanished on the 7th day. After studying the effects of the sample brought by Aadhmi, I also came to the conclusion that some sort of radiation is emitted from Emberonium, leading to its own disappearance and the destruction around it. But my uncle Prem and I had been with Emberonium in Prapancha for nearly 2months. There was no radiation from Emberonium then. So, Emberonium must have become activated only when it had entered the earth's atmosphere. Up to 6days it was not harmful. On the 7th day, radiation which is powerful enough to turn down all living organisms of age above 20years into ashes had been emitted. I understood that Emberonium had behaved like a sleeping volcano. I wondered its power. A pea size Emberonium had destroyed an area of about 1,250 sq.km!"

He sighed and said in a chocked voice, "Aadhmi give me a glass of water." With tear filled eyes he stared the floor. Aadhmi gave him water again.

Suddenly I felt something wet in my cheeks and came to my senses. I realized that I too was crying and wiped my tears quickly. Aadhmi handed me a glass of water now. I was so thankful to Aadhmi as it was so understanding. I drank it slowly as something was blocking my throat and tears ran down my cheeks uncontrollably again.

Now I understand why Professor is living all alone in RV. Now I understand why he becomes quiet when I enquire about his family or relatives. I have always adored, admired and respected Professor. I thought he had everything in surplus and have even envied him. Yes! He is filthy rich. He is very intelligent and energetic. The scientific world looks at him with awe inspiration. But after listening to his painful past, I felt very pity for him. My love and respect for him grew more and more.

———————

16
Research On Gods

I've never imagined that Professor would have such a painful past. I felt very sorry for him. He had lived all alone through his bitter past. Through my watery eyes I could see that Puper is also crying. I think Puper understands what we speak and feel. Now Aadhmi tried to cuddle Puper in the name of consoling him. But Puper very tactfully slithered away from it and leaped on to my lap. I ran my fingers over his fur. He rolled into a ball in my lap. We all remained silent for a while.

Then Professor cleared his throat and started, "After this disaster I spent more time in thinking all alone to myself about life and death. I read many spiritual books. This directed my thoughts to god. I wanted to know about gods, spirits and spiritual world. Do gods have life and death? Is anybody immortal in this world? What happens after our life? Is what we call death, really the end or a beginning? Even Puranas and Idhihaasas could not answer me. I went on a practical search for gods. I did not search god by doing Thapas or Dhyana or prayer. I had a different scientific approach to gods. I believed that gods were invisible to us, just because they existed in between dimensions.

I pursued my relentless search for nearly 2 years. I travelled in Prapancha through many dimensions. I finally found Lord Siva after much difficulty. Though I had traversed that same area many times in Prapancha, I had never thought of the existence of a different dimension there. I saw him high above the Himalayan mountain range. He was shocked to see a human being reach him without his knowledge. Of course some people had already seen him on the earth or visited him in his own abode. But all those were under the will of the lord and not just as per the wish of those individuals. In my case, I had simply reached him with the help of Prapancha. So he was quite interested to know how and why I had come there.

I narrated my whole story and explained him about Emberonium. Lord Siva was very much curious to know more about Emberonium. As you know, the Hindu mythology depicts him as the god with three eyes. He has two eyes as normal human beings and a third eye in the middle of his forehead. This third eye is closed always and if he opens it, the powerful flames from that eye could burn anything in front into ashes. He used to open this third eye only when he is angry. So, lord Siva was interested in Emberonium and its ability to burn everything above the age of 25 into ashes.

When I talked with him, I understood that gods are mutants with some special powers. Different gods exist in different dimensions. There are millions of such mutants still unknown to us. These mutants could hear the thoughts of all living beings. They even help the living organisms directly or indirectly. But there are no specific rules for the help to be delivered in time or undelivered. Some mutants can take different forms too. All mutants travel between dimensions as per their will and wish. They have visited human beings and also have apparated a few along with them to their own abode.

The people who had accidentally or incidentally seen such mutants have created their paintings or sculptures or statues and have introduced them to others. Some have tried to pass on their knowledge about these mutants to their descendents or disciples or younger generations. Some have kept this knowledge as a hidden secret to themselves. Such people are given the name as Saints, Mahaans or Rishis. There is nothing as god or religion. How silly it is, that we humans divide and fight among ourselves in the name of religion, which does not exist and gods, who are just mutants. But I found this revelation giving answer to many of my questions.

For example my grandma would sing 'Aandal's Thiruppavai' – a collection of 30 devotional songs in Tamil, about lord Vishnu in her melodious voice during the month of Margazhi. Once I asked her who the poet of Thiruppavai was. My grandma narrated the story of Aandaal. There are evidences for the life of Aandaal in Srivilliputtoor. But her presence under a tulsi plant in a nandavanam and her disappearance all of a sudden, when she entered the holy sanctum of Lord Ranganatha at Srirangam was a mystery to me. But my research on gods made it clear that a person can be apparated from one place to another within seconds by such mutants who had that power. So her birth and disappearance are just apparations from one dimension to the other.

Another danger awaited me. When I wanted to take leave, lord Siva wouldn't allow me to leave 'Siva Loga' because he feared that I would reveal this secret to the whole world. He did not want the world to know that gods were just mutants and not something super natural. So he wanted me to stay there forever. When I insisted on leaving he threatened to destroy me. But after much convincing, I made it clear that it was not my intention to enlighten the world. I pacified him that I had come there on my own venture and I wouldn't make a publicity of me reaching his abode. Lord Shiva wanted to know where exactly I found Emberonium. So I took him to the Kaala Galaxy. Finally he accepted to let me go. From then on, I have searched and found the abode of different gods who are believed to belong to different religions. I have seen most of the gods." Professor took slow breaths and he was a bit calmed down now.

I had been listening to Professor with my mouth open wide. I couldn't believe what I was hearing. Is it possible for an individual to explore like this? Whatever I have heard now is too much to digest. Puper gently jumped from my lap on to the table and walked to Professor. He casually lifted his paw and rubbed Professor's arms. Professor, who was staring the floor, tore his eyes from the floor and smiled at Puper. Puper rolled on the table as though he was doing some funny circus. Professor laughed at his attempt.

Aadhmi placed a fluffy yarn ball on the table and rolled it towards Puper. Puper turned his head away from Aadhmi and acted as though the ball never existed. I casually grabbed the ball and rolled it to Puper. Puper blocked it with his front paw and rolled it back to me. We all laughed except Aadhmi.

Aadhmi moaned, "Why do you behave like this Puper? You always like this girl only! Why do you always play with her?" I chuckled. Puper took his eyes away from the ball and looked at Aadhmi. Then he made a face and sneered. Aadhmi stamped its foot.

Professor and I laughed merrily. Aadhmi shouted, "Why do you laugh like this? Don't be silly!" his tone made us laugh even more loudly. Aadhmi said, "Wait Puper! Bindu will be with you only today. As soon as she leaves, you will have to depend on me only." As usual, Puper ignored Aadhmi. We continued laughing.

17
The Danger Of 4 Meteorites

Coming back to reality, I spoke up, "Professor could those 4 meteorites that you observed through the telescope in the observatory be Emberonium?" Professor thought in silence for a while and then said in a low voice, "May be" as though he was speaking to himself. Suddenly he sprang up and said, "Aadhmi, go to my observatory and try to spot those meteorites. Estimate their size and speed. Trace their present path and predict their expected trajectory.

"Aadhmi replied in a smart way, "Yes Sir! I have signaled my observatory hardware to accomplish the delegated tasks. We will get the report in 20seconds." Professor turned to me and said, "Bindu, when exactly did you hear the voices last?" I replied spontaneously, "Yesterday afternoon at approximately 2.30." Professor's eyes brightened.

Aadhmi spoke up, "Professor the 4 meteorites are extremely huge like mountains. They entered the Milky Way Galaxy at 5 o'clock, yesterday evening. At present they have raced past Pluto. I have traced their expected trajectory and as per their present speed, they will fly past the orbits of Uranus, Saturn, Jupiter, Mars and finally crash at 4 points on the earth. The speed is too high to be predicted. One of the meteorites will crash between Srilanka and Tamilnadu particularly near Rameshwaram; another near the Ellesmere Island; and the remaining two near both the poles. All these four meteorites are of the same size and shape and same speed.

Professor asked suddenly, "Did you say something about 'Adhivega' when you detailed your vision?" I murmured, "Yes Professor. But what is Adhivega?" He replied, "Did I not tell you that I had already met many gods? One among them is Adhivega. Adhivega is neither worshipped by nor known to people of any religion. This mutant has the capacity to move anything between dimensions at a great speed and also to apparate between dimensions. Now I understand how the meteorites are coming towards earth at this incredible speed. This is not a natural phenomenon; it is the work of the mutant Adhivega!"

I said, "Professor, usually the meteorites that enter into the earth's atmosphere, burn down to ashes due to friction and do not cause much damage. Will it happen like that now too?" Aadhmi answered even before Professor could open his mouth, "That happens when the meteorites are of smaller size. But now, considering the size of the approaching meteorites, they could at once destroy all the land mass on earth if they crash on the earth's surface. More over the destruction could also be triggered by the combined effect of the earth quakes, tsunamis and volcanic eruptions that occur because of the collision."

Professor was in deep thought. I was very much perplexed. I asked, "Professor, why did I get this dream? Can there be any special reason? Could there be somebody else on the Earth who have had the same vision?"

Professor replied, "I don't have the answer for any of your questions. May be someone else might have had the same vision. But we are not sure about it. But as only you have got the premonition there must be some reason behind it. May be the gods are behind this too. They can play with our mind and brain at any time."

I burst out with tears in my eyes, "Please Professor, we must do something to save the earth. Can't we make arrangement to shatter the meteorites into pieces using Paari, your giant laser projectile?"

He replied instantaneously, "No Bindu, I don't want to use laser on Emberonium without knowing the true effect of laser on it. The results may be adverse. So we have to think and act. More over as per your dream even when the meteorites come towards the earth with very high speed because of Adhivega, their landing on earth is not going to be a crash but it is going to be gentle because of Anjanai Putra. Hope now you would also have understood that Anjanai Putra is none other than Hanuman. He is also a mutant. You very well know his power and efficiency from the epic Ramayana. So there won't be any considerable destruction because of the landing. The most important danger we have to worry about is the radiation from Emberonium after 6days."

"Professor even if the landing is gentle, won't there be any rise in the sea level if these huge rocks of Emberonium fall into the oceans? Won't these meteorites be a threat to the people living there if they fall on land mass?"

Professor just had his eyes closed for a minute and then spoke quickly, "Yes, Aadhmi will make arrangements for the evacuation of the people in those localities."

Aadhmi replied briskly, "Yes Professor, I will make arrangements as per your plan." I guess that Professor must have given it directions by thinking.

Professor continued, "Well. Evacuation will be taken care of, without alarming the people. The public shouldn't panic. So you can calm down Bindu."

18
The Fest

"Professor should any steps be taken to cancel the International Cultural Youth Fest to be held in New Delhi?" asked Aadhmi.

I too nodded in agreement. "Yes Professor. I think that this critical moment is the time for action and not entertainment."

Professor said in a strong voice, "No! No! The 'International Cultural Youth Fest' must take place in New Delhi as planned earlier by the President. This festival is to celebrate the peace and harmony between nations. India is proud to host this celebration. If that fest is cancelled for any reason, that will be a big black mark to our nation. Moreover after all these arrangements made and practice done by millions from all over the world, we need not disturb such a 'gala time' worrying about a danger that is out of our control."

Puper who had also been quietly listening until this moment stretched on the table and yawned. I think he feels sleepy. Aadhmi said to Puper in a sweet tone, "Puper… I will sing you lullaby and make you sleep. Come to me" and tried to touch him. Puper sprang up and jumped into my arms. Aadhmi shouted suddenly, "Puper! Don't ever think like that!"

Professor asked, "What is Puper thinking Aadhmi?"

Aadhmi mumbled, "Hm…Nothing!"

We both understood that Puper must have thought something horrible about Aadhmi. Though we didn't know what it was exactly, we began to laugh. Aadhmi again shouted, "What is there to laugh?"

We controlled ourselves and I asked, "Professor can you tell me more about Kaala Galaxy and the planet Embera?"

"**Bindu**, when I visited Kaala Galaxy, except Embera all other planets were either completely or partially burnt. We did not know the reason why the other planets were burnt. We found Emberonium rocks only in planet Embera. Embera did not have atmospheric oxygen for breathing. I think that is why Emberonium had not disintegrated and vanished, but remained stable in Embera. I guess that the time taken for reaching its ignition point or state or temperature may be 6days. That is why it burns and disappears on the 7th day when it reaches the earth's atmosphere that has oxygen which is needed for burning. These are still my assumptions and not confirmed laws." I was listening intently.

Aadhmi interrupted, "Professor you have an appointment scheduled for today's evening. You have promised them that you will attend that function. I am supposed to remind you that. Now the time is 5p.m." I looked at Aadhmi with irritation. Seeing my expression, Professor laughed and said, "**Bindu**! Do you want to be late for your own Chithi's 'Valaikappu'? I think the scheduled time is evening 6 O'clock."

Oh! My god! How did I forget this function? Today's unexpected shocks must have numbed me. I have to rush home now. Or else I will be pretty late! I stood up and placed Puper who had fallen asleep in my arms, gently on the table. He opened his eyes, looked at me with understanding eyes and continued his sleep. I felt very sorry to leave him without saying proper goodbye.

Professor said, "Puper is OK. He understands well. Don't worry. You go to the function. I have some arrangements to make. After doing that I will meet you there. But remember! Don't reveal whatever we have discussed here to anyone; whoever it may be your friends or relatives. It is a confidential matter. I am sure that you are trust worthy as always. But please don't leak out anything out of curiosity."

I nodded in agreement to him. Then I bid farewell to Professor and Aadhmi and rushed into my black Audi. I started it and raced to my house. We call our mother's younger sisters 'Chithi'. My Chithi Gayathri is pregnant. This is going to be her first baby. Valaikappu is a ritual performed usually during the 7th or 9th month of a woman's first pregnancy. All elderly and married women perform this ritual for the health and happiness of the pregnant mother and the baby inside her womb.

Usually all friends and relatives are invited to have a get together, to enjoy good food and also to bless the pregnant lady. Today is my Gayathri Chithi's day. All the elderly women bless the pregnant mother by adorning her with glass bangles, applying Chandan (sandal paste) and kumkum (Vermillion prepared from turmeric) on her cheeks and arms and forehead. All delicious food and sweets are prepared and enjoyed by all, including the pregnant mother.

It is believed that the baby inside will feel safe and secure listening to the jingling of the glass bangles in the mother's hands. Those glass bangles will be removed only after the child's birth. The mother is given utmost care and love at this stage so that the baby inside also feels the same and enjoys the happiness of the mother. Professor had been invited to this function already as he is our family friend.

19

Stunning Sister

The drive did not seem long. As I neared my house I could see Indu standing in the front. She is wearing a designer choli. She looks gorgeous in the white dress with red and green color combinations. She is very pretty.

As I got out of my car she said, "Akka, get ready soon. We all are ready and Dad is expecting you." We address our elder sister 'Akka'. I smiled at her and just nodded. I took a moment to admire her from head to toe. She was wearing a beautiful golden chain with sunflower shaped pendant. The pendant had enamel works of dark red and green colour. It was large and prominent. The enamel flower was perfectly matching her dress. She was wearing a pair of gold ear rings with the similar art work of enamel flower. She had a golden bracelet in her left hand. It is just looking as though a red and green color enamel flower with golden stem was wound around her wrist. The same model ring adorned her left hand ring finger. In her right hand she was wearing 6 golden bangles, each with 6 enamel red and green flowers at equal distances.

She had applied make up that perfectly suited her out fit. The bindi on her forehead was studded with red, green and white stones and it rested perfectly in the middle of her eyebrows. Her long silky straight hair was combed neatly and left loose at the back. There was a beautiful matching red and green flower designed clip pinned to her hair. She herself was looking like a fresh flower.

I could not resist admiring her. I said happily, "Indu you look so beautiful in this dress." Indu was putting on her sandals with the same design of stone works. She turned to me and pouted, "But when you get ready you will be better than me. Anyway, thank you!" I just laughed at her ignorance and ran into the house. Actually she is much prettier than me. She has bright and beautiful eyes. She is slim, tall and smart. All costumes perfectly fit her. I am a bit chubby and I have to be very choosy in my costumes.

My thoughts were interrupted when I saw my mother. She is almost ready and is giving the final touches standing in front of the dressing table. Mom was wearing a green colour silk saree with a thin strip of golden border. Mango design was embroidered in golden thread near the border. Dark green stones shone at the tip of each mango. Her matching blouse fitted her perfectly and had golden mangoes embroidered in the sleeves.

She wore a traditional jewel set made of gold and green stones. The jewel set had mango design throughout. A pair of big dangling earrings called 'Jimikki' was dancing in her ears. 8 gold bangles were jingling in both her hands. She had tied jasmine flowers very closely in a special style and pinned them to her hair. As soon as she saw me she smiled broad. She looked very bright and beautiful. She must have spent at least two hours in the beauty parlor for her facial and nearly an hour in front of the mirror with her makeup kit to give such a glow to her face. My mother loves to enjoy the special occasions to the core by making her appearance so gorgeous.

She asked, "Hai Bindu how was the day? What did you do in Professor's house today? How is Puper? What did you eat for lunch?" Only Mom could ask so many questions at a time without expecting any immediate answer. Even before finishing her series of questions she herself will forget her first question. I opened my mouth to say something.

Suddenly I remembered Professor's instructions. So I said, "Puper is fine Mom. Now he even understands what we think and feel. Today

Professor taught me to prepare colloidal solution of platinum. As usual, Aadhmi tried its level best to annoy me." Mom laughed and said, "I have kept your half saree set and jewels in your room. Get ready soon."

My father entered into the room. He was dressed in a silk dhoti and a silk shirt. Seeing me he hugged me and kissed me on my forehead. Then turning to my mother he said, "Hmm, Hmm. Enough Darling. You are already beautiful. You need not waste this much time in front of the mirror. Come on! Let's go. Indu is ready."

Usually Dad becomes a ring master when we get ready to a party. He gets ready quickly and keeps on pestering us to get ready soon. But we three, I, my sister and Mom take a lot of time to get ready during such special events. So Dad has to do the intense job of ripping us apart from the mirror whenever we go out for a function.

He pulled my mother from the dressing table and said, "Bindu it is already late. It is our family function. So we must be there in time to receive the guests. I, your Mom and Indu will go now. You get ready quickly and come there as early as possible. First come and lock the door as we are going to leave now." I replied, "OK Dad" and went behind them to close the door. They hurried out, got into Dad's car and left. I got a message in my phone. It was from Abi Akka. Abi is my cousin. The text read:

Bindu where r u? Come fast. Guests will start to come in 15 minutes.

I sent a reply.
Mom, Dad and Indu are on the way. I'll be there in half an hour.

I locked the house and took bath. I dried my hair with a fluffy white turkey towel. I spotted my half saree and jewels on the table. My mother had kept me some jasmine flower too. The half saree set had a long flowing silk skirt, a blouse and a matching half saree. The silk skirt was in peacock blue colour with a light green colour border. The border was decorated by feathered peacocks embroidered in golden silk thread. A blue colour stone was placed on each eye on the peacock feather. The upper part of the silk skirt was enhanced by sequence work with golden chumkis. The blouse was light green in colour with short sleeves. Each sleeve had a huge peacock design. The jacket had a low cut back. There were two ropes on either side of the back, which could be fastened together. Two golden peacocks with blue and green stones embedded in them, hung at the end of the two ropes. The silk half saree was in a mixed colour of peacock blue, green and gold. It showed different shades in different angles.

I dressed myself in 5 minutes. I combed my hair and tied my hair loose in a single plait. I pinned a shining stone clip with peacock design on my hair. I pinned the jasmine flower below the clip. I applied a thin layer of makeup and kept a peacock designed stone sticker bindi on my fore-head. I looked at myself in the mirror. Something is missing! Ah! I have forgotten the jewels.

I opened the drawer and found the jewels. There was a long thick gold chain with a peacock pendant. The peacock had fully spread its feathers and there were very tiny green and blue colour stones in the eyes and feathers of the peacock. There was a short chain too. The short chain was thin and from its centre hung loosely a peacock similar to the one in the long chain. I took the golden hip chain and hooked it around my waist. Stone peacocks hung at equal distance in the solid gold hip chain.

I put on my golden ear rings. It looked as though a peacock was sitting in my ear lobe and its feathers were hanging down freely. The ear ring also had stone works. In my right hand I put 10 thin gold bangles and at both the extremes I placed two broad bangles with 4peacocks at equal distance. In the left hand I wore a chain bracelet with similar stone peacock. I slid a golden ring into my right hand ring finger. The ring had a peacock mounted on it. Blue and green stones shone from that peacock too.

I wore silver anklets with peacock design. Hundreds of tiny silver balls called 'chalangai' hung from the anklets and made chiming sound whenever I moved my legs. South Indians consider gold as a sacred metal and we never wear it in our legs. So we use only silver for anklets.

20

Naughty Bala

Suddenly my phone rang. It was Bala. I answered it, "Hi Anna!" He shouted, "Hey potato! Where are you? Guests have started to come. Don't pretend to be too busy. Whatever makeup you do will be of no use if the party is over. Come soon potato!"

Bala is my mother's elder sister's son. He is Abi Akka's younger brother. He was born just 10minutes earlier than me. So he believes strongly that he is elder to me and expects me to respect him as an elder brother. We call an elder brother 'Anna'. He always teases me that I am chubby and calls me 'potato'. I replied, "I am on my way." He yelled back, "We miss you potato!"

I snatched my Audi's key from the key stand and rushed out. When I reached my Chithi's house, I felt relieved that not too many guests had arrived yet. The parking lot was free only. Thank god I am not too late. But I know very well that guests will be flooding in soon. The time is 6.15p.m now. I appreciated myself for getting ready this much quickly and entered the house after parking my car.

Bala was standing in front of the reception table. There were many large trays on the table. There were large fresh red Ooty Roses on a tray; neatly tied jasmine flowers on another tray; another tray had Rose water, Chandan and Kumkum; another tray had a heap of sweets and all were arranged neatly to receive the guests.

Bala was very smart in a graphic Nehru jacket and black jeans. He looked taller than me. He keeps on growing now. Two years back he was shorter than me. As soon as he saw me, he chuckled in a teasing manner and closed his mouth. I walked towards him. Only when I went near him I realized that I have to really look up to see his face. What is he doing to grow tall like this?

Seeing me he tried to control his laughter and said between giggles, "Potato! What are you wearing? The guests may get a heart attack on seeing you." I replied coldly, "I hope you are not blind Anna. I am wearing a half-saree." Again he chuckled, "Oh! Oh! It looks as though a potato is wrapped in a blue colour cloth." I gritted my teeth in anger. He is another Aadhmi in annoying me. I have to tackle his comments. I quickly snapped him, "Did you see yourself in the mirror Bala? You look like a bamboo stick wearing a shirt and pants. Moreover you don't have the guts to wear a traditional dhoti." He mumbled, "Huh! Who said I do not have the guts? I don't …" Again I interrupted him, "Accept the fact that you don't know to wear a dhoti!"

He began, "Hey potato…" but was interrupted by someone coming from inside calling, "Hi Bindu!" I turned and it was Abi Akka. She was very tall; even taller than Bala. Once she had long thick black hair that fell down like a black cascade below her knee. Now she has a boyish cut. She feels it comfortable and convenient to maintain. She was wearing a black pencil jeans and loose white cotton tops.

A thin platinum chain sparkled in her neck. A watch was in her left wrist and a thin platinum bracelet was in her right wrist. A plain platinum ring adorned her right hand ring finger. She hates the yellow colour of gold. She had been like this since her childhood. White metal and black metal were her favourite. All the golden jewels gifted to her or bought by her parents for her were sent to the locker at once as she never touched them. There was no bindi on her forehead. She repels traditional outfits, traditional habits and customs. But I love being traditional.

I greeted, "Hi Akka!" She exclaimed, "You are so beautiful in this dress. Your dazzling peacocks are attractive. You remind me a beautiful peacock." She casually adjusted my flower and pinned it properly. I replied, "Thanks Akka" directing a stare towards Bala. Bala held his stomach and pretended to control an upcoming vomit and said to Abi, "Akka you must test your eye sight. I shall fix an appointment with the best eye specialist in the town. You must be partially blind or your eye sight must be terribly affected. Such words of praise will never come out from a person with normal eye sight. I feel like throwing up when I see Bindu." She couldn't control her laughter hearing his comments. Somehow she managed a stare towards him and said, "Shut your mouth you monkey. Don't spoil the happiness." She went near him and sat on one of the empty chairs in front of the reception table. She is all set to receive the guests. I said, "Akka I'll see Chithi and come." She nodded, "OK."

I entered the decorated spacious hall. Seating arrangement was neat and comfortable. All ladies were busy with some work or the other chatting and laughing among themselves. Gayathri Chithi was sitting on a podium in the middle of the hall. My Ammamma (mother's mother) was arranging a display of silver trays in front of Chithi. There were many trays in front of Chithi and on those trays all fruits, raisins and nuts were arranged neatly. Especially on a very large tray hundreds of glass bangles were arranged neatly. There was also another tray on which silver bowls containing Rose water, Chandan, kumkum, turmeric, betal leaves and holy ash were kept. There prevailed a pleasant smell in the atmosphere. Small kids were noisily running around and playing happily. All our family members and close relatives were present there.

On seeing me Chithi waved joyfully. She was glowing in her wedding saree and jewels. During Valaikappu a lady is supposed to wear her wedding saree. She looked like a goddess. Usually as soon as Valaikappu is over the mother to be is taken from her husband's house to her mother's house for the delivery. Only after the naming ceremony of the new born, the mother returns back to her husband's house with the baby. So from today onwards Chithi will be in Ammamma's house for at least 7months.

Though she had not applied any make up Chithi's cheeks were very pink and shiny. She smiled sweetly when I neared her. She spoke with a mischievous smile, "Hm! Now I understand why it took you so long to come here. Welcome peacock beauty!"

I smiled and said, "Sorry for not coming early Chithi. Anyway thank you for your compliments. You look more beautiful now. I have no words to describe your serene beauty." We kept on talking sweet nothings for a while. Ammamma too joined us. The hall was getting occupied slowly. I excused myself saying, "I'll be at the reception Ammamma" and came back to the entrance.

21
Diya My Friend

As I walked to the reception, I was delighted to see Professor Ramanujam talking with Abi Akka. There are still a lot of questions circling inside my head and I could clarify them now. But is it possible in this crowded atmosphere? I walked towards them.

Professor saw me and said, "Bindu you look so beautiful in this half saree. This is the special dress of Tamil Nadu. But nowadays it is very rare to see girls in this costume. I am so happy to see you in this dress. It would be better if Abi too had worn a Half-Saree."

Maybe I was really beautiful. Professor always loved the traditional way of dressing. Abi Akka repelled tradition. So, she smiled sheepishly. I said, "Thank you Professor. Please come in and get seated." He excused himself from Abi Akka and walked with me towards the hall. Bala was found to be nowhere.

I asked Professor in a very low voice, "Professor I have a doubt. As far as I know, I think drilling beyond a depth even for research purpose is not allowed in the poles. All nations have signed pacts to protect the polar region. But the meteorites are going to fall on the poles too. Wouldn't it be an immediate danger to the earth?" He suddenly laughed and I couldn't make the head or tail out of it.

He explained, "Bindu! Those facts are all built up by us. We scientists made up those facts for a purpose. See! The poles have a number of varieties of metals and minerals in great quantity beyond our imagination. If the predatory human population knows about it they will scrap it all out and what will the forth coming generations have? So we scientists made up this theory for the betterment of future earth. But still there are some brainless people who call themselves 'scientists' and try to smuggle the resources from the poles." That is incredible. I am sure if such rumors were not created the human population would have made the two poles an exquisite tourist spot and thereby polluted it.

I asked, "Professor, can you tell me if life is possible in any other planet?" Professor smiled at me and said, "I think this is not the apt time. I'll say it to you in a couple of days. Bindu! Hmm... Can you skip school tomorrow? I have got a lot of things to say, show and teach you."

I sometimes went with Professor during school days to assist him in his researches. The last time I did this was when we created Puper. My school liberally allows me for this because it is a matter of pride and prestige to have one of their students as an assistant to the world famous scientist Professor Ramanujam. I said energetically, "Sure, Professor!" As we neared the hall, we saw Daddy. He walked over to us.

Daddy exclaimed with joy, "Hello, Professor Ramanujam! Welcome. How are you and your researches?" Professor Ramanujam exclaimed back, "Hello, Thirupathi! I am fine and everything else is well as usual." They shook their hands. I came to know of Professor personally only through Daddy. Being a Bank Manager my father helps Professor Ramanujam with his accounts. Dad and Professor Ramanujam are really close. Professor considers Daddy as his son. They started their conversation and I took leave from them and walked over to the reception.

I saw Abi Akka and I went near her. She made a face and said, "Why does your Professor bother about me? I can wear whatever I wish and I believe we are in democratic India!" I said, "Akka, he is one hundred and three. Old people always want everything to be traditional. So, never mind his words." trying to comfort her. She rolled her eyes.

Suddenly a familiar face appeared in the entrance. It is Diya. She likes me very much and I like her too. She is our family friend too. I always help her in her studies. While we study, she is very thorough with her answers and recites them spontaneously. But as soon as she enters the examination hall everything vanishes from her memory. She says that she feels very anxious and tensed when she sees the question-paper. So currently I am working to help her come out of her emotional disturbances.

Diya wailed joyfully, "Hi! Bindu!" She almost ran to me and hugged me heartily. Looking at me through her rectangular framed glasses she exclaimed, "Wow! You look superb in this dress" and winked at me. I couldn't control my laughter. Diya is very innocent and she simply admires me for everything. She was so lovely in a purple colour choli.

I said, "Diya you are awesome in this costume. Tell me how many people fainted on the way seeing you?" With a funny smile on her face, she began to snap pictures of me in her cell phone. I shouted, "Hey! What are you doing?" She announced, "You are so pretty in this dress and the whole class will talk about you tomorrow as I am going to show these pictures to them! "I felt quite embarrassed and shy. Why is Diya behaving like this? If I had known that she would put me into trouble like this I wouldn't have come in half saree. None of my friends or classmates wears half saree nowadays. They will certainly make fun of my outfit in the class tomorrow."

I ran near her and tried to snatch her phone saying, "No Diya. You are not doing anything! You can't exhibit my photos to anyone." I grabbed it skillfully. She placed her hands in her hips and asked questioningly, "Why not?"

I replied in a funny tone, "Because I will not draw the diagrams for you in your science record note" and moved my left eyebrows up and down swiftly. She pouted and raised her right eyebrows.

With a defeated expression she said, "OK. I will not reveal anything about your gorgeous dress in the class. But Raj will." I questioned, "Raj!"

Diya said excitedly, "Don't you know that Raj will also come today? He kept on saying about that in the class." Oh! God! Raj's parents are also our family friends. I love and respect uncle and aunt. But I don't want my class to know about my outfit. I don't know what to do now. Do I really look like a potato as Bala said? I felt humiliated. Somehow I collected myself and said, "OK Diya. You please get inside and get seated in the hall. I'll join you soon."

As she moved away she saw Abi Akka on the way and again wailed, "Hi Abi Akka! How are you?" Abi Akka said warmly, "Hi Diya. I'm fine. Welcome dear" and soon Diya went in. I saw Diya's parents approaching. I welcomed them and directed them in. I saw Raj's parents enter in. I was relieved that Raj was not with them. I went towards them to receive them. They are our family friends from childhood. Aunty pinched my cheeks gently and said, "Sorry for being late sweety! Raj is coming with Bala. They will be here in no time." Without knowing the impact of what they had said they happily went in. I felt like they had thrown a bomb on me.

22

The Twin Nuisance

Oh! No! Already Bala is in full form to tease me. If Raj joins him, no one can control him. It will be better if I don't get into their vicinity. I stood behind a pillar and peeped out to see Raj and Bala enter in. They were walking hand in hand. Raj was laughing at some crazy joke that Bala might have cracked. Did Bala make fun of me? Ok! Let me escape from their vision. I quickly said to Abi Akka "Akka, I am going to the dining hall." Without waiting for her affirmation or reply I just ran away leaving her behind with a puzzled look.

A grand delicious feast has been arranged and I saw the guests enjoying that happily. I saw Professor eating and my mother was serving him payasam, saying something funny to make him let out a roar of laughter. I started to serve ice-cream to everyone.

When I crossed my mother, she exclaimed with wide eyes, "You look so pretty my darling!" Only now we both are meeting after their departure from home. She scanned me from head to toe and smiled with satisfaction. Suddenly I saw Raj entering the dining hall. I stopped serving ice-cream, gave the tray to my Mom and rushed out through another way. As I was running down the steps I felt a hand grab mine. The grip was firm and strong. I turned with bewilderment to see who it was. To my dismay and shock, it was Bala.

He smiled wickedly and said, "Hey potato! Where are you running stealthily? Do you know that I got a company now?" If Raj had come with him, then I am dead. I scanned the area behind Bala. There was no sign of Raj. I let out a sigh of relief.

Bala grinned mischievously and said, "Hey potato! See the guests are complaining that ice-cream is over. It's all because of you. I know that in the name of serving ice-cream you might have swallowed as much as possible. How many times should I tell you not to steal and eat ice-creams? Ignoring my advice if you keep on eating chocolates and ice-creams you will transform from a potato into a pumpkin. Tell me! What shall we do now? How are we going to serve desert to the guests who are still flooding in?"

I understood his mockery and said defensively, "Grandpa will take care of that. You need not worry about the availability or shortage of anything in the dining hall," still trying to escape from his firm grasp. He said, "Are you so busy eating that you couldn't even welcome your friend Raj?"

Thank god. Bala is thinking that I am too busy eating. He did not realize that I was actually running away from them. I said, "Bala, Please let me go," in my attempt to escape from him. His grip became more firm. "Where are you trying to run now? How many chicken leg pieces did you gobble?" I must escape from this stupid Bala. An idea hit me. I brought my mouth close to his hand that was holding me. I opened my mouth pretending to bite his hand. He became aware of the impending danger and instantly loosened his grip. I ran away as fast as I could without dashing on the guests moving here and there. Bala also chased me shouting, "Bindu, Bindu…" But I mixed into a crowd of women and escaped from him.

I let out a sigh of relief. Thank god. I have escaped from Bala. Suddenly two palms closed my eyes and I could see nothing. I prayed that it shouldn't be Bala again and touched those hands. I was delighted to feel tiny fingers with rings and some bangles in the wrists. I was happy that it was neither Bala nor Raj. My heart beat rose. Who could this be? I said doubtfully, "Diya, is that you?" She giggled and said, "Yes Bindu. Correct guess!" My heart began to beat normal. I let out a sigh. "Whom are you running from?" Diya asked with concern. I replied, "It is Bala. He is teasing me about my outfit" and pouted. She said, "Don't listen to him. He just envies you as he can't wear a half saree. I assure you that you look great in this dress."

I believe Diya. But Bala's comments have shattered my confidence and I feel too embarrassed now. All the happiness I had when I dressed myself had vanished now. The only thing that I want now is, this news should not reach my class. Diya questioned with doubt, "Bindu, is it Raj standing there?" I gasped. I stood in my toes and searched amidst the crowd. I could see Raj scanning the crowd. Diya raised her hands and waved to him. I pulled her hands down and quickly dragged her away. Diya looked at me in a puzzled way. "Why are you pulling me away? It's Raj!" I hissed, "I don't want to be seen by him and so I am running away from him too!" Diya's eyes widened with a mischievous grin.

She said joyfully, "I am ready for the fun! See Raj is over there. Let's hide." She pointed to one direction and then pulled me in the opposite direction. We headed towards a pillar. Our hands were interlocked. But a crowd of small kids got in the way and ran between us. We got separated. The hall was overflowing with people. I was moving randomly searching Diya and occasionally saying 'Hai' to one or two familiar faces coming in the way. Suddenly I bumped into something or may be someone and dropped my cell phone. I uttered a 'sorry'. I knelt down and began to search it. It was difficult to see my phone between all flowing sarees and legs. Suddenly someone pulled my arms. Again it was Diya.

I stood up quickly and said, "Diya I dropped my phone down. I couldn't find it. Give me your phone. I shall give a missed call to my number." She searched in her clutch and took out her phone. I dialed my number. After a couple of seconds I heard my phone ringing. We followed the sound and moved in that direction. Someone who was showing his back to us was holding the phone. We happily rushed towards that boy. But as soon as we neared him we froze in shock. It is Raj! Raj had my phone in his hand. He must have taken it from the floor. He still has not seen us. But he was looking all around. I and

Diya looked at each other not knowing what to do. We turned back and walked away stealthily. I quietly ended the call.

Raj must have found out that it is my phone by this time. I have set my own image as the wall paper! How stupid of me to do so! Now he could have seen Diya's name as I have made a call from Diya's phone. I dragged Diya out of the crowd and when we were about to step out, we received a call from my number. I and Diya froze and looked at each other like idiots. Suddenly right behind us I heard Raj's voice, "Hey Bindu, is this your phone? Are you searching for this?"

23
Raj's Friendship

Well. That's it. He has found us. I signaled Diya to turn back and get the phone. She turned back and smiled sheepishly at him. He said, "Hi! Diya!" and walked past her and came front. His mouth fell open. Diya said, "Raj! She is beautiful, isn't she? But it seems that Bala is teasing her," in a complaining tone. Ignoring my stare he kept on looking at me as though he was in a trance.

When Diya shook his shoulders hard he said, "Yes! She is beautiful! Bala must be doing it just for fun." I snatched my phone from Raj and tried to move. Raj stopped me and said with wide eyes, "Bindu you look really pretty in this half saree. I couldn't identify you in this make up, costume and jewels. You are amazing!" I didn't know what to do or tell. His direct admiration was quite embarrassing and I felt my cheeks turn pink.

He added with concern, "Are you alright now? You fainted yesterday." I cleared my throat and replied, "I am fine now." After all, Raj is not like Bala finding pleasure in teasing me. Thank god! I felt a burden melt down from my mind. I felt comfortable now. He is the same Raj, my childhood friend. We began to chat casually and moved out.

We came to the garden decorated with lights and sat on a table set in a corner. I shared to them, "Diya! Raj! I won't be coming to school tomorrow." Both were puzzled and they asked together, "Why?" I replied, "Because I am going to RV to carry on some important research work with Professor." This is something that happens often.

So Raj just listened in silence. But Diya said, "I will miss you Bindu." Still Raj was immersed in some deep thought. I wondered how he could shut down his nonstop FM radio mouth.

I shook him from his dream and said, "I have to meet Professor. He was in the dining hall last time when I saw him. I am going to the dining hall. Are you two coming with me?" They nodded in agreement and we three walked towards the dining hall. On the way we saw Professor and my Dad coming out together. They were casually talking something. Professor seemed to be relaxed.

Raj had always wanted to be Professor's apprentice. He had envied me since I joined as Professor's assistant. I thought that it would be the best moment to introduce Raj and Diya to Professor. So I walked with them towards Professor. I could see the excitement in Raj's eyes. He always had huge respect, reverence and admiration for Professor. Even before I came to know of Professor, Raj was his fan. Raj was obsessed with Professor, his scientific inventions and researches. And he was more obsessed with Aadhmi. We went to Dad and Professor. As soon as we neared, Dad took leave with a pat on Raj's back. Raj smiled at Dad.

We three were alone with Professor. I introduced, "Professor I would like you to meet my friends, Raj and Diya." Before I could tell anything more, Raj exclaimed, "Professor it's a great pleasure to meet you today. This is the best and unforgettable day in my life. I am your great fan." And he kept on babbling. Diya rolled her eyes. Professor shook Raj's hands with a warm smile. Raj's face was like that of a small kid who had seen his favourite 'super hero'. Diya had to wait patiently for Raj to let Professor's hands off. Professor shook Diya's hands too and casually talked with them about their studies and family.

After some time, I cleared my throat and said, "Professor, when can I come tomorrow." Professor replied, "Bindu, I won't need you before 12 O'clock. So you can start after 11.30am. I said, "So I shall come from my home at 11.30am." Professor said at once, "No Bindu.

You can go to school as usual. I shall send Aadhmi to pick you up from school at 11.30am."

Oh! My god! Aadhmi will create trouble at school. He will certainly be mortifying me in front of everybody. I opened up cautiously, "Professor may I come to RV myself at 8 O'clock?" He replied with a puzzled look and teasing tone, "Why do you want to come there when I do not need you? Your service is not needed before 12 O'clock genius! So you can attend school." So I gave up and said, "OK, Professor!" But I pouted.

Again Raj came closer and began to talk to Professor with awe respect. Professor signaled me that he wanted to talk to me privately. I scanned for Abi Akka among the guests. When she saw my searching eyes she quickly understood and rushed to my rescue.

I said, "Akka can you please take Diya and Raj to the dining hall. I'll have a word with Professor and be there in 5minutes." Without demanding anymore explanation she simply tried to take them away.

But Raj continued to protest, "It's OK Bindu. As I have met Professor just now, I don't feel hungry at all. I have a lot to share with Professor and I shall eat later. Even if I don't eat today I will not bother. Diya if you are hungry you can go with Abi Akka."

I rolled my eyes and now Diya came to my rescue. She pinched him and dragged him away. Diya is the only person who could control Raj. Abi Akka couldn't control her laughter seeing the puzzled and disappointed expression in Raj's face.

24

Crazy Bala

Professor spoke to me in a low voice. "Bindu we suspect that the approaching meteorites are Emberonium. That can be confirmed only when they land. If it is confirmed, then you have to accompany me in an important mission; a very secret mission too! I have got permission from your Dad. I have informed him that we are actually very busy in our research on creating mammoths. You say the same reason. Is it clear?"

I nodded affirmatively and said with much hesitation, "Professor, may I come in the morning itself? I want to skip my school." He looked at me quizzically with piercing eyes and replied, "No Bindu. If I find out the meteorites to be normal, you need not come at all. If it is confirmed I need you to work on a program to guide the younger generation. Aadhmi will assist you in that. Someone should take the responsibility to be the leader to control the chaos and bring order. I can't imagine the damage of the impending danger." His voice choked and he couldn't speak anymore. He became very serious as his mind had drifted away from the joyful present to the nearing future.

I understood his condition and said, "OK, Professor!" in a comforting way. He left soon and I rushed inside. There is no crowd now. Almost all the guests had left and only close relatives were sitting here and there and chatting.

I entered the dining hall. Raj and Diya were about to eat and as soon as they saw me, they summoned me there. Their parents had already finished eating and were having a happy chat with my grandparents. Abi Akka had finished eating and she offered to serve us. I sat with Raj and Diya.

Suddenly Bala appeared. His eyes were showing his deliberate intention to make mischief. He whistled happily as he saw me sitting to eat. First, Abi Akka placed a big fresh green banana leaf in front of me. Bala ran towards us and said to Abi Akka in a dramatic tone, "Abi Akka such a small leaf won't be enough for Bindu. Don't you know that she eats a lot" he stretched the word 'lot' too long. Abi Akka rolled her eyes and shrugged her shoulders. She simply behaved as though he never existed.

Bala came to me and spoke in a very sweet accent like a little girl, "Oh! My little sister! How many times will you eat here? You know, we should eat dinner only once a day. Just because it is a wonderful occasion and you got too many delicious items to eat, you cannot eat dinner 5 times. How will there be anything for Raj and Diya if you gobble like this?"

Raj chuckled and Diya made faces. I haven't eaten anything since I came here. Why is this idiot embarrassing me by saying that I have eaten 5 times. This Raj is also chuckling like a buffoon for this silly joke. I wanted to say something harsh to Bala. But before I could open my mouth Abi Akka came to defend me.

She curtly said, "Shut up Bala! Still there is lot of food here. You know very well that Bindu has not eaten yet. It is you who has eaten three servings of biriyani. I never saw you leave the dining hall since you entered in monkey!" At once Bala made monkey face and jumped around Abi Akka like a monkey making everyone laugh.

Abi Akka sprinkled water on our leaves and we wiped away the water with our hands. First she kept a sweet meat in our leaves and then a hot spicy cutlet. Bala was not ready to give up.

He said much more dramatically holding his chest, "Akka! There is a limit for telling lies. What you said about Bindu is unbelievable and what you said about me breaks my heart. Oh! My heart is aching!"

Abi Akka did not control her laughter this time. I and Raj joined her too. Diya chuckled and covered her mouth. She liked Bala and she kept on blushing too. Bala said very politely, "Akka please give me the privilege of serving my dear sister some biriyani" but snatched away the biriyani vessel from Abi Akka. He placed two big servings on Raj's leaf and Raj gasped in shock.

He shouted, "Bala! Are you crazy? How can I eat this much at a time?" Bala patted Raj's shoulder dramatically and said, "Don't cry my boy. See how thin you are! Eat well! You have to become strong. But don't worry; you can never come near Bindu's size. She will be unbeatable however you try to defeat her in this regard."

How irritating this Bala is! Can't he shut his stupid mouth and let us eat in peace. I felt my stomach rumble. I frowned at Raj as he was merrily laughing. At once he stopped laughing and smiled sheepishly as though trying to ask sorry. I glared at him. Bala kept one full serving in Diya's leaf and before he could serve again she covered her leaf with her hands and shook her head. Bala commented, "How did you become Bindu's friend? You are such a poor eater and she is just the opposite. You have to learn how to eat from Bindu." She just blushed with her head down. Myself and Abi Akka passed glances.

Bala came to my leaf and said, "Bindu! Though you have already eaten 5 times, I am generous enough to give you food now. No other brother will take care of his sister like this with love and affection" saying so he placed just a small spoon of biriyani. I frowned. Suddenly Bala shouted, "Aah! Aah! Leave me! Leave me!" It was Periyamma; my mother's elder sister; Abi Akka and Bala's mother. She had Bala's ears in her hands. Seeing her he over reacted. "Aah! Amma! It's paining!" periyamma said strictly, "Bala I shouldn't see you here until they finish eating. Get lost somewhere! Hey where are you running with the vessel? Hand it over to me." Diya, Raj, Abi Akka and I laughed merrily. Periyamma served me biriyani. We all enjoyed the delicious dinner chatting and laughing. It was about 9.00 pm. We went up to see the hall almost empty. Mostly everyone was gone. Only our family, Raj's and Diya's parents were there.

Raj said to me dreamily, "How nice it would be if I were Professor Ramanujam's apprentice? I could learn a lot from him." Suddenly he held my hands in his and pleaded, "Bindu, thank you so much for introducing me to him today. Will you make arrangements for me to visit RV one day? I have heard a lot about RV from you. But I want to see everything in person. May be Professor Ramanujam will identify my talents and choose me to be his assistant too!" Oh! God! He has started his nonstop FM radio. He will not stop now. How can I fulfill his wish at this critical moment? Already Professor has so much to worry about. I don't want to annoy him with Raj's nuisance. I felt helpless and did not know what to reply him. But he did not expect any reply at all. He kept on babbling well immersed in his dream world. I sighed helplessly.

Diya ran to us and dragged away Raj saying, "Raj! How many times should we call you? Your Mom and Dad have already gone to the entrance. We are the last guests to leave. Come on you lazy buddy." She waved good bye to all specially to Bala. Now, only our family was there. We started cleaning up the mess. Bala continuously tried to make fun of me and Abi Akka kept on saving me. Abi Akka is doing her college in London. She had come for attending the function and she is leaving today. We both cleaned the hall and when it was over she said, "Bindu, can you drop me at the airport?" I said, "Sure." She bid goodbye to her parents, then to our grandparents and my parents. Bala helped us load her luggage into my car and ran in as he was needed there.

We both got into my Audi and I began to drive. The airport was a few kilometers from there. She still had ample time. So I drove very casually. We reached the airport and Abi Akka said, "Thank you Bindu. Take care of yourself. I'll miss you." She hugged me. I said, "I'll miss you too Akka!" I could feel her tears on my shoulders. I controlled myself and pulled away quickly. I shouldn't make her feel weak and lonely. I said softly, "Bye Akka! Happy journey!" She waved and I waved back. I quickly turned and walked out without turning back. I didn't want her to see my tears. How stupid and weak I am! Why are we such emotional idiots?

I was composed when I drove back home. Again my thoughts returned back to the discussions I had with Professor today. Thousands of questions lingered in my mind now. I felt as though the entire burden had come back to my head. The fun and laughter we had a little time before seemed very distant now. What arrangement has Professor made to evacuate the people from the spots where the meteorites are expected to fall? Is it possible to move them out without creating any suspicion? More over the meteorites are not tiny to be hidden from commoner's vision. What explanation could be given to them? What about the other scientists? Haven't they noticed them by this time? Where are the meteorites now? When will they fall? How will be the landing? I thought that my head would split if I think of so many questions at a time.

When I entered my house Dad was watching TV in the living room. Seeing me he asked, "Bindu, is everything fine? Did you drop Abi at the airport? Has she boarded the plane?" I replied, "Yes Dad. I dropped Abi Akka at the airport. But I did not wait there. As soon as I dropped her, I bid her farewell." As I was about to move towards the bedroom, something in the TV caught my attention. I walked to the couch swiftly and sat near my Dad. My eyes widened on seeing the headlines. Automatically my hands locked with my Dad's.

'Due to an emergency warning from the International Weather Prediction Center, the central and state governments have jointly worked hand in hand to evacuate thousands of people from Rameshwaram in south Tamil Nadu and the northern parts of Srilanka. The Srilankan and Indian governments have summoned military jets to ferry people to safer locations. Thousands of people are flooding out with their movable possessions. The reason behind the evacuation hasn't been leaked out. Government officials act

deaf to the enquiry of the press and the public. The situation is very normal in all other parts of the state and the whole country.

Similar condition is prevailing in Ellesmere Island. Almost all the population of Ellesmere Island has been evacuated. There hadn't been any pre-warning or information.'

Oh! God! Then the meteorites are surely coming! Professor must have made arrangements for evacuation. By this time all the lead forecasters of the weather services meteorological departments will be very busy. It will certainly be a sleepless night to those people. Will the approaching meteorites be Emberonium? My head began to swirl. Should I talk to Professor now? No. He never encourages me contacting him as he may be involved in some serious research always. If he needs me he will certainly call me. I let out a sigh of relief.

My Dad asked me suspiciously, "Bindu, do you know anything about this? Got any idea why the people are being evacuated?" I answered quickly, "No Dad. I come to know of this only now. I don't know anything about this." He passed me an 'I don't believe you look.' But I evaded his questioning eyes and moved to my room mumbling, "Goodnight Dad." I just wanted to lie down.

I removed my jewels and packed them in their cases neatly. I removed my clothes and slipped into my night wears. I walked to our bed room. The lights were already turned off. I figured out that Mom and Indu must have fallen asleep due to tiredness. I turned on the night lamp. Mom was fast asleep on the king size cot at one end. On the other end, the lower bunk of our bunk bed was occupied by Indu. So I climbed up to the upper bunk. My head was aching. I punched my pillow to a comfortable position, placed my phone by my side and relaxed on the bed. Soon I went to deep sleep and all thoughts were shut off.

25

The Landing

I suddenly felt a tremor in my sleep. I rolled over suddenly and my head dashed 'Bam' on the metal railing. Ouch! It hurt! I couldn't open my eyes. But bright light was piercing through my eyelids. Someone must have turned on the lights. I woke up and sat straight. I picked up my phone. The time was 2.15 am. Mom, Dad and Indu were awake. Was the tremor my dream or real? I got down from the upper bunk. I touched my forehead and gently rubbed it. I could feel some swelling on my forehead.

Indu was gibbering to Mom, "I think that it is an earthquake Amma. We have to run out. May be we must get under a table and protect ourselves. May be all our neighbours are outside in the streets." Dad held her tightly and comforted her. When I passed them a questioning look, they just shook their shoulders and we came out of our house. Just as Indu said all other people in our neighbourhood were on the street.

Mom, Dad and Indu enthusiastically joined the crowd outside and got seriously involved in the hot discussion. Many ideas, guesses and suggestions flooded out from our neighbours. I just leaned on our portico wall and watched the gathering. The meteorites must have fallen. But have they fallen on the predicted spots or elsewhere? Had the evacuation been really useful or futile? Are the meteorites made of Emberonium? What will be Professor's plan to save the world now? Suddenly the sound of approaching siren interrupted my thoughts.

Cops came into our street with blaring siren and announced in their microphone:

'Everybody please go inside your houses. The tremor is due to an important science research. The situation is under control and there is no need to panic. There is no danger. You can all get into your houses and carry on your routine. We request you to co-operate for your own safety and security.'

They insisted everyone to get in their houses and waited until the street was empty. As we went inside Indu exclaimed, "The research must be some sort of nuclear explosion. The noise and shake was tremendous. Certainly some buildings must have shattered to pieces. I hope that today will be declared a holiday."

I said curtly, "Don't imagine anything Indu. Come in without clattering like a monkey." Ignoring me she ran behind my Dad, shouting, "Daddy certainly today will be a holiday. Let us see if there is any announcement regarding the declaration of holiday. Please turn on the TV. Let us watch the news."

When the three sat on the couch, I went to my room to brush my teeth and refresh myself. Then I sneaked to the terrace. I wanted to know if there was any visible difference in the sky or nearby areas. I stealthily climbed the stairs that lead to the over head tank and to my dismay I found nothing indifferent. The sky was very clear and spotless. The stars were twinkling numbly as usual. There was no sign of the meteorite or its path. Suddenly I heard my mother's call and I climbed down carefully and raced down swiftly shouting, "Yes Mom!"

Still they were sitting in front of the TV and as I walked in my Mom moved to make place for me on the couch. In a news channel a video coverage was being telecast. A female reporter was standing with a mike and behind her was some black barricade. She reported:

'Right now I am standing in front of the barricade. Officials say that there is a research being conducted by the scientists here and this area is totally restricted. The military has installed this huge barricade and it seems to be towering up even higher than the Eiffel tower. The barricade covers the shore of Rameshwaram fully and extends up to the northern part of Srilanka'.

She whispered as though she was saying a secret in a funny way, **"May be they are rebuilding Lord Rama's Bridge"**.

'Up to this Moment no reporters or media people are allowed to even peep into the barricade. Government has confirmed that the situation is under control and all schools, colleges and government offices would function as usual. Stay with me to know more.'

Suddenly her eyes widened and she blurted out:

'Now our President Dr.Abdul Rahman is coming out of the barricade and let us listen to what he has got to share with us.'

She started running with the mike and the camera followed her. There was a small door in the barricade that was heavily guarded and the President came out of the door. He was wearing a grey colour safari suit. The reporter extended her mike in front of him and questioned, **"Mr. Rahman, can you explain to the public what the real situation is? Already people had been evacuated based on weather predictions, but now this huge blockade has come out of nowhere and it is announced that it is some scientific research. Could you please tell us what the true story is? Is the government trying to hide something dangerous?"**

She talked very fast and questions flooded out like bullets from an AK47. President Abdul Rahman scratched his forehead and after a moment said, "As per the information from our leading scientist Professor Ramanujam, there is…" before he could finish, the reporter exclaimed, **"What? Professor Ramanujam! Is Professor**

Ramanujam here? Is he the brain behind this research? So will he give the explanation now?" The reporter was quite impatient and irritating. Even I was annoyed by the way she interviewed the President without expecting the answers. She reminded me of Raj, the nonstop FM radio.

But the President was cool headed. He answered patiently, "Hmm…. No. Professor Ramanujam is not here. He is neither responsible for the research here. But he has explanation to all your questions and he will face the media shortly. I think you have to excuse me now." The reporter was quite disappointed, but not ready to give up. She continued, "**Mr. President, will the media be allowed to enter this barrier? May I please have a look with my crew inside?**" Even the cool headed President was taken aback by this request. He answered quickly, "No! It is not possible to allow anyone inside now. I can assure you that the nuclear research conducted here is completely harmless. You see, the evacuation was made only as a precaution. There is no immediate danger. The barrier had been constructed only as a safety measure in case of any radiation."

She still continued, "**Mr. President, it is confirmed that a similar barricade adorns Ellesmere Island. What do you think about that? Are the world scientists doing this research together?**"

He nodded thoughtfully, "May be… and that's all I could tell you now. Thank you!" and saying so he walked briskly towards his vehicle and his body guards kept him safely protected from the mob of media people. The press photographers tried their level best to take as many snaps as possible. The President left in a second with the sirens blaring.

The reporter came back into the screen. She had been lucky enough to break the wall of body guards and reach the President for the interview. She again started with pride, "**This little chat with our President has provided us the confirmation that we are safe at present. Stay with us to know more from scientist Ramanujam**" and ended with an artificial smile.

Dad switched on to some other channel for more information. Mom asked me, "What will Professor say about this? Is he involved in this research? Do you have any idea what is going on Bindu? I called you only to show this and ask what it might be." I answered very carefully without showing any emotions, "I don't know anything about this Mom. I am as blank as you in this regard. May be I'll ask Professor when I meet him today. Where is Indu?" and I moved in search of her.

26

Monday Morning Syndrome

When I entered the bedroom there was a huge mass of blankets on the lower bunk bed and a moaning sound came from inside the mass. Ah! Ah! I think Indu has got her usual Monday morning syndrome! Basically Indu doesn't hate going to school or learning. But she behaves very peculiar on Mondays. On Sundays she wakes even before sunrise and enjoys her day to the core from the beginning. She used to say happily, "An early bird catches its prey" and wink at me on a holiday. But the reverse happens on Mondays. She would try her level best to skip school by pretending to be sick. May be it's because my mother encourages it. Whenever she pretends to be sick, my mother simply allows her to stay home to take rest.

One Monday Indu pretended that she had high fever and my innocent Mom prepared porridge and kept it in a bowl near Indu's bed. To justify her acting Indu wanted to show Mom that she had high temperature and she dipped a thermometer into the bowl. But alas! What happened you know! The bulb of the thermometer burst due to the intensive heat and Indu got 'special treatment' on that day. Another day, unable to bear her acting, Mom called our family doctor and I couldn't forget how swiftly Indu jumped out of bed and got ready to school, as the doctor approached her with an injection. It's good that she is afraid of needles!

She must be disappointed that today is not declared a holiday. I dug into the pile of blankets and explored. Finally I got her hands. Her hands were shaking violently. Well! I must believe that she has shivers and chills. She held my hand tightly and spoke between false shivers, "Akka! My body…. is aching….inch…by…inch. I think I have a deadly fever like malaria or dengue. May be some mosquitoes must have blessed me with this…" I cut her short, "Nice imagination and excellent acting. You can be nominated for the Oscar Award! Now stop pretending and go to sleep. It's just 4.30am. You have ample time to rest" and I hopped on to my bed.

There was a message from Abi Akka in my phone. It read:

'Reached London safely'

I was happy to know that she has landed safely. I did not feel sleepy. Indu was pretending to snore. So I informed this message to Mom who had started to cook in the kitchen. Dad was sitting on the couch and snoozing. I switched off the TV and went to my room. I took out the English project that I had prepared last week and began to read it. I am 100% sure that there would be a perfect clone of my preparation from Hana as she had borrowed my project earlier for 'reference'. According to Hana the meaning for 'reference' is taking a neat copy. I usually never bothered about this habit of her. But this time Yen was right behind us when Hana returned back my project and he was staring with his prying eyes. He might create some problems.

I revised my lessons and packed my bag to school. My mother came with hot milk at 6.am. She said, "I have finished cooking and your lunch bags are ready. Wake up Indu and get ready to school. I'll just rest for a while." Fantastic! Now I have this wonderful task of waking up Indu. I thought of a plan. I went near Indu and bent down closer. I said controlling my laughter, "Hey Indu, good news! At last the government has declared today a holiday. You need not lie down in bed and waste a wonderful day." The very next moment all the blankets were on the floor and Indu was jumping here and there like a crazy monkey. She had no symptoms of the deadly fever that she spoke about an hour ago and was looking as healthy as a horse. Here smile extended from her left ear to right ear.

She shouted joyfully, "I am not going to school today!" I asked with concern, "But are you alright now Indu? You were very sick before some time." As though she remembered something, she controlled herself and slightly coughed and said, "Thank you Akka! I feel much better now." She happily hopped to the living room and switched on the TV. Casually she flipped the channels until she got her favourite music video. My sister loves the singers Eric Dixson, Dustin Swagger, Evan Hover, Isabel Lawrance, Veronica Stiles, Victoria Blooms and the famous boy band Uni Direction. I liked Uni Direction too. But I am not as crazy as her. She sat comfortably on the couch in a relaxed position. Dad must have gone out for his usual morning walk.

I sneaked into the bed room to inform Mom about Indu. When Mom came into the hall with me, Indu was enthusiastically dancing and singing along with the singers of the band. In the mean time I heard Dad's footsteps. He stormed into the room and yelled, "Indu, why are you watching TV so early in the morning on a working day? Go! Go and study your lessons. How many times will you watch this music video? Dixon Swagger or Victoria Blooms is not going to help you in your life. Only your studies will help you. Go and study. Then get ready to school!"

Very casually Indu said, "Dad, don't you know that today is declared a holiday? I am in my holiday mood and I am enjoying my time. She happily did her favourite step of rowing a boat from Uni Direction." Dad gave a puzzled look and asked her, "Who told you so?" Indu stopped dancing abruptly and blinked like a lost child. She understood the reality soon and anxiously flipped over to news channels and scanned the running scrolls. I chuckled merrily. When she had confirmed that today is a working day, her face drooped down. She turned angrily towards me and came running towards me. She held a lock of my hair and began pulling hard. I couldn't control my laughter. But my Mom intervened and released me from her hold. I waved her 'bye' and escaped from there.

There was no more commotion as Dad was at home. If he hadn't been at home, then certainly Indu would have kept on chasing me around the house, ignoring my mother's calls. She can easily cheat my Mom by cajoling her, but my father does not fall a prey to her 'puppy dog face'. He strictly insists discipline at home. Indu frowned; showed faces; she pouted; and cursed me to her heart's content. Finally she gathered her books from her cupboard and sat down to read her lessons. I had a doubt in solving a problem and my Dad helped me solve it. I worked out some more problems to make myself thorough with the concept. Mom was watering the plants in the garden.

At 7am she came in and said, "Get ready to school fast." Daddy got ready in a jiffy and he came first to the dining table. I joined him soon. Mom served us hot Idli, spicy chutney and sambar. When Indu saw Idli in our plates, she pouted. Mom made crisp Dosas for her specially. She is always a pet to Mom. Dad was ready to drop us at school. Dad asked me, "Professor asked permission yesterday to take you with him for an important assignment. When will you leave school today?" I replied, "At 11 O'clock Dad." "What project are you working on now? He said that you are trying to create another extinct animal. What is it?" I said, "It is a mammoth Dad. This also belonged to the ice age." Dad said with concern, "Whatever research you do, be careful. Don't get involved in any dangerous researches. I have read the biography of Marie Curie. Though she got Nobel Prize, she died because of the hazardous radiations from her research. I am not an expert in science. I don't know what you are working on. But I know that experiments are not easy matters like selling policies and insurance plans. They can be fatal sometimes. I am worried about your safety. Please take care of yourself. I have given you freedom to pursue your field of interest and you should know to use that freedom wisely."

Sometimes I have felt that Dad showers more love and concern on me than Indu. I was moved by his words and swallowing hard the lump in my throat, I said fighting back my tears, "OK Dad. I'll take care." Mom kissed us 'goodbye' and we three jumped into Dad's car.

Dad dropped us at the school gate and waved 'bye'. We waved him back and walked in. Indu cursed me and showed faces. She moved away from me stamping her foot. I tried hard to control my laughter and showed her an emotion less face. Suddenly she saw somebody and waved happily. I turned back to see Niranjana.

Niranjana was standing in her sports costume. She must have come earlier for her tennis practice. Niranjana is Indu's BFF. I too like her. But she always comes to our house to enjoy with Indu. They both turn our house into a music club by playing loud music and dancing to their favourite songs especially for the Uni Direction's songs. They wish to become pop singers in the near future and turn my life a living hell by their horrible singing at present. May be I am allergic to Niranjana for this reason. They both locked hands and moved away chatting something happily. I envied Indu for her care free life. She never worried for anything. She was always cool and happy. She always enjoyed everything that comes in her life. Her anger and sorrow are short lived. Suddenly the bell rang.

27

Sleepy Raj

I ran towards the class with my school bag on my back and my lunch bag oscillating in my hand randomly. Through the window I could see that Mrs. Crow was marking attendance. So I raced to the class. First hour is Mrs. Crow's English class. Though Mrs. Crow resembles her name in her appearance, she thinks herself to be a peacock. She is tall and lean; she is pitch black in colour; I think she never combs her hair because her hair is always clumsy. There are one or two cymbals in the class, who add oil to the fire of her pride. I reached the class entrance and started panting for breath.

I politely said, "Excuse me Madam." She raised her head from the register and said, "Bindu, principal said that you will be on leave today?" in an enquiring manner. I answered, "Yes Madam. I will leave at 11 O'clock." She nodded and moved on.

I entered in and scanned the class for an empty seat. When she was busy taking attendance, I saw Ann playing some games in her cell phone. We are not allowed to bring cell phones to school. But I have seen her often with a cell phone and she is least bothered about being caught. Ann was sitting with Usha and they both smiled at me. Raj and Diya were sitting behind them. Raj was obviously snoring. Diya waved happily to me. I waved back secretly to her. The seat next to Hana was vacant and I sat near her. She smiled at me. Yen was sitting on a bench towards Hana's left

In the pretext of taking class, Mrs. Crow began to bore us with her flash back. She used to correlate each and every topic in the lesson with her own life experiences and torture us by narrating her flash backs. I couldn't control my laugher when I turned to see Diya was preoccupied with the enthralling occupation of inserting thin rolled sheet of paper into Raj's ears. She was seriously involved in that work, while Raj was very busy sleeping. I chuckled and threw a small eraser on Diya. She was startled, but smiled at me when she saw me. Mrs. Crow was deeply immersed in her past. She was dreamily narrating an incident to depict her greatness.

Yen was scanning the whole class with his evil coal black eyes. Suddenly he sprang up and interrupted the class. Ann and usha were startled and they nearly dropped the phone. But Ann caught it and showed a thumps up signal to her slaves. They laughed victoriously. Ann put up a heroic expression on her face and kept the phone inside her bag.

Yen said, "Madam, Raj is sleeping!" At once Diya stamped his foot and Raj sprang up from his place with sleepy eyes. He was looking like an alien with two white paper sticks protruding from his ears. Diya saw me and we both chuckled. Not knowing how he looked like and what had happened, Raj stood with an innocent expression on his face.

"Raj, did you sleep?" questioned Mrs. Crow. Raj responded instantaneously, "Yes Madam" and blinked like an idiot. And the whole class let out a roar of laugher. Mrs. Crow's face looked very horrible when she was angry. "So you are not afraid to admit that you are sleeping in my class?" Diya muttered something to Raj in a very low voice, without moving her lips, but scratching her head.

Raj somehow composed himself and answered, "No Madam, I slept at home and here I am listening to your wonderful past. How is possible that you had such good qualities even in your childhood madam?" Mrs. Crow always loves to be praised. So she was easily flattered and she asked him to sit down. Raj still hadn't noticed the paper roll from his ears and everyone was laughing at it. I stared at Diya and she removed them at once with an apologizing look in her eyes. He did not realize that too. Why is he so dull today?

28

Hana The Copy Cat

Yen again started, "Madam, Ann and Usha are playing games in Ann's phone." Ann and Usha stood up. Ann opposed, "No madam", clearly and boldly. They both showed their empty hands to prove their innocence. Yen persisted, "Ann dropped the phone into her bag just now. I saw it." Mrs. Crow walked stylishly to Ann's place; grabbed her bag; turned it upside down and found out the phone. She ordered Yen to escort Ann and Usha to the principal's room. Mrs. Crow began to advise us. We had no other go than to nod politely to her advices.

Then she asked us to submit our projects. When we were busy, submitting the projects on her table, Yen entered the class. After submitting my project, I walked back to my place. Yen went near Mrs. Crow and murmured something to her. She listened keenly to him nodding her head periodically. Then she had a shocked expression on her face. I, Raj and Diya passed questioning glances.

Mrs. Crow walked clumsily towards the pile of the submitted handwritten projects and searched for a while. She took out two projects after some time. There was an expression of satisfaction in Yen's face. What is he up to? This idiot has no other work than to interfere in other's business. I hate his looks and behavior.

When I looked at the picked up projects I was completely puzzled. I recognized one of the two projects as mine. Mrs. Crow scanned both the projects and her face turned red in anger. She shouted my name furiously. I walked to her. She looked at me angrily and asked, "Why have you copied Hanna's project?" I was taken aback. Stupid Yen! This brainless idiot has assumed that I had borrowed Hana's project when he saw me getting back my project from her. He thinks of himself as a super detective. But he is a stupid detective. Mrs. Crow is too naïve to believe this mindless monkey and doubt me.

I replied patiently, "No madam! I haven't copied anyone and my project is the result of my true hard work and sleepless nights." She raised her eyebrows in a suspicious manner.

I kept my looks straight and said boldly, "Madam, if you find any similarity between my project and Hana's then I think that it is Hana who is to be questioned, because, it is she who borrowed my project for 'reference'." Yen was smiling in a vile manner. Mrs. Crow shouted Hana's name. Hana stood up in a humble manner and reported, "Yes, madam."

Mrs. Crow questioned, "Hana, did you borrow Bindu's project for reference?" Hana bit her lips and stood still like a statue. She began to release water from her instantaneous Courtalam falls and made a puppy dog face. It is not the first time I see her fake crying. Mostly all the girls in my class are experts in acting like innocent angels, crying readily whenever they want to seek excuse from their mistakes when caught red handed. So the same happened here too.

On seeing Hana's puppy dog face Mrs. Crow melted. She said, "OK, I understand that you really feel sorry for your mistake. Hereafter you must do your projects on your own and you should never copy from others. I excuse you this time. All of you sit down." So Hana escaped without any trial and she secretly showed me a 'thumbs down' signal. I pretended that I did not see her.

29
Aadhmi's Visit

Soon the bell rang. Ann and Usha returned back to the class. Ann was heroically explaining the girls what had happened in the principal's room. The second period was Maths and we were very busy during the Maths period as usual. We felt relieved when the interval bell rang. The next two periods will be science practical session in the lab. I rummaged in my bag for the record note.

Hana came very quietly near me and asked, "Bindu, can I borrow your science project paper presentation for reference?" I would have said a spontaneous 'sure' believing that nothing is wrong in helping a classmate. But the experiences I had in the first period were fresh in my mind. I don't want her to exploit me recklessly. I don't want her to steal the fruits of my serious efforts and focused hard work. I decided to confront her. It is time that I stood stubborn against her. So I started, "I am sorry Hana."

She was shocked as she had not expected this answer. Her disappointment was clearly visible from her expressions. This is the first time she has got a 'No' from me. She looked fazed and questioned, "Why?" as she couldn't give up. She has underestimated me that she can take me for granted. It is time that I taught her a lesson.

I started in a determined tone, "Mrs. Mathi announced this project last Tuesday. What were you doing throughout the last week? You were simply enjoying your time. I have spent all my time in surfing over a number of websites to collect the necessary information and compile them in a presentable order. I have read and reread the content to give it my personal touches and modify it. Then I have made a fresh handwritten copy of that with all the unnecessary decorations expected by Mrs. Mathi. But you come and casually get mine for 'reference'. Actually what you do is take a copy of mine and enjoy the benefits of my hard work. That is not a good habit Hana. If you want to refer, you can go and borrow someone else's please."

But Hana persisted, "No, Bindu. I just wanted to have a glance of yours. Others will never lend me anything. So if you hand it to me today I will return it safely to submit tomorrow."

My rage surged to its peak. I controlled myself and questioned calmly, "Aren't you tired of copying my thoughts and views. Why don't you try something on your own?"

Hana tried her final weapon. She made a puppy dog face and began to shed tears like an overflowing Courtalam falls. She said between sobs, "No Bindu. I have never copied yours ever in my life. You have mistaken me." I understood that talking to her is a waste of time and I declared, "Don't lie Hana. I think I have heard enough from you. I don't want to be late to the lab session" and began packing my things. She showed a guilty expression as she continued crying. Am I very rude to her? Should I console her now? I think she deserves this treatment. I walked out of the class swiftly, looking through the corner of my eyes. I could see some girls approaching Hana to console her. They gathered around her and hid her from my view.

I did not bother to turn back. I heard two pairs of feet following very quickly behind me. May be it is Hana's friends. They may expect me to apologize to Hana and console her. So I quickened my steps. Suddenly a hand fell on my shoulders. I was startled and I turned back. Pooh! It is only Diya and Raj. I was pleased to see them.

Raj chuckled and said, "Wow! That was awesome. At last you have got the courage to deny her demands." I smiled just a little. Diya added, "Bindu, she deserves it. I have always hated the way she steals your hard work and gets good name for herself. That 'drama queen' knows how to convince the teachers and escape from punishments.

But today you taught her a valuable lesson. It was amazing!" As I wanted to divert the topic, I commented with a grin, "Not as amazing as Raj in Mrs. Crow's class!" Diya chuckled. Raj was embarrassed and he laughed shyly.

I walked between them chatting sweet nothings. As we neared the lab, we saw Mrs.Toad standing in the entrance of the lab. She hates students being late to the lab and she is very creative in giving exclusive punishments to the late comers. We wished her and Raj started, "Good Morning Mrs. To…!" I pinched his arms as he was about to say the word 'Toad'. At once he managed and finished, "…Mathi" with a silly smile. I and Diya giggled. Raj has totally forgotten her real name 'Mathi' and casually was about to use the nick name 'Toad'.

We walked to our table and stood in our respective places. Diya, Raj, Ann and I shared the same table. All the apparatus necessary for the 'salt analysis' was arranged neatly on the table. There were reagent bottles neatly arranged on the shelves; Test tube stand with test tubes and boiling tubes; a spatula; a test tube holder; A tray containing only bottles of concentrated acids was on the common table and a cleaning brush near the wash basin. There was a watch glass with a salt in front of everyone's place. Each student will be given a different salt. We have to identify the name of the salt and confirm the same, through many tests. It was a piece of cake for me, for I used to identify most of the salts seeing their colour and observing their texture.

When all the tables were completely filled, Mrs. Mathi began to instruct us regarding the discipline and safety measures to be followed in the lab. She kept on insisting that we should be very careful while handling concentrated acids. Raj was showing us a 'boring' signal when Mrs. Mathi noticed him and shouted "Raj, can you tell me the confirmatory test for nitrate?" Raj stood blank for a moment.

I scribbled 'brown ring test' on the table. At once he answered, "Brown ring test madam" and let out a sigh of relief. She nodded reluctantly, staring wildly at him. Raj whispered to me, "Bindu, don't expect me to thank you. I have helped you once and you have helped me now. It's done. We have no commitments now." I just rolled my eyes. Mrs. Mathi announced, "Now you can start identifying your salt. Make it fast. The one who correctly identifies his or her salt quickly will be given a pen."

Observing the colour of my salt, I identified it as copper sulphate. I did the confirmatory tests for the acid and base radicals and rushed to her to give the answer. She observed the test tube and said, "Very good!" with satisfaction. She announced, "Students, as usual Bindu has identified her salt and confirmed it first. I would like to present her this pen." Some cheered; some clapped their hands; and a few rolled their eyes.

She gave the pen and said, "Start writing the procedure. Don't forget to clean your place in the table. After writing the procedure, get it corrected by me." I nodded in agreement and rushed to the table. My task starts now. Some students passed their watch glasses with the salt to my table secretly. I identified the salt and wrote the name in a piece of paper and sent it back. Raj and Diya were busy doing their confirmatory tests. I finished writing the procedure in half an hour.

Suddenly I heard some students gasp in surprise and some call others and say, "Hey! Look there!" My eyes widened when I peeped from my place. It was Aadhmi. It must have come to pick me. It said to Mrs. Toad, "Excuse me Madam, I am Aadhmi. Professor Ramanujam's robot. I have come here to…" before it could finish a group of girls and boys ran towards Aadhmi shouting, "Hey! It's Aadhmi!" And fell over it.

To my dismay Raj was the most dominating character there. He was literally hugging Aadhmi and looking at it with admiration. All were trying to touch Aadhmi. They behaved as though they have seen their favourite pop star. Through the crowd, I could see Raj happily shaking Aadhmi's robotic hands. A girl lamented, "Oh! God! I don't have my camera to take a snap with Aadhmi. At least let me get an autograph from Aadhmi." Seeing all this commotion, Mrs. Toad stood puzzled. Everyone tried to get a glimpse of Aadhmi and the lab became clumsy.

Mrs. Toad bellowed, "All of you go to your places!" in very high decibels. But no one paid attention to her. She tried to pull the students away from Aadhmi. But that effort was fruitless. It looked as though Aadhmi was a huge magnet and the hovering students were iron pieces. Aadhmi was on the floor, trying to crawl out of the over powering mass. I couldn't believe how Aadhmi had so many fans. I realized that I was the only person who hated it and tried to humiliate it. Suddenly all the students moved away from Aadhmi with 'Ooh!', 'Aah!', 'Ouch!' and 'Gosh!', sounds of pain and surprise. Some shrieked, "Aah! It hurts!" I was completely confused. What is happening now?

Aadhmi explained in his robotic tone, "Sorry for the mild electric shock. My safety mechanism has suggested the apt treatment. The electricity passed out is not dangerous as very low voltage is used. There is nothing to panic. You will be free from pain in 5 seconds." Mrs. Toad began to 'shoo' away the girls and boys. Students retreated to their places with a look of disbelief. Still Raj was standing near Aadhmi. I was very much irritated by his behavior. But what has happened to his hair? All his hair stood up straight like needles pointing in all directions. Girls began to laugh secretly and then openly seeing his pose. His eyes were transfixed somewhere and he stood like a show case doll. I and Diya giggled. Aadhmi said, "Err… this boy must have got some extra shots as he was too close up on me. He will be alright in 2 minutes." Well, Raj deserves it.

It was surprising to see the girls still look at Aadhmi longingly. Most of all, Priya! Priya was shedding tears of happiness on seeing Aadhmi. She is an introvert. The tall curly haired girl Priya shouted, "Aadhmi, I am a great fan of yours! I am delighted to see you!" and again tried to move towards him. But Mrs. Toad caught her midway and warned, "Priya, if you don't calm down now, I will get you expelled not only from my lab but also from school." Priya came back to her table. Now, Raj who had recovered from his shock started to prattle, "Aadhmi, I met Professor yesterday and I am lucky to meet you today. Convey my regards to Professor and inform him that I will ..." He stopped abruptly as Mrs. Toad gave him a blow. The lab attendant dragged Raj to his place. Raj still prattled, "We'll meet soon Aadhmi." He still looked quite funny in the way his hair stood out.

Somehow the class came into control. Still girls were looking at Aadhmi as though he was a 'Teen Sensation'. Mrs. Mathi analyzed Aadhmi from head to toe while Aadhmi did the same to her. Mrs. Toad was allergic to modern technology and she hated modern gadgets. It was very lucid from her looks that she disliked Aadhmi. She frowned and said, "What do you want and what the hell are you?"

Aadhmi replied in his mechanical tone, "Hello Mrs. Toad," no sooner did Aadhmi say the word 'toad' than the students clapped their hands in joy. Well, Aadhmi must have read the minds of the students here and got her name. Mrs. Mathi looked puzzled. "I have come here to escort out Bindu. I was instructed that she is in the lab. Though you hate me to the core; and you wish to stamp me with your foot; and you want to throw me in the dust bin; there is no time to execute your plans now." Well, Aadhmi has read Mrs. Toad's mind too. "We have to report to Professor immediately. So, please send Bindu with me."

Mrs. Toad was taken aback. She somehow managed and shouted, "How dare you call me 'toad'? I am Mrs. Mathi." Aadhmi an ardent lover of Kiran Bedi, the first woman IPS officer of India, has a peculiar habit. Whenever it hears the word 'dare' he used to say the title of a book written by Kiran Bedi. So Aadhmi happily answered Mrs. Toad in a majestic lady voice, "I dare! It is always possible." The whole class laughed again. Wow! It is quite interesting to watch Aadhmi test the patience of Mrs. Toad.

Mrs. Toad shouted angrily, "Shut up!" Aadhmi responded in a robotic tone, "Wrong command. I cannot obey your orders. You are not my master. You are disturbing me from executing the order given to me. I think you need to be instructed in a different way." Mrs. Toad said, "Oh! You are going to instruct me? I am the controlling authority here and you want to instruct me. Who gave you permission to enter into the school premises now?" Aadhmi said, "The principal of this school granted me permission to come here. I understand that seeing me irritates you very much. I will not annoy you if you let Bindu come with me now." With an irritated look, she said, "Go and wait out. She will come." Then she came to me and said in a low voice, "Bindu take this damaged piece of iron out of my lab as early as possible. Make sure that I never see it in my life again."

Aadhmi shouted from out, "I can hear you Mrs. Toad." Mrs. Toad rolled her eyes. This created a roar of laugher again. As soon as I came out, Aadhmi stood in the entrance and facing Mrs. Toad, it raised its right hand and pointed its index and middle finger to its eyes and then to Mrs. Toad. Students understood his action and shouted in a loud chorus, "I have my eyes on you!" merrily. I could hear Mrs. Toad stamping her foot as we both ran away from the lab.

30

Sorna

I rushed to my class room to collect my school bag. Even before I could reach the class Aadhmi raced ahead of me and was ready with all my things. I had to meet the principal and inform him about my departure as per our school rules. So I went into the principal's room to complete some formalities. In a few minutes Aadhmi and I were walking towards the entrance together.

I wanted to clarify my doubts about the meteorites with Aadhmi. It might know much information even more than Professor. So even when we were walking in the school corridor, I opened up, "Aadhmi are the meteorites…" It interrupted me cautiously and said in a serious tone, "Bindu, you may clarify all your doubts as soon as we reach RV." I nodded and ran with Aadhmi silently.

My mouth fell open when I came out. Aadhmi had come in 'Sorna'. Sorna was the only car that Professor had never allowed me to drive or even explore. I looked Aadhmi enviously, when it opened the driver's seat door and sat in. As I entered into the car, I was puzzled to see the interior. There was no steering wheel or key slot or gear system or accelerator or even a brake pedal. There was no difference as driver's or passenger's seat. Now I get why Professor had never allowed me near Sorna.

Aadhmi just placed its palm on the plain black dash board and said, "SAPS". Just a rectangular flat panel was visible to my eyes now. Suddenly a voice recognizer responded, "Welcome to SAPS Aadhmi. Who is this with you?" Aadhmi replied, "This is Bindu, Professor's apprentice cum assistant." The voice boomed, "As per protocol, the new subject's bio-metric details must be recorded."

Aadhmi said, "Bindu, place your palm on the dash board." I obliged as said. There was a buzzing sound for a minute. Then the voice asked, "Destination code?" Aadhmi asked me, "Bindu, do you want to go home before we leave?" It's really nice sometimes that it could read my mind. I nodded and Aadhmi said my address very fast in a robotic tone.

Sorna began to move but even without the slightest starting sound. Is there any engine here or not? It glided fast and smooth like a skateboard. I observed the interior with hungry eyes. The seat covers were woven in golden threads and embroidered with platinum threads. The interior was fully decorated with artistic works using pearls, diamonds, rubies, emerald, jade etc. it was very grand and beautiful. The cushions on the seats were very cozy. Is the car moving or not? To my surprise Sorna was very fast indeed. In no time I was in my house.

Aadhmi said, "Sorna can move even faster than this. But Professor had ordered me to reduce its speed to minimum when it is used in front of the public. You will open your mouth if you know the true potential of Sorna." Even without knowing much about it I have started to love it. I saw a back pack at the back seat and wondered why Aadhmi had brought it. At once it replied, "There is some really important stuff in it. We may need them at anytime." I just lifted my shoulders and asked, "Would you like to come in Aadhmi?"

Aadhmi preferred to stay in the car. I rushed in; dropped my school stuff; changed into a purple chudi; grabbed my phone and kissed my Mom 'good bye'. My Mom shouted, "Your lunch bag is heavy. Why don't you take it with you and eat it later?" I did not shout any answer back. I happily got into Sorna again. "You are happy to escape from your Mom's food. Is it that much bad?" When will it stop peeping into my thoughts? I did not want it to underestimate my Mom.

So I said, "Familiarity breeds contempt." Aadhmi chuckled in a funny way and ignoring my stare it declared the destination as 'RV'. As the car began to move, Aadhmi said casually, "Your science teacher's thoughts give me a suspicion that she may be mentally retarded." I laughed out happily, but pretended to be modest and said, "Don't talk unnecessarily Aadhmi." It said, "Human beings think one and say out something else. It is possible for you. Why don't you too accept it and enjoy the truth?" Oh! God! It has read my mind again. I nodded my head in a gesture of defeat and said, "Sure! I believe she is!"

Aadhmi has not started a quarrel with me up to this minute. It is very polite and friendly with me. This is unbelievable! Some thing seems fishy! Within a few minutes of the fabulous ride, we reached RV. Sorna moved in and stopped in front of Professor's residence. No sooner did Sorna stop, Professor came towards it with Puper walking by his side. Professor looked very stiff and rigid, immersed in some serious thoughts. I got down. Puper ran towards me as soon as he saw me. I knelt down and lifted him. Professor said swiftly, "Bindu, get in quick. Let us talk on our way to the meteorite."

31

Visit To The Meteorite

I cuddled Puper and got in. Professor and I were sitting in the back seat with Puper in my lap. Aadhmi was busy with something shiny like a ribbon in its hands. It was hunched in its seat with its concentration fully converged on the ribbon.

When Professor coughed to get its attention, it stood straight and said, "Reach the uploaded designation." Sorna began to move at once.

Professor leaned back comfortably and said. "As in your dream, the meteorites have landed very smoothly without causing any disaster. I have confirmed without any doubt that the fallen meteorites are Emberonium. I have talked to Abdul Rahman and made some precautionary arrangements with his support.

We expected that the meteorites would crash on the earth at any time after 12.00 midnight. I contacted some of my trustable friends all over the world and informed them about the approaching meteorites. More over the heads of the meteorological department from all over the world had already started discussing about the fast approaching peculiar meteorites. All were puzzled about the size of the meteorites. We had a teleconference. I convinced them with the forum of scientists that as per our calculations though the size is extremely bigger the meteorites are not an immediate threat to the earth. The meteorites landed precisely at 2.14am. I was with the President here yesterday at the time of the landing. You would have really enjoyed the sight. With the support of the meteorological department, military personals and hundreds of hardware of Aadhmi, we constructed a barricade around the meteorite here and at Ellesmere islands. That work was completed swiftly by about 2.30pm so that nothing could be caught by the prying eyes of the media. You might have seen that in TV. As the Polar Regions are having almost nil or very thin population we did not bother to cover them up. They are cold and remote and also protected by treaties. So I am sure that the uncovered meteorites will not pull commoner's attention. The Presidents of all the nations wanted us to give them the assurance for the safety of the public. They wanted to avoid any forms of chaos. You must see the meteorite that has fallen in Rameshwaram first. This is the first day the meteorites have entered the earth's atmosphere. I believe that they may show their adverse effect only on the 7th day. So I am sure that we have got some time to work out our plans without disturbing the public."

Again Aadhmi was busy with the shiny ribbon. It looked like a belt with a thin buckle. Puper who was on my lap gently rubbed his head against my hand. My cell phone slipped and fell down. At once Puper took it by his mouth and stuffed it in his mouth. I was shocked and shouted, "Puper! What have you done?" He was taken aback and he spat it out instantaneously. I looked at him angrily. He gave me an irresistible 'puppy dog' face that drove away my anger. My phone was soaked in his saliva. When I showed a disgusting face, Aadhmi volunteered to clean my phone. Wow! What has happened to Aadhmi today? Has Professor made any special modification in its behavioral properties? Aadhmi retorted quickly, "No change has been done by Professor in me. I am the same old version." I did not dare to think of anything else after that.

Suddenly my eyes caught something and I was dumb struck. It was the barricade. Wow! We have covered such a long distance in just 15minutes. Miraculous! The reporters who were scattered here and there with their crew, rushed towards Sorna as soon as they noticed it. When it came to a halt they surrounded Sorna. A number of guards in uniform came running and cleared the crowd of reporters. We came out of Sorna. Aadhmi placed his palm on the panel and said, "Switch to micro mini mode" and quickly got down with its back pack. In a second Sorna shrunk to the size of a small button. It looked like a golden shirt button. Aadhmi took it and kept it in the back pack.

I had Puper in my arms. Though he was heavy I did not feel like leaving him down. Aadhmi came closer to me and handed back my sparkling clean cell phone. I spilled out a 'Thanks' and smiled at it. The reporters tried to break the wall of guards and approach us. When that failed, they began to fire us with questions and extended their mikes towards us expecting our reply. But Professor walked straight towards the barricade ignoring them and I had to run behind him. The whole place looked like a military base. We crossed three check points and neared a small door in a corner. The guards there saluted Professor. They checked my ID and even Professor's. Then a senior officer like person came towards us smiling at Professor. He opened the small door and let us in. I expected the interior to be dark. But it was well lit with flood lights. I couldn't guess the size of the meteorite. It was not like a piece of rock at all. It looked like a huge mountain. It was so tall and huge that I could not see the top of the mountain.

Professor said, "This meteorite has covered the gap between Rameshwaram and Srilanka completely. Don't you think it is funny Bindu? Once lord Rama built a bridge to Lanka with the help of Vanarasena. But today, this meteorite has linked India and Srilanka without the aid of any helping hands. If you climb over this meteorite and walk, you can certainly reach Lanka. But I don't know if it would be comfortable to walk over." The rocky surface was uneven. So I just kept on walking by the side of the meteorite with my mouth wide open and did not try to hide my amusement. I had no shame in behaving so because, it seemed to be just extending and never ending. Professor said, "You can touch it and examine it. It resembles a spongy material." I let Puper down gently and he began to wander around casually. I went closer and touched the meteorite with the curiosity of a child. When I pressed a little bit harder, my hand sank in. It felt like a rough sponge. But Professor had said that Emberonium was too hard to be chipped off from its mother rock and he had taken just a pea size Emberonium with much difficulty!

Aadhmi said without lifting its head from the collar it was working with, "Emberonium is hard only when it is out of the earth's atmosphere. Once it enters the earth's atmosphere it becomes soft and weightless like a sponge. We observed this property only when I brought back Emberonium the second time from Kaala Galaxy for Professor's research." How many mysteries and wonders does nature have? Professor added, "Yes. Though it is soft like a sponge it has considerable weight. If you smell it, it resembles vinegar. The most reliable test to confirm that this meteorite is Emberonium is using highly concentrated sulphuric acid on it. You can test it by yourself."

I bent down and smelled it. It smelled like vinegar but was denser and powerful than the odour of vinegar. Aadhmi took a small thick glass bottle from its back pack. It handed me a small glass dropper with some concentrated sulphuric acid taken from the bottle. Professor warned me, "Be careful Bindu. Just a drop is enough." I cautiously got the dropper and placed a drop on the meteorite. My eyes widened when the single drop of acid began to corrode the rock very fast. Soon there was a depression nearly the size of a foot ball. Wow! Then the whole meteorite can be dissolved by spilling concentrated sulphuric acid on it. Thank god. There is a solution to each problem and the solution to this huge problem is so simple! Unbelievable! I shouted in joy, "Professor, you are a genius! Let us take immediate action to dissolve the meteorites." But wait! What's happening now? Is anything wrong with my eyes? I observed keenly and to my horror, the Emberonium that had dissolved and formed a depression had started to develop from the same spot. My eyes widened in shock. The foot ball size depression was filled in seconds and it still continued to grow. It projected out like a small surface, and then kept on growing until it reached the size of a heap. Puper looked puzzled observing the mounting of the meteorite and hid behind my legs with quizzical eyes.

Professor let out a sigh and said, "Sulphuric acid is not the remedy to our problem Bindu. It is only a confirmatory test. The acid enriches the growth of Emberonium, that too multifold. The barricade and protection in this area is only to protect this meteorite from morons trying something different in the name of research and causing any other unpredictable damage. People could do everything unimaginable if it is left open. They may even make it a picnic spot." I just nodded. I still could not come out of the shock. There is no way to get rid of Emberonium.

Professor continued, "President Rahman has asked me to meet the press today. But I am in no mood for it. So I hand over the task to you. Just give them only the basic information delivered by the President yesterday in a different form. Don't open up your mouth to answer any of their silly questions. They may drill you with all sorts of questions to pull out words from your mouth that could feed them with some information to fill their columns tomorrow. Don't fall a prey to them. Just walk out. I will take care of the rest." I looked at his face. He seemed pretty serious. So I alerted myself and followed him. We walked for nearly 15minutes and scaled the vastness of the meteorite with our eyes.

To me it seemed that Professor was not concerned about getting rid of Emberonium. Why? Aadhmi answered, "Professor thinks that it is time to clean the earth. He believes that it is not good to act against the will of the gods. He is not worried even about his own death. Ancient world needed wise seniors who were store houses of information and knowledge. Whenever there was a problem to be solved only the aged persons could give the solution. So they were valuable assets to the society. But today, all information is stored in indestructible forms." I turned to it and asked angrily, "Is a person just above 25 aged to you. What is the logic behind 25? I don't think it is fair to sweep off all the population above 25.I can't imagine a life without my parents, relatives and family members. Moreover we don't need elders only for knowledge and information. We need them for the love, affection and the blessings they shower on us."

Aadhmi chuckled, "It is you who saw the gods and goddesses in your dream. You should have asked them then. What is the use in asking me now? You are a sentimental fool Bindu. You are not thinking practical like Professor." Seeing us lagging behind Professor stood and waited. I ran to him and joined him. Aadhmi will drive me crazy if I am alone with it for some more time. Soon we returned back to the entrance. My heart began to race as we neared the gate. The guards opened the door and we stepped out. All still cameras and video cameras engulfed us hungrily. The flash of snaps made me close my eyes. Professor signaled the guards and moved forward while we followed him. We stood comfortably under a tree to face the press. 6 guards stood around us for protection. Aadhmi had moved away to get ready Sorna. I stood watching them with Puper in my arms.

As soon as he cleared his throat, the mob became silent to listen to him. He began to speak very casually, "Good afternoon, everyone. I now present you my young and energetic assistant Bindu, to give you details about what is behind this blockade. I am not in a situation to address the press today. I request your cooperation. Thank you." Saying so, he began to move swiftly from the crowd, guarded by the 6 gunned men who ran from a nearby shed to his escort as soon as he moved. The moment he left, the crowd of reporters turned towards me. I felt quite embarrassed to face them. But I have to keep up Professor's reputation. I held Puper tightly for support.

The 6 guards formed a half circle around me. The media people were held beyond the circle. They were pushing one over the other noisily. When I opened my mouth to speak, I realized that only air was gushing out of my mouth and I couldn't hear my own voice. As I cleared my throat, silence fell up on them. I tried hard to sound casual. I said with confidence, "Good afternoon everybody. Scientists were doing a research on creating a new substitute for bio-fuels. Basically it was a nuclear research based on chain reaction. The chain reaction has become unstable and has lead to the tremor. There is nothing dangerous. There is an excessive outburst of the desired product. The conditions will become stable soon. We expect it to be stable in about 6days. Once the conditions are stable the barrier will vanish. Until then I request the media to provide full support to the scientists and the government by not writing any imaginary stories and frightening the public. At present no intruders are allowed in so that the research could go without any disturbance. The useful outcome of this research will put an end to the exploitation of our natural resources. I have nothing more to tell you. Thank you."

Questions flooded in. "Is there hazardous radiation inside?" "How many scientists are working inside?" "Is this the same research as in Ellesmere islands?" "Are you holding the extinct animal created by you and Professor?" "What project are you working on now?" "Are you involved in this failed experiment?" I was startled. When did I say the word 'failure'? "Will there be any more explosions and tremors?" "Are there any deaths hidden from the media?" "If it is quite safe why not we go in?" "Is this research that much important? We believe that millions of government money is used for this?" "With the International Cultural Youth Fest to be hosted in a few days, is it wise to conduct such dangerous experiments? Won't this spoil the reputation of our nation?" "Are you related to Professor Ramanujam? Why is he giving much importance to you? What sort of relationship exists between you and him? Are you comfortable working with him?" "Do you get paid for assisting Professor Ramanujam?" "What is the use of creating an extinct species?" I remembered Professor's warning. Though I wanted to shout back at them, I controlled myself and walked swiftly towards Sorna. Before the rabble could come near Sorna I got into it. As soon as I got in Sorna moved in a fraction of a second as though it had waited eagerly for my arrival.

32

Puper's Talk

I felt my heart thumping still. My palms were cold and watery. Puper's hair was stuck together in clusters where I had held him. Aadhmi laughed, "Don't scold the reporters like this. They have done their duty. They had to ask all nonsense to provoke you. But you were smart to come without answering them." I did not respond to Aadhmi. Professor said without any emotions, "You managed well. Nice imagination too." I smiled uncomfortably. We were heading towards RV. Aadhmi continued, "You are so angry because you are very hungry. Just wait 5 more minutes to enjoy your favourite tomato rice prepared by me." Only after Aadhmi's words, I heard my stomach rumble. Aadhmi gave me a tray with two bowls of soup. "This is only the starter" it added. I thought a hearty thanks to Aadhmi. It replied, "You are welcome."

We reached RV before we could finish the soup. Aadhmi took us to the dining hall quickly and served us delicious tomato rice and kichdi. It kept saying, "Usually Professor would have eaten his lunch by this time. We are late today." I enjoyed the food without a word. Puper happily ate the fish specially cooked and served to him. We finished our lunch quickly. We moved to the living room. Aadhmi reminded, "Professor, you must meet the President today. When shall I fix the appointment?" Professor thought for a minute rubbing his forehead and then said, "Call Rahman now. I thought of visiting him in his place. Now I think it is better if he comes here. Let me invite him here."

Wow! Am I going to see President Abdul Rahman now! Fantastic! I adore the simplicity and intelligence of our President. He is a gem of a person who has dedicated his life to the welfare of the society. He is a role model for all the younger generations. No other President in Indian history has ever had the support and respect of the youths like him. He is similar to Professor in scientific knowledge and skills. He had always been an inspiration to me.

Professor spoke in a friendly way, "Hello, Abdul!" Then he was silent for a while just nodding his head and suddenly he burst out into laughter. He said in between his laughter, "Now it's your turn to tease me and pull my leg. Just enjoy that! Hmm, Abdul where are you now?" He listened intently and nodded. Then he said, "OK, come to my valley. When can I expect you? Let your visit be a secret. Don't feed the media." Then he listened for a while and laughed heartily, "Oh! You saw that? ... Yeah... yeah! That's my assistant.......You can meet her today and tell that in person.....She is very intelligent and reliable. In fact she will be in charge of the mission. ....Well, let's discuss everything here. .....Yep! She will also be coming. ....fine! Meet you at 3O'clock."

Professor seemed much relaxed after his small chat with the President. He turned to me and said, "Bindu, the President will come here in an hour. He was very happy about the way you faced the media!" I smiled nervously. This day is really remarkable. I am going to meet the President! Puper was jumping across my legs and playing happily.

Aadhmi came in and said victoriously, "Ta….Daa!... I have made a gift for Puper and you will really be happy than him for that Bindu," and showed the shiny ribbon like collar. There was a small rectangular metal bar like structure fixed in the middle. It was silvery white and bright too. What is so special about a neck band? And more over I don't want to chain Puper like a pet dog. Aadhmi answered quickly, "Don't underestimate this neck band. It is not just a collar, it is a thought decoder. It's a techno-band! This wearable computing reads the wearer's brain waves. From now on you can hear what Puper wishes to say or even thinks! It will act like a voice chord."

Puper opened his eyes widely and stared at the ribbon. Aadhmi gently lifted Puper and fastened the collar around his fluffy neck. It began to adjust something and then placed Puper on the floor saying, "It's done!" Puper looked at me merrily. Professor looked at Aadhmi proudly. Still I heard nothing. It would be so nice if Puper could speak. I want to know what he thinks about me. Two minutes passed without any change. Aadhmi looked puzzled. Again it lifted Puper and opened the rectangular box like device and made some adjustments in the IC units. It took out a micro chip and replaced it with another. Puper ran towards me, jumped on to my lap and sat comfortably. Aadhmi again fastened the belt around his neck. Puper rubbed his soft face against my hands and looked at me. A voice came from the rectangular box, "I love you Mummy." The voice was so sweet.

Mummy! Puper is calling me 'Mummy'! Why should he call me Mummy? Professor let out a roar of laugher. I questioned him, "Puper, have you been calling me as 'Mummy' all these days?" Puper answered energetically, "Yes, Mummy." It was so nice to hear his voice. But I wasn't comfortable with the word 'Mummy' though I had done all the works in creating Puper under Professor's guidance. "Why do you call me 'Mummy' Puper?" Puper answered, "You were continuously talking with me, when I was in the incubator. I have been listening to your voice since I was able to hear. When I opened my eyes, you were the first person I saw. So you are my Mummy. I love you Mummy." I was moved by Puper's love and affection. I hugged him tightly and said, "I love you too Puper."

Professor was moved by this sight. He was delighted to see this expression of love from Puper. Puper turned to Professor and said very sweetly, "Please Grandpa, shall I go with Mummy today and stay with her?" We both burst into laughter as he called Professor 'Grandpa'. Aadhmi said, "I know his thoughts already. I have laughed enough and now it's your turn." Professor continued laughing and said, "I am happy that you think of me as your Grandpa. Still, you can't go with Bindu. Her mother will not allow you inside. Their house will not be comfortable for you to stay." Puper pouted. I said, "Professor, my father is going to Delhi on an official trip. He will not be at home tonight. My mother is very eager to see Puper and she will be excited if I take him home. It will be a pleasant surprise to my Mom and sister if Puper stayed with us tonight."

Professor mused for a while and then nodded his consent. Puper jumped here and there happily, shouting slogans of victory at the top of his voice. Aadhmi said, "Come on Puper! Tell Bindu what you think about me!" Puper scratched the floor with his front right paw gently and said shyly, "Thank you Uncle! I love this gift." We burst into laughter again. "Is that all you got to tell about me? I expected a lot from you," complained Aadhmi. Puper said in exasperation, "That is the problem with you, uncle!"

33

President's Visit

Suddenly Aadhmi alerted, "The President has come." When we rushed out the President was getting out of a vehicle that was a replica of Sorna. He walked very energetically towards Professor and hugged him. They greeted each other and walked in with their arms locked together. The President laughed merrily and said, "Ram, I lost my body guards as you said." Professor slapped him on his shoulders playfully. I did not think that they were this much close! Professor introduced me, "Abdul, this is my trust worthy assistant Bindu." The President exclaimed, "Oh! The bold girl who acted as your right hand today! Hello! Bindu! Very nice to meet you! I have heard a lot of wonderful things about you. How are you?"

How simple and friendly he is, irrespective of his power and authority! He had very powerful and intelligent eyes. No wonder the whole nation bows to his charisma! No wonder it is possible for him to bring about miraculous changes in administration! No wonder even the corrupted politicians respect him and accept his orders! India is in wonderful hands at present. I said politely, "I am fine sir. It is a great pleasure to meet you. I am a great fan of you!" He laughed heartily, "Oh! You are very smart. I am happy that I have got the chance to meet you here."

He noticed Puper standing by my side and said appreciatively, "Oh! It has grown a lot. I saw it when it was just 10 days old." Puper greeted him, "Welcome Mr. President!" President Abdul Rahman was surprised and exclaimed, "Wow! It talks! Hats off to you Ram! You are really enjoying your life with such inventions and researches. I crave to come back to this life. But the burden of responsibility has tied my hands now. I miss the days when we both used to do researches together. Golden are those days, when science was the passion for both of us."

Professor replied, "It's just the artificial voice chord and sensor. The credit goes to Aadhmi. It is waiting to meet you too." The President happily held Aadhmi's hands and walked in chatting happily with it. He was vibrant, optimistic and perfect. Each and every action and movement of him was perfect. He walked smart and swift. One could feel the positive energy radiating from him. Mom, dad and Indu will be happy to know that I met the President. I have a lot to share with them today. Raj and Diya will be excited to know this. Professor seemed to be quite relieved with the President Abdul Rahman around. We went into the living room. Aadhmi had specially set a small round table with 3chairs; 3glasses of water and 3notepads. Professor is indeed very serious about this discussion. What is the role to be played by a school girl like me here? We sat comfortably in such a way that one could face the other two easily. Puper stood by my chair. He looked very energetic.

Professor started, "Bindu, just listen patiently to what I say now. Don't ask any cross questions. I don't think that I may have any other chance to explain everything in detail to you. Puper tried to play with me and jumped on to my lap. He wanted me to pay attention to him. He constantly tried to distract me towards him. Aadhmi said, "Bindu, it would be better if you handed him over to me." Puper gave a bewildered look towards him and said rudely, "I am being with you all other time when mommy is not here uncle. I am really bored of you. Don't try to keep me away from Mummy when she is here." President laughed loudly and said, "Oh god! Imagine the things that would be going on in the minds of all the animals in the zoo! It is so pathetic to live a boring life!" It seemed that Professor was not in a mood to enjoy Puper's pranks. He looked Puper in his eyes and said,

"Puper, we have to discuss something very important now. I need your co-operation too for the success of this mission. Be smart. Aadhmi bring him a chair too. Let him be seated alone." Puper looked at Professor with understanding eyes and settled down quietly on the chair provided to him immediately by Aadhmi. He kept his attentive eyes on Professor and not on me.

Professor said in a serious tone, "Abdul thank you for the trust you have in me. You have given me full freedom and acted according to my will up to this moment. I assure you that it is surely for the safety of the people." President said, "Ram, without asking any questions I have acted as per your guidance. I have even lied to the media and public. If anything turns out wrong, the whole nation will lose its faith in me. I was really shocked to see the enormity and peculiar nature of the landed meteorite. I read the report you faxed me about the disaster this spongy rock could do. What do you call that? Hmm,…Yeah! I got it! Emberonium! It's unbelievable! I have never seen or heard about anything like this in my life. Should we bring it to the notice of the SAPS? Should we not alert the public? And when did you know about this and how did you come to know of this? I am really worried about the lives of billions of people all around the world who are aged above 25. Is there any possibility that we could alter this age limit at least to above 50? Please tell me the truth now."

Professor said in a very clear voice, "Yes Abdul. Whatever I have informed about the true nature of Emberonium is hundred percent true to my knowledge. I think it is impossible to save the huge population that is going to meet its end on the 7th day. I am worried about the younger generation that is going to live after that. I have made plans to maintain order and discipline in the life of the youngsters even after the death of the elders. I have chosen Bindu as the leader for the survivors who are going to live after our demise. The survivors are to be called 'Phoenixians'. I and Aadhmi have created a program to guide the Phoenixians. Aadhmi has accurately estimated the population of all the human beings below 25. They will be the future Phoenixians.

Each Phoenixians above the age 16 will be allotted a duty depending on his or her ability, potential and skills. From 16 they are considered as 'Senior Phoenixians'." He stopped for a second and took a sip of water from the glass.

President Abdul Rahman was paying rapt attention to him with his hands rested on the arms of the chair. His face was held in his left hand with the index finger stretching across his left cheek; thumb holding the lower jaw and the other three fingers covering his mouth partially. It looked as though he was immersed in deep thought. But his eyes were watching Professor intently. After wetting his lips Professor gave an 'Is there any questions look?' around. As nobody opened our mouth he continued, "These seniors must take care of all the younger ones like infants and juniors. The junior Phoenixians will attend school when the adult Phoenixians will take care of all the duties of the government. I want some preplanning and training to be given in this regard."

'School'! Why should juniors go to school? I opened up, "Professor, can't the juniors stay in huge communities and develop their skills without any studies. I say this because mostly children hate schools and it will be impossible to make them attend school without the aid of parents." Professor chuckled and said, "Well! I am also a person who is against the 'board and chalk; 4 wall jail' type of schools. But only the place named school gives the perfect atmosphere for learning. So, even when we call it a school, nothing will be forced on the kids. Good qualities, moral values and aesthetic skills will be developed gradually in a friendly atmosphere. So attending that school will not be a pressure and will only be a pleasure. Now Aadhmi will continue." Puper was listening to everything very quietly. What role has this little darling got to play in the future? I wondered.

Aadhmi came in between me and the President. Light rays of different colours emanated from Aadhmi's eyeballs to cast a huge virtual map of the world on the opposite wall. There were millions of shiny white dots on the dark background of the map. Aadhmi started,

"I have plotted all the youngsters from 16 to 25 years as white dots on the map. They form the total adult Phoenixian population. I have also sorted them out separately as male and female. But at present the Phoenixians are not going to be biased on the basis of their gender. All will be given equal responsibilities. I have already created an ID for all the future Phoenixians, except the ones that are yet to be born within the following six days. This ID is based on their DNA. The jobs, to be allotted to the adult Phoenixians, have also been planned." Puper watched everything with wide eyes. Could an animal brain understand any of these?

Aadhmi answered, "Don't forget that we have taken steps to develop artificial intelligence in him, apart from his basic animal instincts. He understands everything quite well." Puper stretched out on his chair and let out a lengthy yawn. "Though I am fascinated to listen to this I also feel sleepy Mummy" saying so he let out another yawn. I had to try hard to keep me from yawning. Is it true that yawning is infectious? In the class room also I have seen many students yawn when one starts it up. Aadhmi said curtly, "You must sacrifice your nap today buddy boy!" and began to continue.

"By analyzing the DNA, the senior Phoenixians with strong muscles, broad shoulders, healthy and strong physique are identified and given specific code numbers. They have been assigned the duty of security and maintenance of discipline. They will maintain order in the Phoenixian community. Those who are interested in agriculture, nature, farmlands, animal husbandry and also fit for physical work will be assigned the duty of cultivation. Providing all sorts of natural food and food products to the Phoenixians will be their role.

The ones who have passion for fashion, who are creative, innovative and imaginative will be designated the duty of dress designing and manufacture of clothes. They will be responsible for the production of costumes and apparels for the Phoenixians. Those who are interested in numbers, calculations and maintaining money will be the bankers and policy makers. They will take care of commercial activities too.

Those who are interested in constructions, precise in measurements and accurate in designing structures will be the future engineers.

Those who have the patience and intellect, to motivate, to guide and educate the others and bring out their inherent capability will become teachers. Those who are having good memory power; as well as interested in biological science, anatomy and physiology of human body; and who have the delicate touch that could cure ailments will be chosen to be nurses and doctors. The ones with healthy body and service mind will take care of all the service departments. The adults efficient in administrative field and having a logical thinking will be allotted the department of administration." We all were listening with admiration. When Aadhmi explained everything it also showed an animated visual of the expected scenario.

Professor coughed lightly and said, "Let me take it from here Aadhmi. This is actually not as simple as it looks. The most important task is to train them initially for these activities and bring out the best of them. Finally when the Emberonium burns the rest into ashes on the 7th day, all the remaining Phoenixian population will be collected in an organized way with the help of the thousands of mini robots called stanno-tech-robots that are currently being manufactured by the hardwares of Aadhmi. Abdul, I need many more helping hands in accomplishing this task. These stanno-tech-robots or the ST-bots will play a very important role in helping the younger generations."

As soon as I heard this my stomach churned. I felt very uneasy and my heart became heavy. I tried hard to control my tears, though what I heard was the anticipated brutal reality. Aadhmi touched my shoulders and said, "You cannot afford to be emotionally weak now Bindu. This is the time that Professor is expecting you to exhibit your courage and mental strength. He trusts you and has kept all his hopes on you." The President closed his eyes and clasped his fingers. Is this great scientist praying God now? I wondered how Professor has managed to veil the secret he knows about gods from his friend's questioning and curious mind.

Professor continued, "Steps will be taken to ensure non-stop supply of food and water. Care will be taken to make certain that no more valuable lives are lost for any reason. For that we need many well planned and organized work forces. The younger generation may be in great panic and loss then. So here, the stanno-tech-robots will play their role by bringing all the junior Phoenixians together and taking care of them. The same mini robots will play the role of guiding the senior Phoenixians and bringing their inner strengths during that critical moment. Work is in progress to create at least 100thousand mini-robots before the stipulated time. But we are still analyzing if this number will be sufficient."

President Rahman interrupted, "Ram, won't there be any more danger from Emberonium after the 7th day. You have already informed me that it disintegrates and vanishes on the 7th day with the mass destruction of lives. But will there be any poisonous gases or harmful radiation left behind in the atmosphere? Will the earth be safe enough for the existence of human life? I have this doubt because you have conducted your researches earlier, with only very small quantity of Emberonium. Consider the vastness of the Emberonium that has landed today. What if the earth's atmosphere becomes unstable and unfit for human survival?"

Professor thought for a while and it seemed that he was searching for the right words to express himself. "Your doubt is very valid Abdul. I have also thought about it. But from my research I have confirmed the disintegration of Emberonium without any doubt. But considering your suspicion, I have already thought of a backup plan. Most probably there won't be any need to go for it. But there is no guarantee that the atmospheric conditions will remain unaltered. Well, what might be the solution suggested by you if the situation turns out to be like that?"

President Abdul Rahman said immediately' "In that case, we are in a critical situation to find another planet suitable for human existence at once. If there is any such habitable planet known then, we have to take immediate measures to send everybody there. All nations could put all their scientific knowledge, intelligence, research skills and available resources to execute this mission. If such habitable planet is not identified then, we can think of building habitable colonies in the moon. Giant size chambers with artificial atmosphere can be set up on the moon. That may take too much time, isn't it?" He pondered for a split second and added, "Or at least we can build space ships huge in size and number to take them to a safer distance away from the earth. The space ships can linger in space until the earth's conditions come back to normal. Why not build huge space stations with all supplies? Why not save all the people on the earth irrespective of their age? We can get the support of all 'super powers' and seek the aid of their scientists too."

Professor cut him short and said, "I already knew that these words will come out from you. You are a very sensitive man, who wants to do good even to your enemies. You will never be confined to the safety of yourself or your nation alone. You have a very broad heart to think about the safety of each and every soul on the earth, unlike me. I am ready to accept the will of the nature. But you are not." Puper turned to watch Professor's face and the President's face with fear in eyes. Its eyes resembled that of a small child watching the heated argument between its parents.

"Ram, what are you talking? Do you want me to sit with folded hands when there is a possibility of saving millions of lives? What is wrong in trying all the other means and ways? I think we are wasting time in hiding this secret from other nations and the public." burst out the President. Puper automatically jumped from the chair to my lap and held my hands. I comforted him gently without showing my emotions out.

Professor started convincingly, "Think practically Abdul. Is it possible to build huge space ships to hold the population of the earth permanently within this short span of time? Is it possible to take all age groups to space without any prior training for space travel? Do we have enough raw materials for the construction works and enough fuel for the travel? OK. Let us imagine that there is another planet with an atmosphere suitable for human existence; Imagine that we have constructed hundreds of mega size; safe; space travel planes based on your secret prototype; do you think that it will solve all the problems and save all lives? Think of the chaos it will create when the news is leaked out. People will panic and try all means to get into those planes. All the corrupted leaders, dons, politicians, each and every soul with power or money will try to misuse their weapons to save their own lives. You can see the worst of human behavior when there is a threat to their life. Not all people on the earth are noble and selfless like you. If you want to erase human population, the first thing you have to do is to announce the impending danger openly. And moreover what makes you believe that all the selfish 'super powers' that have never joined hands to reduce pollution and save the resources of the earth will join hands with you now for a common cause. They will try all their means to show their supremacy and take secret steps to save only those who are in their priority list. Your so called 'super powers' will certainly exhibit Darwin's instinct 'survival of the fittest' and even create another world war due to the outburst of their prejudice and hatred" and ended angrily.

He took the glass of water and emptied it in a second. He signaled Aadhmi for more water. My mouth was also completely dry. But I dared not to move. Puper and I were like to tiny rabbits in the midst of two ferocious lions roaring violently. Aadhmi took the glass of water and pressed it in my hands. Aadhmi, you are my savior. Thank you so much. But still it is a miracle that it is behaving well to me. President Abdul Rahman never spoke a word, but kept on thinking silently. After calming himself down, Professor continued, "You see Abdul, here we both are not concerned about our individual lives. But we are worried about the world. I want a better world. Let the youth take charge. Let them bring out an uncorrupted society. Let the old leave way to them. I want your whole hearted support in this."

President said with a sigh, "OK, Ram. I know about you. I give up. Now I am completely depending on you. I trust you with my whole heart. I believe that whatever you are planning will be for a positive result. Tell me what I should do." After much hesitation Professor spoke up, "Abdul, as I believe you I reveal this to you. What Aadhmi showed us now is plan A. I have named it as mission 'Yuva Sansaar'. I also have plan B for back up. But I don't have the courage to reveal that to you now. I am very sorry" and bent down his head.

President Abdul said sternly, "Ram, we all are going to die in just 6 more days and still you want to play hide and seek with me. I have no time and energy for that now. Throw away your unnecessary hesitation now. Look at me and answer me." His eyes focused a piercing look on Professor. Professor couldn't bear the intensity and said slowly in a low voice, "Will you believe that I have discovered another planet where human life is possible long back? Will you believe that I can make arrangements to send the Phoenixians to that planet if earth becomes inhabitable? Please Ram, don't ask me for any other details regarding this. But what I say is true!" President Abdul Rahman's face was in terrible shock first. Then it bloomed in pleasure. His eyes widened in wonder and admiration. He seemed as though he was mesmerized by something magical. He stood up as though he was in a trance. His eyes were wet. Puper was startled and confused to see that. He held me tightly.

He rushed to Professor and stooped to hug him. He hugged Professor and shook his hands with joy. He shouted happily, "I am blessed Ram. You are a rascal. You have never revealed this to me even when we had done space researches together. I suspected you! Yes! I always had a feeling that you knew something wonderful already. Now the cat has come out of the bag. I am happy! I am delighted to know this my friend. Well! What other pleasant surprises are you going to give me?"

Aadhmi interrupted them placing 3 large glasses of freshly prepared orange juice on the table and saying, "Juice time Professor." It placed a bowl of milk for Puper. Puper saw the two great personalities' faces for a moment. Then he jumped on to the table and began to slurp his milk. Seeing that, they both laughed and took their glasses. I let out a sigh of relief and leaned forward to take a glass for myself.

I have never seen Professor so angry ever. I was a bit frightened to be with them when they were discussing something very important like this. They both drank their juices happily and President Abdul Rahman turned to Aadhmi and said, "Thank you Aadhmi, your preparation is as delicious as usual. The taste will linger in my tongue for a long time." Aadhmi said dramatically, "You are welcome Mr. President." Even Puper laughed at the funny voice imitated by Aadhmi.

After a moment the President asked, "What shall we do about the International Cultural Youth Fest Ram? Shall I call it off?" Professor answered, "No Abdul, as we have discussed earlier, the Fest should be held as planned. But just make arrangements that more people participate in it and enjoy that. All interested candidates must be given chances to exhibit their talents. The grandeur of the event will be a wonderful distraction to the public."

Our President Abdul Rahman is a lover of all forms of arts and an adorer of artists. He had even insisted that the school students should learn at least one art form for their own well being. So he was really happy to host the fest. He replied, "Well. I will ensure that the boarding, food and security arrangements are perfect to the guests from all nations. Let the students keep on practicing as usual to rock the stage!"

Professor continued, "Abdul, I need your help in two aspects. I need the aid of our military air force for an important purpose. The stanno-tech-robots that are being created now must be evenly distributed all around the world in the spots already chosen by us to take charge and guide the youth after the calamity. Only your power and authority can execute this. The robots must reach each and every nook and corners of different nations without creating any suspicion. Secondly I need the support of ISRO to speed up and monitor the works that are being done by the hundreds of hardwares of Aadhmi. But they must not know the reason behind their work. All available eminent scientists from all over India must be brought by you to RV. Aadhmi will take care of the rest. I will be happier if you could visit here periodically and follow up the developments."

The President nodded enthusiastically and said with confidence, "Done. This is not at all a problem. I think these works are not going to be as difficult as building the barricade. What a tension! But I really appreciate the soldiers who rose to the occasion and helped us in executing our plan. OK, it's getting late Ram. I think I must leave now. Or else my body guards will come here with their sirens blaring! Let's meet at the SAPS. My opinion is that the SAPS must know everything about this mission 'Yuva Sansaar'. This mission is not for the welfare of our nation alone. It aims at the welfare of the whole earth. I believe SAPS will join hands with us and help us in this mission. Why not we try?"

He looked at Professor with pleading eyes. What is this SAPS again? Professor just thought for a while and then nodded saying, "You are a man of hopes. I wish you good luck my friend. I will be really happy if this works out. Let's meet again at SAPS and see if the wind favours us.

We walked out with the President to bid farewell. As before Professor and the President were chatting and laughing heartily as school boys, playing all along the way. Aadhmi opened Sorna for the President. We all stood there waving until Sorna disappeared out of our sight.

Professor sighed, "I did not intent the meeting to be like this. I have a feeling that I have missed something. I am not satisfied with how the discussions went today. I am not even sure whether I conveyed all the messages correctly to Abdul. This is the problem with me. I don't know to handle people. Aadhmi, remind me that I have to talk to Abdul today night. It is very important. I have to clear many things by that talk. Was I very rude when I spoke to him? I should have controlled myself."

Aadhmi replied casually, "Mr. President has no ill feelings Professor. In fact, he was very happy that you came out emotionally. He believes you from the bottom of his heart. His one and only regret is that he couldn't join you in your researches." Professor laughed in a relaxed manner.

34

Raj's Prank

Suddenly my phone rang. I excused myself and attended the call. It was from Raj. Oh! The school must have been over as usual at 4 O'clock and he might have reached home. I answered, "Hello! Raj!" He shouted enthusiastically, "Hello! Bindu! Do you know what we are doing now? We are actually watching you!" What? Watching me? I turned around here and there to search him.

Suddenly a girl voice shouted, "We are watching you in TV. Wow! You are holding Puper too. I love him. How wonderful it is to look at him. Will I ever get the chance to hold him in my hands?" What? Is it Diya? Has she gone to Raj's house or has he gone to her house? They must be watching the coverage at the meteorite site. Again Raj shouted, "Bindu, did Professor say anything about me? Have I impressed him? I have expressed my desire to work under him in all possible ways." I rolled my eyes and said, "Professor did not say anything about you Raj."

His enthusiasm was drained at once and he said in a low voice, "Did Aadhmi talk about me?" Why should Aadhmi talk about him? Raj said with laugher, "I have pasted a sticker on its back. Did Aadhmi find out the sticker and enquire about me?" I scolded angrily, "You idiot! Why did you do so? And when did you do so?" He laughed, "Then only Aadhmi will remember me! I pasted it when I hugged it in the lab." I couldn't control my laugher. Diya was munching something and said, "Hey! You didn't tell me that you were going to the barricade! Tell me how it was. Hey! Idiot! Don't take from my plate, you monkey!... This stupid Raj!" Well as usual Raj must be snatching and eating her snacks. They both began to quarrel and I could hear only bits of their shouts with a lot of breaks. Finally Diya spoke triumphantly, "I beat him to a pulp as usual. How dare he is! I have come to his house as a guest and he doesn't know to play a decent host! Silly monkey! Hmm!...Aunt's 'onion bajji' and chutney is delicious!" I laughed again visualizing the scenario that would be going on there. I missed them very much. I too wanted to be with them there. After chatting with them for a while I disconnected saying that I have to talk to my mother.

All the while Puper was jumping here and there and playing around me. He also joined me whenever I laughed without even knowing the reason. He was like a small baby reflecting the emotions of its mother. I called my mom and informed her that I will be late and she need not worry about my safety as Aadhmi will drop me as usual even if it is midnight. I enquired if Indu had come home. The ear-piercing sound of the pop music in the background confirmed her presence. My mom insisted me to try to come home earlier before the departure of my dad to Delhi. I didn't inform her about Puper's stay. She would really be surprised! I imagined how my mom's eyes would widen in glee as a small girl, at the sight of him and laughed to myself. I came back into the house with Puper to know from Aadhmi that Professor had gone to the lab and we had to go to the lab to discuss more.

Aadhmi was standing near the wall high window and watching the evening sun trying to go behind the huge mountains. RV was shining bright and sparkling like red gold, by the setting sun. When I saw Aadhmi I was remembered of Raj's silly act and I began to laugh. I went and stood behind Aadhmi to check if there was a sticker there. Raj had really pasted his favourite comic-hero's sticker there and I laughed uncontrollably on seeing that holding my stomach. Aadhmi turned to me and stared. Then suddenly it extended its hand back at an odd angle and peeled off the sticker. It said to me, "You need not laugh this much for such a silly matter. I don't understand human beings! Laughing instantaneously and crying instantaneously! That boy Raj! As there was a huge crowd around me and there were too many thoughts to be read, I missed his action! I like him too!" I laughed again. What's the wonder in two crazy creatures liking one another? Aadhmi complained, "You don't understand my value as I am at your service by Professor's order. A day will come when you will understand my true value and importance." I wondered why Aadhmi is taking my teasing very serious! Aadhmi said suddenly, "Professor wants us to come to the lab immediately. Let's go now."

Aadhmi walked before me to the lab. I walked slowly with Puper. When Aadhmi was out of our eye sight, Puper exclaimed, "Mummy Emberonium was so big! Will we go there to see it again?" I laughed and said, "I think there won't be any need to see it again Puper." He said, "I liked the outing and travel Mummy. I was happy to see different people there. When will you take me out again?" I replied, "Don't worry dear, I will take you out today itself. Today you will see many different faces and everybody there will like you very much."

Puper said with hesitation, "Mummy, I hate uncle Aadhmi." I enquired, "But why?" He said, "Aadhmi tries to cuddle me and that irritates me." May be Puper has misunderstood the funny quarrels between me and Aadhmi. Aadhmi has been behaving in a very supportive and polite manner to me lately. I can never hate Aadhmi. So I did not want Puper to have any ill feelings over Aadhmi. I said in a pacifying tone, "Puper, you need not hate Aadhmi. Aadhmi takes care of you perfectly always. It is your protector and it is no wonder that it loves you. It has taken care of you since your birth. It wants to be closer to you. There is nothing wrong in it. Moreover you must not hate anyone in the world. You must be kind, gentle and polite." I felt that it was my responsibility to advice him and guide him in the right path. Puper mused for a while and then replied, "OK, Mummy. I will obey whatever you say." I lifted him happily and hugged him. We reached the lab soon.

When we entered the lab, many hardwares of Aadhmi were working around busily. Professor was moving around and observing the works. When he saw me, he signaled me to come to him. I ran quickly to him. He said, "Bindu, who were you talking with then?" I replied, 'Professor, it was my friend Raj and Diya. Hmm.. I introduced them to you when you came to ….." "Oh! Well, oh! That enthusiastic boy! I remember him very well. He was very much interested in all my works. What do you think about him?" he asked briskly. What would I think about him? Why is Professor asking me this question? Why is Raj important now? Professor was thinking something to himself and continued, "We need more trustable persons for the success of our mission. I was thinking if we could use this boy Raj for our works. He was really eager to help me and join our team. How are his scientific skills?"

I let out a sigh and said casually, "His scientific skills are as good as mine Professor. He takes the 'ALL INDIA SCIENCE TALENT SEARCH EXAM' every year and ranks first or second competing with me. He has wonderful scientific knowledge and application skills." He still was thinking something seriously and said, "I will inform you how we can get him involved in our works when the right time comes." Aadhmi walked in briskly and said, "Professor, I have set the table for tea, outside. Please come out and take a break." Professor nodded and said, "Bindu, come on. Let us discuss over tea." When we came out of the lab, the atmosphere was filled with the chirping of the birds returning to their nests before sunset. Aadhmi had arranged a small table with three seats. Setting sun was beginning to give a dark shade to the trees and mountains around.

There was a tray on the table. The tray was loaded with chinaware set, which included a beautiful jug with intrinsic works of art, 3 cups and saucers with the same type of artistic work and 6 small bowls of the same design. One bowl had sugar cubes with a small shiny tongs; the other had fried cashew nuts; the next one had some roasted almonds; there were some biscuits in another bowl; another had milk in it; and it looked as though there were some fried fish in the next bowl. We sat listening to the sounds of the birds and enjoying the dominating smell of the thick woods around us. Puper was happy to be let loose and free. He began jumping into the bushes for fun. Aadhmi handed us both two cups with steaming hot 'masala tea' and placed the snacks bowls in front of us. It called out for Puper. "Puper come here to enjoy your milk and fried fish." Puper came running to the table. He said, "Thank you uncle" and began to cherish his milk and snacks.

Professor sat back on his chair munching the almonds and enjoying the smell of ginger from the masala tea. I was relishing the taste of the crispy cashew nuts in my mouth. He took a sip from his cup and spoke, "Bindu, once I was working on a project with Abdul. Our aim was to build the fastest space ship for our nation. Though I had 'Prapancha' many years before meeting Abdul, I couldn't reveal that to him. Prapancha was an outcome of our family's researches and hard work. So I did not tell him anything about Prapancha. Abdul is not a man of secrets. When I showed him my special Sorna out of my true friendship, he just made a similar one to all the presidents and the lead scientists around the world. So I did not dare to tell him about Prapancha. But still we worked together and designed rockets and space ships for our country.

After the death of my family you are the one and only person to whom I have shared the secret of Prapancha. I think of you as my great granddaughter Bindu. I have considered you as my family. Puper interrupted, "I too know the secret of Prapancha grandpa." As Professor was in a relaxed mood, he laughed and said, "Of course Puper! I think of you also as my family." He turned to me and said, "Bindu, now the future Phoenixians will need a large number of Prapancha to transfer them safely to any other planets or even galaxies. I have asked for the help of all Indian scientists from Abdul only for this purpose. You should be by my side throughout this mission. I think, you need the help of your best friends too. You must be the pioneer for the Phoenixians. Even in my absence, Aadhmi will assist you and obey your orders. It will act as your left and right hand in all your accomplishments. I have imparted all the knowledge I have acquired, to Aadhmi. Currently we have worked and designed an important gadget called 'Suethae' for the younger generation."

Aadhmi reminded, "Your tea is perfectly hot to be drunk Professor. You may regret later that you had not taken it at the right time." Professor responded, "Oh! Thank you Aadhmi!" and began to drink his tea. I savored my tea with the company of cashew nuts, almonds and biscuits too. All were too delicious to resist. Puper had finished his milk and fish long back. I broke a biscuit into small bits and placed them before him. He too enjoyed them to his heart's content. Suddenly Professor's cell phone rang. He became very attentive on seeing the number and attended the call briskly. "Yes, Abdul." He listened quietly for a while. Then spoke up, "Well, no problem at all." Then he listened nodding his head and said, "You need not worry about that Abdul. Aadhmi has made all the arrangements. We have hundreds of hardwares of Aadhmi too. … Yeah! We can manage." Then he let out a sigh of relief and said, "Thank you Abdul. I am waiting to receive them. Thank you my friend!" He disconnected with complete satisfaction on his face.

Then he said happily, "Scientists from ISRO are coming now to RV. I have to do some preliminary works in the lab with Aadhmi. If this works out then our burden will be reduced a lot. OK, Bindu, I think now you can leave and come back tomorrow. You need not go to school tomorrow Bindu. I will send Aadhmi to pick you up." Then he turned to Aadhmi, "Drop Bindu and come back as early as possible. We need to reschedule the works." Puper asked very politely, "Grandpa, can I go with Mummy now?" Professor laughed and nodded, "OK, Puper. But behave yourself and be a good boy." We walked to the portico as Professor walked briskly into the lab. Aadhmi took Sorna for the ride. On the way it said, "Tomorrow I will come to pick you up at 9am. I will show you a prototype of Suethae and demonstrate its operations. Be ready tomorrow Bindu." I nodded in response. Aadhmi dropped us at my house within 5 minutes and departed at once in a hurry.

35

The Sleepover

When I entered into my house, the sound system was in its maximum volume, vibrating the glass windows. Puper clung to me tightly. I comforted him and called for my mom. I was pretty sure that dad was not at home. My sister dare not listen to music with such volume in his presence. She would seek her ear phones. Mom was also found to be nowhere and that puzzled me. I tip toed to my room and hid Puper behind my table. I asked him to stay hidden there for a while so that I shall show him as a surprise to mom. He too accepted and nodded his head. I door of my sister's room was vibrating violently. I opened it gently and peeped in. my eyes popped out. The lights were switched off except for some disco light illuminating the room in periodic flashes. I had to struggle hard to accustom to that dim lighting. I saw three figures dancing like monsters to the music. One will surely be my sister; sometimes, my mom goes crazy and accompanies Indu to my horror; but who is this third figure? I squinted my eyes to identify the third one.

Suddenly the third figure rushed to me and jumped over me tumbling me down. Thank god, the figure was a girl and she began to laugh like a maniac. Oh! My god! This is Diya! "What are you doing here Diya?" I had to shout louder than the music. "Tomorrow the whole school will be practicing only for the 'Cultural Fest'. We have no homework! I went home; got permission from my mom to go to Raj's house first and then stay with you here!" she shouted joyfully with full energy in a very high decibel. I could not converse in this noise pollution. I moved towards the music system, approximately guessing the path in the semi darkness and switched it off. Then I put on the light. The trio covered their eyes overreacting to light like vampires! I ignored their acting and asked Diya, "When did you come here?" She said happily, "After talking with you, I did not stay much longer in Raj's house as he had to attend his keyboard class. He dropped me here and went to attend his class."

Mom asked with concern, "Bindu, shall I bring you something to eat?" Diya added, "Yes Bindu, your mom's 'carrot halwa' was very tasty. You can eat it now. Don't miss it. Because, by the time I go to sleep, I would have finished it completely" sounding as though she was warning me. I said, "No mom, my stomach is heavy now. I will eat everything later." Then I turned around here and there and started in a very serious tone, "Mom, I think dad has not yet left to Delhi. Please, listen to me patiently. I am going to tell you a very important secret. We encountered a serious problem today. There was a freaking accident in our lab." I gave a pause. Indu, mom and Diya were listening with panic stricken eyes. I continued seriously, "A very dangerous, hazardous product was formed as a result of that accident. It would be too risky to have it in the lab. So I had no other go than to bring it to our house." They three shouted together, "What? Why did you bring it here?" I hushed them and pleaded, "Why are you shouting like this? You will alert the whole area I think. Please come and have a look at it. Then let us decide how to dispose it."

The three held hands tightly and walked behind me with fear filled eyes. I struggled hard to control my laugher and hid my face from them. I lead them to my room. They dared not to enter my room and peeped in. It seemed that their eyes would pop out at any time. I bent down; lifted Puper from behind my table and suddenly showed him in front of them. They shouted in horror at first and after seeing Puper, their eyes widened in wonder. Indu and Diya let out shrieks of joy and rushed in to snatch Puper from me. Puper was bewildered and he clung tight to me. Seeing his reaction, they laughed wildly.

Mom shouted, "Shut up your mouth girls. See, he is disturbed by your shouts. See how frightened he looks!" at them and then turned to Puper and said, "You come to me dear. Don't panic." Puper looked at me with fear in his eyes.

I comforted him, "Puper, this is my mother. She is my sister Indu and this is my friend Diya" and introduced them to him. Puper went readily to my mom and then to Indu. He looked at Diya indifferently. When she snatched him from Indu, he tried to pull out her spectacles. Indu and mom were quarrelling to cuddle him. Indu won and she said, "Let me show him around. Puper I will show you my pet fish 'Rocky' and cat 'Lolo'. I will also show you my mango tree and neem tree. Let us swing in the neem tree. Puper replied, "OK, Indu. I like you very much. But what is a swing?" They three gasped in surprise as they did not know that we could hear his voice now. Mom shouted in joy, "How is it possible Bindu. How can he speak?" I explained, "It's just a wearable computing mom. The techno-band around his neck can transform his brain waves into sound waves." She nodded still watching Puper with wondering eyes. Indu's eyes filled with tears as she listened to his words of love. She hugged him tightly and said, "I too love you very much da. What a sweet voice you have! I will show you what a swing is." Mom went with Indu and Puper.

Diya and I came to the living room. Diya switched on the TV; took the remote and reduced the volume very much; then she sat leaning back comfortably on the couch and said, "Do you know what happened at school after you left? This Raj ..." She began to laugh childishly. I sat near her and said, "Diya, what is it? If you tell me we can laugh together." She again started, "This Raj no, he ..." She began to laugh uncontrollably again. I made a face at her. She tried to control her laughter with much difficulty and then burst out laughing. I said in a warning tone, "Diya!" She nodded and closed her mouth. Then she said, "Bindu, after you left today, Raj showed your pictures in the class to all our class mates. He kept on babbling that you looked very gorgeous, beautiful, magnificent etc. He used all known adjectives to describe your beauty." I looked at her sternly and asked, "What? What pictures?" She said, "He showed the photos taken during your Chithi's Valaikappu. He commented that you looked great in half-saree!"

I was very angry that Raj had behaved like this in the class. I controlled myself and asked coldly, "How did he get my photos?" Diya asked with fear in her voice, "Are you angry Bindu? I did not think that you will be angry for this matter. It was funny for me and Raj." I again asked sternly, "How did he get my photos?" She said in a guilty tone, "Sorry Bindu. I think Bala has sent them to Raj and Raj had brought his cell phone to school." I asked, "I was there during the morning session. You both were with me throughout. Why didn't you inform me then? When did he show the photos to others?" Diya said with tear filled eyes, "I am sorry Bindu. I did not think that you will take it this much serious. He showed it during the lunch hour." I understood that it was not fair to fire her with any more sharp questions. I calmed myself down and said in a controlled voice, "OK. Leave it now Diya. I don't want to spoil your mood when you had come to my house. I will deal that idiot Raj myself later." I did not want to irritate myself by talking about that. But Raj will get nicely from me for his stupid behavior. Idiot! I cursed him in my anger. I will catch him, hang him upside down and throw plates on him.

At once Diya became normal and began to chat with me happily again. She asked me all of a sudden, "Is there something very serious behind the barricade? I am your friend. I know very well that you lied in front of the camera today. I could sense that something is really wrong. But I don't want to push you. I want you to know that I am always there for you and you can share anything to me at any time." I fought back my tears and said, "Thank you Diya for your understanding. I will surely tell you when I am given the permission. I am happy to be with you at present. Let us not open up anything heavy." She hugged me to comfort me and said, "It's OK Bindu. Everything will be alright. Whatever be your problem, I will pray for you." I smiled happily at her.

I heard my dad's car. He came rushing in. I said, "Hai dad, Diya has come and she is going to stay here today." He smiled at her and said, "Welcome Diya. Feel at home and enjoy your stay. Right now I am in a hurry to catch my flight to Delhi. Bindu, where is your mom?" without waiting for my answer, he moved in removing his tie. Diya asked, "Will you come to school tomorrow? Tomorrow is no books day! We can enjoy freely without any boring class room activities!" I said slowly, "No Diya. I have to go to RV tomorrow also." She asked quickly, "Then when will you practice for the Cultural Fest?" I said, "Diya, at present I am not at all worried about the cultural fest. Something more important is haunting me." She looked worried and confused. After thinking for a while she asked gathering her courage, "Then who will be the 'Master of Ceremony' Bindu?" I said in a comforting tone, "Don't worry Diya, I will surely give you a clear picture tomorrow. Don't put all heavy matters in to your tiny brain and squeeze it hard. Be cool as usual." She let out a sigh and said, "OK. As you say!"

My dad came with a briefcase followed by mom and Indu. Puper was happy in her arms. My dad came to me and kissed me goodbye. He waved to Diya and warned my mother, "Lock all the doors and windows and be safe. Take care of the children. Don't join with Indu and behave like a school girl. Be responsible. I will come in two days." Puper asked, "Is he serious like this always?" to Indu. She said, "Sshh..." to Puper and smiled at my dad. My father said, "It is weird to see a talking animal!" My mother pulled my dad and dragged him out before he could give any more comments. I heard his car leave.

Mom said, "Come on children, let us all have dinner and then go to sleep." Indu started, "Mom, shall we play for a while after dinner in the terrace?" I suggested, "Why not we have dinner at the terrace?" Mom said gleefully, "I grant OK to both the suggestions." All shouted a joyful 'Yeah!' as loud as possible. We carried a carpet, water bottles, plates, table spoons, hot packs with chapatti, and channa masala gravy and tomato chutney with us. We went to the terrace and marveled the sight of the full moon. Clouds of different shapes were moving here and there and periodically hiding the moon. We spread the carpet on the floor and placed everything in the middle. We sat around and ate our dinner chatting noisily. I tore a chapatti into pieces, dipped them in tomato chutney and gave them one by one to Puper. He enjoyed them happily. Indu never left him down. He was locked in her arms. Diya stuffed her mouth with chapatti and channa and said, "Hmm.... Hmm... Yummy! Aunty, now I understand why Bindu is very chubby. If you cook delicious food like this and serve me every day, then I will also grow soon in the X-axis and compete with Bindu."

I pinched Diya and she shouted, "Ouch! Am I not telling the truth?" Puper said, "Don't be mean Diya. You need not tell any truth. Mummy is not chubby. Mummy is very beautiful. You are only lean like a stick. You look like a flag post I saw on the way. You are only stuffing 4chapattis at a time." Diya bowed with artificial respect to Puper and said, "I am very much frightened of you Puper! Your mummy is very lean like a thread! Are you happy now? How furious he becomes if I talk anything about you! See Puper! Your mummy is not my friend anymore. I will not talk anything about her." My mom said, "Enough! Don't talk unnecessarily while eating. Taste the food and eat properly."

Suddenly Diya said, "Aunty, I forgot the 'carrot halwa'. It is on the dining table. Shall I bring that too?" and without waiting for my mom's reply she rushed down. She returned with the halwa container and a spoon. She announced, "Bindu and Indu, you can eat your mom's preparation any day, at any time. As I am the guest, I think I can take this fully for me. Puper said, "Am I not a guest too?" Diya looked at him and said, "Considering your size and age I think what you had eaten is more than enough for you. Don't overload yourself and suffer in pain in a new atmosphere Puper. Don't you want to go back to Professor safely tomorrow? Control your tongue and be healthy my boy!" Puper flared in anger and his hair stood still. Indu whispered, "Bindu, I think he has got 'Goosebumps'. What should I do now?" I laughed and said, "Take it easy Puper." Indu asked slowly, "Mom how is it possible for Diya Akka to be so lean when she keeps on grinding something always?" Puper laughed uncontrollably at her comment. Diya said to my mom in complaining tone, "See aunty! This Indu is teasing me and this Puper is enjoying that!" Mom said in a comforting tone, "Just ignore them Diya. Come sit near me." Diya poked her tongue at Puper and went near my mom.

After eating we cleared the vessels and put them in a corner. We cleaned the carpet and spread it again. Indu, Diya and Puper began to play hide and seek, with just the water tank to hide behind. I asked my mom, "Mummy shall I lie down in your lap?" She caressed me with love and I rested my head in my mom's lap and was lying down on the carpet watching the sky. I did not want to think of anything that is going to happen in the future. I just wanted to enjoy the present. I tried to count the stars. Mom rubbed my hair in gentle strokes and I was slowly going to sleep. Suddenly Puper jumped over me and nestled in my mother's lap shouting frantically, "Help me mummy! Help me! Diya is coming to catch me!" Diya and Indu were giggling and running around the water tank. With shouts of laughter they too came running towards us and landed on the carpet, panting for breath. I opened my eyes and cuddled Puper. Diya and Indu also occupied the remaining place in the carpet. Full moon was now shining brightly with no clouds to veil its glow. The whole surrounding was very quiet with muted sounds of traffic on distant roads. We did not want to break that silence. There was a gentle breeze and the weather was becoming cool. After some time mom whispered in a low voice, "Children, shall we go down. Bindu wake up." I felt it too difficult to move my legs. Diya had crossed her legs over mine. Puper was lying like a fur bag between Indu and Diya. I woke them both without disturbing Puper.

Mom, I and Diya collected everything we had brought up; Indu lifted Puper like a baby and took him to the bed room without disturbing his sleep. She cuddled with him in her lower bunk. I and

Diya rested our sleepy heads on the king size cot in the corner. Diya's eyes closed before we could mumble a 'goodnight' to my mom. I could hear mom doing something in the kitchen. I turned to Diya to say good night. She was snoring already, with her spectacles still on. I removed her specs and placed it on the small table nearby. The very next moment I too went into deep sleep and we all slept like logs. My cell phone alarm rang at 6 am as usual. I woke up and scanned the room in search of Puper. He was neither with me and Diya in the king size cot, nor with Indu in the lower bunk. I heard voices from the kitchen. I tried hard to free myself from the strong clutches of Diya's bony hands and legs. Finally I slid out of her grip and walked out of the bed room. I refreshed myself and went to the kitchen.

As I had guessed, Puper was chatting happily with mom and they both were laughing periodically. Seeing me Puper smiled broad and rushed to me. He ran happily between my legs and said, "Good morning Mummy. I drank milk and ate crispy rusks. They were very tasty." I lifted him and rubbed his fur. I asked him, "Did you sleep well Puper?" He nodded and said, "Hmm. Yes. I slept well mummy. Everything is very comfortable for me here. I want to stay here with all of you forever mummy." I smiled and said, "Let us see if it is possible. We have to get permission from Professor for that. So don't dream of anything now itself." My mom asked as usual, "Have you brushed your teeth Bindu. Shall I give you some tea?" I nodded, "Ok mom. Where did you sleep and when did you sleep mom?" She replied, "I did some cleaning works in the kitchen after we came down. When I came back to the bed room only the upper bunk was free and I had no other go than to climb up and sleep there. Throughout the night I had a feeling that I may fall down at any time. When I climbed down at 5.30am Puper also woke up and came behind me."

I placed Puper on the dining table and drank three glasses of water. Puper jumped down and began to watch Indu's pet fish in a tank on the shelf. I informed my mom, "Mom, Professor has asked me to come to RV today in the morning itself. I have to leave with Puper at 9 am." My mom said, "OK, Bindu. Then Indu and Diya must get ready to school. Wake them first. Diya has brought her dresses. She said that no books are needed today. So let me pack them lunch alone. When they are ready, please drop them at school before you go." I thought if there will be enough time to drop them and then said, "OK mummy. I can drop them. Aadhmi will come only at 9O'clock to pick me up." Puper asked eagerly, "Mummy, may I come with you to drop Diya and Indu?" I nodded with a smile and said, "Yes, Puper."

Mom handed me a cup of tea. I sipped the tea and read the newspaper. The barricade was in the headlines. The hot topic of the news was the carelessness of the scientists to carry on such dangerous experiments in populated areas and causing discomfort to the public by asking them to evacuate all of a sudden. I read the newspaper fully and then went into the bedroom to wake up Diya and Indu. First I went to Indu and murmured gently, "Indu, Indu…" She rolled but did not open her eyes. But opened her mouth and began to babble, "Oh, Niru…Yes! Yes! That was fantastic. I loved that song too. But Zuil's hair was really beautiful!......No,….They were nice…Yes,…..Still I vote for Uni Direction. That…. Black….shoe.." and she drifted back to sleep. Well! Indu is dreaming about her favourite British boy band Uni Direction and her friend Niranjana. How silly she is to think of them even in her dream! I shook her violently. I know that it will be of no use. The best way to wake her is to use water effectively. I brought a glass of water and poured it slowed over her closed lids. She opened her eyes and on seeing me she began to shout, "How many times have I warned you not to pour water to wake me!" She began to chase me to beat me and I ran around the house. While running itself I explained, "I tried to wake you by other means, but it was of no use. So I used this technique as usual. Don't be mad at me. There is some important news about your favourite singer Zuil in the newspaper." As soon as she heard this she went to see the paper, cursing me. I again went into the bed room. Diya was still sleeping. Even Indu's loud yelling has not woken her up.

She was snoring gently and her mouth was wide open. I took a hanky, and gently lowered it into her mouth. When it touched her tongue, she shook her head suddenly and got up. She sat straight and spat out as though some insect was in her mouth. But still her eyes were closed. She scratched her head fiercely and then lay flat again and went back to sleep. It was really funny to see her. I murmured in her ears in Mrs. Mathi's voice, "You fool! This salt is not lead nitrate. Did you study the procedure at home properly or not? Get out of my lab!" Diya began to answer in her sleep, "No madam, I studied madam. I did the confirmatory test too. Sorry …." She was about to cry in her sleep. I ran my fingers in her foot. She giggled and said, "Oh Puper, don't do like that. It tickles!... oh! It tickles!" and she continued to laugh. I shouted, "Wake up Diya. Wake up. It is not Puper! It's me." she shuddered off from sleep and looked at me drowsily. I said, "So you dream about your science teacher and sleep talk too!" She laughed sheepishly and ran to the bathroom laughing in a silly way.

I watered the plants in the garden with Puper. He was chasing the butterflies and the small birds. When I came in Diya was reading the newspaper. Indu was nowhere. I asked her, "Where is Indu?" She pointed the bedroom in a secret way with a mischievous look in her eyes. Ahah! Indu must have gone again in to continue her sleep. I said to Puper, "Puper, go to the bed room and see if Indu is sleeping. If she is sleeping bite her legs and drag her out of bed." Puper happily took up his mission and ran to the bed room shouting, "Sure Mummy!" Diya chuckled. Puper came running to me in a few minutes and reported, "Mummy, Indu is getting ready. I dragged her to the bathroom and did not allow her to come out at all." We all laughed at puper's sincerity.

Mom shouted, "Indu! Diya! It's getting late. Come and have your breakfast and go to school. Your lunch bags are ready." They were ready in their uniforms and I was wearing a long flowing skirt and plain white cotton tops. The black colour skirt had neat chumki works. A thin platinum chain with a very small heart shaped dollar hung almost invisible in my neck. My small handbag was slung across my shoulders. There was nothing much in it. I just had my cell phone, a hanky, a note-pad and a pen. Mom served us hot idiyappam and chicken gravy. We finished our delicious breakfast quickly and got into my Audi to go to school. We were chatting and laughing nonstop all along the way to school. I dropped them at the gate and returned home. Puper was not at all ready to part with Diya and Indu. I was not in the mood to pacify him. So he kept very quiet on the way back home. I parked my Audi at the portico and went for a stroll in the garden with Puper in my arms. I believed that he would be distracted a little. He became normal and began chatting with me normally. I had all my ears to the gate. As soon as Aadhmi came I shouted, "Mom, I am going with Aadhmi. Please lock the door as soon as I leave" and ran to Sorna without waiting for my mom's reply.

36

Kankan Suethae

Puper was not really happy to come with us to RV. He said with pleading eyes, "Mummy, will you please bring me to your house today night also. You see, I did not say 'good bye' to your mother. I did not even say 'thanks' to her. But I have said 'I love you' many times. But that is not enough. Before I could say a word, you simply brought me into the car." The way he said this would melt even a stone hearted person. I felt very sorry for what I had done and I said, "I am extremely sorry Puper. To compensate for this mistake I will bring you back with me. I will get permission from Professor so that you can be with me wherever I go." Puper was very pleased and he shouted, "Thank you mummy! I love you!" Aadhmi spoke seriously, "Today you may be quite busy Bindu. Professor is in the lab right now. He has asked me to bring you there directly. Hope you have had your breakfast. So without wasting a minute we have to go to the lab." I nodded in agreement.

When I went to the lab I was surprised to see that none of the hardwares of Aadhmi were working there and Professor was also not there. Aadhmi explained, "The scientists from all over India came to RV yesterday and all are working with my other hardwares in the production section of the lab. This research section will be exclusively for Professor and us." Soon Professor walked briskly into the lab. Aadhmi might have informed him about our arrival. I and Puper wished him, "Good morning Professor" and "Good morning Grandpa" together; He accepted our greeting with a smile and a nod and sat in front of a demonstration table. Puper walked towards him and played around his legs. Professor lifted him and placed him on the table. Then he asked me to be seated and took out a very small cube from his coat pocket. Its five faces looked like metallic silver and the sixth face was black. Professor said, "This is the prototype of the gadget we have named as 'Suethae'." He handed the mini cube to me. I observed it closely. What could be the specialty of this gadget?

Aadhmi explained, "This black colour side has a biometric sensor to identify the true owner. Each Phoenixian will be given a Suethae. The Suethae can be opened only by its owner. The biometric sensor will analyze the DNA and react to the user. The Suethae you are having now is only a prototype and no DNA identification code is installed in it at present. So you can open it now. Bindu, just touch the black face of the cube." There was space only to place the index finger tip and I placed the tip of my index finger on the black surface. Suddenly, the cube opened out into a small black panel. When I touched the panel, it became active and a virtual screen radiated from it. A voice boomed from Suethae, "Dear Phoenixians! Yes! From now onwards, you will be addressed so, as you are like the phoenix that rises out of its pyre. It's the time for you to rise and shine. Now you have lost your parents, elders and beloved ones. Don't panic. You are safe and no danger awaits you. You must understand and accept the fact that you are alone now."

Aadhmi touched the black surface. The message paused. Professor started, "My plan is to create one Suethae for each Phoenixian including you. As soon as the calamity occurs, the stanno-tech-robots will spread out these Suethae. The Suethae will already have DNA identification codes and they will go in search of their owners and identify them. They are designed in such a way that they can fix themselves as a band around the wrist of their owners. It will look like a bangle or a Kankan. So it can be called as 'Kankan Suethae' also. Once the Suethae reaches the owners, they will teleport them to the nearest Prapancha available. The whole Phoenixian population will be kept safe inside the controlled atmosphere of Prapancha. Once the earth's atmosphere becomes stable, they will be sent out to lead the Phoenixian life. If the earth's atmosphere doesn't become stable, all the prapanchas will begin their journey at the same time to the safer planet. Once they reach the space, all the prapanchas will be linked together as compartments and will form a whole unit. During this process all the Phoenixians will be guided by the ST-bots. The first important work of the Suethae is teleporting. The process of teleporting will take place within a fraction of a second, so the Phoenixians will not even know what had happened to them. Then the Suethae will explain everything to them and prepare them for the Phoenixian life by instructing each and every individual."

"How many prapanchas are ready now Professor?" I inquired. He said, "A minimum of 100 prapanchas is my immediate target. But we may need a maximum of 650 Prapanchas. Thanks to Abdul, the scientists have come already and they are working on it. But they still don't know what they are creating. Prapancha can alter its size to accommodate just one person or hold thousands at a time. Each Prapancha will be under the care of at least 10 ST-bots. There will be easy communication facilities between the prapanchas. So all the young people will be teleported to the nearest Prapancha and they can communicate with any of the younger generation of their family in any other Prapancha through telepathy."

Professor touched the black panel now. The voice continued, "Leave the past behind with courage. It is your time to rule the earth. This Suethae will guide you in this new world of Phoenixians. This Suethae is an important asset that should never be lost forever. This should be kept very safe. This Suethae will help in the smooth functioning of the world. Phoenixians must obey the rules of Suethae. Suethae is like your ID proof. All sales and purchases will be possible only through Suethae. To know more about Suethae and clear your doubts go to the help option." The voice stopped and a home screen appeared on the virtual display.

Aadhmi explained, "Once the Suethae has made its first contact with its owner it can read the brain waves of the owner even when they are away and help them accordingly." Aadhmi just flipped its hand in mid air. Suddenly the Suethae became active and started narrating the whole theory about Emberonium; its nature; how it had come to earth; how the seniors have demised; and how the owners have come into Prapancha. The Suethae also gave an animated explanation about the ST-bots. Finally the home screen appeared with many icons.

I asked with hesitation, "Professor how are we going to care of food supply? Is it possible to feed the Phoenixian population when they are in Prapancha?" Professor said, "Aadhmi and the ST-bots will collect all the available perishable and non-perishable food items that could last for months. The perishable food items must be given to the Phoenixians first and then the remaining food items must be used. Later on the Phoenixians will take care of the cultivation." "How could a Phoenixians get food or water when they need?" I asked again. Aadhmi chuckled and said, "Bindu, only you can worry about food and water under such critical circumstances!" At once Puper sneered and said, "Don't be mean uncle. Most of the Phoenixians are going to be young children who need to be taken care. Feeding them becomes the responsibility of the senior Phoenixians. That is why mummy is enquiring about this in detail." I laughed in pride as Puper tried to defend me. Aadhmi chuckled again and commented, "You may think so great about your 'mummy'", it gave an extra special stress to the word 'mummy' and continued, "But I know she is concerned about herself."

Professor said curtly, "Aadhmi, there is nothing wrong in worrying about food. Human being's first need is food and water. So Bindu is right in clearing her doubts. Don't give unnecessary comments now." Puper showed a 'thumps up' to me and a 'thumbs down' to Aadhmi. Professor turned to me and said, "Initially one can get food and other supplies freely with the help of Suethae. Later on, once the Phoenixian organization has become effective all their needs can be purchased only with the help of their Suethae. Particularly the senior Phoenixians can never get anything without their Suethae. Each senior must work and they will be credited points according to their works. For each purchase, points will be debited from their accounts, once their purchase is done. Well, you can try it yourself now."

I observed the icons on the home screen. There was an icon with a shopping bag symbol. I gently tapped the air pointing to that icon. A new screen appeared with icons for list of items. Again I clicked the icon that read food items. Another screen with a very long list of items, their images and rates appeared. The list extended to many pages. I clicked at the item code for 'cookies.' I was puzzled. What will happen now? How will I be delivered the cookies I have chosen? Aadhmi pointed to the screen and explained, "Bindu, can you see this aperture here? It is a teleporter. Once a Phoenixian selects a product and wishes for it, the ST-bots receive the information and feed it to the master teleporter. At once the desired product which is in storage is delivered by the master teleporter to the Suethae and it reaches the Phoenixian through the teleporter icon." As Aadhmi had explained, a beam of light shot out from the aperture. Aadhmi directed the beam to the table. Suddenly a pack of cookies appeared on the table like a magic show.

Are they real or virtual? "Try them Bindu!" Aadhmi encouraged me. I took the chocolate cookies pack. It was real! I opened the pack. The contents looked really tempting. I broke a piece and gave it to Puper. Puper tasted it and said, "Mmmm....Mmmmm.... it is very delicious mummy! I like it very much!" I took another piece and put it into my mouth. It melted in my mouth and the taste was delicious. I gave another cookie to Puper and when I gave one to Professor, he laughed and said, "No thanks Bindu." I was about to take another bite of my cookie. But Aadhmi stopped me saying, "Hmm! Bindu! It's enough. In the name of tasting, you will empty the whole pack." I rolled my eyes. Puper frowned and said, "Uncle if you mess with mummy, I will throw plates on you!" We all including Aadhmi, burst out laughing as he imitated my 'throwing plates' style.

Again Aadhmi moved his fingers pointing home. The home screen appeared again. Aadhmi showed another icon and said, "This menu 'occupation' will give the Phoenixian the details about the duties to be performed by that individual. The particulars related to his or work like the timings, the credit points for each hour of service etc will be provided here. It will tell you about the training camps and the activities to be performed there." He showed me each and every icon and explained in detail the applications associated with it. I asked Professor, "Professor, what about the clothes? Will the Phoenixians need any space suits or special protecting accessories?"

Professor said, "Now we have made certain modifications in the Prapanchas. As the atmosphere inside Prapancha is controlled, there won't be any need for special costumes. The ST-bots are creating as many costumes as possible for the junior Phoenixians. But the senior Phoenixians who are going to do different activities must be given a special costume; it should be something like a uniform. It should be able to withstand the atmospheric changes in case they have to explore new habitable planets. I think you can design this basic costume with Aadhmi. You can discuss and decide the colour, material, the pattern etc. Do you have any other doubts?" I thought for a second and asked, "What will be the source of energy for the ST-bots and Suethae Professor? Will they not run out of energy?" He pointed Aadhmi and said, "All the hardwares of Aadhmi, Prapancha, ST-bots and Suethae are powered by tritium cells. All these gadgets have the inbuilt facility to use solar energy too. The ST-bots and Suethae are designed and manufactured in accelerator laboratory using wonder material graphene and stanene. They are protected by topological insulators. So they will never run out of power."

He thought for a while and said, "All the hardwares of Aadhmi will also come with the Phoenixians in Prapancha. They will also assist you and act as protector and defenders. If there is a need they will fight for the safety of the Phoenixians until their destruction." Aadhmi reminded as usual, "Professor, the time is nearly 20'clock.

You are already very late for lunch. I did not want to disturb you in the middle of such important discussion. So I did not remind you. Now, please if you permit I shall serve you lunch and we can resume after lunch." Professor nodded, "Yes! Yes! You are right Aadhmi. Let us have lunch Bindu." He touched the black panel's corner. It transformed itself into the silver cube. He picked it and put it in his coat pocket. We all began to walk to his house.

37

Designing The Phoenixian Uniform

We finished our lunch quickly and came back to the lab. As soon as we entered into the lab, a hardware of Aadhmi informed Professor that all the scientists had been provided lunch and the work was going on in full swing. Professor said, "Bindu, when you both work on designing the costume, I shall go to the production section and monitor the level of progress." I nodded and Puper said, "Grandpa, may I come with you?" and without waiting for his answer, he started to run behind Professor.

I am not a good costume designer like Indu. But I can give a try. Aadhmi took me to the designing table. It got a call from Professor and it rushed to Professor. So I have to design it all alone now. I switched on the designing machine. The designing was by virtual method. We can cut and stitch the virtual images of the fabric. After we have framed the shape we require we have to just confirm it. One prototype will be given as output. If we are satisfied with the prototype the required number of costumes can be fed to the 3D printing system and we can get as many costumes as we want. I thought that a simple white full hand shirt with full trousers will be a decent costume to choose. The senior Phoenixian uniform should be simple and sweet. White is a symbol of peace. It could give some solace and calm down the junior Phoenixians. I chose a material produced using nano technology. That material was soft, wrinkle free, smooth and silky. It was a bit shiny too. It was dust resistant and stain resistant. I clicked on the virtual cloth and then clicked on the available designs to see the availability of any design based on my imagination. Many designs appeared on a virtual screen. I clicked on the one that suited my imagination. I coupled the material and the design option. A prototype of the desired model came out of the 3D printer. All I had to do was to add a logo. I flipped through many logo options and finally clicked on the picture of a colourful 'phoenix bird'. I confirmed my selection and finalized the position of the logo in the shirt. I placed the shirt on the printer and closed. The shirt came again with a small phoenix logo printed on the top left corner in the front and a huge phoenix at the middle of the back. The logo looked very bright and beautiful with the white background. I took the costume and observed it. To me it seemed 'OK'. But I wasn't sure whether Professor would like it.

Suddenly I heard footsteps, sounds of laughter and voices approaching the lab. To my surprise, Aadhmi opened the door wide for Professor and the President to enter. Puper followed them behind. I happily greeted the president and he was happy to see me there. Professor asked me, "Is the costume designing over Bindu? Abdul came with more scientists today and he wished to see all the works related to the Phoenixians. So I brought him here too. He has already seen the Suethae. You can show the costume to Abdul if what you are holding in your hand is the model." I felt quite shy to show that to them. Simply I had done some experimentation and I did not want that to be scrutinized by a person I respect very much. I felt embarrassed. Aadhmi motivated me by saying, "It's OK Bindu. There is nothing wrong in showing your first attempt. It is after all your first design and we are not going to use it for a fashion show. Show it please."

With much hesitation, I spread the costume on the table. They all surrounded the table. Puper shouted eagerly, "Mummy, have you designed fur costumes?" I imagined all the senior Phoenixians wearing only fur clothes. It will be OK for the people in colder regions. I imagined the condition of the people in hotter regions and laughed at once. Puper looked at me and asked, "Why are you laughing mummy?" I explained, "Puper, fur clothes will not be comfortable for the Phoenixians who will live in hotter regions of the world. The material should be suitable to all climatic conditions. So I have chosen the material that acts as a thermo wear in colder regions and behaves as pure cotton in hotter regions. This nano material also reacts to the atmospheric conditions and gives comfort to the wearer."

The president looked at me with sharp eyes and asked, "Bindu, Why have you selected this phoenix bird as the logo?" I replied slowly, "Sir, we the younger generations are going to be like this phoenix soon. God has decided to give us sorrow and pain by killing our parents and elders. It is like destroying our roots. Our respectable elders are going to burn into ashes right in front of our eyes. But I am sure that we will not succumb to the loss. We will not be heartbroken. We will rise from their ashes with courage and power and continue to live our live with faith and confidence. I wanted to symbolize that and so I chose this logo. Whenever a senior Phoenixian touches this logo, he or she will get the inspiration to carry on their duties with self assurance and poise." Professor and President Abdul Rahman clapped their hands with tear drops ready to cross their barriers. Professor shook my hands and said, "We are really moved Bindu. I am proud that I have chosen you as a pioneer to the Phoenixians and you have the true spirits of a leader. Keep it up my dear." I never thought that my answer would bring such emotional disturbance to them. Aadhmi commented, "The material chosen is the best choice. I really appreciate it Bindu." Puper was very much excited and he jumped happily into my arms and said, "I love you mummy. I am happy that you have impressed everyone." I was relieved that my work has satisfied them.

Professor asked, "Aadhmi, should we go for any more designs?" Before Aadhmi could answer, President Abdul Rahman said, "This is quite good in all aspects. Then why should we waste our time in the same task. Tell me more about 'Kankan Suethae'. Aadhmi explained more about the different functions of the Suethae for about an hour. Then the talk drifted casually to other general matters and the president happily shared about his school life, the impact of his teachers on him, his service in the teaching field etc. His narrations were in a very simple and lucid style and we all were laughing to his jokes forgetting our burden for some time. Aadhmi brought us fresh apple juice and we all enjoyed it happily in the lab itself. Puper was given specially roasted mutton. He relished it to his heart's content.

When we were chatting casually, this question suddenly came out from me. "Sir, the world is nearing its end and the children will lose their parents in just 5 more days. So why not you declare a nationwide holiday to schools, so that the children can enjoy more time with their parents." President laughed and said, "School children are always childish. I thought you were too matured. I did not expect this from you. But you are also still a small child expecting parental affection. Well, Bindu, I find a logical point in your saying. But for a better tomorrow, what the Phoenixians need is not the happy memories with their parents, but the growth of knowledge and wisdom. We do not know precisely what development occurs in a child's brain every day. The knowledge acquired may be too little or very high depending up on their opportunities, sources and atmosphere. But that acquisition is very important now. In my point of view, not even a single day of school should be missed by any child." I understood and accepted his point. I was glad that he did not ask me to go to school.

Aadhmi served us tea and the usual array of snacks at 6O'clock in the lab. The president left after tea reminding Professor that he should not forget the SAPS meet scheduled the next day. Again I wondered what SAPS could be, but did not ask anything as they would have talked about that to me if I should know about it. Professor went to the production lab. Again Aadhmi demonstrated many more applications of the Suethae. We had dinner with Professor at 8.30pm in the dining hall. Professor said after dinner, "Bindu, please be ready at 7.30am tomorrow. I will send Aadhmi to pick you up. I think it is better if you take Puper with you. He is more active with you. Is there any discomfort in having him in your house?" I shook my head violently and answered quickly, "Puper is most welcome in my house Professor. It's really a pleasure to be with him. Thank you for sending him with me."

"I still have some works in the lab. OK Bindu, see you tomorrow," saying so Professor left. There were 10 missed calls in my cell phone. The calls were from mom, dad, Diya and Raj. I had it in the silence mode and forgot that totally. First I called mom and informed her that I was on the way. While going in Sorna I called my dad and enquired about his health. He said that he was fine and he missed me. There was no other important message from him. I thought I could speak to Diya and Raj after I reached home. Aadhmi dropped me and Puper at home. Aadhmi left at once. I rang the bell and waited for my mom to open. Indu came and opened the door. She rushed and scooped Puper in her arms. Usually mom attends the door. My eyes searched mom.

"Mom was not feeling well and she slept early. She tried to call you in the evening, but you did not attend and she kept on worrying about you," she answered my enquiring look. I said, "I talked to mom when I saw the missed call. She did not tell me anything about her sickness Indu. I am sorry. If I had known, I would have tried to come earlier. I feel tired. Shall we go to sleep?" "Wait, wait, now only I have got Puper. Let me play with him for a while and then sleep. If you feel sleepy, you can join mom." I nodded and started to the bed room. Indu asked Puper, "Shall I give you some rusk to eat now Puper? Are you hungry da?" He saw her fondly with shiny bright eyes and said, "No Indu, I am not hungry. Shall we go and see your mother. How does she feel now?" Indu hugged Puper and said, "How loving and caring you are! I missed you da! Come let us see mom." She locked the gate and door and came into the bed room.

When we entered the bed room mom was snoring very feebly and was immersed in deep sleep. We did not want to disturb her. I went to my room and changed into my night wear. I thought of climbing on to my bunk and then changed my mind. I stretched near my mom in the king size cot. Suddenly Indu also joined me. Though the cot could accommodate 4people, I pushed her and said, "Go to your bed. I am tired and sleepy. I am not in the mood to quarrel with you." She said, "Shh… Shh… Why are you shouting like this? I will go to my bed after you answer my questions." I touched my mom's forehead. Her temperature was normal.

Indu asked, "Will you come to school tomorrow at least? Our principal wanted to meet you regarding the youth fest and he asked me if you could meet him tomorrow." I replied, "No Indu. I couldn't come tomorrow too. Please inform our principal that I will surely come to school the day after tomorrow. Was he angry with me?" She said with frustration, "Why is he going to be angry when the great Professor Ramanujam himself calls him and asks permission. How come you become an apple to everyone's eye? I condemn this partiality." I chuckled and cuddled Puper. She violently pulled him from me and moved to her bed. Puper looked at me with his glowing eyes and said, "Good night mummy. Sweet dreams." I smiled and said, "Good night Puper." I fell into deep sleep in no time.

38

Professor's Past

I woke up at 6am. Mom was not in bed. Indu was sleeping in an irregular shape with her mouth open wide. I tried to close her mouth. But she opened up again and again, and I gave up my effort and went out of the bed room. Mom was doing yoga in the hall. Puper was stretching himself and giving her company. "Good morning mom! How do you feel now?" Are you alright?" She bloomed on seeing me and said with a smile, "Good morning Bindu, I am fine. Just had a slight cold and fever yesterday. I feel very brisk today after a good sleep yesterday night." I was happy that mom felt better now. Puper said cheerfully, "Good morning mummy. I am also doing yoga." I laughed and said, "Very good! Keep it up Puper!" He giggled happily like a small girl.

"Mom, I have to leave early today. Today also I can't attend school. Aadhmi will come at 7.30am to pick me up. Can you drop Indu at school?"

"Don't worry Bindu, Diya's mom will come to pick her up today. She only dropped her here yesterday evening too. So you can carry on with your works."

I called Raj and Diya and talked with them for a while. They shared what had happened at school. All were busily involved in preparing for the 'International Cultural Youth Fest'. They really felt the school boring in my absence. I promised to meet them at school the next day. I got ready quickly and woke up Indu. Puper was very busy chatting with mom and moving around with Indu. As I had to leave early, mom served me Idli and chutney. I had my breakfast and insisted Puper to have his breakfast also soon. He obliged and was happy to eat rusk and milk. When we were done, I heard the ringing of the door bell. Aadhmi had come. I rushed out saying 'good bye' to mom and Indu.

On the way Puper casually began to sing a song sung by Uni Direction. I was shocked. Just two nights at home! Indu has made Puper sing her favourite song! I asked Puper, "How did you learn this song Puper?" He said proudly, "This song is sung by the British boy band Uni Direction. You slept early yesterday night. Indu played this in her I-pod for me yesterday night. She kept on talking about them and I know many more songs also. Shall I sing them too mummy?" I wanted to dash my head on a wall and throw plates on Indu and her 'Uni Direction'. Without knowing my feelings, Puper said enthusiastically, "I really love their voice and I am a huge fan of them!" and began to sing another song. Puper just resembled Indu's style and accent while saying this. I was fuming with anger. Not even two nights! Just one night is enough for her to spoil my innocent Puper! Aadhmi chuckled and asked, "Why do you hate this band of singers? It is interesting to see you getting angry. Actually the band is really nice and I like them too." I controlled myself and said, "Enough Puper. You can sing later." Puper looked at me with disappointment. Thank god the journey was over and we were in RV. As soon as Sorna stopped Puper jumped out and ran in search of Professor. Aadhmi shouted, "Puper, Professor is in the production lab." I went with Aadhmi to the lab. Aadhmi had made the entire set of costumes of the same model and had stacked them. A dummy was dressed in that costume. I felt happy that the costumes will be very majestic and will give a smart look to the Phoenixians.

I and Aadhmi worked together and added some more applications to the Suethae. We collected the list of people below 25 years who have completed or were learning medicine and nursing. We saved their list in the medical aid app. We made similar collections for all branches of engineering, agriculture, information technology, polytechnic, teaching and arts. When the work was accomplished, Aadhmi informed Professor about the completion of the task and it listened to Professor intently for a while. Then it said to me, "Professor has another important assignment today. We have to travel a bit now. I'll go and get ready Sorna. Bindu, you please go to the production section and take charge of Puper. When Professor has given instructions to the scientists there, you all can come to the portico." Saying so Aadhmi left the lab. I moved to the production section. I could hear the sound of many machines working at the same time. When I opened the door, hardware of Aadhmi handed me a helmet and a coat. I put on the helmet and coat. Puper was moving around Professor's legs restlessly and was trying to get his attention. No sooner did he see me than he ran to me and jumped into my arms.

Professor was wearing a metallic helmet, shielding glasses and a protective coat like all other scientists working there. The glass looked very peculiar. I walked towards Professor carrying Puper and on the way I bumped on to something and shouted, "Ouch." But I couldn't find anything on my way. When I extended my hands, I could feel some metallic structure in the shape of a huge capsule. Puper said with wonder, "Mummy, it's quite noisy here and I was also constantly hitting on something. I don't know what it is!" I was also puzzled. I began to walk carefully, spreading out my hand to feel if there was anything on the way. All eminent scientists of India were there. I dared not to disturb them and kept watching them from a distance. I have seen the photos of many of the senior scientists in magazines and journals. Even one or two among them had come to our school to deliver special lectures for us. I have met some of them in a few science meets when I went with Professor. I had talked to a few of them.

Professor finished his works and came to us. "Bindu, many prapanchas are ready now and they are kept in invisibility mode. So put on the special glasses that are in your coat pocket, so that you will be able to see them." I bit my tongue. I might have dashed over one of those prapanchas on my way. When I put them on, I gave out a gasp of surprise even without my knowledge. There were nearly 70 to 80 glass capsule like structures arranged here and there. They looked like huge glass beetles that could accommodate two adults inside them. I removed my glasses and placed it in front of puper's eyes. He said, "Mummy, what are they? They are beautiful. Did I collide on them? Why were they invisible to me before?" Professor said, "Because, they are made of reflecting glasses and are set in invisibility mode. OK, now we have an important work. Bindu, today I am taking you to London to meet a very important person." A hardware of Aadhmi removed Professor's coat, helmet, and glasses and collected them from me too. Did I listen to his words properly? Did he say 'London'? "We are leaving to London right now," said Professor and walked fast.

What? London? How can I go to London without my passport or visa? Why did Aadhmi not tell me anything about such plans? I ran behind him and blurted out angrily, "Professor, Aadhmi did not tell me about my journey and I am not prepared for it. I don't have my passport or visa! I haven't informed my parents too! So it is impossible for me to join you now." He laughed and said casually, "Just stay calm Bindu. Let me show you how everything is possible when you are with me. We can reach London by Sorna." I was completely puzzled. Aadhmi also had said that he will get ready Sorna. But how is it possible to go to London by Sorna.

I tried to stay composed without bursting out my emotions because I was sure that Professor is a man who keeps up his words. He has a perfectly preplanned and scheduled life style. If he has made some sudden arrangements then that must be really important. Maybe now we are going to London to discuss with someone about the steps to be taken to protect humans from the impending danger. Wow! When I go to London I may even get chance to meet Abi Akka if time permits! But who are we going to meet? Seeing the confused look on my face, Professor patted my shoulders and said, "We are going to meet Dr. Malik." My eyes widened in wonder. What? Dr. Malik?

The world famous scientist! Research co-coordinator! A pioneer in medical researches! And the owner of 'Malik' pharmaceuticals! The owner of 'Malik towers', the tallest building in London. Am I going to meet that powerful, all rounder personality? All world famous scientists and researchers in medical field are acquired by his company and his 'Malik pharmaceuticals' stands the first in the production of medicines in the world. May be he might have also done researches relating to Emberonium and has some solution to the problem. That is why Professor is in a hurry to meet him.

We rushed to the portico and got into Sorna. Professor was immersed in his own thoughts and he said suddenly, "I have to talk with you Bindu." Aadhmi looked at Professor waiting for instructions. He gave a puzzled look reading Professor's thoughts. Professor said, "Bindu, you must know about Dr. Malik before we meet him. I think you must have the freedom to choose whether you wish to come with me or not. So I am going to tell you about my life. This was some 70years back. After the demise of my family, I lived a very lonely life with only Aadhmi and my pet dog Rex with me. Soon Rex also died due to ageing. I was left all alone with Aadhmi. My loneliness was gruesome. And you know how difficult it is to live with Aadhmi!" We both chuckled. Aadhmi pouted. We both laughed. And Professor said comfortingly, "Sorry Aadhmi. Such comments are only for fun and they come from my lips. But from the bottom of my heart the truth is that you have been my better half throughout my life till this date, and you will be so forever in my life. You are not just a robot, but my family." Oh! God! This is too much and this is more than enough to make Aadhmi be in cloud nine!

As he expected Aadhmi was pleased and satisfied. Professor continued, "OK. Coming back to my life, my loneliness led in search of friendship and love. Yes! I fell in love. I met Celine at a conference and fell in love at first sight. She was a remarkable scientist and we had the opportunity to work together. She was from London and I felt that she was the angel sent from heaven to comfort me. She had big blue eyes and curly blonde hair. To me she was the most beautiful woman on the earth and I did not wait long to open up my mind. She accepted me as a good friend first and soon I tried hard and stole her heart. We were married when I was 30. She was just one year younger to me. We lived a happy life in RV. God blessed us with a beautiful baby girl. She was a replica of Celine and we named her 'Rose'. I thought that I was the luckiest person on the earth." His eyes were closed and he seemed to be enjoying the vision of his wife and daughter behind his closed eyelids.

What? Professor was married and had a family in the past! Where are they now? Professor cleared his throat and looked at me and said, "In the same conference I met Malik too. He was a young and energetic chap. He was interested in everything and curious to know more. Though he was 10 years younger than me, he became my close and true friend. Oh! I am sorry. You will understand better if I say 'Dr. Malik who resides in London'. Dr. Malik was my friend then." I was excited. Dr. Malik! Wow! What a pleasant surprise! The world famous scientist Dr. Malik! In the world of inventions and researches Dr. Malik is a renowned name. I knew, Dr. Malik was living in London and I have read all his books and of course, I admire his scientific knowledge as I admire Professor Ramanujam.

"Malik was more ambitious. He craved for name and fame unlike me. Though we three did many researches together, I never discussed or shared any of my secret researches with Malik. Malik was very much eager to find a cure to ageing and control ageing. His aim was to look young forever. He began to concentrate more in medical field and soon he attained the name and fame he had craved for. His company stands the first in medical researches since then. He is the master brain behind this success. He had always questioned me about life, death, after life and immortality. I believe he wanted to be immortal too. He believed himself to be the king of human race and he wanted to rule the world. He always had a doubt that I knew something very important and I was hiding that from the world. He had tried to convince me to let out those secrets so that human life can be more painless and happy. But I knew the catastrophe that would come from the exposure of my researches and I paid a deaf ear to him. He could not extract any information from me. But I shared all my discoveries including those about gods and the different dimensions to Celine. I hid nothing from her. I asked her also to be careful with Malik. Though he was my friend, I had some intuition that kept on warning me about Malik.

Celine was a devoted mother. She began to spend most of her time with Rose. She expected the same from me too. She wanted me to spend time with the family; make a lot of friends and give a social environment to the baby. She did not want the baby to live a lonely life like me. But then, I was very much interested and seriously working on a project named 'Patchi Gragha'. The research occupied my mind completely to an extent that I even forgot Celine and Rose sometimes. I would have promised to take them out or have fun with them. But would easily forget them and be involved in the research in my lab. Celine kept on warning me that I was testing her patience by this behavior." He covered his face with his hands to wipe off his tears.

I was worried now. What is haunting him and causing him pain like this? I looked at Puper and he looked back with a puzzled look. He continued, "I still remember the day. It was Rose's first birthday. Celine made many plans to celebrate that day in a special way. I think women live in a world of fantasy while men live a practical life. I did not have the slightest enthusiasm or eagerness like Celine about that day. I was preoccupied with my research. I wanted Celine to know more about my research when she needed me to be a normal husband to enjoy all the tiny pleasures of life. She wanted me to cherish each and every moment of Rose's childhood. But she met with failure as I did not know the value of what I had got then. Celine had asked me to come from the lab early to spend some quality time with the family. As usual I forgot that totally and was in the lab."

Now I understand why Mom shouts at Dad for silly matters. What seems silly to a man's brain may be much more important to a woman. My Mom also expects my Dad to be early home from office and spend some time with us. Whenever my Dad is with us during a picnic or outing, I have seen Mom's face glow with some sort of happiness, pride, love, satisfaction and pleasure. May be ladies don't expect big things from men, but just sharing and caring about the family. Professor Ramanujam might have been a good lover but not a husband and father.

"Celine stormed into the lab with Rose in one arm and a big bag in the other. She shouted in a fit of rage, "This is the limit Ram. I have tried my level best to be your wife. You have behaved like a typical Indian man, who just takes his wife for granted. I am not for that. You have always disappointed me and I have convinced myself during all those occasions. But today! Today is our daughter's birthday and you can't even remember that. What is wrong with you Ram? We have everything we need. But still you are not ready to enjoy your life. Why the hell do you rot in this lab? You don't have to work for money or name or fame. You are least bothered about all these as you have them in plenty already. How were you when you loved me? You were always behind me like a tail. But I don't expect that now. Can't I have my rightful time with you as a wife? You are making me sick. I am fed up with you. I have given you as many chances as possible. Being with the metal pieces in RV, you have also lost all your emotions. I need a change. I need to be away from you. I just can't keep on complaining and grumping always. I am going to my Mom. You can freely carry on your research without any disturbance from me."

"I was just dumbstruck by her emotional explosion and did not know what to do. Before I could convince her, she took Prapancha and flew off. It took me some time to realize what had happened. Celine had left me and gone to England with our daughter. I might have been an irresponsible husband and father. But that doesn't mean that I can live without them. Life is not possible for me without Celine. I have to apologize to her. I had to wait for a flight to England. When I tried to contact her, she was not ready to talk with me. I was happy that at least they were both safe in her mother's house in London." I think Celine must have reached England in minutes as she had gone in Prapancha. What was this Aadhmi doing then? Could it not do anything to stop her?

Aadhmi said defensively, "I tried my level best to stop her and convince her. But she behaved as though I did not exist." Who needed this useless explanation? Professor said, "Nobody can be blamed for my mistakes. I am the one and only reason for the failure of my marriage. Bindu, there is no use in pointing at Aadhmi now. I am responsible for everything that happened in my life. I craved to meet Celine and convince her. So I went as early as possible to her mother's house. When I went there the gate was ajar and the door was not closed. I entered in slowly as there was no response for my calls and I heard Rose crying too.

When I entered into the bed room hesitantly I was shocked to see Celine lying down in a pool of blood. There was a dagger pierced in her stomach. Our daughter Rose was standing near Celine and crying loudly. I held her in my arms and consoled her. I checked Celine's pulse rate. Though it was low, I was happy that she was alive. I had to act immediately to save her. When I was about to move suddenly Celine's hands held my leg in a tight grip. I knelt down and took her in my lap. With much difficulty she opened her eyes and I questioned her hastily, 'Celine, what happened dear? Who did this to you? Please stay with me. Nothing will go wrong. I will get some medical help now.' Tears rolled down her beautiful blue eyes. She said in a low voice, 'Malik came here and asked me about your research papers. I was not ready to answer him. He threatened me that he would kill Rose. In my attempt to save her, I got hurt. Don't believe Malik. I want you to do only one thing for Rose.' I nodded with tears in my eyes."

Oh! My God! Is Mrs. Celine alive or dead now? Had Professor lost his true love forever? Professor continued "Celine said, "Promise me that you will never come in the life of Rose forever. I don't want you to see her or talk to her or even gather information about her. Never

ever try to contact her or try to claim her in the name of parentage. I ask this to you for the safety and security of my daughter. This is my last wish.' She held my palm in her hands tightly. Before I could speak, she was dead and gone, leaving me in total despair. I hugged Rose and cried for the loss of my love. I have not only lost her, but also my life. I felt that I was a dead man too. Though I know that Malik had killed her, I had no proof for that except Celine's last words. I know that those words are not enough for the law to take action against him.

I did not say the truth even to Celine's mother. That poor lady even suspected that I had killed her daughter. But evidences proved that I was not guilty. She was very much angered that I had taken away her daughter and was not ready to allow me touch her granddaughter. I too did not persist as that was Celine's last wish. That scoundrel Malik attended the funeral like an innocent soul. He did not know that I had met Celine and talked to her just before her death. He believed that I was unaware of the truth. I controlled my anger when he consoled me and shared his condolence for the loss. The police had to close the file as they could not get any clue about the suspect. I had to bear the pain of losing Celine and Rose at a time."

Professor was crying now bitterly. I realized that I was crying and wiped away my tears. Puper was crying too. He dug his face in my lap. I comforted him by gently rubbing him. If Dr. Malik had killed Professor's wife, why is he still maintaining relationship with him. Where is Rose now? Now she must be at least in her 60s. Is she alive or dead? Is she married and does she have kids. If she had, then at least Professor may have grandsons or granddaughters. Is there any contact between Rose and Professor?

Aadhmi answered in a low tone, "Professor has never met Rose since the death of Mrs. Celine. He had never tried to contact her. But initially he sent money and gifts to his mother-in-law's address. But as they were returned back just as sent, he stopped that too in a few years." It was difficult to stay composed after listening to his miserable life. Professor wiped away his tears and said, "I did not claim Rose, because I wanted to punish myself. I think that I deserved this punishment. I threw Malik out of my circle too. But he often contacted me during the release of any new medicines or research results. He is sometimes interested in mutants and mutation and he has approached me many times to clear his doubts. I have helped him many times as the new products he was about to launch had been really useful to humanity and rejected his requests sometimes as I sensed that there was something fishy behind it. We have to meet in science fests and conferences. I talk to him as I converse with any person I know and I have to accept that there is contact between us for the sake of the world."

He sat back and closed his eyes. What I have heard about Dr. Malik was circling in my head. A villain? A murderer? How can he do injustice to a person who had accepted him as friend? What did he want to know from Professor? I hate Dr. Malik to the core. I had a huge reputation for him and admired him. I have even wanted to meet him at least once in my life time. But now as I had known his past I feel like throwing plates on him. Even that is not enough for this murderer. I feel like killing him with my own hands. I feel so sorry for Professor. Does his daughter know about the existence of her father? Will she believe and accept him if she comes to know of him? I let out a sigh thinking such questions for which I don't have any answer.

After a few minutes, Professor opened his eyes and said, "Now tell me Bindu, are you ready to come with me to meet him?" I had no fear for Malik. Why should I be afraid of him? I have promised already that I will be with Professor in all his activities. There is no second thought in it. So I agreed and Professor said to Aadhmi, "Let us go." Aadhmi said, "Professor, please stay back so that I shall fasten your seat belts." When Professor and I leaned back, seat belts extended from the sides and fastened themselves automatically. I wondered what may be the need for seat belts. Puper asked pathetically, "What shall I do uncle? There is no seat belt for me." He was seated in my lap. I covered him around with my hands and said, "My hands are your seat belt Puper. I will take care of you." Aadhmi said, "Puper, if you come to the front seat, you can have your own seat belt." Puper replied, "It is quite comfortable here uncle." I cuddled Puper and checked if my cell phone was in my handbag.

Aadhmi kept his palm on the flat panel and said, "Switch to invisibility mode." As soon as it said so, the golden exterior of the car was covered with some sort of reflecting panel shields and it was no more the shiny Sorna. The reflectors camouflaged it with the surrounding, thereby making it invisible. One has to give a second look carefully to identify the presence of Sorna. Again Aadhmi said, "We choose flying mode to reach the desired destination." At once the bonnet of the car elongated into a sharp beak. The boot projected out like a tail and changed its shape. The panels spread out like wings on both the sides and the shape of Sorna had changed completely. It looked like a mini plane now. Sorna started running on the road; took off from the ground and soared high in the air. The tyres went in and Sorna was completely sealed now. A radar screen appeared on the panel in the dashboard. It was so miraculous. As it was invisible and produced no sound too, no one took notice of it.

We flew over Pakistan, Afghanistan, and Turkmenistan and soon over the clear blue Caspian Sea. The view stole my heart. I did not want to have any serious discussion inside and miss the wonderful sight. So I pointed out and made Puper also watch the captivating sights. The radar showed our path over Ukraine, Belarus, Poland and Netherlands. The aerial view was a feast to our eyes. The North Sea came into view. Suddenly something strange happened. Sorna tilted forward and began to stoop down. Something must be terribly wrong. We were falling down at a very high speed with Sorna facing down and shaking violently. I was afraid that Aadhmi had lost control of the vehicle. We were literally falling towards the sea. Sorna plunged into the water splashing water all around. Puper held me tight and shouted in panic, "Mummy! Mummy! Are we going to die now?" I hid my own fear and said in a comforting tone, "No Puper, certainly not. Don't panic! Aadhmi will take care of everything. Am I right Aadhmi?" Aadhmi just chuckled. Soon Sorna was completely surrounded by water. I controlled myself as Professor was composed except for a quizzical expression on his face. Another glass shield was around Sorna now and it was moving under water like a submarine.

Aadhmi appreciated me with a smile on his face, "Well Bindu, you have showed your courage by comforting Puper, though you had a rush of adrenaline in your body. Surpassing your body's defense mechanism you have controlled your emotions and stayed cool. I like it." I stared at it and let out a sigh of relief. Only I knew how my heart was racing! The journey underwater was really amazing. Puper shouted, "Mummy! See that giant squid! Oh! My god! Sharks too! Look here! The huge colourful fish! Grandpa I have never seen such huge fishes in our aquarium too!" I never moved my eyes off the window. The wonderful magic of the underwater world mesmerised me. All the sea creatures moved off suddenly when Sorna approached them. Their movement was so swift that I had to avoid even blinking my eyes to have a glimpse of them. Professor asked with pride, "Do you like this underwater ride? I did not expect Aadhmi to delight you today with this surprise." Puper answered enthusiastically, "Wow! It is wonderful grandpa!" Aadhmi said, "They were very upset after listening to your story. I just wanted to cheer them up and I came deliberately under water to distract them!" Puper said in a complaining tone, "But uncle, I thought you had lost control and you were going to drown us in the sea because of your poor driving skill." Aadhmi rolled its eyes. Professor and I laughed out louder.

Soon Sorna came out of water and began to fly high again. In a while we were flying over England. My heart was filled with happiness and pride. Will anybody believe me that I had experienced such a memorable journey and come to England? Indu will die if she hears this! It has been her dream to come to England and meet her favourite boy band the Uni Direction. If she had come with me, she would have shouted in joy! Finally we flew over London. I marveled at the sight of the London Bridge and the mighty Big Ben! The Thames spread long like a sapphire carpet! It was shining beautifully. Sorna flew over a building that seemed to be the tallest one. There was a helipad and it landed like a feather on the roof. Aadhmi said, "Professor we have reached the Malik towers." The journey had not been too long! Wow! It seemed to me that we had travelled at the speed of our thoughts. I remembered what Aadhmi had told me earlier about Sorna's speed.

We all got out of Sorna. At once we were surrounded by a team of 20 armed men in black uniform. Aadhmi said to me, "Malik owns the tallest building in London and it is called as Malik towers. He is filthy rich and you will think of the riches in RV as nothing compared to that you are going to see here. First we have to cross this security check to enter in. Professor has already informed Malik about our arrival." I was certainly not in the mood to enjoy the riches of that scoundrel Malik. I controlled my anger and did not respond to Aadhmi. Puper who had got down and stood stretching himself was taken aback by those guards and he jumped into my arms wildly.

Professor asked casually, "Bindu, do you have your ID? You will need it to enter in. The whole place is under tight security." I bit my tongue and gave an expression of a lost child. Professor always insists me to carry my ID and cell phone in my bag. I usually forget my ID. Aadhmi chuckled, "Did I not tell you Professor that she is forgetful. But I have brought a copy of her ID." It handed me my ID heroically. I thanked Aadhmi and smiled guiltily. Again Aadhmi is so sweet to me. The ID had my photo; it declared all my personal details; and confirmed that I was Professor Ramanujam's assistant. Professor handed over his ID too. Aadhmi minimized Sorna as usual and kept the small gold button into its back pack. We all were scanned thoroughly from head to toe and were taken down in a lift to the reception. Money was spent lavishly to add richness to each and every inch of the tower. Almost all the items in the building were black in colour. May be Dr. Malik is a lover of black colour.

We were seated in the grand reception. Even the sofas were black in colour. The receptionist attended a call; kept on listening intently for a while and then nodded her head. Then she said in a low voice, "I'll explain the situation to them" and came towards Professor. She said politely to Professor, "Professor Ramanujam, though Dr. Malik has given you appointment at this time he is engaged in another important meeting now. He will be delayed a little. We are really sorry for the discomfort and inconvenience. He has requested you to stay for a while. He has promised that he will meet you as early as possible." She then gave a readymade smile and asked, "What would you like to drink now Professor, coffee or tea?" Professor said, "Oh! No thank you! We don't want anything now. We are comfortable and we will wait."

She walked back stylishly to the reception and began to shape her nails. A tall black man in black suit got out of the lift and neared her. Seeing him she smiled broad and began to chat happily. "Where is the meeting going on?" she asked casually replacing the nail file into her black colour hand bag. He said with irritation, "As usual his family has come to pester him for money. His family is more than enough to torture him to death. They believe that he has some chronic illness and would die soon. They want him to write his will." She said expressing her pity, "Tch..Tch.. So pathetic! He is a terror to all his employees except his shadow Elsa. But his family is a terror to him. How much may be the value of his assets?"

Asking this question, she began to apply a fresh layer of lipstick over the already existing neat coating. The tall black man said at once, "He is worth more than 800 billion today. He has already paid a huge amount in the form of cash and assets to all his wives after divorce. But they are not satisfied. None of his children or grand children is intelligent enough to succeed his throne. He trusts no one too. So they try to extract as much as possible from him." She said interrupting him, "This is what everyone knows in common. I heard that he is worth more than that. He keeps on writing wills and tearing them apart as per his mood swings. What does he think in his mind? Does he think that he will live forever?"

He gave a shocked expression and said as a warning, "Shh… Shh… be careful! Don't talk unnecessarily and put yourself into trouble. Control your tongue when you are here." She just waved off his warning and said in an undisturbed tone, "OK, leave it. Shall we go to a movie today evening?" He smiled with enthusiasm, "With pleasure. I'll come to your apartment to pick you up." He left soon and she began to pay her attention to the computer screen in front of her.

Professor said in a low voice, "I want to know what Malik knows about Emberonium. I must also discuss some important matters with him. You all can stay back here or come with me inside to meet him." Puper said angrily, "I will come with you grandpa. I will tear him into pieces as soon as I see him. He is a killer and I will protect you from him." Professor laughed and said, "You need not be emotional Puper. I have never revealed that I know the truth about him and we have a cordial relationship. Please don't spoil the meeting Puper. I wish the same from you also Bindu. You can be with me, if you are just mute watchers. OK." We nodded to his condition without a word. Then he suddenly said in a warning tone, "Puper never open your mouth in front of anybody here. I don't want to put you in danger by exhibiting your specialties! Even Malik may wish to acquire you if he identifies you as a master piece. So don't spill out even a single word from your mouth as long as we are inside Malik towers."

Soon an old man wearing a black suit entered in and guided us to another room. There was a tall lady dressed in a bodycon skirt teamed with a shirt and blazer. She was also dressed in black colour. We were asked to wait there. I had a feeling that we were being watched. He said something in a very low voice to her. She took charge of us. She led us to the 50th floor and made us to sit in a conference hall. Is Dr. Malik going to meet us here? The tall lady in the formal costume opened the door of a nearby room and I was able to see a tall girl. I couldn't see her face as she was turning back. She was wearing a pair of denims and a loose pink colour tops. The first person to wear a colourful casual wear! What a wonder in Dr. Malik's all black Malik towers! I began to watch intently. She had boyish cut too and that reminded me of somebody.

The tall lady went near her and began to whisper in a very low voice. I tried to read her lip movements. The lady in formal costume said," You have to distract and entertain the visitors. They are really important for Dr.Malik." I couldn't read the colourful girl's lips as her face was still turned back. They argued for a while. The tall lady said, "They were not expected. We expected only one guest. Dr. Malik wants you to handle them in particular. I don't know the reason why he has chosen you specifically for this purpose. Just obey his orders." Saying so she came towards us, cursing, "All because of the importance Dr. Malik gives to this silly girl! What does she know about the important works we have?" She excused herself saying, "Dr. Malik's assistant will take charge of you from now on," and she got into the lift. The girl in pink tops came into the hall and said cheerfully," I welcome you to the Malik towers!" and she froze in shock.

39

Liar In London

Her face became pale the moment she saw me. It was Abi Akka! What was Abi Akka doing here? I was furious. She had never told us that she was Dr. Malik's assistant. She is a liar. Why should she be the assistant for this evil man? She stood completely frozen in shock. I stared at her. Even though I was angry at her I was afraid that she will tell Mummy and Daddy about my little trip to London. Never mind! I could make it up by telling that we had come to London to gather some information about mammoth DNA or something. I am an expert in making up things. But I can't forgive this liar. What? Is Abi Akka alone a liar? I have also lied to her then! I have hidden a lot of information from my family too. If she is a liar, then I am also a liar. Well! A pot must not call the kettle black! So I have no rights to blame that she is a liar. But before she points her arrow at me I should attack her. I have to create a scene.

So, I said in an angry tone, "Abi Akka! You are supposed to be in the university now!" and she backfired at me," And Bindu! You are supposed to be in India attending your school!" I replied, still trying to keep my voice angry," I am doing research to create a mammoth. So the school has given me permission. And I am not alone here! I have come with Professor." Abi Akka exclaimed, "Oh!.." she paused for a while as though she was searching for the right words and then blurted out, "Then... then... my university has also given me permission to be Dr.Malik's secret assistant and help him."

I was actually happy to see her. But I have to put up some scene so that she wouldn't doubt me. I busted out as I began to walk towards her," You little liar! Have you ever told me that you were his assistant? Why have you hidden it from us? You cheat! Fraud!" She was a little bit shocked to see that I was furious. Have I over reacted and spoiled the show? She replied defensively, "Well Bindu, I hope the word 'secret' gives explanation for that. Dr. Malik's men approached me with an offer that I would be paid a lump sum to be his assistant. The one and only condition they insisted was that I had to keep my service here as a secret."

Has she lost her mind? Does she think that it is really safe to work in a place without telling that truth to her family? She is in a foreign country and is staying here under student visa. How can she simply ignore her studies and work here without informing anyone? How will anyone know if something wrong happens to her here? Is Abi Akka such an irresponsible and thoughtless person? I was filled with anger and fear for her safety. I shouted in a fit of rage, "I will never trust you! How could you hide it from us? How long have you been working here? Do you understand that you are not cheating your family but yourself? Do you think that it is safe to accept such a job just for money?"

She replied, "Bindu, I have informed my friends and roommates here. And the university has given me special permission as Dr. Malik is a very influential person. I joined here just before four months. I myself am not sure why I had been chosen as Dr. Malik's assistant. Actually I don't have any special work here and Dr. Malik just gives me some assignments to refer about some new elements. That is quite boring for me and I am already in a mood to get out of here." Still I was not ready to give it up. I exaggerated," Four months! And not a word about this job! I hate you Abi Akka! You should have said about this to me at least!" She really wanted to console me. So she said in a pacifying tone, "I'm really sorry Bindu. Hereafter I will never keep secrets from you! Please don't embarrass me in front of others. Let us have our personal talks later." Now she is really taking it seriously! I think I should put a full stop to my drama. She is really thinking that I am angry. So I tried to act a bit cooled down.

So, I said," Ok! I understand you. I was really shocked to see you here. I had plans to meet you at the university without prior information and give you a pleasant surprise. But your presence here has disappointed me. Don't mind if I had over reacted. I am sorry too!" She let out a sigh of relief holding her heart. She was really relieved that I had ended the drama. Secretly I was happy that she had not questioned me much. I was really delighted to see her and I happily hugged her. A very weak and bony lady in full black slim suit was staring at us from the entrance of the hall. Her bony body looked bonier in her tight fit costume. When did she come in? How long had she been watching us? To me she looked like a watch dog. I think it would be more appropriate to call her a watch dog. Why is she so thin? She looked as though she would faint and die any moment. She looked so weak. She casually moved in like a black cat and seated herself in a chair. She kept on continuing her stare.

I did not know what to do. I asked Abi Akka in a whisper, "Who is that watch dog?" Abi Akka gave me a warning stare and said, "Sshh… be careful Bindu! Don't play your nick name games here. She is Dr. Malik's body guard. She is always with him. She is given the same respect as Dr. Malik here. Don't ask me anymore." So I just ignored watch dog's presence and casually introduced Abi Akka to Puper. Puper never spoke a word as instructed by Professor earlier. How smart he is! He seemed to like Abi Akka. Abi Akka is not so fond of animals. So she just stood a step away and smiled uneasily at Puper. "So I think this is the tiger you created," she said as she had to say something. I understood her feelings and lifted Puper and handed him over to Aadhmi. Puper did not fuss as he was intelligent enough to sense her feelings towards him. She said a nervous 'Hi' to Aadhmi. Aadhmi nodded but never talked anything. Abi asked in a whisper, "Is this the robot you always talk about? Is this the one that always irritates you? Is this the one that meddles with you always?" I felt quite embarrassed now. I even felt irritated by her behaviour. I tried to signal her to be quiet and stop her talk, but she wouldn't pay attention to them. She doesn't know that Aadhmi has become my friend now.

I already know about Abi Akka's aversion for Professor Ramanujam's advice. So I have to be cautious and I shouldn't allow them to interact too much. Professor said in an energetic tone," Hi! Abi! I'm so delighted to meet you again." Abi Akka put up a fake smile which only I could identify and said with false enthusiasm, "The delight is all mine Professor!" I just wanted to stop their conversation. So I interrupted," So, Akka! Do you go to college nowadays?" She replied spontaneously," No, the university has given me permission to be here. So I live here at the eighth floor in Malik towers helping Dr. Malik with his research."

What research is she helping him in? Why has Malik chosen Abi Akka as his assistant? Will there be any special reason behind it? Is there any hidden plot behind it? As far as I know, Abi Akka is not so good in science. Her field of interest is English Literature. And that interest had made her talented and well versed in English literature. That is the reason why she got admission in The Oxford University. Everything is strange now! She had dreamt about learning in The Oxford University for ages and now she is getting special permission from her university for assisting this evil scientist. Unbelievable! Puper ran away from Aadhmi and jumped on to my lap. Abi Akka moved a foot away nervously. Puper's eyes met mine. I could understand that he was hurt by her dislike for him. But still as it is her nature, I couldn't help it. I cuddled him to express my love for him.

Professor Ramanujam excused himself to make a phone call to President Abdul Rahman. I was glad that he moved away, so that I need not be the buffer between Professor Ramanujam and Abi Akka. Aadhmi walked behind Professor Ramanujam. So I, Abi Akka and Puper were left behind. I and Abi Akka started to chat. She told me that she had seen me on the TV and that she was really excited. Puper was remaining mum. We were talking till another heavy built man in black suit came over to us and informed us that Dr.Malik was coming there to meet us. Professor Ramanujam came back with Aadhmi. Within a few minutes, I heard a heavy pair of footsteps. The sound was becoming louder and louder. I think that must be Dr.Malik. Suddenly a huge figure appeared opening the door. It was Dr.Malik. He looked very fat, tired and sick. It seemed that he couldn't carry his own weight. How could be the owner of such a pharmaceuticals not take care of his health? He even struggled to walk properly. He was breathing heavily for even his slightest movements. I had a feeling that he suffered from malnutrition. As soon as he entered, the watch dog stood up and moved towards him. He held her hands casually and began to move towards us. It seemed that he trusted her very much and felt safe in her presence. His hair was black in colour and he had big brown eyes which were piercing. He had a very sharp nose. He had a big smile on his face as he said a brisk, "Hi! Ram! I'm really sorry for the delay. I was caught up in some family issues." He hugged Professor Ramanujam. Professor looked so tiny near him.

I saw Professor Ramanujam's face. I couldn't read the expression in Professor Ramanujam's face. I've never seen him with that expression. It was so eerie. I couldn't correctly judge what he was feeling. But it was evident that he was in pain. Who wouldn't be in pain if they have to act in a very sweet manner to the one who killed his loving wife? Murderer Malik's face was overflowing with smile. Probably he is comfortable as he believes that Professor Ramanujam doesn't know his true colour.

After hugging Professor Ramanujam Dr.Malik came to me and said with a plastic smile, "Ahh….You should be the famous Bindu Thirupathi the creator of the Saber tooth. I have heard a lot about you!" I eyed him with disgust.

He was looking at Puper with his evil eyes. I hated Dr.Malik. Puper was grinding his teeth. I spoke to Dr.Malik, "I have heard wonderful things about you too." Well! Really wonderful! A world famous scientist and a murderer! Will anybody believe that there is a monster behind this innocent smile? He is an expert in acting! He could be titled as the 'Drama King'! I hated him to the core. Abi Akka eagerly introduced me as her sister to Dr.Malik. He was delighted to know about it. Dr.Malik said that he wanted to talk privately with Professor Ramanujam.

40

Snooping Around

He smiled at the watch dog and said, "Elsa please take care of the guests when I have a little talk with my friend Ram." So, the lean watch dog's name is Elsa. Why is he taking Professor alone? Why not we join them? I looked at Aadhmi so that he could give me some answer. I wanted Aadhmi to at least accompany Professor. But it never opened its mouth. So, they both left. A man in white laboratory coat wearing glasses came in and requested for Abi Akka's help. She said," Bindu I'll come in a few minutes." So, I, Puper and Aadhmi were left all alone. Nothing was alright. Something was fishy. Why would Dr.Malik appoint Abi Akka as his assistant? I couldn't control myself. I decided to do something on my own. It was quite irritating to see Aadhmi sit like a statue. Now it is the time for me to become Nancy Drew. The watch dog was waiting at the entrance to monitor us. I have to snoop around a bit. I started to walk towards the lady. Aadhmi tried to stop me, but I paid no attention to it. Puper was sleeping like a ball on a chair. Well! I got no company now.

    I walked straight to the lady. She was staring at me. I asked her with a puppy dog face, "Excuse me, I need to use the restroom." She said, "Go straight and take the first left in the second right." Hurrah! Somehow I escaped from that room. I thought that she would escort me and I would have to go ninja on her on the way and prove my fighting skills. But never mind! No action scene for Nancy Drew this time. I'm usually not a lover of fight and action but a fight with that watchdog could add up to the action stunt for this Nancy Drew character. I have gone for a couple of Karate classes. I cannot fight an expert but a weak opponent like this skinny and bony watchdog will be a scoop of ice-cream for me.

Now I'm going to snoop around. I have to find the board which says 'NO ENTRY 'or 'NO TRESPASSING' or 'PROHIBITED AREA'. I have read these sleuthing techniques in this wonderful book '101 ways of spying specially designed for dopey'. Though I'm not a dope that book has helped me escape from the watchdog.

I walked past many rooms. They were all ajar. Usually wide open rooms don't have any secrets. So I decided to enter some confined room. My intuitions told me that the basement should be the best spot. So I got into the elevator and went to the basement. In a few minutes the elevator door opened. I got out of the elevator and walked around the basement. It was strangely empty! Maybe I should try the other floors. I made my decision and got back into the lift but my attention was caught by the voices. They were male voices. I looked around but I couldn't see anybody. It was so strange. The sound of the voices was increasing steadily. There was a big barrel of oil. I decided to hide behind it. I heard footsteps. Without having a second thought I hid myself behind the big barrel. I couldn't see the persons but their voices were audible. I was completely puzzled. Where are the voices coming from? I was clueless.

Suddenly something strange happened. The cement floor at one end of the basement slid in and a flight of stairs appeared from below. So actually this is not the real basement. Two men emerged out from the stairs. One was fat and the other was a bit lean. The fat man let out a big sigh, "Phew! We are suffering like this because of this stupid Malik. Always asking us to rebuild that same spaceship again and again! He always travels in it in search of something he doesn't know. I am sure he is nuts. He has no family as he doesn't know to maintain relationships. We have to work as slaves to this heartless monster. And the worst of all is that we cannot proudly say that we are working for this Dr.Malik. We have to maintain our work as a secret! How strange! We cannot even meet our family and live a happy life. This mass of flesh has no love to anybody except himself. Why the hell does he torture us by keeping us away from our family? If I get the chance to escape from this hell, I will just run away! Even toilet cleaners will be happier than us in the outer world. And see we never get leave at all, not even for Christmas or New Year! It has been 10 years since I saw my family! How long have you been in this hell?"

The other man, who was listening patiently, began to burst out now. He said in an exhausted way, "I have lost all hopes of escape from here. I have been under captivity here for the past 15 years. I am afraid that I will die here itself like my senior Anderson. He was a good friend to me. He helped me in many ways. He tried his level best to escape from this secret jail. But in vain!"

The first man asked suddenly, "What does he do to himself in the secret lab? Whatever he may be doing to him, I don't think that it is doing anything to improve his health. Is he trying all the new medicines in his own body?"

The second one said, "I doubt that he is up to something very big. Our mind has no power to imagine what he might be planning. As far as I know all the medications he had taken for remaining young has made him so indifferent as he looks now. And recently, he is very serious about finding something in the space." The two men walked past the barrel towards the elevator. Gradually their sound faded and soon I heard no more sound of footsteps or human voices.

I guess Dr.Malik should be a very bad employer. Now I was sure about three things. One, Dr.Malik had a secret research lab. Two, he had a spaceship and three; he is randomly roaming about the whole Galaxy in search of something. I have to find out what he is searching for. I swiftly made my way towards the flight of stairs. I climbed down the marble stair case. It went really long.

Soon the stairs lead to a dark room. My intuitions told me that I had to proceed further. I opened my bag and took my phone out of it. I turned on the flash light in my phone. I could see in the dim light that the room was almost empty. I walked around the room trying to find a door way or something.

It was evident that there wasn't any doorway in that room. The whole room was so dusty. The walls were decorated by spider webs. But something was strange. One of the four walls was free of spider web. It gave me a spark. Some secret passage should be there. Under the light from my phone it seemed normal. I went to the centre of the wall and placed my hands on the wall. It was smooth and even everywhere.

Suddenly I felt a hole at a particular point. I brought my flash light near the small hole to get a clear view of it. It was very small. Only my fingers could fit inside it. So I inserted my index finger into the hole after examining it for a while.

I could feel something. It was a very small button. Without having a second thought I pressed it. Suddenly a beam of light ray entered the room. I observed closely without making any sound. The light ray had entered in through the small opening in a secret door. I neared the door and peeped through it.

Wow! There was a huge space ship like structure. Nearly 500 men were working around it. The whole place was well lit and people were busy moving around and assembling the machinery. It looked as though I had entered a space research centre. Some of them looked like scientists and many were only workmen. They just obeyed the commands of the ones who looked like scientists. There were giant screens showing the trajectory of a rocket. Many drawings showing designs of space ships and rockets were displayed on some screens. I thought that Dr. Malik owned only a pharmaceuticals company. But what I see here proves his special interest in space research too. I had to report this to Professor Ramanujam. I didn't dare to go in and do any heroic act. I was sure that, it will lead me to trouble. So I decided to go back as quiet as I had come. I walked back to the elevator. I appreciated myself for being a very good sleuth.

I rushed into the elevator and reached the 50th floor. I walked fast towards the conference room. The watch dog standing at the entrance caught my eyes. She was staring at me with the same look. I entered into the conference room. I saw Aadhmi, Puper and Abi Akka. Puper had woken up. He was yawning like a baby. Abi akka looked really tensed. As soon as she saw me she looked a bit relieved. She ran towards me and asked," Bindu! Where did you go? Were you snooping around the building? I was really frightened. I saw you on the surveillance camera. You were roaming about randomly!" I replied," Akka, I was going in search of the restroom. It is nowhere to be found." Abi Akka let out a sigh and she said," I'll take you there. Come on" I walked with her. Puper tried to follow us. I said, "Puper, please stay with Aadhmi. I will come in a minute." He went back with a disappointed look.

While we were walking she asked to me in a low suspicious voice," I saw you entering the basement from the elevator. What did you do there?" I stopped walking and froze for a micro second. Has Abi Akka understood that I had seen something at the basement? Is she simply checking me? I decided to pretend innocent as far as possible and replied calmly without showing my fear, "Abi Akka, I was really searching for the restroom. I think the basement doesn't have any restroom." She said to me," Oh! I was worried because I couldn't see you after that because there is no vigilance camera in the basement." Thank God that they don't have any vigilance cameras in the basement!

"Bindu, I want to ask you something. Do you know something about an element that can keep people young forever and make them regain their youth?" Maybe it is what Dr.Malik is searching for with the spaceship. I replied," No, Akka, I don't know." She just pouted. She thought to herself for a moment and then said, "Is there any such element that could help people remain young forever? I had never studied even the periodic table in my science book thoroughly! I hated science and loved only literature. But now I have to search an element that could give a person everlasting youth! How is it possible? That is the assignment Dr. Malik has given me! I have surfed the net for all the websites that enlighten us about the known elements and I am still blank now. I haven't got the answer to his question. So I thought you could help me as you are interested and well versed in all branches of science." I had a suspicion that Dr. Malik has chosen Abi Akka just because she is my cousin. He might have planned to reach Professor's secrets by reaching Abi Akka and thereby me! If my guess is correct, Abi Akka is in grave danger! I felt that some tight knots were becoming loose now.

She shook me from my deep thought and said, "Hey! Don't worry if you don't know the answer. Here is the rest room." I nodded and I just went in to create a scene. In a few minutes I came out. I asked her slowly, "What does actually Dr. Malik expect you to do?" She said casually, "He questions me about something called 'Kaala Galaxy' the name that I had never heard before. He searches for some element he calls Navjavaanium. Have you heard about that ever before Bindu? I think that he has mistaken me for a science nerd! I will soon quit this job. I am waiting for the right time." I was shocked to hear the word 'Kaala Galaxy'. It is one of the discoveries of Professor. How did Dr. Malik come to know of it? What else does he know? I replied," Never heard about it. "I also added," Akka, if you find something fishy here please call me any time. I am not at all happy to leave you here and go. Would you like to come with me now?" She said, "Don't worry Bindu. I will take care of myself. No one can harm me just like that. I have been treated here with respect till this date. I don't feel insecure here. I am quite comfortable except for the fact that this job is not suitable for me."

We came back to the conference hall. Puper rushed to me. I lifted him and cuddled him. Aadhmi was sitting as before. Abi Akka said to me," Bindu, I have got some works. I don't think that we will be able to meet again before you leave. So I wish you 'Good bye'. Don't worry about me as though I am a small child. Remember I am your elder sister. I can take care of myself," and went away. I sat down near Aadhmi. I was worried about Abi akka. I can't underestimate Dr.Malik. I knew what he is capable of from Celine's grievous end.

Suddenly Aadhmi said," Bindu, What you think about Malik is absolutely right. I read Malik's mind." Wow! My suspicion is correct! Aadhmi spoke, "He has investigated a lot about you and recruited Abi as she is related to you. He actually wants information about 'Navjavaanium'. Abi doesn't know about his evil plans. Did you really go to the basement and see what is going on there?" I think Aadhmi must have read my mind. I just made a nod and said, "Aadhmi, can you tell me about Navjavaanium."

Aadhmi started, "Professor sent me to collect samples of Emberonium from planet Embera in the Kaala galaxy. I found two planets very close to each other. Embera and Yuva Graha were those two planets in Kaala Galaxy. Just as Emberonium is present in Embera a bluish green element was present in Yuva Graha. Professor named it as 'Navjavaanium'. To our surprise life also existed in Yuva Graha. But all the creatures were just young ones. We could find no fully grown adult. They said that they were young forever and immortal too. They said that their youth was due to the consumption of the bluish green element in their planet. We understood that Emberonium had nil effect on the life forms in the Yuva Graha as all were young forever. The reason for their everlasting youth was the presence of an edible element present there. That edible element is the bluish green Navjavaanium. But professor's researches made it clear that Navjavaanium is not compatible with the human body. It becomes unstable and an explosion occurs due to a chain reaction, because of which, not only the body of the in taker, but the whole planet may blast into fragments. Initially professor wanted to use Navjavaanium for the welfare of the mankind. Later predicting its adverse effects, he dropped his idea. But still secretly we are conducting researches on Navjavaanium in RV." Maybe, Dr.Malik had come to know about Emberonium and its effects. In order to survive the radiations he wishes to lose his age by finding Navjavaanium.

Aadhmi started, "Bindu, your assumption may be correct. But I can't be sure that he knows about Emberonium. As far as I know,

Malik's greatest wish is to live young forever. So he might be searching Navjavaanium for that purpose." There are many possibilities. But I am sure about certain things. I have to stop Dr.Malik from finding Navjavaanium. Dr.Malik had killed Celine in search of Navjavaanium.

41

A Chat With Murderer Malik

Problems never come single. A problem always comes hand in hand with more intense problem. What else would I come to know about today?

Suddenly Professor Ramanujam and Dr.Malik walked into the room. Professor's walk was not stable and he was slightly stumbling as he walked. Professor had never been like this before! He is always steadier than I am. It was really strange. Aadhmi rushed to catch him and it made him sit on a chair. Malik said very kindly, "Aadhmi professor seems a bit tired. I think you can make him take rest for a while in a couch in the next room. Make him feel at home." Without speaking a word Aadhmi attended professor.

Suddenly Dr.Malik said to me," Bindu can you lend me your ears for a second?" Oh! God! Has he found out that I was snooping? I must sound brave and bold while talking to him. If he is about to meddle with me then I should treat him in such a way that he will never ever forget that until his death. I got up from the chair couch and walked towards him. He escorted me to a nearby room.

He started to speak," Bindu, Do you know something about Navjavaanium? I know that you did a bit of snooping in my building. So, I hope that you might have done the same with Professor too!." Oh! God! I am caught! I should not panic. I should play cool. I said in a cool casual tone, "What is Navjavaanium?" He said in a scornful tone," It is an element". I exclaimed," Oh! Element! I don't remember seeing it in the periodic table. I will surely convey the valid information if I get to know of them."

He said with an irritating smile, "But to your kind information, you need not worry about conveying me any information! I have got whatever I need from your respectable professor Ramanujam. Won't you ask me how I did it? Well! Well! You are already in a bit of shock! So let me not strain your tiny brain! I hypnotized him!"

He laughed hysterically and shouted out loud like a maniac, "I will achieve the greatest ambition of my life. I will live forever and be the king! This silly loser has made my search easier by coming to my place and delivering all the details of his research. I never expected this shower of luck on me. You know, he believed me when I lied that I had found out a chemical combination that could nullify the effect of the Emberonium that has landed on the earth. This savior came here to give his life and save the earth! What a pity! I am not at all bothered about what this Emberonium is going to do to the earth. Because now I know where Navjavaanium is! When I become young nothing could disturb me. I will rule the world! I am the king of this world! I know well that you don't know where Navjavaanium is. So I spare your life and even forgive your snooping." He made a scornful expression.

Why is this man so mean? I felt pity for Professor Ramanujam who had fallen a prey to his plots. I put up a very rude face and spoke to him, "Oh! You talk about forgiving! I too remember an event from your life which could make your reputation reach its peak." He exclaimed, "Really!" I said, "Yep. I know very well that it is you who did the holy job of killing Celine Ramanujam with a dagger and making baby Rose motherless." He couldn't speak anything. I said," I hope you remember it crystal clear!"

He looked like he was under some shock. He is also a human being. He has heart and his own conscience. I didn't want to stop. He is in the intention of pricking me, but after what I am going to say he is never going to get the slightest idea of hurting me or Professor Ramanujam or Aadhmi or Puper or Abi Akka. Of course Aadhmi is an exception. Dr.Malik looked really perplexed. I continued," I think you remember how you pierced the dagger into Mrs. Celine; I think you remember how you tortured her to give information about Navjavaanium; how you betrayed your close friend Ramanujam; how you left the little baby crying killing her mother right in front of her eye!"

He was shocked and he said," You don't have any proof!" I butted in," I have! Can you believe that professor was there with Mrs. Celine when she died? When he came to her house, she was about to die. She died as soon as she told Professor who the murderer was and what the reason for the murder was. And to his surprise it was you! Professor's best friend! The world will be very happy to know about you." He was really shocked and surprised. But in a moment he was composed and said casually, "I am very sorry that you are such an innocent soul to believe that I will feel sorry for a murder committed in the past. Celine's murder is just one among the hundreds I had done! But I can't believe that professor had been kind to me through all these years even when he had known that I was the one who killed Celine!"

I challenged him, "You think you can win by cheating. But that is impossible. I assure you that you will meet your pathetic end soon!" and quit that room at once not wanting to see him or hear his talk anymore. He continued laughing victoriously. I ignored him and approached professor. Aadhmi said, "Sorna is ready. Let us move. We have another meeting. The President called and professor was not in a condition to attend the call. I attended it. We have to go to SAPS now. I will explain about SAPS on the way." I nodded and we escorted Professor Ramanujam who was now drowsy, to the elevator. Puper followed us. I could feel the eyes of the watch dog Elsa staring our backs.

42

The Bermuda Triangle

We reached the top of the building and got into Sorna. Professor instantly fell asleep. Sorna started to move. As we were moving out of London, Aadhmi checked if Professor Ramanujam was asleep and it exclaimed," Wow! You gave a nice blow to Malik. It was awesome." I was just smiling.

Puper said in a pleading tone, "Can I open my mouth and speak now?" I laughed and said, "I am longing to hear your voice dear." He said, "I am very hungry mummy." I realized that we have a stomach only when he said this. At once Aadhmi took out and gave hot soup cups and some sandwiches from its back pack. We thanked him and gobbled them hungrily. I wanted to get the answer for the question that has been circling in my mind for a long time. So I asked, "Aadhmi, now tell me what this SAPS is."

Aadhmi started with a question, "Bindu, have you heard about The Bermuda Triangle?" I have read many articles and watched many movies based on The Bermuda Triangle. So I nodded. Aadhmi continued, "Yes, just as you know, The Bermuda Triangle has been referred to as 'The Devil's Triangle'. It is located in the western part of the North Atlantic Ocean. It is believed to be a hub of strange activities as it has played a role in the bizarre disappearances of a number of aircrafts as well as surface vessels. In popular cultures these occurrences have been attributed to strange paranormal activities or even to extraterrestrial entities." Oh! My god! I know this already. But what is the connection between the word SAPS and this Bermuda Triangle.

Aadhmi said, "There is connection. Listen patiently." And it began to speak in the tone of a news reader, "One of the earliest documentations of an unusual disappearance was recounted in an article on September 16th 1950, in the Associated Press. The article was written by Edward Van Winkle Jones. Two years after the publication in Associated Press, Fate magazine published an article 'Sea Mystery at Our Back Door'. This article covered the mysterious loss of planes and ships. The article went on to explain the first description of this phenomenon as the Bermuda triangle. From these first articles, many books and theories emerged claiming to explain the unusual phenomenon surrounding the Bermuda Triangle. But none of the theories are authentic."

I gave a puzzled look towards Aadhmi. It said, "Wait Bindu. Now, listen to the true theory. It may be even difficult to believe. It was Professor Ramanujam who created the Bermuda triangle!" I shouted out in shock, "What? That is not just a building or a machine to be created by humans. It is a natural phenomenon that is still a mystery to the scientific world."

It nodded but continued, "The Second World War came to an end in the year 1945. For a world filled with peace and harmony, treaties and pacts were not enough. So the UNO decided to form the 'Secret Association of Presidents and Scientists' shortly called as SAPS. The SAPS includes the Presidents of each nation and the lead scientists of each nation. If the situations demanded the scientists were allowed to bring their assistants with them. Ensuring the safety and security of the world was the common motto of the SAPS. All the presidents and eminent scientists usually discussed about the approaching natural disasters, the border problems between nations, the nations that could be a threat to the world peace and the terrorists who could invoke calamities that could be dangerous to the common people. They arrived at possible solutions to the approaching problems here. In the beginning the SAPS meeting was conducted in the south pole as they thought that no civilians would come there. It was their headquarters.

But it was not like what they had imagined. There were a lot of disturbances. The SAPS did not want the world to know about their secret activities. So SAPS was in need of a new headquarters.

In 1949 Professor Ramanujam selected a particular location in the western part of the North Sea and he created a portal like thing. All the presidents gave their nation's support in this secret activity. He fixed an area. The area enclosed in this portal could not be analyzed by satellites. An object that has once entered the portal cannot get out of it. But Sorna is an exception. Sorna was invented by Professor. He designed one for each member in the SAPS. The SAPS meet twice every month. In situations of adversity, the SAPS is called for an instant meet.

The interior of the SAPS is so enchanting that a person who once visits it never has the heart to go out of it. When the SAPS head quarters was created, many ships which crossed it entered the portal. The sailors were enchanted by the beauty of the headquarters and they refused to leave it. Even if they try to leave it they will be destroyed by the security system in the SAPS. Only the Sorna can get in and get out of the Bermuda triangle safely. The crews of the ships that had disappeared are employed in the head quarters. They are assigned works according to their caliber and talent.

There is a decoy of the SAPS in the surface of water. It is a floating island. The SAPS is underwater below the floating island. The SAPS is completely covered by water. Edward Van Winkle Jones was a good friend of Professor Ramanujam. So Professor asked Edward Van Winkle Jones to publish article about the strange disappearances which were partly true, in order to create a fear among the people. It led to many superstitions and scientific hypothesis.

The Chief Country is the leading country in SAPS. The country with the highest rate of growth is declared as the Chief Country. And the President or Ruler and the lead scientist of that country are the President and chief scientist of SAPS. Currently England is the country with highest rate of growth, and it is the Chief country. So, Malik is the chief scientist and Prince Hamilton is the president of the SAPS."

43
SAPS

Puper and I were amused by the history of the Bermuda Triangle. I was always attracted to the mystery behind the Bermuda Triangle. But I have never imagined that there would be such a big history behind this. It was really nice to know about SAPS. I was really eager to see the SAPS.

The Bermuda triangle is the region between Puerto Rico, Bermuda, and Miami. Sorna flew past Slough, Reading, Swindon, Bristol and Weston-Super-Mare. Suddenly Sorna plunged down into the sea water. We travelled under water. I was really enchanted by the wonderful undersea life. They were widely different from the undersea life in India.

We sped across the Atlantic Ocean. When we neared the western part of the North Atlantic Ocean, something was really strange. The water was murky. The weather reflected cyclones and tornadoes. The sea was really rough. I could feel the jerk. I saw through the widow. The whole sea was covered by bubbles. It was really weird.

Maybe we were caught up in a bad storm! Aadhmi understood my fear and said," Don't worry Bindu, we are entering the portal. The portal is designed this way. In a minute we will be in SAPS. The jerk and murkiness lasted for a while. After we crossed the portal we saw the clear blue sea surrounding us. It was really awesome!

Aadhmi said," Lady and cub I welcome you to the SAPS. In no time we will be reaching the head quarters of SAPS." I saw Puper. His mouth was wide open and his eyes were bright with amazement. Puper said to me," Mummy this is fantastic!" I was just smiling at him.

A round ball which was fully lit came into my view. It was really beautiful to look at. My mouth fell open. It must be the head quarters of SAPS. It was under the shadow of something. I looked up through the glass window. Something big was floating above us. Aadhmi explained," That is the floating island." And Puper exclaimed, "Aah!... Wow!.."

Aadhmi said to me," Bindu, let us not tell Professor anything about what had happened in the Malik Towers. He would have forgotten what had happened. Let us just tell him that he fainted all of a sudden and as per president's instructions we had to bring him here. Let us not tell him about the spaceship you saw in Malik Towers. Now you, I and Puper should develop 'Yuva Sansaar' without Professor's help. Currently he has a lot of stuff going on in his mind. So let us not burden him." I and Puper agreed.

As we reached the SAPS Aadhmi gently woke up Professor Ramanujam. He was confused and we told him that he had fainted suddenly, while he was talking about Dr.Malik's family with him. We came near the underwater building. The same female voice as in Sorna greeted us," Welcome to SAPS! May I know who has come?"

Professor Ramanujam replied to the voice," I'm Professor Ramanujam. As usual Aadhmi has come with me. This time, my assistant Bindu Thirupathi is accompanying me. The SAPS had requested me to show the Saber tooth tiger, so Puper a saber tooth tiger is accompanying me."

The voice questioned," May I know on what basis your assistant is coming today." Professor replied," She has come to explain the SAPS about the impending radiations which will destroy the earth." The voice spoke after a long pause, "Is it so important that she should meet the SAPS right away?" Professor Ramanujam replied," No, actually I will be explaining the SAPS about the impending danger and if it is not sufficient she will have to interfere because she knows about that more than I do." The voice said," OK! You are welcome!"

Aadhmi explained," Actually national leaders from all around the world will be coming today, and that is why they are not ready to let you in. But, don't be afraid, it won't be a problem". Suddenly an opening was formed in the building. Sorna moved in slowly. Once we entered in, the opening closed. The surrounding water drained out and the door of Sorna opened.

A young girl was waiting for us. She was dressed fully white, in a formal three-piece suit. She had long black hair. Her brown eyes were bright and shrewd. She greeted Professor," How are you Professor?" Professor replied to her," I am fit as a horse. How are you Gemma?" So Gemma is her name. She looked very vibrant and energetic. Gemma replied, "Fine, Professor!" Professor introduced her to me, "Bindu, this is Gemma and she organizes the activities of SAPS." I greeted her, "Hi, Gemma! I am Bindu." She had a really friendly face. She said, "Hi, Bindu!"

She seemed to be really friendly with all. She talked with Puper and Aadhmi too. She lifted Puper and cuddled him with love. She told Professor, "We got information that some of the members will be delayed a bit due to unavoidable reasons. So, if you want you can be relaxed in your office." She escorted us somewhere. On our way Aadhmi explained to me," There is an office for each nation that is a member in SAPS."

We walked with Gemma and on our way we saw many people doing all sorts of cleaning and arranging works. I guess they must be the crew of the disappeared ships. She left us in front of a door and rushed away saying that she had to receive the President of America. We entered the office room. The lobby had a big map of India indicating that it was the Indian office room.

We walked past the lobby and entered a new room. It had two big desks. I guess one was meant for the President and the other for the lead scientist. We entered the next room. There was a big couch in the next room. Professor Ramanujam slowly walked to the couch and sat there. Aadhmi compelled him to eat some sandwiches and have the soup. After eating a little professor fell asleep. Puper slept on the floor near the couch. I sat on another couch in the first room. Aadhmi was making a phone call to the President Abdul Rahman. Aadhmi gave me a laptop from his backpack and I began to develop the other important features regarding 'Yuva Sansaar'.

44
SAPS Meeting

After a while Gemma walked in with another man who was carrying a tray filled with jars of coffee, tea, milk, snacks etc. He left placing the tray on the table. She saw that Professor Ramanujam was sleeping. So she decided to give me company. She asked the reason for my visit. I explained her, the whole theory about Emberonium with some modifications. She was shocked, but she believed me. She was really worried about the world's end. We were talking for a while. Gemma explained to me," Bindu, I am not allowed to let you in as per the rules and regulations of SAPS. Members from all around the world will be coming here today. You will be called in only if it is necessary. Or else you have to stay confined to this office room. But you seem to be a really sweet person and I like you very much."

I learnt that she was eighteen years old and she had reached SAPS during her voyage from England to America. Their ship had accidentally entered the portal. She was five then. Since then she has never seen the outer world. She had been given proper education and training. She has learnt more than thirteen languages. So the SAPS decided to appoint her as the coordinator for the SAPS meeting. She has been staying in SAPS for the past thirteen years. She has been missing a company like me and shared everything with me. She said with dreamy eyes, "I don't remember much of the outer world seen by my own eyes. But I am kept connected to the outer world through the media. I know more information about politics and the history of all nations than a person of my age in the outer world. Though I don't feel sorry for living here, I just miss one person. I miss my friend. I had a friend named Liam Nialson before I came here. He was my best friend. The one and only person I still crave to meet from the outer world is Liam. I had a wonderful life back in England. When I was eight years old, my parents who were serving happily here, died due to some unknown disease. So now I have no one to show me true love and affection here. I have become accustomed to the life here. There are also some people of my age here and we get together and have fun. Sometimes we use the SAPS member's shuttles and go to the floating island to have fun. This part of the sea is deserted always and vessels come rarely to this area. So secrecy is maintained always. All things needed for the people inside the SAPS comes from outside through shuttles. Shuttles visit SAPS only twice a month."

I understood that she meant the vehicles like Sorna as shuttles. Suddenly a young man came in and announced that Dr.Malik and the King of England had arrived. So Gemma excused herself to receive them. Puper woke up and stretched. I gave him milk and some biscuits. After a while President Abdul Rahman came inside the office room. He was really delighted to see me. We talked for a while about mission 'Yuva Sansaar'. He gave some valuable suggestions for the development of the schooling system in the new world. He was advising about how to maintain law and order among the Phoenixians. I promised him that I will lead the younger generation in the right direction. Soon he left to meet the other members.

Aadhmi and I began to continue our work. I was very happy and relieved to have Aadhmi's support. It was really nice that I and Aadhmi don't have much of conflicts now-a-days. We help each other. In fact the mission Yuva Sansaar has brought me and Aadhmi closer. We have joined our hands together to work for Yuva Sansaar. It's really good to have a reliable friend during times of crisis. I kept thinking about my family, Raj and Diya too.

After a while I heard an announcement," Attention please. Good afternoon everybody. Welcome to SAPS. The meeting commences in five more minutes at the conference hall in the eighth floor. The members are requested to assemble in the conference hall. There is also a special visitor today. You will be seeing the animal which was extinct for a million years. Reporting to you is Gemma Collins, your faithful meeting organizer."

So, Aadhmi woke up Professor Ramanujam and I compelled him to drink some black tea with a squeeze of lemon. Aadhmi lifted Puper in its arms. It said, "Today all the scientists and presidents have invited you as their special guest. They have been asking professor to bring you here since you were born! So you are a kind of VIP today!" Puper laughed happily with pride. They got ready for the meeting. I was really interested to see the proceedings of the meeting. But, as Gemma had said, I couldn't attend the meeting and I had to wait in the office room. Aadhmi said, "I will leave them in the conference hall and return soon. You need not feel lonely and I assure you that you will be free of boredom too!" Again it has read my thoughts and has given solution to my immediate problem. I have started to somewhat like Aadhmi!

The trio went away. I sat down on the couch and I began to design a program for the education management as per the President's guidance. Suddenly Aadhmi came in and said in a secret voice, "Bindu! I have got a surprise for you! Guess what?" Normally if Aadhmi had a surprise for me then it was something very dangerous or it was some kind of plot. I can never under estimate Aadhmi. It always meddles with me. I said to it, "What is it?" Aadhmi said, "Do you want to listen to the meeting or not? "I really wanted to listen to the meeting. But how could I do it? I said to Aadhmi, "Yeah, but how…" Aadhmi butted in, "You want to listen, isn't it? OK! Then you have to promise me something." I exclaimed, "Promise!" It said, "Bindu, I will tell you a secret when the time comes and you have to keep the secret from Professor Ramanujam." I replied, "Sure!"

Aadhmi said nothing more. I was really shocked, so I questioned it," Aadhmi, how am I going to see the meeting?" Aadhmi didn't respond and that aggravated my anger and I shouted," Aadhmi, you rusted piece of iron and nickel! I am asking you a question and you have to answer me! You told me that I could see the proceedings of the meeting. Please tell me how I am supposed to do it?" I think I over reacted. But Aadhmi didn't mind about it. It said to me," Cool down Bindu! Cool down! Aadhmi has a way for everything." I was really annoyed, so I shouted," What way?"

Aadhmi explained to me," Have you ever seen my invisible camera." It was really absurd. How could someone see something which was invisible? So I said to Aadhmi," I can't see invisible things!" Aadhmi said," Exactly! It is the same for the members in the meeting too!" Wow! So we are going to use the invisible camera to overhear the proceedings of the meeting. Aadhmi corrected me," It is not 'Overhearing' it is 'Overseeing'." I just rolled my eyes.

Aadhmi said to me, "When I left professor and puper in the conference hall I also left my flying invisible micro mini cam there. Right now it will move all around the conference hall and act as our eye." Aadhmi pulled the lap top I was working with and worked on it for a minute. Then it said triumphantly, "Well, now the invisible camera, linked to this lap top will start its work." I looked at the screen eagerly. There was a big round table in the center of the big conference hall; many people were sitting around the table. I noticed Professor Ramanujam and President Abdul Rahman. Puper was nowhere to be seen. I identified most of the people as Presidents and scientists. They were all talking among themselves.

Suddenly Gemma made an entrance and announced," Good afternoon everyone! I welcome you all to the SAPS meet." I spotted Dr.Malik who was busily talking over the phone with someone. He seemed really tensed. Aadhmi took out a remote like device that resembled a joy stick, from its backpack and said, "We can even control the movement of the camera from here using this voyager." It focused Dr. Malik's face. I tried to read his lips. He was saying with frustration, "Don't disturb me unnecessarily like this. I am really fed up with you. You are a leech, trying to suck me out. I have already paid you through my nose. Don't call me forever." Saying so, he switched off his mobile and then smiled uneasily at the Prince of England, who was watching him. Then he turned his face to the other side and cursed, "Useless idiots, I should first get rid of this pests." And he shook his head violently like a maniac. What is actually going on inside him? His behaviour was very peculiar. Gemma came and stood near Dr.Malik. She bent down and asked him something in a very low voice. I tried to read her lips. But she was bent down so low that I couldn't see her face at all.

Gemma announced," Professor Ramanujam has kindly accepted our request and brought his creation 'Puper' for giving a feast to our eyes! The amazement is that Puper belongs to the Saber tooth tiger species, which is believed to be extinct. One saber tooth tiger is extant because of the sincere efforts of Professor Ramanujam and his faithful assistant Bindu Thirupathi." Professor was smiling and he said," The credit goes to Bindu." There was a big round of applause. Professor was really generous.

There fell a sudden silence as Gemma raised her hand. The focus lights pointed to the entrance of the room. The lights focused on Puper. Puper made a majestic entrance into the room. He looked really nice and smart. Everyone was applauding. They were all surprised to see Puper. I could hear a number of exclamations. They were all really surprised to listen to Puper's voice.

Puper walked to Professor Ramanujam and stood near his chair. He was between Professor Ramanujam and President Abdul Rahman. When the awes and exclamations had come to an end, Gemma said," That was really remarkable! We have more. We have to be patient and we should listen to what Professor Ramanujam is going to tell us. It is a very intense matter. I know that everyone is confused about the sudden call of the meet. But Professor Ramanujam will give you explanation for it" and she sat down.

45

Intrusion

Professor got up from his seat and began to explain to the gathering about the impending danger. Of course he made some modifications. He said in a clear voice," Good afternoon everybody! I have come here to share a few words with you about the danger which is awaiting the world. I and my assistant Bindu came to know about the four meteorites that were approaching the earth. As soon as the meteorites landed on the earth, President Kalam and I made arrangements to create barriers around the meteorites with the help of the Indian army, to prevent the panicking of the civilian population. I would like to thank the President and the military force of the Ellesmere Island to have joined hands with us in creating the barricade in Ellesmere too." They were all listening with eager ears.

He explained," The meteorites have landed near Rameshwaram in the southern part of India, in the Ellesmere Island, in the North Pole and the South Pole. The meteorites are not just ordinary meteorites. They are really dangerous. They are made of an element known as Emberonium. You may not have heard about it. The element was discovered by me once upon a time, but I didn't make any attempt to bring its discovery to the notice of the world, because of its dangerous nature. It has a very strange nature. It has the power to create radiations to burn all the living things above twenty five years into ashes."

He hid most of the truth about Emberonium. He didn't say a word about the Kaala Galaxy and the planets in it. He hid the truth about the planet Emberonium. He did not explain how he discovered it and moreover he did not reveal a word about the Gods. Maybe he thinks that the Gods may be outrageous if they knew that Professor Ramanujam had revealed the secret about their existence. The meet didn't seem to believe Professor Ramanujam and they began to chatter among themselves complaining that Professor was building up a story or something. They didn't believe a word from Professor Ramanujam's mouth. They began to gossip.

Professor Ramanujam explained the gathering," You may think that it is impossible for such a thing to happen. Actually, my researches have confirmed that the radiations will outburst in exactly three more days. We cannot do anything to save the whole world but we can do our best to guide the younger generation who survive the radiations. In order to guide the younger generation who will be called Phoenixians we have created a project called 'Yuva Sansaar.' I have trained my assistant to be the leader of the surviving younger generation."

Suddenly someone butted in," Shut up! Old man! We don't want to listen to the fairy tale your assistant has narrated to you. Go and try to say it as a bed time story to your great- grandchildren. And I am sure they will find it really boring! Oops! I am really sorry I forgot that you don't have a family!" and he laughed loudly. I identified him as Prince Hamilton of England. Dr.Malik was chuckling. I understood that Malik was behind this nuisance. I wanted to break their facial bones by throwing plates. I think Puper was thinking the same as he was grinding his teeth.

The President of Russia got up and pacified him. He said to Professor Ramanujam in a very polite way," Professor why didn't you bring the discovery of the element to our notice earlier?" He looked at Professor in a very pleasing way. Professor replied to him, "Actually, I discovered the Emberonium a long time before the SAPS was formed. So I thought that it was unnecessary to talk about the past. Moreover we were busy with our regular tasks of executing a number of new plans and revolutions. So I thought that it would be a big distraction. And Emberonium would have been a big threat to human life if it had reached the wrong hands. If the anti social elements had known about its existence, then they would have easily chosen that as the wonderful tool to create unpredictable disaster."

The President of Russia said, "Then……, Professor Ramanujam, as you have already saved the world many times under adverse conditions, SAPS always trusts you. Could you please tell us now what the SAPS must do to join hands with you in your mission?" It was so simple. Professor began to speak, but before he could open up Prince Hamilton got up from his seat suddenly and burstout, "What? You people are going to listen to the fairy tale spun by this brainless old man and his silly assistant!"

I began to boil in anger. He is dead if he calls Professor Ramanujam as 'old man' again! A woman got up from her seat and said, "Can't you get Prince George's point of view! Do you people believe this story? Don't we have any other job? Are we supposed to drop all our important duties and work for this Old man believing his silly words?"

My patience has a limit. How dare they call Professor Ramanujam as 'old man'? Prince Hamilton said again, "The meet is over. So let us go home and take care of the important jobs we have to take care of without wasting our time listening to this 'old man'". This is the limit! He is dead! I lost control of myself! In a fit of anger I raced to the elevator and sped fast to the conference room.

Before I could realize what I was doing I was inside the room in no time surrounded by the members of SAPS! They were all staring at me! But their look of shock or horror had no impact on me. My heart was beating fast as I was fuming with anger. My one and only intention was to make the people who dare to talk against professor shut their mouth. I know the seriousness of the impending danger and I wanted to strike at the point. I had neither fear nor hesitation. Words flooded out of my mouth uncontrollably. I did not have the patience to be gentle and polite to the gathering. I didn't realize what I was talking. Aadhmi who had come behind me to stop me stood at the entrance helplessly. It did not dare to enter in and interrupt.

I couldn't remember what I talked. All I remember is that I was uncontrollably angry. I was expressing my views strongly in front of the gathering of the most famous personalities from all around the world. I didn't know what I was speaking. Only after exploding and draining out all my emotions and feelings I stopped. I talked nonstop for about 15 minutes, pouring out my anger and frustration on the people trying to insult a genius like Professor Ramanujam and thereby blocking his attempts to save the human race. I wanted to explain them the steps taken by him until that moment and the importance of the world to understand him and not underestimate him.

Only when all the words had spilled out of my mouth and I had nothing more to tell, I stopped. It seemed to me that I had come out of a trance. My heart was still racing. What have I done! I stood like a statue without knowing what to do! Have I spoiled everything? But everyone in the meeting had a different reaction. They were looking at me with their mouth wide open. They were absolutely in shock. Soon they recovered and began to discuss among themselves. The presidents and scientists from different nations scribbled notes and passed them on to Prince Hamilton, the chief of the SAPS.

Suddenly Prince Hamilton stood up and said, "Dear SAPS members, I am really sorry for the confusion and commotion created here. Thank you Bindu Thirupathi, for bringing into light efficiently the need for immediate action. SAPS will do its best to help your mission 'Yuva Sansaar'. I am extremely sorry professor Ramanujam. SAPS gives you full freedom to send as many numbers of your representatives to any nation at any time without any questioning. All nations are ready to send their eminent scientists and their military power to assist you. Most of the scientists present here have given their consent to join you in your mission. With this the meeting is over. You can have further discussions individually with the Indian president, professor Ramanujam and his assistant Bindu Thirupathi."

I still can't realize what I had spoken. But, I could realize that it had created a great change in Prince Hamilton. No one messes with

Professor Ramanujam! Gemma winked at me with a broad smile and showed a 'Thumbs up' sign. I stood there pathetically without knowing how to react. President Abdul Rahman patted me on the shoulders and said, "Well done my child! You have held your flag high! That was really excellent! You have changed the fate of the world today! You really are a brave girl! You deserve to be the leader of the Phoenixians and I am satisfied again that you will guide them. You have got the power to control people, change their minds and lead them." I smiled at him uneasily.

Many hands patted my shoulders and shook my hands. Many people wished me and none of those faces were registered by my brain. The one and only face registered in my mind was that of professor Ramanujam. He was happily looking at me with tear filled eyes. Secretly he wiped his eyes. Gemma came to my rescue. She said with enthusiasm, "Congrats! You have done a wonderful job! You brought them under control by your fearless speech!" Puper ran to me and jumped on to me and shouted happily, "I love you mummy! I love you! I am so proud of you!" Aadhmi whose mouth had fallen open came back to its senses and said appreciatively, "Phew, I was afraid that you will spoil everything. But you were awesome! Hats off to you!" Wow! Have I given such a rebellious speech? It is incredible!

Dr.Malik had a grim face. He looked really tensed and he said something to Prince Hamilton angrily. Prince Hamilton looked at Dr. Malik with disgust, but Dr. Malik ignored it and took out his cell phone. He began to talk with to someone in a hurry. With my lip reading skills I was sure that he was calling Abi Akka to get ready the space ship. I could make out words like 'space ship', 'Abi', 'Emberonium', 'Navjavaanium', and so on. If he is going to reach Yuva Graha and find Navjavaanium and use that to bring back his youth then the problem will become more serious! We will get another added responsibility to stop Dr. Malik from consuming it. I have to make myself prepared to face another problem.

The President of America appreciated Professor Ramanujam that he had a really efficient assistant. He promised that NASA scientists will be sent to RV to help him in Yuva Sansaar. The crowd that had gathered around Professor and President Abdul Rahman was dispersing slowly. President Abdul Rahman shook Professor's hands and took leave after saying that he would come to RV and help him in all the works. The members of SAPS began to leave the head quarters. Professor held my hands gently and whispered, "You have proved that you are my family. Thank you!" I had no words to say as I actually did not know what I had done.

Aadhmi asked, "Professor shall we leave now?" Professor answered enthusiastically, "Yes! We have got all the nations' support now. So we have a lot to do! RV will be buzzing with activities. Be ready to become busy!"

Gemma bid me 'good bye' with a heavy heart. She said that she felt too close to me within a short time and that she would miss me. I too had the same feeling. Maybe, she will become my best friend in the future. We took leave from SAPS and boarded the Sorna.

46
Trouble

We came out of the Bermuda triangle. Professor Ramanujam had a contented look on his face. He was very calm and relaxed. He held my hands warmly, lay back on his seat and closed his eyes. There was a sense of relief in him. I was feeling tired and weak. My body craved for rest and sleep. So I went for a little nap cuddling Puper.

I had a restless sleep first. I did not know if I was awake or asleep. My head was swirling. I was running over thoughts that made my head burn like anything. The first thing that was haunting me was the safety of Abi Akka. Then the second thing is if Dr. Malik gets Navjavaanium and consumes it before the emission of radiations from the meteorites all our hard work to create Yuva Sansaar will be in vain. Because, even the Phoenixians will be dead along with the adult population due to the nonstop nuclear fission reaction from Dr. Malik's body. He himself will act as a massive nuclear bomb and destroy the whole earth. The world will be no more. I was afraid that he may even try it on human beings without bothering about its disastrous after effect. So, I have to prevent this notorious scientist Dr.Malik from ruining the world. Soon my thoughts were blurring. I fell into a deep sleep.

Everything was completely dark and really peaceful. Suddenly some sound was annoying me. It was my phone. I was really reluctant to open my eyes. I didn't want to put a comma or full stop to my sleep. I just wanted to continue it. Filled with unwillingness I opened my eyes. It seemed like late evening. Puper and professor were not disturbed by the sound and they continued sleeping. Aadhmi turned back and said to me, "We are crossing Pakistan and entering India."

I took out the phone from my handbag. The call was from Abi Akka! At once I became fully alert and attended the call. I could feel the fear and panic in Abi Akka's voice as she said my name, "Bindu...!" She said in a low but serious voice as though she was conveying a secret. I understood that something was wrong and that she was in trouble. So, I said to her in a comforting tone, "Akka, is everything alright?" I could hear her sobs. She is really in trouble. If Dr.Malik is the reason for the trouble, then he is dead!

After a couple of sobs she controlled herself and responded to me in a very low voice, "Bindu, Dr.Malik is behaving a little strange today. He asked me to send a spaceship to some Galaxy known as 'Kaala'. He said that he could not go as he had another important meeting. But he gave the path and the destination to the scientists helping him in this project. So with their help I sent a crew in the ship which you saw in Malik Towers. You know Bindu, that ship is unpredictably fast. As per his instructions I ordered the crew to collect terrestrial samples of the greenish blue coloured planet.

When Dr.Malik came back from his meeting, he was very angry and tensed. He called for an immediate discussion with his team of scientists and I was also called. He said so many unbelievable stories about the world's impending end. He said that the people above 25 years are going to die and he could survive only if he consumes this greenish blue element which he calls Navjavaanium. I am really frightened. He is really forcing us to hasten up the search. I feel that he is doing something illegal. He is behaving like a maniac. He shot down two scientists who talked against him, right in front of my eyes. He has warned everyone that we will meet the same fate if we disobey him."

Of course, he is a maniac! He is a villain! I replied to her patiently, "Abi Akka, don't panic! Do you have your passport with you?" She replied, "Yes, I have all my stuff with me here." I continued, "OK.

Then take your passport and valuables and get out of Malik Towers when you get the chance. Board a flight that departs to India at the earliest and come to India as early as possible. Don't show your tension out. Play cool and wait for the opportunity to come out without rousing any suspicion. I think there is no immediate danger to you now. If you have any problem in executing this plan, then I will come there with Aadhmi to rescue you."

She said, "Bindu, now everybody is busy with the proceedings in the research station. So I think that there will be no problem in sneaking out of here. I believe that I can escape from here and reach India." I cautioned her, "Abi Akka, I have to confess something to you now. I am actually working on a mission to save the world now and that was the reason for our visit to the Malik Towers today. This mission should be kept as a secret and it shouldn't be known to our family. It is a very serious issue and I will explain it in detail when I meet you. But please don't tell anything about my visit to London or about Dr. Malik to your parents or my parents. Please help me Abi Akka. Don't say a word about this to our parents. Once you come to India everything is going to be alright. Don't panic. Be cool." She accepted and I hung up the phone.

Professor Ramanujam was sleeping soundly. Aadhmi said to me, "The way you guided your sister was really nice. We will make arrangements to save her. But if she gets caught, you should act in such a way that hurting your sister Abi doesn't affect you." The mere thought of this scenario made my stomach churn. Aadhmi asked with concern, "Can she manage herself or should we return to London now? If you feel that we should help her at once, we can plan something and execute it immediately." I thought over Aadhmi's idea. But I did not want to mess up things further. So I answered, "Actually, Abi akka is a very courageous and confident person. In fact, she is stronger than me. She has secured a black belt in Karate. I know that her punches and kicks are really strong. So when she is subjected to a fight or something the victory is on her side. But now her opponent is Dr.Malik, who is a murderer, backstabber and notorious scientist. He may do anything to harm Abi Akka. The problem is becoming bigger and bigger. I need someone else to help me. We need a bigger team to monitor things."

Aadhmi said, "Bindu, that boy Raj really seems to be intelligent and shrewd. I feel that he will be very helpful in executing our plans." I nodded and accepted its view. I said, "You are correct Aadhmi. Moreover today I made a lot of modifications in our Yuva Sansaar mission. In particular I have designed and added up many more apps to the Suethae. It is going to have a wonderful reformation. The Kankan Suethae will be useful only to the Junior Phoenixians. But for the Senior Phoenixians I have designed another version which will act like a back pack. There will be a lot of storage facilities in this back pack model. I am still working on it to get the maximum output. It will be a positive growth regarding convenience and comfort. You will really like this change. So definitely we are going to need some more help."

Aadhmi said, "Well, I have already gone through all your works and I appreciate the changes. Well, tomorrow I am going to ask Professor Ramanujam to make arrangements to recruit Raj. Also he will really love to work with you!"

That was not a bad idea. Raj was very active and intelligent too. He is very creative and innovative too. So he will be really helpful. He would accept this opportunity. In fact he would love to be Professor Ramanujam's assistant.

After a while we reached my home. I walked into the house as Sorna fled away with Professor, Puper and Aadhmi inside it. Mom asked me with sleepy eyes if I needed anything to eat. I said a big 'No'; walked drowsily into the bedroom and collapsed on the king size cot with my phone next to me.

47

A Friend In Need

My phone rang and woke me up. I felt really tired even though I had slept all night. It was ringing continuously. Someone was calling me. I really began to hate my phone. It was 4 am! Who the hell is calling me so early in the morning? It was Abi Akka. God! I totally forgot about her. Is she alright? If she is calling so early then something should be wrong. She said in a low voice, "Bindu, I know that I am disturbing you in your early morning deep sleep. But I have no other go." I said in a sleepy and croaky voice, "It's OK Akka." She said hastily, "Listen, I thought that I could feed you some information about the activities of Dr. Malik as long as I am in Malik Towers. At present, Dr. Malik is still very angry that his team has not yet reached the destined planet. He is eagerly waiting to get good news from them. I have no problem here and I am being treated well as usual. When I secretly snooped around the different floors of Malik Towers I found out something peculiar. Nearly abnormal looking creatures were locked in cells in a floor. It looks as though they are kept as captives. I think some medical research is being done on them. I could not predict if they are human or any new form of creatures. That floor is under tight security." There was a pause and I heard no sound.

In a moment her voice resumed, "I just checked if anyone was coming. There is nobody here. Coming back to the point, I also suspect that some other medical research is being done in Dr. Malik's body. A team of nearly 50 doctors are working on him at regular intervals. I don't know what they do to him. But I see that periodically a heavy dosage of medicines is pumped into him intravenously. He is being monitored by them continuously. Those doctors are experts in their own field. His body conditions are also being monitored and recorded. When I went through a file I could not make the head or tail of it. But either he is being treated for some illness or some new medicines are being tried on him and he is being observed to check if his body could accept them. And his shadow Elsa never leaves his side. I have never seen him or her sleep or feel tired. She looks as though she is made of stone. She looks like an anorexic person because she gobbles on something at regular intervals. But maintains the same zero size. Not even zero size, she is in her minus size. I have been spying on them without their knowledge. I really played cool and have made him a fool!"

The information she shared with me made me fully alert. I was wide awake listening to her. I was sitting erect now. I felt that I could get an idea of what is being done to him, if I could see one of his medical files. I asked her if it would be possible for her to mail some information to me. She was really in a detecting mood and she readily agreed. I gave her some instructions regarding what is to be done. She listened to my instructions very keenly and patiently. Then suddenly, she said in a more whispering voice that she would call me later as someone was approaching. I was looking at the disconnected phone for a while and then let out a sigh. I was really worried about Abi Akka because, her 'playing cool' tactics are really terrible. I know that they are really poor and pathetic. It will add up to her safety if she actually doesn't do her style of 'playing cool'.

Mom was snoring in a very low rhythm. I searched Puper for a second and remembered at once that he would be in RV. Could I go to sleep again with this much fresh information sparkling in my brain? The information kept on rewinding in my mind for a while. After tossing around this side and that side for about half an hour I began to feel sleepy and my eye lids closed slowly. Suddenly my phone rang again! Oh! God! I saw the caller. It was not Abi Akka but Aadhmi! Why on earth is it calling now? Why do people enjoy ruining my sleep? Not only people, but also robots! I couldn't sleep hereafter. Abi

Akka had already woken me up! And now Aadhmi has got the baton in this relay race! I could never sleep! I attended the call. Aadhmi spoke in its robotic tone, "Good morning Bindu!"

'Good morning!' Wow! What a bad morning! The time is just 4:15am and I am badly in need of some more sleep! I feel tired and sick! But Aadhmi wishes me 'good morning'! I wish I could throw plates on Aadhmi's metal head. But I know that it won't be any good. One thing will surely happen. The eating plates will be out of shape. They will be bent and dent. Nothing can affect Aadhmi's metal body. It is made of the strongest alloy of metals.

Aadhmi said to me, "Professor has granted permission to involve Raj in our mission Yuva Sansaar. We have talked to your Principal. He is very happy to send Raj to RV to accompany you in the research. So today Raj will join us." I did not know how to react to this information. I did not know whether to laugh or cry. Aadhmi metal head has no need to sleep at all! But my tiny brain is tired and it needed rest! When did they talk to our Principal regarding this matter? Aah! Yes! I totally forgot that our headmaster wakes up at 3am in the morning. He is a very peculiar man. He wakes up early and alerts his daughters and sons at the same time. He forces them to chant the hymns of the Gods; do yoga and makes them climb the small hill which is not far from his residence. The worst is that he makes them take bath in cold water as soon as they get up, no matter how chill the morning is. In fact, that is our ancient Indian culture and he strictly follows that.

Whenever he takes us out for a camp or trekking or a bird watching trip he does the same to us. So Professor must have caught the early bird and sought his permission!

As there was no reply from my side and it could not read my thoughts too, Aadhmi asked in a serious tone, "Do you feel comfortable working with Raj? Or should I keep him out of this?" I had already planned to throw plates on Raj's face when I see him again for showing my photo to all our class mates and commenting that I was very beautiful in half-saree. So I was eager to meet him and finish the deal. Why should I miss this opportunity? I said in my sleepy voice, "Aaaahhhh…..comfortable..comfortable……"

Aadhmi added, "Well, then inform Raj about this and bring him to RV at 6am. You can tell him everything and bring him prepared for the task. But remember, your principal has been informed that you both are going to work together in creating mammoths. So let him not leak the truth to anyone! Caution him to be careful and ask him to tie his tongue even to his parents!" Without waiting for my reply Aadhmi hung up the phone. I couldn't go to sleep. I lay awake. In my upper bunk Diya was sleeping smiling in her dream as usual, with drool in her chin. Daddy hadn't come back from Delhi. So Mummy might have invited her to stay with us. She might have thought of chatting with me before sleeping. I cannot go to school today also. Raj also will not attend school today. She will miss us very much. So I just wanted to have a chat with her at once.

I couldn't control myself. I decided to wake her up. I pinched her and she blabbered, "Toad……Toad……" I guess she always dreams about Mrs. Toad. I shook her violently. She shouted, "Earth quake! Earth quake!" and again went to sleep. I wanted to wake someone now. So I tried Indu. I pulled her leg and she cried, "Zuil Malik! Zuil Malik! Please sign this autograph book! Wow! ….." Zuil was a member of her favourite boy band Uni Direction. She is dreaming about Zuil. So funny! She will wake up the whole neighbourhood if I destroy her sweet dream!

Well! Who shall I wake up now? Raj! That's it! Without knowing what I was doing, I called Raj. The rings went on one after the other. I realized how silly I was behaving and hung up the phone before Raj could wake up and answer it. In a few seconds my phone rang again. It was Raj this time! I have disturbed him early in the morning and he is calling me back! If someone had called me at this time of the day, I would be happy that I hadn't attended it and I would continue my sleep. But this fellow is calling me back! Unbelievable!

I accepted the call but spoke nothing. Raj said in a hoarse voice, "Hello….." I said, "Hello Raj!" Raj asked with concern, "Are you alright Bindu?" Why is he worried about me? I replied, "I'm fine." He let out a sigh and said, "You never call me usually at this time. So I thought that there must be some emergency. Is everything OK?" Oh! What a concern! Why would I be calling him if I were in grave danger?

I shouldn't have disturbed him. I said with hesitation, "Nothing is wrong Raj." He said in his sleepy voice, "Bindu why are you calling me so early, if everything is alright?" I had no other go than to open up the topic. So I said to him slowly, "Raj actually Professor Ramanujam has given his consent to acquire you as his assistant. Would you like to join us in creating Mammoth?" In no time he shouted in an energetic voice, "Yeah!!!!Sure! Shall I come to your house right now?" Why is he shouting like this? I said quickly, "No, I will come to pick you up at 5.30am. We shall go together to RV. Even our principal has granted you permission to skip school." He retorted, "No! I will go to Ramanujam Valley right now. I will meet you there when you come." I said to him, "Wait! You can't get into RV without me." Without waiting for my explanation he said, "Then I will come to your house and we shall go together from there." He is not going to give up. So, I said to him, "OK Raj, I will come to your house right now and take you to R.V. So get ready soon."

I took bath and refreshed myself. I wore a green colour cotton tops with simple bead works and light green coloured pencil fit pants. I left a note for my Mom and Diya. It read

Dear Mom,

    I have to go to R.V to continue the research. Don't worry about me. Take care. I love you! Diya, I am sorry for leaving so early. I will explain everything when I come back. Raj is also coming with me to RV. See you soon. With love

Bindu.

I jumped into my Audi and raced to Raj's house which was not too far. In a few minutes I reached Raj's house and I could see that Raj was waiting in front of his house. He was dressed in a hoodie top and jeans.

He was smiling at me as he greeted me, "Hi! Bindu!" How dare he is to show my photos and make a big publicity about my outfit throughout the class and smile at me innocently! He is dead! I just smiled back at him. He got inside the car swiftly and we started towards the Ramanujam Valley. He said suddenly, "You look really beautiful in this dress." Now he is commenting about my dress! He is really dead! I put the break and slapped him. He shouted in shock, "Aaaahhh!..." I frowned at him and he was puzzled. He questioned me with the shock still on his face, "Why did you slap me? Are you crazy?"

"Who is crazy? Me? You little monkey! How dare you show my personal pictures to others without my permission! Did I give my consent for that? You have gone to each and every person in the class and told that I was beautiful in half saree. Can't you keep your mouth shut?" I yelled angrily.

He looked really shocked and he said to me innocently, "What! You slap me for telling the truth to the class! Bala said that you will be happy if I do so! I kept on telling him that you looked very beautiful in that dress and he suggested that I say that to everyone to please you! Is there something wrong in it?" I felt like dashing my head on a wall and yell loudly.

I controlled myself and asked, "So you will follow everything what Bala says?" He again answered innocently, "Not everything. But anything regarding you as he is your brother and I believed that he knows you in and out." I said in a composed tone, "Well! Hereafter don't seek Bala's advice regarding me. That will be the greatest disaster to you. Moreover never comment about me to others." "Then what do you want me to do?" This idiot will never understand anything. I said in a frustrated tone, "Just keep your mouth shut Raj! Whatever you feel you have it to yourself. Don't irritate me by proclaiming that to others." He covered his mouth with his hands and nodded his head like a small child. Though I felt like laughing on seeing this I controlled myself and turned my face.

48

Planet In Andromeda

The fight came to an end. He questioned me, "So, Bindu how are you creating the mammoth?" I replied to him in a calm voice, "Raj, we are actually not creating any mammoth now." He exclaimed, "What! You are not creating a mammoth! Then why are you skipping school? What is keeping you busy at present?" I asked him to calm down and explained to him, "Raj, listen to me patiently. I am working on something more important and something much more confidential." I explained everything to him. I said everything including my dream, vision, Emberonium, Dr.Malik, Navjavaanium, the Gods, Abi Akka, Professor Ramanujam's past life, mission Yuva Sansaar, Phoenixians and the Suethae. Though he listened with wide open mouth and eyes, he believed me. I said to him, "Raj, I need your help in mission Yuva Sansaar." He seemed to be in a shock. But he nodded in response to me.

I phoned Aadhmi and informed it that I was coming to RV with Raj. Aadhmi replied that it was ready to receive us. I drove towards the Ramanujam Valley while Raj was continuously blabbering about his respect for Professor Ramanujam and the appreciable efforts that he would take to create the Suethae. He was so annoying and I got the same intension of throwing eating plates on him. We soon neared the Ramanujam Valley.

I could see some shiny piece of metal in the dim light waiting at the entrance. I guessed that it was Aadhmi. Raj still didn't shut his mouth and it was really annoying. If I am going to work with this 'chattering human monkey' Raj all day then I am dead! Aadhmi greeted us, "Good morning Bindu! Good morning Raj!" I just smiled at Aadhmi. But, Raj over reacted and he shouted at the top of his voice, "Yeah!!!!!!!!!!!!!!!! World famous robot Aadhmi is greeting me!" Silly boy Raj! He is really annoying. I just rolled my eyes.

The sun was rising steadily and RV looked really beautiful under the rising sun. I could see the fields and the forest area extending to a long distance. They were shining ` under the rising sun. As we stood in the entrance, enchanted by the beauty of the Ramanujam Valley, Aadhmi said to me, "Bindu, there will be slight modification in mission Yuva Sansaar." Modification! What does Aadhmi mean by it? I gave it a puzzled look. Raj also became serious and was ready to listen.

"Actually I conducted further researches with the scientists who came here from all over the world and we have found out more about the radiations that would be emitted by Emberonium on the 7th day. Though many theories were put forward, I read everyone's thought and have come to the conclusion that Emberonium is capable of emitting Tera hertz flashes, which are radiations of electromagnetic waves with a frequency between radio waves and infra red rays. Actually Emberonium sends out accelerated electrons on a well defined slalom course with in a Pico second."

Raj shouted out exclaiming, "What! A Pico second! That is trillionth of a second! I have read in an article by the Russian scientist Kapowlov Toopownskey that super fast heating is possible using Tera hertz flashes. They could boil water to a minimum of 600 degree Celsius in a Pico second." I looked at Raj in admiration. Aadhmi patted Raj and said, "Well said Raj! You are absolutely right! But the Tera hertz radiations from the meteorite will be much more powerful I believe. So the Emberonium will cause complete disaster in a Pico second and this confirms that the earth's atmosphere will be certainly affected. So we are forced to go for a change of plan."

Aadhmi explained to us, "As per the new plans we need not prevent Dr.Malik from discovering Navjavaanium." I blurted out angrily, "What! Then are we supposed to fold our hands and wait till Dr.Malik eats the Navjavaanium? And should we just watch him destroy the whole world including the Phoenixians? I don't get what you are trying to say Aadhmi!" Raj intruded, "Has Dr. Malik found out Navjavaanium now?" I replied, "As per the information from Abi Akka he is still searching its location. But he may consume it the moment he gets it. It is not compatible with human body and it may lead to an unpredictably powerful explosion that may destroy the whole earth. The disaster created by Navjavaanium will be far more dangerous when compared to Emberonium that is going to sweep away the whole population of the living organisms above 25 years."

Aadhmi said to me comfortingly, "Don't worry Bindu, I have worked out a new plan that would ensure the safety of the Phoenixians. Have you ever heard of a Galaxy named Andromeda?" The name was familiar. Yes! Andromeda was the Galaxy closest to the Milky Way Galaxy. Aadhmi read my mind voice and he said, "Exactly! Before seventy five years Professor worked on a thesis that, the 'failed stars' near the sun may harbour hidden planets." Again Raj interrupted, "Failed stars are nothing but Brown Dwarfs. I have read about this research by Yuri Beletsky of Carnegie's University with several teams of astronomers. Their research says that the failed stars have a mass below 8% of the mass of the Sun. This mass is not sufficient enough to burn the hydrogen present in their centre. So they form planetary masses."

Aadhmi again patted him on his back and said, "What you said is right Raj. But too much of explanation is not needed now. Because I actually wanted to come to the main point that Professor had discovered a planet named 'Patchi Gragha' in Andromeda galaxy. It is a habitable planet and people live there. Professor visited the planet. He was received happily as a guest by them and since then he has maintained cordial relationship with the people in Patchi Graha. The planet has a stable atmosphere. The conditions in that planet are suitable for human life. It is just like the earth."

Raj asked enthusiastically, "Are you planning to take the younger generation to that Graha? Will they allow that? Won't they think that it is a form of invasion? Will they be friendly or hostile to us? We need to know more about them like the rules and regulations they follow there; their life style; the availability of natural resources there etc." Though Raj is a chatter box, he has a lot of valid information and he is very thoughtful in analyzing the pros and cons of a plan. I was happy that he had asked whatever I wanted to clear myself.

Aadhmi replied, "Very good Raj. Professor's selection never fails. He is an expert in identifying the scientific minds! Your doubts are really valid and logical. Before a couple of weeks Professor Ramanujam and I visited Patchi Gragha. The current king is Walter Scott. He is a nice person. The people living in Patchi Gragha are not wild and unfriendly. They have the features just like human beings. The only difference is that they have wings and they can fly. Other than that they are just like human beings in all aspects.

Whether Dr.Malik destroys or does not destroy the Earth, the earth's atmosphere is going to be highly affected by the Tera hertz pulses. Those flashes will remain in the atmosphere for at least a certain period which is unpredictable at present. So we must make arrangements to shift the Phoenixians to the Patchi Gragha. We believe that the people in Patchi Gragha will give us refuge. We could settle in Patchi Gragha and execute mission Yuva Sansaar as previously planned."

I asked Aadhmi, "What steps have been made to approach them regarding this issue?" It answered at once, "Professor Ramanujam was busy working up to 3am and he is still asleep. He does not know about Dr.Malik's evil plans. We have to persuade Professor Ramanujam to talk to the people in planet Patchi Gragha immediately and make arrangements for the refuge."

Now, Raj was listening to us eagerly. I looked sternly at Raj and told him, "Raj, you are not supposed to leak a word to Professor Ramanujam about Dr.Malik's plan and the researches he does in his own body. Professor should not know that Dr. Malik has learnt the location of Navjavaanium." He nodded with fear in his eyes covering his cheeks with his hands. I controlled my laughter. Maybe he was afraid that I will slap him again.

We went past the main gate. Raj's mouth fell open as he saw the constructions in RV. He was exclaiming over every little things. It was really annoying. Could someone make him shut his mouth? I feared that Raj will be of no help to us if he is going to be a nuisance and a complete chatter box. I will be glad as long as he keeps his mouth shut around Professor Ramanujam. Aadhmi said coolly, "I don't feel that his talk is annoying. Why does that disturb you?"

We entered the laboratory and many Robots were working around doing a lot of stuff. The laboratory looked like a factory. It was really different to look at. I sat comfortable in a cozy spot and began to work on the Suethae. Raj didn't do anything. He was just hovering around the lab, exclaiming over each and every thing the robots were doing and it was really irritating.

I called Raj. He came towards me. I said to him, "Raj can you please be mum for a while. I mean, you are exclaiming over everything and it is disturbing me. I have brought you here to help me. So I will be happy if you would help me in designing the apps in Kankan Suethae." He answered enthusiastically, "Wow! I will be really happy to help you. Tell me what I should do. I will complete the task instantaneously like a genie!" I rolled my eyes and then showed him the different applications we have already designed in the Suethae. He understood everything very quickly and managed to show a demo of their usage in no time. Well! He proves that he is an expert!" Then I gave him a lap top and instructed him on the applications that are to be created.

Finally I said, "If you have any more doubts Aadhmi will clear them. Once you finish this task you have to report it to Aadhmi. Aadhmi will give you further instructions. All you have to do now is to execute my instructions without speaking a word unnecessarily." Raj again pretended to be afraid of me by covering his cheeks with his hands. I raised my hands as though to slap him and he moved away snatching the lap top and laughing happily. After discussing for a while with Aadhmi, Raj began to work seriously on the assignment handed to him. We all were soon immersed in our own works.

49
Raj At RV

It was nearly 7 am. My mother called me. She must have finished her Yoga and most of her cooking by this time. She must have seen my note and remained calm. I was so happy that she was so understanding and supportive. She talked to me for a while. Daddy hadn't still returned from Delhi. I spoke to Diya and told her that Raj was joining me in creating mammoth. She was really delighted. She felt very disappointed that we both will not be there to give her company. I convinced her that I will try to come to school with Raj if our work was over. Then I started to continue my work.

After a while Aadhmi announced that Professor Ramanujam had woken up. It will be good if Professor Ramanujam could talk to the people in Patchi Gragha. If the situations really turn bad, we surely will need a planet for refuge. So I was really eager to have a positive change.

After a while Professor Ramanujam walked in and he was really happy to meet Raj. Raj couldn't plant his feet on the ground and he was overwhelming with happiness. He was in cloud nine as he had got the opportunity to work under his idol, Professor Ramanujam.

Aadhmi opened up the topic to Professor Ramanujam, "Professor Ramanujam, do you remember the planet Patchi Gragha?" Professor Ramanujam said casually, "Yeah! It is the planet in Andromeda Galaxy. I discovered it before some seventy five years." Aadhmi continued, "Yes! Professor, can you communicate with the Patchi king Walter Scott and make arrangements for the refuge of the Phoenixians?"

Professor Ramanujam looked really puzzled and he asked, "Aadhmi, what is the urgency to seek refuge for the Phoenixians? They have got the Earth and mission Yuva Sansaar as the first plan."

Before Aadhmi could make up a story, Raj butted in, "Professor, this Dr.Malik will find Navjavaanium at the earliest. If he eats it the whole world will be destroyed. If this happens all the Phoenixians will also die. The Phoenixians could be…" I stamped hard in his feet with fuming anger, and he stopped at once. He is a cracked pot! Always leaking whatever he hears about. I stared at him and he looked at me pathetically in a very pitiable manner.

Aadhmi tried to patch up the breech that Raj had made. It said, "Professor. This silly boy is out of his mind. What we think is that the Earth is too old and it may be severely damaged after the radiations. Moreover the Phoenixians may be haunted by the memories of their past. The Phoenixians can go to a new world and lead a new life without any memories or remembrances about their previous life if they are away from the Earth."

I could say from Professor Ramanujam's face expression that he was not really satisfied with Aadhmi's explanation. But he tried to hide it and he said, "So, you people want to go to a new planet and start a new life." I nodded monotonously. Professor Ramanujam looked into my eyes deeply. So, I said hurriedly, "Yes, Professor!"

Professor Ramanujam gave in, "OK! Then let us make arrangements to talk to the Patchi Gragha for refuge right now. Let us go to the communication room. If there are no solar flares then we can communicate to Patchi Gragha immediately." I let out a secret sigh of relief. Raj mouthed a silent 'sorry' with pleading eyes.

We all walked to the communication room. It seemed to be a long walk as the communication room was in the farthest end of RV. I was determined to throw plates on Raj if he rattled anymore. Soon, we entered the communication room. The communication room was like a glass palace. It looked really beautiful. I was really happy that Raj didn't exclaim over that.

Aadhmi gave Professor Ramanujam a screen like thing. Professor stood in the centre of the room, holding the screen in his hand. Aadhmi walked towards a big machine and it began to work on it. It looked as though it was trying to match up some frequencies. I and Raj took a couple of steps behind and waited patiently to see what was happening.

Aadhmi announced, "The pathway is clear! We will be able to communicate with the Patchi king in fifteen seconds." I have never believed in aliens. But today right in front of my eyes I am seeing Professor Ramanujam communicating with them. Suddenly the screen came into life. A man's face appeared on the screen. Soon I could see the whole features of the man from head to toe. He looked handsome. I could see something white behind him. They were like feathers. I guess they were his wings just like Aadhmi had told me previously.

The man had oval shaped face. He had lovely, long eyelashes. His eyes were green. He had curly brown hair. He had sharp and long eyebrows. He had really beautiful cheeks which formed very cute dimples when he smiled. He was tall and well built. He was wearing a coat of some shiny material and it resembled me the shields used by men in ancient times. It looked somewhat grand with some peculiar designs. He wore full trousers which were fitting him correctly. He was majestic.

The man spoke to Professor Ramanujam in a language that I couldn't understand. And Professor Ramanujam was conversing with that man in the same language. They were talking like friends for a very long time. It was nearly an hour. And I couldn't get a clue about what they were talking but I could understand that he was Walter Scott the king of that planet.

If I were to lead the Phoenixians after we go to Patchi Gragha, then I will have to learn this unknown language. I am sure Aadhmi will teach me this language. I am an expert in learning new languages. In fact I learnt Korean in a week's time. I can read, write and speak the Indian languages Tamil, English, Hindi, Malayalam, Telugu, Kannada, Urdu and Bengali; and speak Korean, Japanese, Mandarin, French, Latin and Spanish. I have a keen interest in learning new languages.

After sometime Professor Ramanujam finished his conversation with that smart looking chap and he turned towards us. He smiled happily showing a 'Thumbs up' sign and he said victoriously, "He is happy to welcome the Phoenixians to his planet! Though his planet is twice the size of the Earth, their population is just 20,000. So, Walter is happy and proud to have you there and he believes that you people will add up to the colour of their planet."

I was really happy. Now the real problem is to create many prapanchas to ferry the enormous Phoenixian population to that planet. No spaceship could hold the whole population and the supplies necessary for it in one stretch. Aadhmi said comfortingly, "That is not going to be a huge problem when we take into account the support we have got from the other scientists and resources supply we have got from SAPS. The works have progressed well and it is possible to finish everything in three more days." Raj questioned, "Is Dr. Malik also here?" Aadhmi replied, "He is the one among the few scientists who have not shown their consent to mission Yuva Sansaar. Their absence does not hinder our progress in any way. In fact professor is very happy that Dr. Malik has not come here. But Prince Hamilton has sent many scientists with a lot of resources and his best wishes!"

We all laughed happily and Aadhmi asked mischievously, "Bindu, don't you feel hungry by this time? I was expecting you to curse me for not reminding professor about his breakfast!" Before I could give a counter comment, Raj said, "I am really very hungry. I did not even have coffee or tea in the morning! So please Aadhmi, give me something to eat right now. I have no shame in admitting that I am terribly hungry." Professor said, "Yes, let us have our breakfast." We all started to move towards the house. Raj kept on chattering all the way. It seemed that Professor was cool with him. He even seemed to be more close to Raj talking to him very casually. How could he answer all the silly questions and bear with the over reacting of Raj?

I kept pace with Aadhmi and enquired about Puper. Aadhmi informed, "Some scientists from the university of Rochester and Southampton have got professor's permission to observe him. They actually want to analyze his eating habits. Right now they are monitoring his electro-dermal activity using a wearable pad. They are trying to study his mood by the movements from an accelerometer and gyroscope integrated in removable conducive pads. They are also testing on him a new prototype that could identify emotions with accuracy. Puper is happily co-operating with them. He has even made a new friend named Schraefel!"

I was very angry that professor had granted permission to other scientists just like that for their study on Puper. Is he a lab rat! Has professor forgotten that Puper has feelings and emotions? "Are you possessive over Puper? I understand the true concept of jealous, possessiveness and envy from your feelings today. Quite interesting!" I felt very sorry that I had this chat with Aadhmi and moved ahead cursing Aadhmi. Its laughter aimed my back.

As we entered Professor's residence Raj exclaimed seeing each and everything there. I pulled him aside and warned him in a very low voice, "Raj, if you are exclaiming and over reacting for everything, I will make arrangements to fire you. Do you want to go back to school?" He bit his lips and apologized, "Don't threaten me Bindu. I will behave normally hereafter. I won't overreact. It's a promise. I am really excited to be here. Please don't spoil my happiness." I sighed. When we entered the dining room, Professor was already seated. I took the seat near Professor Ramanujam and Raj sat right next to me.

Aadhmi served us hot Pongal and Sambar. We started to eat. I was worried if Puper had eaten or not. Aadhmi said, "Puper has been fed sufficiently by them. Don't worry." I continued to eat quietly. Raj just tasted a mouth and closed his eyes in wonder. He exclaimed, "Wow! Wow! I have never tasted such delicious food anywhere Aadhmi.

Your hands certainly deserve a platinum bracelet!" I stared at Raj. He at once mouthed a sorry and pretended to concentrate on his plate. Aadhmi chuckled. Though I am a slave to Aadhmi's cooking I have never once appreciated its cooking skills. I felt a bit small in front of Raj's openness. Aadhmi whispered with a smile in my ears, "No hard feelings Bindu. I am after all a machine and you need not bother about my feelings. Moreover I have read all your thoughts and I am happy that you really enjoy my cooking even when you have not said it out loud." I rolled my eyes. I actually wanted to relish the food. So I did not think anything further and continued eating.

Professor said suddenly, "Bindu, your principal wanted to meet you regarding the Cultural Fest. So I think you and Raj can leave after breakfast. At present you don't have any important work here. We have planned to check all the Suethae today. So I will be busy with the other scientists and work is in full swing in the production lab. You can have a small change. You can go to your school and meet your principal. If your work is over there then you can come back to RV today evening." Raj stopped eating and became still as though he was given a shock. I nodded my head and before I opened my mouth to say, "OK professor" he began to speak quickly, "No Professor. I have no work at school. Let Bindu leave. I shall stick together with Aadhmi. I will not open my mouth at all. You won't even know that I am present here. I will not be a disturbance to you in anyway."

Professor and I began to laugh seeing the way he spoke. Then I said, "Raj don't worry. You are still in the mission. We will surely come back in the evening." Though he was not convinced he nodded as he had no other go. I first dropped him and then came to my house. Mom had packed my lunch as I had informed her already. She was happy to see me. Indu and Diya had already left to school. So I quickly changed into my school uniform and walked fast to school.

50

Master Of Ceremony

At 10am we were in the indoor auditorium of our school. All our staff and principal were seated on the podium. They were discussing seriously about something. Mrs. Crow….Oh! My god! I have forgotten her real name! Whatever it may be! She seemed very busy interacting with all teachers and the Principal time to time and taking notes in a file. The school pupil leader, the assistant school pupil leader, the students in charge of all cultural associations and clubs, the members of all cultural clubs and volunteers were seated in the front rows facing the podium. All the other students were sitting behind and chatting noisily among themselves. Diya, Raj and I were sitting together in the front row. I had already slapped Raj so that he would not open his mouth regarding our works in RV. He kept on staring at me periodically rubbing his cheeks. He held his mouth shut tight with his palm as he feared that the truth would spill out of his mouth.

Diya said in a very adorable way that she would wait until we give the true reason behind our visit to RV. Thank god! She did not give me the burden of making up any unnecessary stories. Soon Raj became normal and we three also started to chat and laugh happily. The noise of the students' clatter rose to the ceiling. Whenever a teacher requested all the students to maintain silence, we all pretended to obey and maintained a short term silence and then resumed our talking.

Finally our Principal took the mike and said in a clear voice, "Good morning students." Silence fell over the hall. He continued,

"Today we have gathered here to discuss about our performance in the International Cultural Fest for the youth. As you know already, the Fest is a three day program and students from thousands of schools and colleges from all over the world will come to India to participate in this. I am really happy and proud that our school has got the opportunity to participate in the Fest. The celebrities and famous personalities from all over the world will be present there. All the countries will exhibit the exclusive performance of their greatest stars. During such a memorable event it is a pleasure that our school is going to entertain the gathering for 3 hours." The students let out a gasp of surprise and a roar of applause too.

Our Principal waited for the round of applause to thin down. Then he continued with pride, "You are all blessed to perform on that prestigious stage! You are going to be rewarded for your sincere practice for an hour everyday throughout the last month. You have been practising fully for the past two days without any classes and the cultural committee is happy about the development in your performance. You will have practice today also. We have to perform the day after tomorrow. Our scheduled time is morning 6 am. We will conduct as many rehearsals as possible in our school auditorium and before your performance you can have a rehearsal on the stage in the Jawaharlal Nehru Stadium New Delhi if time permits. A special flight has been arranged for all the students of our school tomorrow evening. Those who are willing to come in that flight should give your names and contact numbers to your class teachers. All the teachers will accompany the participants. Of course my presence is also confirmed. The participants who cannot board the flight tomorrow evening in time must come to Delhi on your own with your parents."

Mrs. Crow stood up and moved towards our Principal. She said something in his ears. He listened for a minute nodding periodically and then handed over the mike to her. She cleared her throat and said, "Good morning dear students. The cultural committee has discussed and unanimously selected one student to be the Master of

Ceremony for the 3 hour program allotted to our school." She gave a pause. At once all students hushed many guesses. She silenced us and announced, "The Master of Ceremony is Binduuuu….!" There was a big round of applause. Diya shook my hands happily and Raj was clapping energetically. I was not at all in a mood for any such work and I was not happy with or carried away by the announcement. Suddenly Diya looked at my face and looked at me with concern. She had automatically stopped shaking my hands and questioned me with her eyes.

She asked me, "Bindu, why do you look upset. It is a wonderful chance to exhibit your talent in an international level. But you seem disturbed." I replied, "No Diya. Actually I am not in a condition to accept this responsibility. I have many other important works." She suggested, "Then meet Principal and explain your problem. You know very well how much he considers you! So he will really understand your situation and make some other arrangements. Don't show a dull face for such simple matters." I was very happy that she was with me to boost me and guide me. I nodded cheerfully and waited for the appropriate time to meet him.

Mrs. Crow announced the name list of all the participants and checked if anyone's name was missing. They were asked to assemble in teams as per their event. Soon Diya's name and Raj's name was also called and they left. Then the participants were given a list of Do's and Don'ts. Nothing was registered by my brain. Soon all the students were taken out to the ground and open auditorium in batches by different teachers in charge for practice. Our Principal was giving some instructions to Mrs. Crow and a few teachers. I approached him slowly. When all the others left, only Mrs. Crow was near him. He turned to me and questioned, "Wait Bindu, Mrs. Padma will give you the program schedule so that you can start preparing for anchoring" Oh! Now I get it! Mrs. Crow's original name is Mrs. Padma!

I said in an apologizing tone, "Excuse me Sir! I am really sorry Sir! I actually came to explain to you that I am not in a condition to accept this wonderful opportunity Sir. I am really busy with a new project with Professor Ramanujam." He interrupted immediately, "Yaah! I know very well about that! But this is more important at present. After this event I will allow you to skip school and get busy with your project." Mrs. Crow added, "Yes Bindu! The English literature club suggested your name specially appreciating your oratory skills, time management capability, your stylish pronunciation, accent, flawless flow of words and presence of mind. You manage different situations very well and rise to the occasion. We need such a reliable person for this important task."

Suddenly our dance teacher came forward and said, "Sir actually I had selected Bindu for classical solo performance. Her dance will be the inauguration dance of our slot. Her name has been personally suggested by our chief minister after seeing her performance in the 'Classical Dance Mela' at Chidambaram." He said at once, "Well! Then let her do both the inauguration dance as well as the compeering." Dancing was my passion and I love Bharatha Natyam. I could give an excellent solo performance with just one hour of practice. Compeering needed a lot of co-ordination, timing and my full time presence throughout all the rehearsals and the complete performance. So I decided to make myself very clear.

I said in a pleading tone, "Sir really Professor needs my support for the project. If you want you can confirm that to him and then make the final decision. I can perform the inauguration dance as I have kept on practising dance always." He mused for a while and then nodded his head, "Ok. You have never ever run away from any of the duties given to you until today. So I will consider your situation now. I will make some other arrangement for the Master of Ceremony'. Well! You can do your classical dance alone." I was relieved and I said, "Thank you so much Sir!" happily. I was about to run away when Principal's voice caught me mid way. He said, "Bindu, wait. You must not skip school today and tomorrow. I want your performance to be the best of all. So spend some of your time for sincere practice." I replied, "Yes Sir!" and ran out as early as possible.

I went around the campus in search of Raj and Diya. Most of the students were participating in one event or the other and the whole campus was buzzing with activity. Students were dancing to the music blaring from different music systems. Some were practising singing too. I saw Raj, Bala and Diya standing under a huge Baobab tree and discussing something seriously.

When I walked towards them they did not notice me as Bala and Diya were listening intently to Raj. The fear, seriousness and shock in their eyes told me that Raj had opened up his mouth. I felt drained. I could not bear the panic in Diya's face. I went closer and touched Diya. She turned, but did not respond or react to my touch as she was in complete shock. Suddenly tears began to roll down her eyes. I hugged her at once and held tightly. I said in a whisper, "Shh! It's OK! Control yourself Diya."

Raj looked at me in fear and blinked like a lost child. He covered his cheeks with his hands and began to babble, "I am sorry Bindu. I did not mean to tell them everything. But everything spilled out of my mouth without any control. Please, don't slap me." I looked at him in disgust. But I was too drained to be angry. In one way I felt relieved that they had known the truth now. Bala was very composed. He did not over react. He was in some serious thought.

Diya said with tears, "Bindu, how did you play cool when you had such a heavy burden in your heart? I really felt deep in my heart that you were managing something very serious. But I had never imagined that it could be so severe like this." Bala said in a serious tone, "Bindu, are you sure that Abi is safe there?" He seemed really worried about his sister Abi.

I said confidently, "Yes! She is. She spoke to me even today morning. But Bala please don't tell about this to your mom or dad. They cannot bear this." He said in the same serious tone, "Sure Bindu. I am not Raj. I will never tell anyone even if they slap me. I give you the word that Raj will not talk about this to anyone else. I assure you that we will be by your side always. Even if it is an easy task or a difficult task, we will help you by all means." I felt that these words were not from his lips but from his heart.

Suddenly an announcement brought us back to the school atmosphere. Mrs. Crow's voice reverberated throughout the school, "Dear students, due to some unavoidable reasons the Cultural Committee has selected the following students to be the Masters of Ceremony." All other sounds stopped and silence prevailed in the campus. Mrs. Crow's voice again echoed, "The compeering for the three hours allotted to our school will be shared by Bala, the School Arts Club Secretary; Raj and Ann. Bala, Raj and Ann please come to the office room immediately."

All the students cheered happily. I too joined them with joy. Now Raj and Bala looked disturbed. They said in unison, "What the hell is going on here?" and stared at me. I laughed and convinced them, "Raj and Bala Anna you are really experts in giving lively comments based on the nature of a performance. So you can easily manage." Diya said happily, "Congratulations Raj! Congrats Bala!" and shook their hands. Diya and I dispersed to our respective spots for practice, while Raj and Bala went towards the office room together chatting something very seriously.

I rushed to the Dance Club hall. My dance teacher was already waiting with a team of musicians. I practised nonstop for nearly 2 hours. My dance teacher Mrs. Saroja was very particular that there should be perfect match between the 'Thaalam' and the 'Jathi'. When the bell for lunch break rang, Mrs. Saroja said to me, "Bindu, I need one more sweet female voice to sing during your performance. As most of the singers are engaged in different events, I don't know how to get us a singer now. Can you try somebody known to you? You have to take the responsibility of relieving her from the program she is enrolled now." I said, "Madam, I will try madam. But I am not sure if it is possible." She said promisingly, "OK! At least let us give it a try. If you catch any fish, bring her immediately to me after lunch."

During lunch time Raj, Bala, Diya and I met again and we decided to have lunch together unlike my regular habit of eating alone. A lot of stone benches and tables were under the shade of huge neem trees. I and Diya sat on a bench facing Raj and Bala. While eating Diya said casually, "Mrs. Toad is in charge of our group song. She has selected her daughters and her sister's daughters too. I cannot tolerate the family get together they enjoy there. Moreover Mrs. Toad wants all others to underplay when her children dominate. I don't know what to do. Shall I just escape by saying that I have got severe throat infection or something?" I shouted happily, "Hurray! Diya, don't worry. I have a wonderful solution to your problem." All the three looked at me in a puzzled way. I explained them what Mrs. Saroja had told me. Diya happily agreed to get her name deleted from the group song, and join with my team.

Raj and Bala showed the full schedule and the preparations they have done so far. Suddenly they stopped talking when someone neared us. It was Ann. She cheered artificially, "Hi everybody! Would you mind me joining you?" and she squeezed herself between Bala and Raj without waiting for our reply. Bala and Raj smiled broadly seeing her. Diya gave me a bewildered look.

Ann said with a pout and an artificial tone, "Bindu, I feel very sorry for you! You have been rejected by the teachers from compeering even when you are really talented. It is too bad! See now! Though you think that I am not talented than you, our teachers have understood my real potential and given me the important task of being the 'Master of Ceremony.'" She gave a special stress to the word Master of Ceremony. I just smiled at her. My expression annoyed her.

She said in an insulting tone, "Better luck next time!" I and Diya began to laugh at once. She gave us a puzzled look and then turned to Raj. She started to chirp in an artificially sweet voice, "Raj, I have many doubts regarding our performance. When shall we three meet again?" At once Bala and Raj said together, "Why not we discuss it now itself?" They three began to talk and laugh as though we two had become invisible. I and Diya were fuming in anger. Shameless creatures! How silly of them to laugh like this to Ann. I cursed Bala. Raj will be spoilt if he is in Bala's company. I wished to throw plates on Raj, Bala and Ann's face. They seemed to be in cloud nine. Diya whispered to me," I feel like vomiting. I can't stand this anymore. Shall we quit this horrible atmosphere?" I said, "Wait a minute Diya. I have to bring two monkeys to reality before we leave!" and I emptied my water bottle on Raj, Ann and Bala's head and we ran off laughing together. We ignored Ann's shouts and curses that followed us.

I went for dance practice. Diya came into the Dance Club hall after fifteen minutes smiling victoriously. She neared Mrs. Saroja and said something to her. Mrs. Saroja happily nodded her head and gave Diya place to sit near her. Yes! Diya has come to my team. She winked at me and began to concentrate on the lyrics papers handed over to her. The whole afternoon we had severe practice. When the school bell rang at 4pm I was really happy to go home. All the students seemed very tired because of the tight schedule the whole day, but were still happy and enthusiastic. Indu and I were walking very happily as we had no school bag but only our lunch bag. She was going to sing in the Fest and she was happy that the band of instrumentalists that played for her included Niranjana too. Indu has a very sweet voice than me and she is an expert in drawing too. When we entered home we were delighted to see our Dad.

51

New Visitors To RV

We rushed to Dad and hugged him happily. Indu kept on clattering about what had happened here since he left. He was listening to her happily. I just watched her pour out everything. Mom as usual gave us apple juice and she sat comfortably with us. My heart was filled with mixed emotions of joy and sorrow. I tried to freeze this scene in my mind. I went to my room to refresh. There were 3 missed calls from Aadhmi. Before I could call it, my phone rang. It was Abi Akka. She asked me in a serious and secret voice, "Bindu, why the hell did you tell about my work in Malik Towers to Bala? What about the promise you gave me? What if my parents come to know of this?" She kept on firing me. I just listened silently. When she had finished I said, "I am really sorry Akka. It was that loose talk Raj's mistake. But don't worry. Bala is very understanding and supportive. How are you? How is everything going on there?" She was cooled down a bit and she said, "OK, I am fine. Yet I have not been into any trouble. Still Dr. Malik has not got Navjavaanium. Bala called me and asked me if I was safe. So I became much tensed. Otherwise everything is OK here." Soon we ended our conversation.

  I called Aadhmi. As soon as picking up my call, it said, "Congrats Bindu!" I asked, "Why?" Aadhmi replied, "You are going to dance in the Cultural Fest, aren't you? So I congratulated you." I replied, "All most all the students of our school are performing there. So there is nothing special about me alone. The credit goes to the school." Aadhmi did not give up. It said, "I know you more than anyone in your school. So congrats!" I said, "OK! Thank you! Where is

Professor? How are the works going on there? How is Puper? Did he ask about me?"

Aadhmi said, "Everything is going on here much more wonderfully than we had expected. Prapancha and Suethae are produced at a very fast rate. They are being tested then and there and the stock list is perfectly recorded. Professor is really happy with this progress. You know something? He is one of the guests of honour at the Cultural Fest! Already President Abdul Rahman is hosting the event and professor could not deny his invitation." I was happy that Professor will be there in Delhi with us when we perform. I asked Aadhmi, "Is professor in RV at present?" Aadhmi replied, "Of course! He is eagerly waiting to meet you. When are you coming here with Raj?"

I was silent for a second and then asked with much hesitation, "Aadhmi, can I bring two more visitors with me today? It's Bala my cousin and Diya another friend of mine." Aadhmi said at once, "Wait Bindu. I do not have the freedom to grant you permission. Let me talk to professor and then contact you." The call ended. What a stupid I am to ask all of a sudden like this without knowing the situation there. I felt a bit guilty. As minutes passed, I began to change my clothes. When I came out of my room after refreshing again my cell phone rang. I rushed to grab it. It was Aadhmi. It said, "Bindu, Professor has given his consent. You may bring them with you. But I will scan them thoroughly before they enter in." I replied happily, "That's not a problem. We will be there in half an hour."

I quickly called Raj, Diya and Bala and informed them about this and asked them to be ready. Bala and Diya said that they will wait for me in Raj's house. They were very happy and nervous about their visit to RV. When I came to the living room, Indu was watching TV with Mom and Dad. Her head was in my Dad's lap and her feet were in my Mom's lap. She was sharing the information she knew about the Cultural Fest to them. I envied her childishness and innocence.

I sat on a chair in front of my Mom and informed them that I had to go to RV. "Is Raj coming with you?" asked my Mom. My Dad asked in wonder, "When did Raj join your team?" I replied, "Just today morning Dad. And not only he, today Bala and Diya will also come with me to RV." Indu sat erect at once and shouted, "What? Then I will also come with you. I miss Puper very much. How come you leave me alone and take everyone else with you? I will come with you right now." Oh! God! She has started her adamant demanding. I looked at Mom and Dad helplessly and said, "Indu, I cannot decide as per my wish to take someone there. Professor has called them there for a project. When you become more interested in science and scientific researches you can also come there. But now I cannot take you with me. But I will try to bring Puper here today."

I just said a quick 'Good bye' and rushed out. I got into my Audi and in no time I was in Raj's house. Raj, Diya and Bala were already waiting for me. So we started to RV at once. We entered in after the security check. Aadhmi scanned Bala and Diya exclusively. It said in a serious tone, "Professor has insisted me to be very careful. So please don't mistake me." Diya was very happy to see Aadhmi and nothing else bothered her. I introduced Bala to Aadhmi. "Aadhmi, he is Abi Akka's brother, Bala." As soon as I mentioned Abi Akka's name, Aadhmi looked at Bala with concern and said, "Your sister is so courageous to be there in Malik Towers with that evil man. You must be really proud of her." Bala just smiled and did not react much.

I asked Aadhmi where Puper was. "He is still with those scientists. But he is fine. You can meet him today." We entered into professor's residence. Professor welcomed us happily as he knew Bala and Diya already. He had a small talk with them and soon we went with him to the lab. He asked, "Aadhmi can you give a demo of the final version of our plan so that the new comers will also know about it in detail?" Aadhmi explained with a visual on the virtual screen. "We are still trying to calculate the precise time when the Tera hertz radiations would emanate from the meteorites." The 4 meteorites were displayed on the screen. Their vastness was elaborated.

Aadhmi continued, "Sufficient number of Stanno- tech-robots is ready. Each ST-bot is loaded with thousands of Suethae that will reach their owners in a nano second and form the Kankan Suethae. The Suethae will teleport the Phoenixians instantly to the nearest Prapancha as soon as they come into contact with their owners. Each Suethae weighs just 4micro grams. The required number of Prapanchas is also ready. ST-bots are like humanoid robots and they will attend to the physical, emotional and psychological needs of the Phoenixians." The visual demo was like an animated movie. Raj, Diya and Bala watched it intently and asked many questions to clear their doubts. Aadhmi explained everything to them very patiently. In the mean time I was going through some files sent by Abi Akka. They were the medical files of Dr. Malik that she had secretly taken and sent.

Professor said, "OK! Well done Aadhmi! Now Bindu, you can show your friends the Suethae and demonstrate its different applications." Raj interrupted, "Professor, I know very well about the Suethae. I shall demonstrate that to Bala and Diya." Professor looked at him with a smile and agreed. Then he said, "OK. Then after that Aadhmi will take you to the production lab and show the ST-bots and Prapancha. If they want you can even take them on a ride in Prapancha Aadhmi." Diya gasped in surprise, "Won't the public know about this if we go on a ride?" Aadhmi answered, "All the Prapanchas are made of reflecting panels that make them invisible. So they will not be visible to anyone's eyes unless we choose the visibility mode."

Professor said, "Well. I am leaving to Delhi to attend the Cultural Fest tomorrow morning. All the members of SAPS will also be there. Aadhmi I want you to be with Bindu always and give her protection. So Bindu, you need not come here tomorrow. Moreover most of the hardwares of Aadhmi, all the ST-bots and the Prapanchas are going to be distributed to all nations as per their population. They will be kept in the research centers of each nation. So RV will be completely empty by tomorrow evening. When are you leaving to Delhi Bindu?"

Raj answered in a hurry, "There is a special flight arranged for our school students and teachers that leaves at 6pm tomorrow evening. Though the Fest starts tomorrow morning our school's schedule is only in the day after tomorrow." To me it seemed that Bala was extremely calm unlike his nature. May be the seriousness of the situation has affected him much. As Bala was very quiet, Diya also seemed worried. Only Raj seemed to remain unaltered by the change of the events. Professor turned to Aadhmi, "In case of an emergency you can make use of the ST-bots and Prapanchas available. But ensure that it doesn't alert the public by any means."

Professor shook hands with all of us. He hugged Raj and Bala and we fought back our tears. May be this will be our last chance to have a personal time with him. He said, "Don't forget to have your dinner here. Even if I am busy you must call me Aadhmi. I don't want to miss this last supper!" and winked. I broke out as I couldn't control anymore. Professor patted my shoulders and went without turning back. Diya hugged me and cried too. Bala started, "Hey Potato, why are you crying? Are you worried that Professor will come to eat his share? Is it fair on your part to plan to eat his share of dinner too? Is it right to cry over food when you have to act good? See the timing and rhyming!" and appreciated himself. A laughter cracked open my closed mouth. I pretended to beat him and he ran behind others shouting, "I want to die a natural death, not in an accident or attack." We all laughed forgetting everything.

While Raj, Diya and Bala were busy with the Suethae, I was discussing about Dr. Malik with Aadhmi. "I went through the files sent by Abi Akka. It is clear that Dr. Malik is being injected some chemicals to reverse aging. A team of geneticists are working on him to give appreciable results. They are working on to improve the communication between the mitochondria and the nucleus in his cell." Suddenly Raj who had come near us listened to our discussion and said, "Mitochondria is the power house of a cell and it helps in carrying out key biological functions. It keeps a cell young and energetic. As a living organism ages, in its cells the communication between the mitochondria and nucleus decreases." I knew very well that he was correct. So I inquired, "Is it possible for Dr. Malik to reverse his age below 25 and join the Phoenixian population before the catastrophe?" Aadhmi explained, "Some chemicals can repair the broken network in a cell and restore communication in a cell and improve mitochondrial function. But this treatment cannot produce miracles and changes all of a sudden. The effect will be slow and steady. It is impossible for an aged person to reverse his age all of a sudden. So don't worry about Dr. Malik." It turned to Raj and said, "Raj is your work over? Shall I bring Puper here?" Raj nodded and Aadhmi left.

Soon Puper came running towards me into the lab. Bala was trying to use the different applications of the Suethae and he was busy. Diya was also working with him. Raj exclaimed, "Wow! Is this Puper?" I hugged Puper and nodded. Puper rubbed his head on my cheeks and asked lovingly, "How are you mummy?" Again Raj exclaimed, "It calls you mummy!" I corrected him, "Raj, Puper is not to be said 'it' but 'he'. He is not just an animal with just 5 senses. He has the 6th sense also like us. He is no different than a human baby in his feelings and emotions." He said at once, "Oh! Ok! I am sorry Mr. Puper!" in a dramatic way. I rolled my eyes. But Puper responded, "It's OK. May I know your name please?" Raj opened his eyes in wonder and said with admiration, "Wow! You are unbelievable! My name is Raj. I am a friend of Bindu." Puper said, "Nice to meet you!" Raj laughed approvingly and came forward to get him from me. Puper happily moved into Raj's hands to my disappointment. I thought that he would sneer at Raj. But Puper seemed to like Raj very much. Raj was really sweet to Puper. He gently placed Puper down. Knelt down near him and brushed his fluffy fur with his fingers. Puper was enjoying that.

When Diya and Bala had spent some time with the Suethae, Bala was more eager to see Prapancha and the ST-bots. So we all went to the lab and spent some time there. Aadhmi demonstrated how the

Prapancha could modify itself from a small size to its maximum capacity. Before leaving RV we had dinner with Professor. I was driving my Audi. Raj was sitting near me with Puper in his lap. Bala and Diya were sitting at the back. I asked in a mischievous tone, "Hmm.. how is your compeering training going on?" Raj replied with a mischievous smile, "We are actually enjoying our time with Ann. Bala feels that it is really a wonderful experience to work with the most beautiful girl in the school campus!" Diya gave an angry bird look at Bala and gave a Karate pose as if she was going to attack him. At once Bala shouted, "Hey! When did I tell you so? Are you crazy? I can't get blows from this black belt girl!" Raj and I laughed out loud. Puper asked me, "Mummy, who is this Ann?"

When I was about to answer him, my cell phone rang. It was Abi Akka. So at once I stopped driving and took the call. As usual Abi Akka spoke in a secret voice, "Bindu, I am going to come out of the Malik Towers. Today he shot four of the doctors attending him saying that they were useless and inefficient. He behaves like a lunatic. All are afraid to go near him. So I think it is not safe anymore to be here." I was relieved that she had taken the right decision and said, "OK Akka. Be careful. Bala is with me. Would you like to talk to him?" Bala and Abi Akka spoke for a while and then bid 'good bye'.

First I dropped Bala and then Diya at their place. When Raj got down carrying Puper who was asleep, I called out, "Raj, give Puper to me." He came back laughing in a silly way and said, "I thought that I could have him with me today night as he is quite comfortable with me. May I have him with me?" Though I enjoyed the eagerness in his voice I said curtly, "No way! I don't want to see him a chatter box like you tomorrow. You know Puper is very intelligent and he learns fast. If I leave him with you, you will train him to be a talkative like you. I cannot bear with your nuisance and I dare not give one more companion to you." He looked disappointed, but placed Puper in my lap and said, "Good night Bindu" with a warm smile. I said, "Good night Raj. See you tomorrow" and started my car.

When I came home no one at home was asleep. Indu ran eagerly to me and snatched Puper. She was least bothered that she was disturbing him from his sleep. She happily conveyed me the news that Mom and Dad were also coming with us to Delhi to enjoy the International Cultural Youth Fest. I was delighted to hear the news and they added that most of the parents have planned to come with the students for the safety of their children and also to enjoy their performance on stage. Puper was wide awake now and was happily singing Uni Direction songs with Indu. I packed my dance costume and jewels too. I packed some casual wears and accessories for me. I wrote a list of all the things needed for my journey and performance and verified if I had packed everything as per the list. When everything was satisfactory, I took bath, put on fresh night wear and went to bed. Indu had already cuddled Puper and they both were lying in the lower bunk. I kissed them both 'Good Night' with love and then climbed up to my bed. Soon sleep hovered over me and gave me complete peace.

52

The Nightmare

Puper was reluctant to send me and Indu to school. He wanted to come with us to school. I convinced him, "Puper we are not allowed to bring any animals to school. Moreover today is just a half working day and we will come in just three hours." He happily stood near our Mom and said, "OK Mummy! Come home soon." Indu complained, "Akka, I thought of taking Puper to school and show him to everyone. You know, everyone will like him and he will be a celebrity there. But you spoiled everything. I had brain washed him yesterday night that our school will be wonderful and his life is a total waste if he did not visit it." Now I understand why Puper had insisted to come with us. I stared angrily at Indu and she kept her mouth shut.

The whole morning we all had our practice and rehearsal. At noon the school was dispersed with some final instruction to the participants. I chatted with Raj, Diya and Bala for a while. Then I and Indu rushed home to see Puper. Puper jumped on to me as soon as he saw me. Mom served us delicious coconut rice and cauliflower fry. We three ate to our hearts content. We sat comfortably on the couch in the living room and began to watch the Cultural Fest that had started in the morning. It was being aired live. The stage and auditorium was very grand and the decorations were fabulous. India's best art directors had created an extraordinary magical world on stage. The lighting and sound system was excellent and highlighted the performance effectively. Puper was in Indu's lap. He was excited to see the programs and he kept on asking many questions to her. She answered him tirelessly and feeding him the information about the name and origin of the performers.

I felt a bit tired and sleepy and I lay back on the couch. The softness of the cushion was soothing my aching back. I closed my eyes a minute. Suddenly I felt that if was falling into some deep darkness. I was going down and down and felt that something was not right. I suddenly opened my eyes in fear. But who is this? I could see Gemma! Her eyes were filled with tears. What place is this? And I was taken aback by what I saw next. I saw my own face. It was puffed and red with tears flowing nonstop! Puper was lying on the floor in a corner and was bleeding! What has happened to Puper? I shouted his name very loudly, but no sound came out. Who is lying there? To my horror it was Abi Akka writhing in pain in a corner. I observed the room. It looked like the conference hall in SAPS.

Someone laughed very loudly, wildly and irritatingly. It was Dr. Malik! He shouted like a maniac, "I am Malik! The king of this whole world! I am unbeatable. I will live forever!" and he continued to laugh like a monster. He had something in his hand and he was about to put it into his mouth. I gathered some courage and wrestled with him trying to prevent him from putting that into his mouth. Gemma too joined to help me. Though he was aged and looked weak, he was unbelievably strong. Our efforts were futile when compared to his power. He shouted victoriously, "You can't stop me eating Navjavaanium!" and he swallowed what he had in his hand. I shouted, "NO! Nooooo…." Suddenly Dr. Malik exploded with an earsplitting 'Boom' sound and a scorching brightness. I felt pain of fire for a micro second. It was extremely hot and I was burning. Oh! No! We were dying. The explosion engulfed everything. It is over! Everything is over!

I woke up as someone was shaking me wildly and a familiar voice was calling my name. I opened my eyes with a shudder. I sat upright in a hurry and looked around in fear. I was soaked in my sweat and I was pale in shock. It was Diya. She shouted at me, "Bindu! Get up!

We have a flight to catch! You must get ready soon!" I breathed heavily and looked at her again. She was holding Puper in her arms and was dressed in a lemon yellow colour cotton tops and black jeans. She looked very fresh and the smell of her perfume filled the air pleasantly. Phew! It's just a dream! I was relieved that Puper was alive. I grabbed him rudely and checked if he was hurt. I dialed Abi Akka's cell number and it was switched off. I remembered that she would have sneaked out of Malik Towers and boarded her flight by this time. She will certainly call me as soon as she lands. And what about Gemma? When I am safe and sound here she is also sure to be safe. It is silly to worry about the safety and security at SAPS. Anyway, I decided to talk to Gemma with Aadhmi's permission. I let out a sigh of relief. Oh! Its all a dream! A silly dream! Diya looked at me suspiciously and asked, "Bindu, are you alright? Why do you behave in a peculiar way?" I shook my head and said, "Sorry Diya, I had a bad dream." She sat near me and held my hands with concern. She asked, "What did you see Bindu? Is anything wrong?" I let out a sigh of relief and said with a smile, "Everything is alright at present. Don't worry!"

I got ready in a jiffy. Aadhmi called me and said that he would come to pick up Puper as animals were not allowed in flights. We all were ready. As I had already packed my bag, I was chatting with Diya and Indu casually with Puper running around us and playing happily. We all had some coffee and snacks. Puper slurped his milk joyfully. Mom and Dad were busy giving a final check, if everything was packed up. When Aadhmi came to pick up Puper, I went out to send off Puper and before I could say anything about my dream, Aadhmi read my thoughts and said, "Don't worry about the safety of Gemma. She is comfortable at the SAPS. Professor had a talk with her today morning. Everything is perfect there. Let us wait and see if the situations turn adverse. Anyway we will be prepared for everything. Don't worry." It comforted me again and again and finally left saying, "Bindu, I will bring Puper in Sorna or Prapancha. Meet you today night at the Fest." I stood there watching them leave. I walked slowly and got into my Audi. I traced the steering with my fingers very gently. I took a deep breath to fill my lungs with the smell of the interior of my car. I had insisted that we go to the airport in my car because, that may even be my last chance to enjoy the pleasure of driving it. I know how I loved my car. I had dreamt and longed for my lovely car since I was in 6th grade. Though I had not asked my Dad openly for this he sensed that I had a desire for it. That's my Dad! He loves me that much! Dad had to save a lot to buy me this car and present it as a reward for my achievement in my 10th grade board exam. I got state rank and he was really happy about that. Since I got the key, I have never let anyone else drive it except my father. I have treated it as a part of me. I felt too close to it like a family member. I always had it sparkling clean and shiny. No one can point a scratch on it. I ran my palm smoothly over the dash board and seat.

Soon everyone filled in chatting happily and noisily and their enthusiasm was very infectious. The short drive to the airport was made memorable by our shouts of joy and loud singing. Diya was very happy to be with us. Her parents would join us tomorrow morning. As we neared the airport, I could see Raj, Bala, Ann, Priya, and Niranjana with their parents and most of our teachers. Soon we joined them. My Periyamma hugged me and Indu with affection. Bala kept on taking 'selfies' of himself in his mobile and as he neared me he said in a mocking tone, "Hai, Potato!" I rolled my eyes. Bala can never be tamed. He will always be the same. What fun does he have in teasing me? I wondered. I said in a very composed tone, "Hello, Bala!"

Raj also came near us. Bala exclaimed, "Potato, you are going to dance first. Be careful that you do not break the stage. I have already requested the organizers to make the stage double strong. They also promised me that the stage can withstand the weight of 4 elephants. But poor souls! They don't know about you!" I began to breathe heavily in anger as Raj turned his face in his attempt to control his laughter. Bala was motivated by Raj's act and continued with enthusiasm, "Raj, as we are going to be very close to the stage we must be very alert. We must watch out for the cracks as soon as she starts dancing. We must warn the gathering and save as many people as possible if she creates a tremor!" They both chuckled and I frowned at Raj. He instantaneously stopped laughing.

I warned Bala, "Bala, don't be silly! Be serious!" Bala just paid a deaf ear to me and said, "Raj! Call the ambulance. I am serious!" and he laughed at his own silly joke. Diya came to my rescue and said, "Bala, stop your silly game or I'll go ninja on you and beat you to a pulp!" He pretended to be afraid and hid behind Raj and commented, "Raj I am very much afraid of this Karate Kid. Save me from her!" They both laughed together and Diya said, "OK! This is the end. Don't blame me if you are to be hospitalized!" My Dad came near asking, "What? Who is to be hospitalized? Is everybody OK?" At once Diya managed, "Oh! Nothing uncle! We were just chatting simply" and laughed in a silly way. Bala and Raj showed innocent puppy dog faces. They knew very well that my Dad would never allow anyone to meddle with me even for fun!

When I was about to sit in my seat in the flight, Bala commented, "Bindu, don't come forward or move backward without any prior warning. The flight will tilt to one side if you move all of a sudden and the pilot will panic not knowing the reason for the turbulence. So maintain balance!" I raised my hand to slap him. He escaped quickly and laughed in a naughty way standing out of my reach. Diya held my hands warmly and pacified me. When we reached Nehru Stadium, I understood the true meaning of the word 'Marvelous' 'Grand' 'Fabulous' etc. The arrangements to receive the guests and give them a comfortable stay were perfect. As usual Ann pierced into our group and began to chat with Raj. He was also babbling and laughing as though he was in cloud nine. Ann waved to someone and blew a flying kiss. Why is she over reacting like this? Diya and I looked at each other and we passed understanding smiles.

Suddenly Ann shouted in excitement, "Oh! My God! Isn't he Prem? The winner of 'Voice of India'!" She began to jump with joy.

Diya looked at me and we both rolled our eyes. Indu pulled Ann and asked, "Why do you jump like this? Everyone is staring at you strangely?" Ann ignored Indu and continued with excitement, "I can't believe that I am meeting my dream icons!" Diya pointed at Prem. Almost all the performers who had come there were young celebrities in one field of arts or the other. Some were already world famous and some others were budding super stars.

Ann clung to my shoulders and shouted, "See! See! He is coming towards me! I can't believe my eyes!" Diya and I passed puzzled glances. Prem was smiling and moving forward towards us. He stood in front of us and said very casually, "Hello! I'm Prem." Diya and I have seen his performance in a reality show and other stages. But we did not know him personally. So we were confused and we gave a blank look thinking that he was talking to Ann. Ann giggled like a silly girl and said, "How cute he is! He looks more handsome!" Indu was not a fan of him and she just moved away. When I held Diya's hands to move he stood right in front of me and said, "Nice to meet you Bindu! I have read articles about you in many magazines. I also saw your interview. I am a great fan of you!"

Ann came right in between and shook his hands. She said happily, "Nice to meet you too Prem! I am Ann! Bindu's close friend! I am a great fan of you too! This is the first time I am seeing you in person and I am so excited about it!" Though he ignored her and looked at her impatiently, she kept on talking to him not allowing him a chance to open his mouth. I saw Aadhmi and Puper and I waved to Aadhmi happily. I started to move towards them. At once Prem pushed her force fully to one side and said in a hurry, "I'll see you later Bindu. You seem to be in a hurry. Meet you soon." Before I could say anything, Diya pulled me and we ran towards Puper.

Prem left the spot immediately and Ann joined us. She shouted turning back, "See you soon Prem!" and waved like a Hollywood heroine in a red carpet. Diya whispered to me, "I feel like dashing my head on a rock." We both chuckled. I lifted Puper and we began to walk. I glanced around to see where my Mom, Dad, Raj, Bala and his parents were. Indu was chatting with Niranjana happily. She looked very beautiful in her slim fit jeans and tops. Aadhmi said, "Everyone is safe and comfortable Bindu. I will watch them for you. You can be relaxed." I smiled at Aadhmi uneasily. Suddenly I saw Madhumitha in the crowd. She was a budding rock star and I had already met her in a talent show. She ran towards me and held my hands tightly. She said in a friendly way, "It's a long time since we met! How are you Bindu?" I said, "Nice to meet you Madhu! I am fine!" I introduced her to Diya and Puper too. She was really happy to listen to Puper speak. After exchanging pleasantries and chatting happily for a while she excused herself.

All our team members gathered together. Our IDs were checked and the rooms for our stay were allotted to us. We checked in; left our luggage there and came out to have dinner. Announcements boomed in the speakers periodically:

> **'Good evening everyone! Welcome to the International Cultural Youth Fest! Enjoy your stay and please call toll free number 666 in case of any discomforts. Delicious dinner is served at the nearest food court. The performers are requested to register their attendance at the nearest booth.'**

We all were walking as a huge team. Diya's eyes were searching Bala and she smiled as he ran and joined us. Suddenly Ann caught hold of Bala and said, "How long have I been searching you Bala? Why did you vanish suddenly from my sight?" Diya cursed under her breath. Raj was carrying Puper. I said to Puper in a low voice, "Puper, people are not used to animals talk. So don't speak in front of strangers." Puper nodded. We all had dinner and our parents asked, "Shall we go to our rooms and sleep?" Indu protested, "No way! We have come here to see all the programs and the performers. It's a life time opportunity to see all the world famous artists." I and Diya giggled as we knew well that Indu was eagerly waiting to meet her favourite boy band the Uni Direction. So we decided to go and watch the performances going on.

As we were walking to the auditorium, we saw many stars from all over the world. The whole area was filled with many foreign faces. Our parents were walking slowly and lagging behind us. Aadhmi was accompanying them. Suddenly Puper jumped from Raj and ran in the crowd. I ran behind him in a hurry and lifted him. When I stood up cuddling Puper, a tall boy with curly brown hair and green eyes was standing right in front of me. I said, "Sorry, excuse me" and I was about to move. He was looking at Puper very keenly. He said in a coarse raspy voice, "Hello! Kitten! What it your name? You are so cute!" and he tried to touch Puper. Puper sneered at him and attempted to scratch him with his paw. The boy smiled as Puper's attempt failed and his smile reminded me a guy from Uni Direction. I remembered his name as Steward.

He said with the same smile revealing his cute dimples on either side of his cheeks and said, "What a cute kitten you have got!" and again he tried to hold Puper. Puper opened his mouth wide to bite him. I was irritated by the boy's behaviour and I stared at him. He said, "Ok! Let me see you later" and walked away. I calmed down Puper by cuddling him. Puper asked, "Mummy, why is he calling me 'kitten'? Am I not a saber tooth tiger?" I kissed Puper and comforted saying, "Never mind such silly comments Puper!" The green eyed boy walked towards three other boys who were rolling with laughter and as he joined them, one of them punched him on his shoulders. A boy with blonde hair commented something and Steward shrugged when all others laughed again. I identified the trio as Liam, Richard and Michel. Puper asked again, "Are they laughing at me Mummy?" I tried to read their lip movement. But my vision was being disturbed by the passersby continuously and I answered him, "May be Puper. I am not sure."

As I was about to turn back another handsome boy with black hair groomed up in a quaff, walked towards them with a gorgeous smile. He was Zuil. Steward was still laughing like an idiot. Michel was cracking some jokes and others laughed very loudly. I decided to inform Indu about their presence here. As Zuil joined them, steward said something into his ears and at once he turned his head and stared at me. I suddenly heard Raj's voice. He came panting and said, "Bindu, we were searching for you everywhere." I went with him and joined everyone and before I could open my mouth, Indu shouted, "Akka, look there! It's Uni Direction!" Ann shrieked wildly like a maniac and ran towards them with her autograph note. Diya and Indu asked, "Shall we also go and meet them? We must get an autograph from Zuil!" I said, "If you want you can go. I am sorry. I am not interested in meeting them." They both shrugged their shoulders and ran towards the 5 singers happily.

Raj and Bala insisted, "Why not we join them?" I said with irritation, "Look at them. They are looking very much immature and behave like silly boys. See how they keep on laughing like cracks!" Bala said, "Hey Potato! Don't complain much. All of us behave like this when we hang around with our friends. There is nothing wrong in it. I am really happy that they enjoy their life always." He added fuel to my anger. So I said, "Actually, I just met this boy Steward and it was some sort of a clash." Raj exclaimed, "A clash! Why? And what for?" Puper narrated, "He tried to touch me without Mummy's permission and he called me a kitten! That silly boy paid no reaction to my infuriated response." Raj, Bala and I laughed at the way Puper was saying this. Raj chuckled and asked, "Really. Is it an offence to call you a kitten?" Puper pouted and said, "Mummy, is Raj too making fun of me? Do I look like a kitten?" I said with laughter, "No dear! You don't look exactly like a kitten. But as you are very young now you resemble a cat except for your small saber teeth on both sides. But they are not visible very much now. When you grow up you will be identified as a fearsome saber tooth tiger" and hugged him.

Indu and Diya got auto graph from all the five members and was talking happily with Zuil who was still staring at us. Ann was grinning widely and taking snaps with them. Raj said, "Let us move Bindu. I'll call them and come." Raj moved towards them. Bala asked me, "Is there any message from Abi?" I convinced him, "She may call us any time Bala." Even I was worried a bit about her. But I dared not to reveal it to Bala. Soon Indu and Diya joined us. Ann was still not satisfied with the photo session. Indu said, "Akka, Zuil asked me who you were!" I asked, "What did you tell him?" She giggled in a funny way and said, "I told him that you were my sister. Then he enquired more details about you. I just said your name and Liam identified you as the assistant of the world famous scientist Ramanujam. Zuil was interested to know what you were going to perform tomorrow. I said that you were going to dance!"

I was very much irritated that she had conveyed this much information to them. Above all, she began to see me and chuckle. I was really annoyed and asked, "Indu! What is there to laugh like this? Are you infected by their silly laughter?" She giggled uncontrollably as she said, "Mmm...Nothing! I'll tell you later." I was puzzled and I turned to see the boys. They were still seeing us and laughing like lunatics. Zuil was literally staring at me. I raised my left eyebrows up and gave a stare back. He turned his face and smiled as the other boys mocked him. Ann was now getting auto graph from a ramp walk model named Milton. When we began to walk, she ran and joined us.

Puper asked me secretly, "Mummy, is Ann crazy? Why is she running behind everyone laughing wildly?" I just smiled, but did not answer him. Diya got Puper from me and our parents too joined us. Soon we walked into the open auditorium. It was filled with heads. We occupied the vacant seats and enjoyed the events. Soon Puper began to sleep and droop. When it was past mid night our Principal's text message warned us, "We have our performance tomorrow. I don't want you to be dull and sleepy when you are on stage. Already, we have not got any time for practice on stage here. You people are going to perform directly on stage. So it is better if you all have some sleep and rest. All the participants must be ready by 5am tomorrow morning. You can come from your rooms to the auditorium in vehicles shuttling to and fro. Good night." So we all returned to our rooms in a cozy mini-bus and went to bed calling it a day.

53

Performance On The Stage

Our program was to be staged at 6am in the morning. I was ready in my full Bharatha Natyam costume by 4am. Diya, my dance teacher Mrs. Saroja and all our team of musicians were also ready. We all had some hot tea and biscuits. Aadhmi alerted everybody to be ready. Indu was dressed in a new sandal colour maxi with full sleeves. It had bright stripes and sheer panels. It was paired with a comfy palazzo pants in dark brown colour. She looked like a ramp show model in that costume. Both Raj and Bala were wearing cowl neck sweaters. But Bala had a shawl around his neck while Raj had a soft knit jacket over that. They had chosen bright colours to match up with Ann's grand printed pajamas with kurtis in fun prints. The trio looked more alert as it was going to be their moment. Aadhmi said victoriously, "Puper, as all others are going to be very busy today, you have to hang out with me." Puper was very much excited to see the huss and fuss of everyone getting ready and he said, "With pleasure uncle!" He kept on running here and there watching the different costumes and make ups.

We all came to the auditorium in a shuttle and we were organized as per the order of the performance. The setting was historic and the arrangements were a mix of the modern and the tradition style. My team was taken behind the stage with Raj, Ann and Bala as we were the first to perform. Soon Indu and her class mates followed. In 10 minutes the performers of the first 10 events were assembled behind the stage. Our parents and Principal took their seats in front of the stage. Our teachers were with us to help us in case of any needs. The arena was filled with the enthusiastic cheers of the audience. Diya held my hands. They were wet and cold like ice. She said, "Oh! I feel a bit tensed." Though I too had the same feeling I comforted her, "You are singing wonderfully Diya. Don't panic. Keep going." Indu was very cool and she said with confidence, "I am going to rock the stage today. May be my favourite boy band may even choose me to join them listening to my voice." She spread out an aroma of courage and confidence and that cooled everyone a bit.

I prayed Lord Shiva the God of dance and put on my 'Chalangai' when it was time for me to go on stage. Raj, Ann and Bala had already started their magic of words filled with fun and facts. Their comments silenced the audience and I felt a rush of adrenalin. Mrs. Saroja, Diya and the musicians were already seated in front of the mikes in the side stage. I walked to the centre of the huge main stage. The curtains were down. Ann gave an intro about me and the theme of the performance. Her voice stopped and the screen lifted up revealing the huge audience. I could see Dad, Mom, Periyappa and Periyamma sitting in the front rows to cheer us. They waved happily to me. Suddenly my eyes rested on someone in a bright blue silk saree and my heart beat stopped. It was the world famous Bharatha Natyam dancer 'Radha Nandagi.'

Oh! My God! Am I going to dance in front of her now? I have been worshipping her as my Guru! But have never got the chance to meet her. I felt goose bumps by the mere sight of her. She was my idol and I decided to show my dance skill and impress her. I wanted to win her heart. As soon as the song was played I got immersed in it. I concentrated and performed each move as perfect as possible. I did not miss a beat. I expressed all the 'Navarasa'- the 9 emotions in an impeccable manner. I got involved in the song and its meaning and I made the audience feel the same and enjoy the inner happiness of art. I felt an eternal bliss when the song came to an end. When I bowed to the audience, the applause was deafening that I couldn't listen to the comment given by Raj in praise of my performance. Mom was wiping her tears.

The curtains fell down and I retreated back. Raj showed a 'Thumps up' sign as he was on the other side of the stage. Bala blocked me and said cheerfully, "Hey Potato! Congrats! You managed to capture the audience without cracking the stage. Excellent start for our performance! See how our Principal is jumping in joy!" I laughed and ran down. Mrs. Saroja touched my head and said, "You have brought laurels to me and our school. Excellent performance dear! Keep it up!" I thanked her and touched her feet to seek her blessing. Diya hugged me and I congratulated her performance. We held each other for a while. The next program was Indu's song and we decided to go out and be seated in front of the stage to watch her.

We came our holding our hands together. Seeing us, Mom and Dad waved to us showing the two vacant seats near them. Actually, Puper and Aadhmi who had been sitting there had come out to receive us. "Your dance was awesome! You mesmerised the audience and gave them a divine experience. Professor and President were really proud to see your performance!" Aadhmi said pointing to the VIP gallery with complete bullet proof shield. I said whole heartedly, "Thank you for your compliments Aadhmi" Aadhmi shook Diya's hands and said, "You have a sweet voice Diya. Your voice filled with emotions was very supportive to Bindu's performance." She said, "Really! Thank you! I am really happy that I managed the show!" Puper jumped from Aadhmi to me and said lovingly, "Mummy! Why did you cry and laugh on the stage. Your movements reminded me a peacock sometimes and a deer sometimes. How is possible for you to change your face expressions like that? I couldn't take my eyes off you. You looked very beautiful." I hugged him happily. He complained, "Mummy! Your jewels are pricking me. How do you put on such heavy ornaments and dance too?" I laughed and said, "I don't feel them heavy. In fact I feel very majestic when I put on them." Puper jumped back to Aadhmi.

I approached my favourite dancer Radha Nandagi and bowed down with devotion to touch her feet and get her blessings. She who was watching me without taking her eyes off me was taken aback and she lifted me at once. She held my hands and observed me from head to toe and said in an emotion filled voice, "I know that you are an aspiring scientist. But never imagined that you would have this much love and dedication to this divine art form. I even wondered why they had given you a chance here. But you have given me the pleasure of enjoying a wonderful performance after a long time! You remind me of my early days! Your involvement has melted my heart! God bless you my child!" I couldn't believe my ears. I controlled the tears of joy and said "Thank you for your blessings Madam. You are my role model since my child hood. I have always wanted to imitate you and your style of dancing. It is a great pleasure that I have met you today and received your blessings." She again blessed, "May Lord Shiva bless you grow more and more in the art of dance."

As Bala's voice gave an intro about the following event, Indu took the stage and we quickly seated ourselves in the empty seats. Aadhmi brought a chair and sat near me with Puper in its lap. It asked, "Bindu, how do you impress all the people you meet? That lady was really moved by your performance and do you know what she felt?" I gave it a puzzled look. It answered, "She wanted you to be her daughter! She wished you to be her heir!" I laughed mildly and said, "Though I could impress everyone, I could never impress you and Bala. You both always tease me or irritate me!" Aadhmi replied, "We both are actually playing with you and enjoy it as a fun. Moreover I cannot mess around with Professor Ramanujam like that. I understood most of the emotions like anger, mischief, fun, laughter and disappointment only from my encounters with you!" I gave an angry look to Aadhmi and laughed at once.

Soon Indu's voice captured the audience and she was really a rock star on stage. Her cool body language, synchronization with her troupe and attitude to make the audience join her had a wonderful effect and the whole auditorium was dancing and singing with her. Everyone forgot everything except the foot-tapping rhythm of her song. Music rang out clear into the dawn by the perfect composing of the 32-piece orchestra that accompanied her voice. Her charisma radiated energy to her companions as well as the audience and made everyone vibrate with joy. She got a standing ovation when she stopped and the audience clapped for quite a long time even after she came down the stage.

My mother was wiping off her tears. I was filled with emotions and I had no hesitation to run and hug Indu. She kept on asking, "Was it good? Was it good?" I laughed with tears and said, "You rocked the stage by your amazing performance!" Everyone appreciated Indu and I experienced and understood how my mother feels when I am celebrated by others. Ann's voice reverberated, "Congrats Indu! Your performance was mind blowing!" Raj's voice followed hers and the trio presented all the events continuously without a flaw keeping the audience attention glued to the stage. Our school gave a wide variety. The programs included latest rap and pop to age old Tamil traditional and cultural dances. Our school completed the given 3 hour schedule successfully. It was really awesome to enjoy the event with lakhs of other audience.

It was 9am and our Principal was in cloud nine as our school performance was a great success. He appreciated all the performers again and again. He insisted that all our school students should go and have their breakfast and then enjoy the other programs throughout the day. Some students decided not to move out but manage with the snacks available there. Some of us decided to go and change our costumes and then return after breakfast. There was a small break for the next team to take the stage. So we began to walk out to the shuttling vehicle stops as a huge team. All the performers and teachers were chatting noisily and sharing their excitement about the success of their programs. I noticed the boys from Uni Direction at a distance seated among the audience, tickling one another and laughing. They all were drinking some energy drink from tin cans. Zuil suddenly saw me and gave a weak friendly smile. Thank God!

He has stopped staring at me. There is nothing wrong in a smile. So I just smiled back. His smile broadened adding more charm to his face. We continued walking. Diya whispered in my ears, "Bindu! Steward is coming towards us!" I slightly turned my head. I could see the four other boys still laughing and playing while Steward was in a hurry to reach us. Puper shouted from Aadhmi's hands, "Mummy, that crazy curly hair boy is coming!" I kept my index finger in my lips and said, "Shhh!...". Aadhmi said, "There is no use in running Bindu. He is coming to meet you. He is determined. It is better you talk to him." Steward ran and overtook us. He stood blocking our path and said, "Hello! Nice to meet you again!" and his smile widened from his left ear to the right. That again revealed the cute dimples in his cheeks.

He saw Diya and said, "So Diya and Bindu are friends?" I just nodded. Diya said joyfully, "I met you just once yesterday. It is so nice that you remember my name!" He laughed and shook hands with her. Then turned to me and said, "I surfed in the net about you after meeting your sister Indu yesterday. Hmm.. we got some interesting facts about you!" I did not react. He continued, "You look so different in this costume, accessories and make up. You are very different from yesterday. We couldn't identify if it were you. Your eyes look so beautiful with this make up on." Diya answered, "This is the traditional dance form of India. It must be performed with such costume, make up and jewels. It's me who sang the song when she danced!" He said appreciatively, "Yes! We noticed and identified your voice from the other female voice. You were awesome. The combination was heavenly!"

Though it was a bit embarrassing, I gathered courage and asked, "Did you see my sister's performance? She is a great fan of your band and she even wants to join your team." He laughed and said, "I know that Indu is a fan of us. But do you like Uni Direction?" I thought for a split second and answered, "I am not a great fan of your band like Indu or Diya. But I listen to and enjoy your songs too." He said triumphantly, "Wow! I have finally made Bindu Thirupathi open up after my perpetual attempts! I thought you were an impolite, unfriendly, serious type girl when I failed in my attempts to converse with you yesterday night." Diya said, "Of course, she is a very serious type girl. No one can get into her closer circle just like that. I will beat you into a pulp if you mess up with her!" We all laughed loudly and I could see Zuil staring at Steward as though he was a rival. Why does he always stare at people? His eyes met mine and at once he smiled sweetly. I turned my head quickly.

Steward asked with a beautiful smile, "Why did you not talk with me yesterday?" I pointed to Puper and said, "You were trying to mess with Puper." He exclaimed, "Oh! Your kitten's name is Puper! He is so cute! I love kittens and I thought that they liked me too!" Raj and Bala had walked front and they signaled me impatiently. So I said, "Steward, my family and friends are waiting for us and we have to join them. So if you could excuse us we could carry on." He said, "Oh! Sorry! Let's meet later. Don't miss our performance. It is at 3.00pm." Diya shouted turning back, "Sure! We will be in the front row to cheer up!" and we ran quickly to join our members. Diya giggled and said in a low voice, "Bindu! I think this Steward is flirting you!" I said, "Shut up Diya" though I was trying hard to control my smile. Puper asked, "Mummy! What is flirting?" I stared at Diya and she kept her hands on her head and bit her tongue. I scolded in a low voice, "Diya, what am I to tell this innocent cub? I am not going to answer him! You give him the explanation!"

Diya started with hesitation and was choosing the words, "It is hmm…. Mm… flirting means… it means a boy or a girl talking sweetly to one another!" and breathed heavily. I frowned at her and she gave me a 'forgive me' look. Thank God! Puper did not ask for any more details. We joined Raj and Bala and we all began to appreciate the performances of one another. Raj was praising my dress and make up and suddenly Puper intervened, "Raj! Why are you flirting with Mummy?" Diya slapped herself on her forehead and Raj gave a bewildered look at Puper. We all gave out a roar of laughter and then

I said, "Puper, Raj is my friend. We know each other since we were small kids. He is not flirting with me now. He is just appreciating me as you or Diya would do." Puper still gave a confused look and asked, "Mummy, then is Ann flirting with Bala?" We all roared into laughter again and Diya said, "Never in a million years!" She said in a warning tone to Bala, "Bala! Don't ever dream of that!" This made us all burst out laughing again. Bala came to me and said, "See! Now we are also laughing in a silly way and does that mean that we are immature or stupid?" I gave him an understanding look and signaled him to close his mouth. He shrugged his shoulders and continued walking. Aadhmi came to Diya and said vey calmly, "I still don't get the meaning of that word!" and this made us roll with laughter. Puper and Aadhmi gave an innocent look and we had to struggle hard to control our laughter.

We got into a vehicle and came to our rooms. I changed to a pink colour cotton chudi; packed my dance costume and jewels neatly; removed my make-up and got ready quickly. Everyone was eager to watch the other programs and we had a quick breakfast and rushed back to the auditorium. When we entered in, a Korean rock band was playing and the audiences were wild with enthusiasm. We were too happy to join them. Following them a group of dancers from Russia took the stage. They enchanted the crowd by their fabulous performance. I wondered how the Russian girls bent and stretched like rubber. The dance was a combination of ballet and gymnastics. Then we enjoyed the Thailand traditional dance by a team of 150 performers who were dressed very beautifully in bright colours. The theme of the dance was the battle between two ancient kings. The most amazing thing was that at the end of the dance, all of a sudden 4 elephants also joined them on stage to our surprise. I looked at Bala with wide eyes. Did he really enquire the organizers about the strength of the stage? I looked at him suspiciously. I thought that he was just making fun and playing pranks on me! He winked mischievously and shouted, "Hey Potato, now I understand why the organizers said that the stage could bear the weight of 4 elephants and now it is clear why there was no tremor when you danced." We laughed happily though he was teasing me. But it is still unbelievable!

I tried Abi Akka's number now and then and it was not reachable. I wondered what she might be doing. At about 3pm the British boy band Uni Direction filled the stage with their team and the female audience particularly young girls from all nations became very wild with enthusiasm. Nothing could stop them from running towards the stage. The boy band was very unique and the whole auditorium was singing and dancing with them as though they had cast a spell. They were very casual on stage and everyone was impressed by their performance. Ann, Diya, Indu and even Puper were singing along and enjoying to the core. They had the crowd under their spell for half an hour and still all young girls there wanted them to perform more. Their charm was irresistible. I understood why girls were crazy over them. The volunteers and the security personals had to spend quite a lot of time to bring order again.

Finally they left the stage and the next event was by some school children from Japan. Nearly hundred children were on the stage. They were in their traditional Kimonos and a very different soothing music began to ease the audience. Soon there was pin drop silence among the audience and the magic of melody spread all around. All younger generation who had behaved wild just a moment before were like statues losing their mind to the sweetness of the music and the gentle dance movements. That was followed by a program by South African performers. Our concentration was focused on the stage. Suddenly I heard someone whisper near my ears in a hoarse raspy voice, "Thanks for watching our program. Did you enjoy our song?" I was startled and I turned back to see Steward smiling widely. He casually pulled a chair and seated himself near me. I smiled back and said, "Did you not see the girls go crazy during your concert as usual? Your program was awesome! You reach the audience and touch their heart by your voice. Each and everyone in your band are unique and that adds to its glamour!" He looked satisfied and said, "Thank you for your compliment! That will make all my boys happy!" Noticing Steward, Ann who was seated a few rows behind with her usual gang of slaves, ran and joined us. She shook his hands enthusiastically and shouted, "Wow! You were fabulous on stage! I kept on dancing with you guys throughout your program. Did you notice me? I even came near the stage and clapped hands!" He smiled uneasily at her and said, "Thank you for going crazy!" I and Diya laughed while Ann blinked wondering if it was really a compliment or not.

Then he turned to me. He looked a bit nervous and asked with hesitation, "Would you like to join us for lunch?" Ann shouted enthusiastically, "Of course! It's a pleasure! Shall we move out now?" Diya pinched me secretly and asked with her eyes if we could say 'yes'. I stared at her and she put her head down at once. I said very calmly, "Sorry Steward, we have come here as a big team and we can't leave them and join you. Any way thanks for asking." He laughed weakly with disappointment and said as though talking to himself, "I already said it would happen so" and shrugged his shoulders putting his hands into his pocket. Ann offered, "May be I can join you! I have no commitments now!" Steward just ignored her and walked off. I let out a sigh of relief. "Phoo!" Diya said, "What is wrong in a lunch on?" I stamped her foot hard and she shouted, "Ouch! I said so because your sister will be really happy" and rubbed her feet.

We had lunch with our parents and friends in a food court. The buffet had a wide variety of dishes that could satisfy the guests from all parts of the world. Though lunch time had passed long back all dishes were available sufficiently for all the visitors. Puper enjoyed waffles and pancakes to his heart's content. After lunch we came back to the auditorium and our eyes widened as the whole atmosphere had turned heavenly due to the lightings and the changes in the stage set up. The pleasant evening weather added to the magnificence of the fiesta. We took seats near the entrance as the auditorium was fully occupied. Aadhmi found some vacant place and took our parents,

Ann, Indu and some of our teachers to the front. We continued to enjoy the celebration. But though I was physically present there, my mind was not on the stage. The cheers of the crowd and the merry of the surrounding had no impact on me. I was restless as I was thinking about Abi Akka. Time passed on. But I had an uneasy feeling that something was not right. Aadhmi came towards me with Puper and said, "What is disturbing you Bindu? Did you have any vision again?" I looked at it nervously but did not know what to say. Aadhmi sat near me and said, "Well, let me go in search of your sister to Malik Towers. It will be just a matter of a few minutes with Prapancha at our service." I felt that it was the best idea.

54

Malik's Malice

But suddenly my phone rang. It was Abi Akka! I shouted in excitement and joy, "Hello! Abi Akka! Where are you? Are you fine?" But I couldn't hear any sound from the other side. I started to run out of the auditorium to escape the noise there. Seeing the panic on my face Raj came running behind me. Still there was no response from the other side. I looked puzzled at the phone. Is anything wrong? I switched on the speaker so that we both could listen properly. Except some breathing sound there was no other sound for a while. Without disconnecting we kept running. Bala, Diya, Aadhmi and Puper were also behind us. We came far away from the auditorium and sat inside an empty shuttling vehicle so that we could hear properly without any disturbance.

Suddenly we heard a slap sound. Then we heard Dr.Malik's voice. It seemed really angry and it shouted," How dare you?" Then another slap sound. I froze in shock. What is going on there? I felt my stomach churn. Then I heard Abi Akka's loud scream. Tears rolled down my eyes even before I knew. I heard Malik yelling to someone, "Can't you idiots take care of a girl whose hands and legs are tied and who is gagged? Idiots! She has cut loose her knots and called her sister as though she could save her! Don't you idiots have the brain to at least snatch away the cell phone when you take someone hostage? You useless fools!" I heard a few gun shots. My heart beat stopped. Finally Dr.Malik's arrogant voice said, "Hello! Bindu! Eagerly waiting to see your sister?"

What I had feared has happened at last. Dr.Malik has caught Abi Akka! I could feel tears rolling down my cheeks. God! How am I going to help her? Anger was burning inside me. I clenched my fists. I just wanted to yell at the top of my voice. I will do anything to save Abi Akka from him. I love Abi Akka so much and I can't let anyone hurt her. Bala was in terrible shock and pain. Aadhmi signaled me to control myself and continue to talk.

Dr. Malik continued with a mocking laughter, "Too shocked to talk!" Though I was frightened to the core, I remembered Aadhmi's words and controlled myself. I cannot let Malik know that I feel weak or hurt. What I need is patience and clear thinking. So, controlled my sob and said in a scornful tone," Hello! Dr.Malik, it is really nice to hear your voice!" He was really shocked by my undisturbed tone and he said in a surprised manner, "Oh! I too am happy to listen to your voice. But I think it is the time for you to feel sad and mourn because I have got your precious sister who was helping you from my regime. She had been under my custody since yesterday! Sounds quite interesting! Isn't it?" I felt helpless and anger soared high inside. I wanted to shout 'You rascal! I will kill you if you hurt my sister. I will even make my son Puper rip off your dumb ears from your ugly face!' But I let no word slip out of my mouth.

He again said in a puzzled tone, "Is Abi your real sister or not? Aren't you worried about your sister? I said that I have your sister in my custody! "Raj stood still not knowing what to do. I kept my voice strong and steady and said, "Oh! What a horrifying news! I am really shocked and my heart aches in pain. Are you happy now? Well! Jokes apart, what do you want now?" My behaviour irritated him and he said in a frustrated tone, "What! What do I want? I have captured your sister, and here is another good news that could make you more happy! My team has got Navjavaanium for me and they have reached back gravity! All my waiting is going to come to an end in just a few hours! I will become the king of the world! Malik will be immortal and young forever! Yeah……..!" His sound echoed in my ears.

I said in a scornful tone, "You have got what you need. What have you got to do with my sister? Just keep your filthy hands off her. Release her you wicked monster!" He laughed loudly again like a maniac, "Never my dear! You don't know the pleasure and thrill I have when I kill someone! But I will not kill your sister now. I have another important work now. Still your sister will see the worst as she had dared to act against me." I shouted, "You can't get away with it Malik! Navjavaanium will destroy the earth along with you. What you think as your boon may become a bane!" He yelled back, "Do you think that I am an idiot to believe your stories? I know what to do!" I shouted again, "What do you want me to do to get back Abi?" But the line went dead.

The tears I had fought back burst out forcefully with sobs and Puper tried to console me, "Mummy! Don't cry Mummy!" He too began to shed tears. I lifted him and hugged him. Diya held my shoulders tightly and comforted me. But I felt helpless. Raj took my hands in his and sat right in front of me. He held my hands firmly and said in a comforting tone, "Bindu, there will be a way out for all the mazes. We can surely save Abi. But first of all we must know where she is. Will she be in Malik Towers now?" I shook my head and said, "I am not sure of it." He wiped my tears. Bala snatched my phone and tried Abi Akka's number. Her cell was switched off. He tried again using his cell phone and the result was the same. He thought for a second and said in a confused tone, "How can we save her if we don't know where she is?" Raj said with confidence, "Aadhmi you can find anything and everything. You can surely help us." Aadhmi said helplessly, "I have no link with Abi by any means. May be I can go to Malik Towers and search her as I planned earlier." Bala said impatiently, "I don't think that there is time for that. What if Malik is not at all there?" Raj said comfortingly, "We have no other go. So let us at least start our search from there."

I said with much hesitation, "Aadhmi, I had a dream that Dr. Malik was hurting Abi Akka and Gemma in the SAPS. I even saw myself and Puper in my dream. Is there any possibility of Malik capturing the SAPS?" Aadhmi replied at once, "Let me check with Gemma then." It took out a SAT phone from its back pack and within a few seconds Gemma was on the line. We were disappointed to know that everything was in order there and there had been no unexpected visitors. We all began to consider the next possibility.

Suddenly I remembered something and my eyes widened. I shook Bala and shouted, "Bala! Our gift! Our gift! Do you remember our gift?" He gave me a puzzled look and shot back, "Have you gone crazy? We are worried about Abi and you are talking about some gift! What is it you are babbling?" I wiped my tears and spoke in a clear voice, "Do you remember the platinum chain and pendant we gifted Abi Akka on her birthday." Bala said slowly, "Yes, letter A for Abi embedded with three diamonds for Bala, Bindu and Indu. What is so special about it?" I turned to Aadhmi and said, "Aadhmi I just installed the micro GPS tracker that Professor presented me, on that pendant. Can you track her using your sensor?" Aadhmi became active and it said, "Of course! It is always possible. It displayed a virtual map of the world on the wall of the vehicle and said, "Just give me a few minutes to identify the code of the GPS tracker that was given to Bindu." It opened its palm and worked on a small panel concealed inside. Everyone looked at Aadhmi with tension and there was dead silence in the vehicle.

After 5minutes, a red dot appeared on the map and we were shocked to find the location of the dot. The red dot blinked not from Malik Towers in London, but it was near Ramanujam Valley. Why has Malik brought Abi to RV? What is he doing there? Who else is with him? Aadhmi said, "He could not enter RV. See the dot. It is not inside RV. If he had entered into RV I would have already known it." But to our surprise the dot entered RV right in front of our eyes and Aadhmi exclaimed aloud, "What has happened to the security systems? How could he breach the security checks? Something is terribly wrong. I'll meet Professor and come back. Can you all just wait here?"

We all were completely confused and we nodded without knowing what to do. Bala said, "Bindu, Diya, I think it would be better if you both take Puper with you and join our parents so that you can be safe with them. Raj and I will go with Aadhmi to RV and bring back Abi safely." Raj nodded his head eagerly, accepting Bala's idea. But I and Diya shouted simultaneously, "No way! We are going to RV whether you accompany us or not!" Raj and Bala were shocked to see our response. Puper added, "Mummy, I am not going anywhere leaving you." Now it was my turn to be shocked. But I had no regrets over Puper's decision.

Aadhmi returned within 5 minutes and it said, "I suspected something and that is right. Professor Ramanujam had received a call and he had excused himself from our President saying that it was an emergency. I believe that he must also be with Dr. Malik with or without his consent. The security system can be controlled only by me and Professor. So I am sure that Professor is also with Malik." We were shocked to hear this and Diya asked, "How is it possible for Professor to go there so quickly? Why did he go there?" Raj said quickly, "Don't you remember that it is possible to travel fast and invisible using a Sorna or a Prapancha? Professor need not wait for a flight or train." Diya bit her tongue and nodded her head. Bala asked, "But why should he go all of a sudden to RV even without informing Aadhmi?"

Aadhmi said, "He must be threatened or blackmailed by Malik. Anyway we have to save Abi and Professor. I have informed all your parents that you are safe with me and professor. I have asked them to enjoy the Fest without worrying about you. I said them that Professor has invited you all to stay with him at the VIP's residence and enjoy the events with him as your performance is over. I think they believed me. And even if they are not convinced I am not going to worry about that now. Come on let's move." It took the cube from its back pack and set up Sorna in a minute. Raj sat beside Aadhmi in the front seat with Puper in his lap. I, Bala and Diya occupied the back seats. Sorna switched to invisibility mode and began to soar high.

I asked Aadhmi, "Is there any other hardware of you in RV to help Professor?" Aadhmi replied, "No Bindu. As Professor said, all the robots, ST-bots, Prapancha and Suethae have been sent to all countries to manage the catastrophe. RV is completely empty now." Diya touched my hands and said, "Don't lose hope. Everything will be OK! We must be happy that Abi Akka had tried to convey the message that she is in danger. If not we won't know it even now! It is better late than never." I gave her a faint smile and closed my eyes. Is my dream becoming real again? Will I lose Puper or any of my beloved ones? Though I felt very strong with my close ones with me I also was worried about their safety.

55

RV Under Attack

Soon we reached RV and the mere sight of it from outside gave us a blow. My heart beat rose as I saw the constructions and the forest area burning here and there and it seemed as though an uncontrollable riot had broken out there. Professor's residence was plundered and there was no one around. All the lights were on in the research lab and production lab as though some work was going on there. Many men in black uniform were guarding around the lab and some were also moving here and there doing all sorts of destruction at their will. Aadhmi signaled us to follow him quietly and he sneaked in carefully expecting sudden attackers. All the artifacts in Professor's house were destroyed and the construction was demolished. The melodious Krishna Fountain that I love very much was shattered into pieces. The cars in the gallery were beaten and broken. They were deformed irregularly. Aadhmi showed us the whole virtual map of RV to estimate the number of thugs accompanying Dr. Malik. It seemed that Dr. Malik had come in with a huge team. Hundreds of men were scattered around the lab, the library and even the observatory. Some were inside the lab and Aadhmi said, "I'll go and distract these ruffians first. When I manage them you have to sneak in and save Professor and Abi. Be careful! It seems that Abi is inside the lab. So Malik should also be inside. I still can't read Professor's thoughts. May be he is unconscious. I will clear out these 'men in black' and then come in." We nodded enthusiastically. Before leaving Aadhmi handed its back pack to me and said, "Bindu, you may need an item from this bag in time of an emergency. Just remember to take that item and use it when it is actually needed. I designed this item after our visit to the Malik Towers. Now I have no time to explain anything." And it ran forward. Though we were puzzled we were not relaxed enough to see what was inside. Diya got the bag and put it in her shoulders.

We hid behind trees in the dark and waited for the right time to enter into the lab. Puper understood the situation very well and just followed our actions without being instructed. Aadhmi walked majestically towards the lab and stood in front of the guards. We heard a lot of gun shots. But the bullets hit its body and shot back as though they had hit something impenetrable. Aadhmi ran fast towards the production lab and all the guards followed it. We sneaked in at once and moved very carefully. All the equipments in the lab were shattered to pieces. We watched our steps carefully and moved forward. Suddenly 4men came running towards us shooting with guns at random. We hid behind the tables. They neared us and Puper sprang on them suddenly. Raj and Bala kicked away their guns and I ran forward pulling Diya. Diya gave a karate kick and cut to one of them. He fell down and began to moan in pain. We heard many more footsteps. So we did not stand there and began to move forward in search of Professor and Abi Akka.

The research room with the board 'Secret Research' which used to be closed always was ajar and we heard Abi Akka's loud scream from there. We rushed in. Professor Ramanujam and Abi Akka were lying on the floor with their arms and legs tied up. Their face was swollen and bleeding. There were burn marks here and there in their arms and legs. The watch dog 'Elsa' was standing facing them with her back to us. Diya signaled me that she would take care of her and I lifted a steel lab stool and was ready to hit the watch dog. We moved quickly and I hit her hard with the stool. But the stool hit her and fell away as though it had dashed it over a rock. The watch dog turned back slowly as though a ball had hit her. What is this? My attack had no impact on her! Diya jumped over and kicked Elsa in her stomach. But the watch dog stood steady and Diya was writhing in pain! I ran behind and held her tight. The moment I touched her, I removed my hands instantaneously due to reflex action as it felt as though I had touched a boiling hot pot. My hands were burning. I looked at her from head to toe in wonder. What is she? Why is her body so hot like this? She laughed wickedly and asked in a husky voice, "Am I not hot? I am a hot chick! Aren't I?"

I moved away and shouted, "Diya she must be a mutant. Her body temperature is extremely high. Stay away from her." Diya's eyes widened and she at once began to rummage the back pack Aadhmi had given her. Elsa began to walk towards me laughing like a maniac and her arms outstretched as though she was going to hug me. She said proudly, "You are right Bindu! I am a mutant and my ability is to generate heat whenever I wish. Do you want a friendly hug from me?" I started to run here and there to save myself from the unbearable pain. I was expecting some help from Diya. But she was trying on some crazy white dress she had taken from the back pack. Without thinking I shouted in panic, "Diya where do you think we are? We are not in a boutique! We are in the middle of a fight! Stop trying that dress. Do something and save me!" She ignored my cry and put on that suit. The dress covered her completely from head to toe except for the eyes.

Elsa said, "I hate this 'catch me if you can!' game of you Bindu. Let us end it now!" She had come closer to me and when she was about to touch me, Diya came in between us and she gave a heavy blow on her neck. Elsa shouted in pain and tumbled down. She looked at Diya unbelievably. Diya winked at me and said, "It's thermo proof. I remembered Aadhmi's instructions!" The watch dog managed to get up and Diya ran in time to give her a kick. Diya began to shower nonstop blows on Elsa. I ran to Professor and removed his knots. He was too weak and tired to move. I helped Abi Akka and she hugged me tightly and said, "I knew you would come to save us Bindu!" We both lifted Professor gently and made him sit on a chair and wiped the blood on his face. I gave him a glass of water to drink. Abi Akka said in a hurry, "Bindu, Dr. Malik is inside this locker room searching the results of some secret research Professor Ramanujam had done already. Let us get out of here before he comes back."

We decided to hold Professor's shoulders and walk him out. But he stopped me and said, "Bindu, I must hand over something very important to you. Malik is searching this inside. He doesn't know that I have it here. He took out a small golden egg from his coat pocket and handed it to me. Keep it safe. Aadhmi will help you out about this later." I just got it and stuffed it into my jeans pocket. We were about to walk out lifting him. "You can't leave in a hurry like this without bidding farewell to me Ram!" came Dr. Malik's voice from behind. We three froze like statues. He came in front of us and slapped Abi Akka hard. She fell down and Professor also stumbled to one side. Suddenly Puper rushed in and he sprang on Malik from behind. He held on to his shoulders and bit his left ear. Malik shouted in pain and he fell down struggling to pull away Puper. Suddenly an ear piercing scream came from Puper and he was thrown away by Malik. Puper hit the wall and fell down like a rug doll. I ran to him with my heart thumping hard; lifted him to my lap and turned him. I burst out crying seeing the blood gushing from a cut in his stomach. Tear drops fell down my cheeks and dripped on Puper. With much difficulty he opened his eyes and then closed them slowly without another word from his mouth. "Aaahh! Nooo!… Puper!" I cried so loud that the building would crack. I took a huge piece of granite slab that was lying near and I ran to Malik ferociously. His face was soaked in blood on the left side and a piece of his left ear was lying down. I began to smack him with uncontrollable anger. I hit him again and again on his head and his attempts to save himself failed. I stopped only when there was no more movement in him. I kicked away the dagger that was held in his hand. I took the gun which was in his pocket. Professor began to walk to the door holding on to Abi Akka. Diya and the watch dog were still fighting. The watch dog was strangling

Diya's neck and Diya was gasping for breath like a fish out of water. Her eye balls were protruding out and it seemed that she was losing the battle. In order to save her I shot the watch dog without hesitation.

A bullet pierced her back. She turned back staring at me and began to walk towards me like a zombie. I shot her again and this time it hit her forehead. But still she continued to walk with the blood dripping from the bullet hole in her forehead and hiding her vision. I thought about her mutation for a split second and then ran towards the huge cooling tank in the lab. It was a huge tank filled with water always to cool certain experimental set ups during our researches. The temperature of the water in the tank could be lowered to freezing level in a second. She was following me. I stood near the tank and moved away just in time to let her fall into the tank. As soon as the water touched her body it evaporated and vanished. The full tank evaporated quickly to half its content and she stood up again. I shot her continuously in her heart and head and she fell into the tank with a scream. I ran at once to the regulator and decreased the temperature. The water in the coolant tank changed into to ice immediately and the watch dog froze with the water. She was captured in the huge ice block with her eyes wide open in fear and horror. I let out a sigh and walked throwing away the bullet less gun.

When I came to where Dr. Malik was lying, I was shocked to see that he was not there. But there was blood on the floor and the small piece of his left ear was also lying there. I searched for everyone in panic. But I couldn't find anyone. Even Puper's dead body was not there. Suddenly two men came running towards me firing their guns. The reagent bottles on the glass shelves shattered to pieces and I leaped on the floor to escape from the splashing acids and chemicals. The guards walked me out with the gun pointed to my head. When we came out, I was shocked to see Dr. Malik kicking Raj and Bala hard. Why are these two idiots not fighting back? I got the answer as 4 of his men in black uniform were pointing their guns at Professor, Diya and Abi Akka. But Puper was nowhere. What is Aadhmi doing out still? How did Malik escape after being smashed by me like that? What was more shocking and surprising to me when I saw Malik, was that his left ear was normal and full as though it had grown back. Yes! His ear must have regenerated back! The mysterious medical research must have been done on him to give him this ability. He has made himself a mutant too!

Seeing me Malik wondered, "Oh! Bindu! Welcome back! You are still alive! Ram I thought that your beloved assistant was waiting for you in hell or heaven with her cute pet! But she is very determined than I had expected. You all can die together after seeing my success." He laughed victoriously and took out something blue in colour from a glass container. Is it Navjavaanium? He boasted, "Do you identify this Ram? This is what you have been hiding from me for years! This is what made me kill your beautiful wife! You are a loser Ram! You are a pathetic loser! If I were you I would have made myself young and lived happily forever. Anyway better late than never! Watch the true magic of your discovery Navjavaanium! Let me eat it now!" Professor shouted, "Don't do that Malik! Don't destroy yourself and the earth!" Malik put it in his mouth with a wild laughter and swallowed it immediately with greedy eyes. We were watching him with fear.

He seemed normal. He laughed like a maniac and shouted, "See! Right in front of your eyes I am going to become invincible!" But suddenly, he began to shake violently and he fell down and began to roll here and there in pain. Even his men were panicked by the sight of it and they backed away with the gun still pointing at us. He scrubbed his face fiercely as though it was burning and he was struggling hard with his back to us and face on the floor. His huge frame began to shrink slowly and after a few minutes he became still. When he stood up slowly, we were surprised to see a very smart and young chap. Our eyes widened in wonder. When I saw the face of Malik, it seemed familiar to me in a different way. He resembled someone else's face. He was very handsome and attractive though his costume was very loose and did not match his cuteness. The young Malik jumped in joy and he observed himself in wonder. He touched his arms and face with admiration.

He laughed meanly and shouted, "Eternal bliss! I am young again! The secret had been hidden by your stupidity Ram! Oh! You are to be addressed with respect now as I have become very young! Shall I call you 'Grand pa' old man? You know I feel very young and energetic. I want to do something very active to burn my energy! I need my punching bags!" He began to jump here and there like a kick boxer and suddenly punched Raj on the face with force. Raj spat blood and he covered his mouth in pain. Bala bent down near Raj and Malik kicked him from behind. Bala turned back and shouted angrily, "You coward! Fight like a man! Let me handle you one to one." Abi Akka was crying bitterly seeing them. Malik laughed mockingly and said, "Nice cinema dialogue! I'll never fall a prey to this dialogue you little imp!" and slapped him hard on his face.

Professor pleaded, "Malik! Leave them alone. I have told you everything about my secret research and you have become young now. What else do you want more? And whatever you need is to be got only from me! Why the hell do you torture these innocent kids? Let them go." Malik came closer to Professor, looked sternly at him and said, "I torture them to give you an emotional blackmail. You are least bothered about yourself. But you worry for them. You must handover the most valuable thing that you were hiding from me. Until then I will torture each and every one of them to death. Come on! Tell me whose death you would like to see first!" and laughed wickedly. Professor spat on Malik's face and said in anger, "You coward! You back stabber! When will your thirst for blood and life end?" Malik wiped his face very slowly and slapped Professor hard very fast. Professor stumbled and fell over a man holding the gun behind him. But he managed to snatch the gun from him and shot him immediately.

Aadhmi entered in suddenly and shot two of Malik's men in a jiffy. Diya kicked off the gun from one man with her left leg and knocked him down with her right hand. At once Abi Akka acted fast and bit hard in the hands of the other man holding the gun and tried to grab his gun. In her attempt to snatch the gun and in his attempt to not let off the gun they were moving here and there at random and bullets fired from that gun aimlessly whenever someone's finger pulled the trigger. Raj and Bala began to tackle the one who was fighting now with Diya. Malik lifted Aadhmi and threw him like a toy. I ran shooting at Malik and he was not bothered about the shots at all. He came towards me laughing and snatched the gun from me very easily. Even at that critical time I wondered whose handsome face he resembled. He gave a kick in my stomach and I hit a pillar hard and fell down. He aimed at Professor and I stood up with much difficulty and tried to push off Professor. But the bullet pierced my shoulders and I fell down with Professor. Malik kept on shooting continuously and I felt fire piercing me in my hip, thigh and leg too. I thought I had saved Professor and turned to see him. But Professor was soaked in blood as it was oozing out from his chest and abdomen. I cried out loud, "Someone help Professor please!" Diya and Raj ran to us and I lost my senses when Raj held me.

56

Good Bye To The Earth

Bright white light was piercing my eyelids and some unrecognizable whispers disturbed me. I opened my eyes with much difficulty. Eager faces of Raj, Bala, Abi Akka and Diya were looking at me and they smiled broadly at me with tear filled eyes. I looked at them questioningly and tried to remember what had happened. I looked around to see where I was. It seemed that I was lying on a stretcher in some cabin and through the glass window I could see only darkness. Is it a hospital? But it looks quite empty for a hospital! I asked, "Diya where are we? Where is Professor, Aadhmi and Puper?" She just cried quietly without answering me and I shouted with irritation, "Why are you crying like this? Let me find them myself!" and I tried to get down. A sharp pain rose from my hip when I tried to move and I let out a cry. All hovered around me in panic and Abi Akka said, "Don't strain yourself Bindu! You are hurt!" I remembered the bullets I had received.

Suddenly a peculiar voice interrupted, "May I have a look at PX1? Has PX1 gained consciousness?" I could hear only the voice but no one was visible. All moved around to give way. A stanno-tech bot extended its pole like legs to the level of the table and injected some medicines into me. It said in a robotic tone, "PX1 I have pumped in some pain reliever for the time being. Soon you will be shifted to the recovery medical section. You must rest in the regeneration tank to gain back your health after your surgery." Something struck my mind and I shouted in horror, "Are we in Prapancha now? Are we really in Prapancha now?" Tears rolled down my eyes and I cried uncontrollably, "Is everything over? Is everything over? Diya tell me what happened." The ST-bot shrunk down its legs and rolled away. Diya came to me and consoled me by hugging. She was also shedding tears quietly. Between sobs I asked, "What happened? When did we come here? Where is Aadhmi?"

Aadhmi walked in and stood by my side. I shouted uncontrollably, "Aadhmi why did you not come in to save us quickly? What held you out so long? Puper is dead because of you! He sacrificed his life in his attempt to save me!" and cried as I could not hold back my tears. It said without any emotions, "Bindu, when you all were inside the research lab I destroyed all Malik's men who were out very quickly. Tackling them was not a problem to me. But when I read Malik's thoughts, I understood that he had threatened Professor and made him terminate mission Yuva Sansaar. The Suethae, Prapancha and the ST-bots had been deactivated from our lab. So the ST-bots will just remain idle and without the Kankan Suethae teleportation of the Phoenixians was impossible. So I was in the production lab reactivating everything. That was the reason for my delay."

I interrupted, "Where is Professor? Is he alright? What happened to the earth?" Aadhmi placed its hand on my head and said, "Don't strain your tiny brain with so many things at a time. The ST-bots had inbuilt Tera hertz pulse sensors which would activate them right before the radiations. When you went unconscious, the whole Phoenixian population was teleported by the ST-bots into the Prapanchas. Everyone in RV except Professor and Malik were teleported to this Prapancha by their respective DNA coded Suethae." Only after listening to Aadhmi I noticed the Kankan Suethae in every one's wrist including mine. I touched the light metal band and wondered how this small device had shifted millions of Phoenixians into Prapancha within a nano second.

Aadhmi answered, "That's the result of the intelligence, creativity and hard work of Professor! All the Phoenixians are safe in Prapancha as per our plan. All the smaller units of Prapancha have been linked now and we are in an interlinked unit now. Now we are travelling in space with the help of super cryogenic engines. ST-bots have taken full charge and are maintaining order." The thought of my parents brought tears in my eyes. I closed my eyes and tried to contact Indu through telepathy. She received me at once and was happy that I was awake. She said that she would come to see me immediately. What had happened to our parents? How would small children feel if they had seen their parents turn to ashes right in front of their eyes. Aadhmi explained, "Teleportation took place before the mishap. So none of the Phoenixian saw anything horrible that would haunt their memories throughout their life! Are you satisfied now?"

I cried without any hesitation and said out loud, "Thank you Professor! Thank you for everything you have preplanned and done for the betterment of younger generation!" I held Aadhmi's hands and asked, "Did you see the calamity Aadhmi? Is there any possibility that humans are still alive there? Was there any other ill effect from Navjavaanium as we feared?" Aadhmi shook its head uncertainly and said, "I am not sure of what might have happened in the earth. At the preplanned time Phoenixians were teleported and we left the earth. The human beings on the earth may be or may be not alive." I shouted in shock, "What an irresponsible answer is this Aadhmi? What is the use of our mission when there is no harm to earth?"

Aadhmi interrupted, "There was a powerful heat wave when we took off and to be inside the earth's atmosphere seemed quite dangerous. I am sure that what we have done now is absolutely right! We shall send back some ST-bots back soon to observe earth and the Phoenixians can return back if everything is OK! Don't shout and strain. Stay calm!" I rolled my eyes. Indu came running to me with tears in her eyes and she hugged me. I winced in pain. Aadhmi cautioned her, "Indu, be careful with your delicate sister!" Indu backed at once and said, "Sorry Akka! I love you very much and I don't want to lose you too. Is it true that our earth is destroyed? Did you know about this already? Is this the dream you shared with me one day when we were walking back from school?" I just nodded with tears in my eyes.

I said with a broken heart, "Puper is no more Bindu." She shouted in shock, "No! It can't be! What happened?" I said, "Malik killed Puper right in front of my eyes." But I remembered that Puper was missing there and I asked, "Aadhmi! Did you see Puper's dead body?" Aadhmi said, "Bindu stop straining yourself! You are physically hurt badly. At least keep yourself mentally strong and healthy." Puper is dead! He is never going to be alright! Dr.Malik killed my son Puper! Young Malik! Whose face was it like? And suddenly I thought about Zuil and his beautiful face! His brown eyes and black hair! I asked Indu, "Hey, Indu, what did Zuil ask about me to you? You said that you will tell me later!"

She began to giggle like an idiot and said, "Oh! He asked if Raj was your boyfriend!" I stared at her and she began to laugh loudly. Raj and I exclaimed at the same time, "Boyfriend!" Bala asked mischievously, "Potato! Do you have any such plans?" I and Raj shouted at the same time, "Never in a million years!" Bala said with laughter, "See! You both seem to think alike and make a good pair!" I stared at him and shouted, "Don't be stupid Bala. Raj is my best friend forever!"

At once Bala hugged Raj; shook his hands; patted him on the shoulders and said, "Congrats Raj! You are really very lucky! Thank God! You have escaped from her! I was really worried that you or she may say 'Yes'. But I am happy for you that you are not in her hit list. Long live happily my friend! Mark this day in your life! This is going to be the best day of your life! Potato has confessed clearly that she is not your girl friend. Choose a good looking girl and enjoy your life. We are really lucky enough to be with all beautiful looking girls under one roof now! I will join hands with you and search my soul mate too!"

Diya gave a wild look at Bala, began to take quick angry breaths, searched for a weapon here and there and as she could find none, she finally gave karate kick to Bala. He began to run around my table to protect himself and everyone laughed forgetting our losses. Aadhmi said with concern, "I think fun is enough Phoenixians. Leave her to rest." Diya said with a puzzled look, "Why Aadhmi, all the ordeal has come to an end at last no? Everything is over!" Aadhmi said calmly, "No Phoenixians! This is not the end! This is the beginning!"

Two ST-bots came in and began to take me away with the stretcher. I entered another section that read 'Cell Repair and Replacement' and the door closed behind me hiding the eager faces of my beloved ones.

EMBERONIUM IS NOT THE END
IT'S THE BEGINNING

COMING SOON
PAST PLUTO

Printed in Great Britain
by Amazon